THE
LOW BIRD

THE
LOW BIRD

DAVID L. ROBBINS

THOMAS & MERCER

Text copyright © 2016 by David L. Robbins
All rights reserved.

Published by Thomas & Mercer, Seattle

www.apub.com

Amazon, the Amazon logo, and Thomas & Mercer are trademarks of Amazon.com, Inc., or its affiliates.

ISBN-13: 9781503940925
ISBN-10: 1503940926

Cover design by Brian Zimmerman

Cover Illustration by Chris McGrath/Alan Lynch Artists

Printed in the United States of America

First edition

For the veterans of the Mighty Pen Project, and all the men and women of the Vietnam War.

And for little Tess and Hugo, who remind me that I am likable.

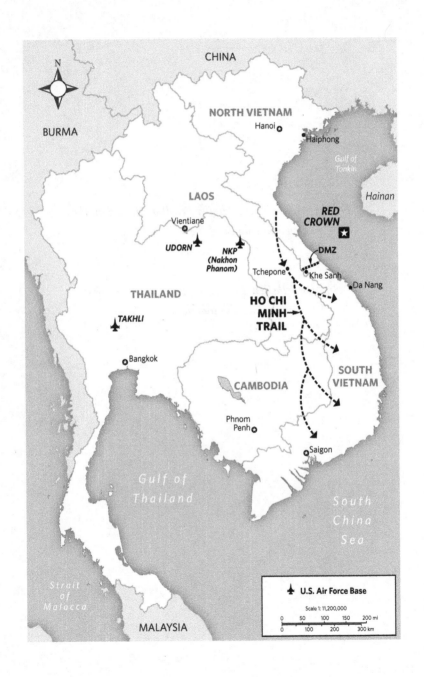

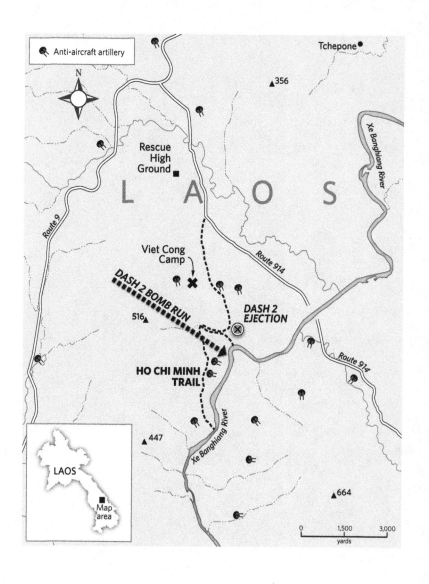

Anti-aircraft artillery

N

Tchepone

▲356

Xe Banghiang River

Rescue High Ground

L A O S

Route 9

Viet Cong Camp

Route 914

DASH 2 BOMB RUN

DASH 2 EJECTION

516▲

HO CHI MINH TRAIL

Route 914

LAOS

Map area

▲447

Xe Banghiang River

▲664

0   1,500   3,000
yards

AUTHOR'S NOTE

The Low Bird is the fictional account of a massive effort to rescue a downed jet pilot from the Lao jungle during the Vietnam War. My novel is based, in large ways and in small ones, on actual events, some foolish or hilarious, many terrible, all exciting. Each incident jumped out at me during my research, insisting on inclusion in the narrative. While based in part on actual events, the statements, actions, and motivations of characters are fictional and should not be attributed to any actual person, living or dead.

At the end of the book, you'll find annotations describing which depicted episodes are inspired by actual events, plus the time and location of their occurrence. The more unbelievable the event, the greater the chance it actually happened. Enjoy *The Low Bird*.

DLR
Richmond, Virginia, 2016

CHAPTER 1

January 2, 1968
Near Khe Sanh, Vietnam

In the dark, Minh could barely see the soldiers on the narrow path with her. Walking through the thick jungle, she kept her head down to stop the unseen leaves and barbed fronds from scratching her cheeks.

The four soldiers, all officers, had placed her and the Chinaman in the center of their line. They were not heavily armed; only the officer in front carried a rifle, the others just had pistols in their belts and dispatch cases with silver buckles around their chests. They were not expecting to meet an enemy and were not looking for one.

Behind Minh walked the tall Chinaman, a guest in the regiment, an adviser. Neither she nor any of the men on the path came above his shoulders. Did they eat that much better in China?

It had been the Chinaman who'd requested Minh's company. He had approached after her sundown performance, while she and her troupe stowed their banners and bamboo flutes, and the day's last sticky heat pressed on the green valley. He said only, "Come with us." The words fell from such a height that Minh felt honored.

The Chinaman's Vietnamese was excellent. Walking with the smaller soldiers, his long strides fell out of step with theirs. His voice was deep and swooped over their heads.

"You sing beautifully," the Chinaman said behind Minh, without provocation.

"Yes, she does," the regiment officer trailing him pitched in quickly.

She let the dueling compliments hang. As if they were fog, she walked through them, and some clung.

The two soldiers in front of her stopped. The one nearest turned to offer water from his canteen. Minh had not been asked to carry anything, not even her own water. She accepted.

In the darkness, the two officers at the rear approached too fast, crumpling into Minh and the others on the path until all had stood still. The officer at the front of the line opened his leather case to remove and unfurl a rolled paper. He pulled out a small flashlight. With the light cupped to mask it, he checked the sheet. He glanced around, ran a finger over the paper. Minh marveled that anyone could know anything about their whereabouts in such blackness and overgrowth.

While they were stopped, with her throat moistened, she proposed a song. This was why she'd been asked along.

The officer returned the map and torch to his case.

"No louder than a breaking stick. Understand?"

This officer squatted on his heels in the fashion of a peasant. He was a leathery man. Most of the regiment was like him, sun-stained, a sign of labor. He was the sort of soldier touted in the songs she sang, exalting how work made the Vietnamese people honest and selfless. Minh had been pale as a beggar orphan in Hanoi, pretty enough. The *Trường Sơn*, the Ten Thousand Mile Road, had browned her and made her sinewy. She was still pretty, but in the way of a paddy girl now.

The other officers squatted in the path; the crane-like Chinaman folded his legs under him. Minh held her fist over her mouth to mute a small cough that cleared her throat.

She thought first to sing a love song. Had she been just with her countrymen, she would have. The only entertainments her troupe was allowed to perform were folk dances, flag routines, and songs of loyalty and martyrdom. It might be nice for the officers to hear her sing softly of the heart, of loss and redemption, a song of a few instead of a nation. But the Chinaman was here to report back to his masters. Minh had to sing of courage and dying and country.

She folded her hands. No need to emote or dance in this darkness. She drew the first breath of the tune, a deep breath because she must sing quietly.

> *The guns' sounds spread over the southern land.*
> *It warms our beloved country.*
> *I want to fly to the South*
> *To kill all the barbarous foes.*
> *I climb the mountains.*
> *The rocks abrade my feet.*
> *Stones don't hurt me at all.*

Minh unclasped her hands to signal the song was over. She stood still, as she would do onstage in daylight; she did not bow because that would be seeking to receive credit for the song, credit that belonged to the fighters in the lyrics. In the dark the Chinaman said, "Beautiful."

Before any more could be said, somewhere high above the ceiling of leaves and branches, the night sky popped. Minh held the breath she'd taken but had not expelled to say thank-you. It froze in her throat, though her mouth hung wide open. She gaped upward with the officers and the Chinaman at the amber light suddenly shafting through the canopy, shimmering and jittery. On the ground, the light crawled over the officers in small bits like glowing pests. The light shifted as the hissing flare drifted down.

The Chinaman was the first to leap to his feet and he, too, hissed. "Americans."

Before the officers could rise, the snap of another flare joined the first. The glow through the trees doubled, and the ground around Minh's sandals turned a livid orange. The officer with the lone rifle became frantic and confounded, trying to swing it off his back into his hands; he looked as if he were swatting at the bugs of light.

A shout broke through the tree trunks and scrub and the unwavering grass under the false suns. Minh did not speak English, but she knew the sound of a frightened man.

The officer with the rifle managed to level it at his waist. He would have looked cavalier and capable in that posture, but he shook too much. Seconds stretched. The orange shivers of light crept upward, up tree trunks and into the leaves, up the bodies of the standing, frightened officers, the Chinaman and Minh, while the twin flares descended.

"What do we do?" whispered the one with the gun. It was terrible to see this man, the one with the only drawn gun, asking what to do. The others had not yet reached for their pistols.

The American voice on the other side of the brush and tall grass called out more urgent gibberish above the sputtering, falling flares.

The officer with the rifle at his hip heard something Minh did not. The American sounded as scared as she was, and why not? The American did not know how many of his foes were on the other side of his voice. Perhaps a gun in the hand makes a man more sensitive to these things, because the officer heard danger. He fired first, blindly, into the bushes.

His gun blazed away, wrecking the brush left and right, up and down. Tracer rounds like red devils spurted out to find the American voice. The officer's bullets shredded leaves and splintered low branches, but in the blasting, Minh could not tell if any Americans had been struck. The Chinaman stepped in front of her just as the answering fire came.

Behind the Chinaman's back, she could not see any flashes from the enemy's weapons. She only heard their roar and the evil zip of hundreds of bullets. Her hands flew to her throat, as if by instinct to protect her one grace. All the officers began to ripple like flags in a wind. One bravely, finally, reached for his pistol, but did not get it out from his belt. He sank to his knees, still fighting to draw the gun as he toppled over.

The Chinaman was the last to go down. Minh, still with her breath clutched in her chest, flung her palms against his broad back to prop him up against the rounds slamming into him. She screamed for him not to fall. She dug under his armpits but could hold him up no longer than a moment. In that fortunate instant, the Americans stopped shooting. The Chinaman slipped from her grasp, moaning a gassy wheeze at her feet.

Overhead, one of the orange flares was finished, the other sputtered. The jungle waited, cloaked and ragged. The last severed leaves tumbled around her, one balanced on her shoulder. Minh released her breath slowly, like cigarette smoke. She stood above a mound of twisted, wadded bodies. Horror padded toward her, a tiger of fear slipping through the night, drawn by the killings. Minh bit her lower lip, a pain to wake her up. She fought to quell her darting eyes, her quaking hands, and her feet, which wanted to run. She stretched out her arms as if she were in traffic, she bid everything to grow still, the horror, too. She listened for a clue to the Americans' next move; she heard nothing. Mist from the guns rolled past, her nostrils stung at the gray stink of powder. Every night bird held its tongue, the insects folded their wings. She was left alone with the silent, invisible Americans.

Six months ago, she'd had a bout of malaria and seen her own death in a fever dream. She saw it now. Because dying was familiar to anyone who had walked the Road, Minh kneeled into the copper stench of splashed blood and began to breathe again. The bullets meant for her had struck the Chinaman from his head to his boots. His face was squashed like an eggshell, viscous between his open eyes. She, a singer, had liked his deep voice and was sorry she'd not told him this. The officers fared no better, all had been riddled. The Americans were lucky shots.

Why did they stay mute? Why didn't they advance? From the sound of their voices they were only twenty, thirty meters away. But the Americans were blind, too, and afraid; maybe they had some of their own dead. In the darkness, Minh did not know what the Americans would do next, so she didn't know what move to make in response. The hushed seconds beat on.

Minh blinked. That stirred her. She knew what to do. She'd played many parts, comic and tragic. She was practiced at playing the heroine.

Already on her knees, she cleared her throat, as if she were going to sing instead of move. She waggled her hands above the Chinaman, repelled by the rents and gore on his black pajamas. Once in a Hanoi alley she'd rifled through the pockets of a drunk to steal his money. It was common in the songs for the hero to come from hard times.

The Chinaman and the regiment officers hadn't told Minh why they were out walking in the dark tonight. She'd had no curiosity about it, just did what she'd been told and kept them company, a pleasant singing girl. Maybe the Chinaman picked her because he would have tried something later. She wouldn't have let him, though she might have let him feed her well before she refused. Vietnamese soldiers didn't make passes at the girls in the troupe, they didn't even make lewd comments. The punishment for fraternization was demotion and self-criticism. Minh and the performers of the Trail sang of honor to those passing on the Road. Defiling a singer would be an assault on honor. Minh had not had sex since she'd walked south from Hanoi—not in a year.

She unsnapped the Chinaman's case, pried out another map with grease-pencil marks on it. Now she knew why they were out here. The regiment was planning an attack on the Americans. They'd come to see the lay of the land, the lanes through the trees, inundations, high ground and valleys, how best to approach the enemy camp at Khe Sanh. Even with their maps, in the dark the four officers and the Chinaman had wandered too close. When Minh sang for them, had the Americans heard?

Before she moved again, she keyed her ears into the jungle. After the tempest of their bullets, the Americans were holding their ground. They didn't want to be here, either. They weren't looking for a fight. But they would fire at any sound.

She could wait until they left. What if they crept forward? The snap of a twig, the swish of a branch, what if they came?

Minh might run and be shot in the back. She could sing to soothe them, announce she was a woman and become their prisoner. No, she would not do this, survive to be questioned and a traitor. She'd sung too many songs of sacrifice not to believe the words.

In the flickering feeble light of the last flare, she could make out little of what was on the Chinaman's map. The papers might be important to the Americans if they were found with the bodies. Expelling a deep breath to keep the blood stench from clouding her senses, she dug into the leather cases of the four officers. She averted her eyes from the worst wounds. No patriotic songs could capture what this looked or stank like. In the cases she found more maps and a scribbled booklet. She gathered them all.

After one last effort at calm, then a rising breeze and a far-off chittering monkey, Minh backed carefully away from the bodies. She did not wish she could do more, like fight the Americans or shout curses at them or drag away the corpses to be buried properly and have the Chinaman shipped home. Minh bothered with none of that as she stole away. She was already doing more than she'd thought she was capable of.

When she had retreated twenty meters on the path, Minh turned to run full tilt, clasping the documents. Her eyes probed into the dark but her ears focused behind, the skin over her spine prickled for a bullet. She ran without measuring the distance or direction; the undergrowth and spiny leaves scratched her face with her arms full of secrets. Only when she felt she was far enough away from the Americans did she begin to cry. She did not slow down.

Minh was aware only of whipping branches and the pump of her breathing. The dark jungle offered to hide her, but in her panic and hurry she stayed on the path. She ran past calls for her to stop, calls in Vietnamese. She burst into the camp, sightless beyond her tears. Without meaning to, or seeing him in her way, she rushed into the arms of a man in a white shirt. He was tall, not so much as the dead Chinaman. He caught her and took her to his chest, pulled her against him until her legs stopped driving. Laying his cheek atop her head, he cooed, or perhaps sang, *It's all right, it's all right.* Minh's sobs broke like the malaria and left her floating. The arms in the white shirt did not let her rise, or fall.

CHAPTER 2

July 15, 1968
Above the Laos–Vietnam border

During his year of training for Vietnam, Sol had dropped bombs only on sand, a year of blowing up grit and salt on the Nevada flats. Below him now were trees on fire, a stream flowing with flame, maybe an unseen monkey or wild pig getting cooked. In the desert, his bombs had made only pale pillars. Those blasts drifted away; those were practice. Vietnam was different, this place burned. Sol pulled the stick hard, kicked the rudder to bank left. With the Thud carving fast on its side, he peered down at the black-and-orange fireball of napalm, the boiling scar of it. One of the magnesium igniters flew high, a lovely arc of white.

Sol didn't like this, destroying trees, spoiling good water.

"Seems a waste."

Dash 1 crackled in his helmet. "Not when it's on target. Good job, Dash 2."

"Roger."

"This time, your run-in heading is one-eighty, with a left break. I want four snakes fifty meters west of your smoke. We'll try a low release on this one."

"Dash 2 copies."

Sol sharpened his turn and soared to six thousand feet to approach out of the north. His F-105 Thunderchief, made to be extremely fleet at low altitudes, scratched twin contrails on the morning off the wing tips. The sun in his cockpit was the same as it was last month over the Nevada desert, a yellow unseen anywhere but Earth's hottest places.

The tight turn cranked up the g-forces. The capillaries in Sol's flight suit stiffened around his legs to keep the blood from pooling in his lower half. Until he leveled out, his eyesight sparkled. To the west over Laos, the planet bent greenly, blankets of mist stabbed on the peaks of karst mountains. Eastward lay the China Sea, rounded blue and immense and safer to fall into than Laos, should he be shot down. Ahead, the ebony coils of his own napalm smoke marked his next target. Over his head, watching with the sun, Dash 1 glinted against the sky.

Sol toggled the switches on the intervalometer for weapons delivery, the stations, sequence, and quantity. He carried four snake eyes—Mk82 five-hundred-pound high-drag bombs—one pair off the right wing, another off the left. He lowered the nose under the horizon, checking speed and altitude.

Dash 1 radioed. "Dash 2, you are cleared hot."

"Copy, Dash lead. Four eight-one snakes at twelve o'clock, fifty meters Whiskey from smoke. Low release. Dash 2 is in hot."

Sol pushed the throttle up to 90 percent military, the power the Thud could fly without afterburner. The ejection seat pushed into his back as the jet surged. He eased the red dot of the gunsight pipper over his smoke, then nudged the nose just to the right of it. The altimeter clocked off his altitude: four thousand, three, two. At one thousand feet, scorching at five hundred knots just above the forest, Sol pickled his bombs. The Thud bounced with the weight gone. He hauled the stick left and back to a climbing bank into the blue of Southeast Asia, bounding to six thousand feet, where the sapphire sea came into view through the tiny g-force firecrackers in his eyesight.

Sol leveled off. Moments later Dash 1 eased into formation fifty yards off his wing, nodding inside his cockpit.

"BDA one hundred percent, Dash 2." Dash lead was giving him a perfect bomb-damage assessment. On trees. "Let's RTB." Return to base.

"Copy."

Sol shadowed Dash 1's bank away, holding formation, chasing the jet's silver undercarriage. In the turn, Sol looked back to see his craters. The concussion from the bombs had done nothing but snuff the fires from his napalm.

On the way back to Takhli AFB, Sol intercepted calls from two O-1 forward air controllers, FACs, slow and low-flying Cessnas trolling for targets over enemy territory. The first FAC had spotted three trucks in the open on the Ho Chi Minh Trail in Laos and had broadcast for fast movers to hit them. The call was snatched up by a circling flight of Navy A-7s off a carrier. The second request, a TIC—troops in contact—in support of a Marine squad in a close-quarters firefight, could have belonged to Dash 1 and 2, but they were low on fuel, so they turned it over to a pair of Fox 4s out of Udorn.

At Takhli, Sol touched down first; Dash 1 was checking him out from takeoff to landing. Sol set his F-105 down gently, neatly. Though he'd brought home most of his twelve thousand pounds of ordnance, he was satisfied, his first armed flight in Vietnam completed. Dash 1 landed behind him.

All returning combat aircraft at Takhli had to taxi first to the de-arming area. Sol headed that way, riding the pleasing hiss of his jet engine at low power, the thrill of so much held back. He halted on a painted yellow X. Sol held up his gloved hands where they could be seen by the waiting ground crew, waggling his fingers. This way he couldn't accidentally fire a missile or pickle a bomb on the runway while the armorers slid the firing pins back into his ordnance.

The shirtless and browned ground crew did not rush forward. They waited, arms crossed, staring up at Sol's cockpit.

A voice sizzled in his helmet. "Dash 2, Takhli tower."

"Takhli tower, Dash 2."

"Dash 2, turn your nose."

Sol bit back a curse before he thumbed the mike. "Copy."

He goosed the F-105's throttle and toed the pedals to nudge his Thud and all its leftover firepower away from aiming straight at the control tower.

"Thank you, Dash 2."

The four-man de-arming crew shot him sarcastic thumbs-up before disappearing under the wings. Sol knew none of their names.

When he got the okay from the crew chief, he taxied to Thud Row. Sol eased into his slot, one of fifty United States Air Force Thunderchiefs on the ramp at Takhli Royal Thai Air Force Base. Another shirtless crewman, this one scrawny, guided him with red flags. Sol shut down the engine when the airman crossed them. While Sol popped the hinged clamshell canopy, a tall ladder was rolled up to his fuselage. An airman climbed to the top to assist Sol with his straps and buckles and held his helmet.

Heat tumbled into the opened cockpit, thick as rain. Nevada had been hot but not like this open-oven-door-in-your-face, this dish-rag humidity. Sol stood, freed from the ejection seat. His throat was parched from pressurized oxygen, and his legs had stiffened from two hours' rushing around at near supersonic speeds looking for a fight he and Dash lead did not find, until they pretended one.

Captain Friedman sauntered across the steamy pavement, already parked and dismounted from Dash 1. His Nomex flight suit was unzipped at the chest, helmet tucked under his armpit. He was wiry, short, built for flying. Friedman wore aviators and a gray buzz flattop. He took long strides for a small man, looking like an ad for Air Force pilots, sweatless and acclimated to Southeast Asia.

Walking, Friedman called out, "We'll get 'em tomorrow, Major."

Stepping off the ladder, Sol felt the heat in the tarmac come through his boots. He lowered the zipper on his own flight suit, slid on sunglasses to stop his squinting in the Thai sun, and tucked the helmet under his armpit. Friedman stood a head shorter, molded swarthy and dark when measured against Sol's blue-eyed Maryland paleness, a captain to Sol's rank of major, and a good five years younger. Sol dealt privately with his annoyance that, though he'd landed first, Friedman had beat him out of the cockpit, making it appear that Sol was mimicking him.

"You flew a nuke?"

Friedman set the first round of beers down on the Officers Club table. He collapsed into his chair as if his legs had gone rubbery. More sarcasm?

This was the statement Sol had made a minute ago, just before Friedman rose to fetch the beers: "I flew nukes."

"Yes." Sol kept his answer short to let Friedman set the tone. Sol was the FNG. The fucking new guy. A certain amount of feeling out was to be expected in the squadron; Friedman was just the first.

"What was that like? I mean, damn. Wait."

Friedman pivoted in his chair away from Sol to motion for the attention of another table of pilots. He vectored the four of them over to the table. The men were all of a type, short and crew cut, captains with early-gray flecks at the temple, each with a simmering kind of energy, confident, like an idling engine. They grabbed chairs from other tables and crowded in. Sol's eyes went to the name tapes on their uniforms, theirs went to his, and that was the introduction. Friedman kept waving them into their seats like a ground crewman until all were parked.

"Sol here flew a fucking nuke."

Hands came off beer bottles, the pilots sat back.

"No shit."

"Where?"

Sol shrugged. He'd become the center of attention at a table of combat Thud pilots. All he'd done so far in Vietnam was rid the world of some timber.

"Germany for five years. One in Japan. Spent the last year at Nellis."

"You mean to tell me, son—"

This pilot, a round-faced Irishman named Beach, who, judging from his accent, hailed from the Deep South, leaned into the center. He extended one arm into the middle of their ring. Beach moved with the slow-blinking torpor of the heat in Asia and of Alabama or wherever he came from, like someone reserving his vigor for more important things. He was a captain, Sol a major, yet he still called Sol "son." Clearly rank wasn't of much importance around this table.

Beach hoisted his index finger, as if to say "excuse me."

"You mean to tell me"—with drawn-out drama, he turned the finger down—"one button"—Beach lowered the finger to the table—"and kaboom. Good-bye, wherever the fuck."

Sol nodded with gravity. "Good-bye."

Beach, still pressing the table, shook his head, rendered ponderous by the notion. The other pilots nodded, too, gravely, asking and answering for themselves if they could do what Sol had done, be ready to drop a thermonuclear doomsday device, a weapon of global war.

Or were they screwing with him? Was ferrying one big bomb around Europe, Asia, and Nevada—a bomb that never got used—anything to compare with dropping a bunch of smaller ones every day on Hanoi and over Laos?

Beach turned his hand upward; his imagined mushroom cloud dissipated. He opened his palm to the real, smaller war they were in, cold beers on the table.

"So you figured you just had to come and get you some of this."

The pilots all laughed. One said, "Some real flying." Friedman patted Sol's shoulder. All Sol had to do was laugh with them, poke a little fun at himself. Maybe say, "Hell, yeah," and raise his beer, simply name them his betters until he could become one of them.

Sol began to tap the tabletop repeatedly with the nail of his middle finger. He gazed at the tattooing finger.

He said, "Actually."

The Thunderchief, the fighter bomber they all flew, was actually designed for his former mission, not theirs. The F-105 was the first supersonic fighter-bomber built from scratch around a single operational profile—to fly low at Mach 2 under Russian or Chinese radar, then deliver a single nuclear device on a population center or a hardened military target. In a world aflame, the F-105 was to be one of the torches.

Sol fixed his gaze on his finger pecking at the table. Beers that had been lifted in mirth froze in midair, waiting on him. One pilot asked dimly, "Actually what?"

Beach cocked his round head. "Major?"

Sol heard the use of his rank instead of his name, or even *son*, the mood souring quickly. He should abort, pull out right now. But which way—jink left, jink right? He'd played no sports at the Air Force Academy, was not on the parachute jump team. He'd trained as an engineer and he flew as one, by the numbers. Sol had loved his tour flying Nuclear Alert out of Germany and Okinawa, had respected the responsibility of the nuclear bomb in his hands, and, no, he'd not requested Vietnam. Debriefing over beers at the Officers Club had been Friedman's idea.

Actually, the F-105 had lost its job back home. The combo of B-52 long-range bombers, intercontinental missiles, and submarines that could launch tactical nukes now formed the core of America's nuclear capability. The F-105 had been shunted off to Vietnam.

The bomb bay of the Thunderchief was huge, constructed to fit one big nuclear bomb, not the massive fuel tanks jammed into the planes today. In Europe and the States, Sol had flown the original version of the 105, a lighter and less muscular jet than what he found waiting for him in Vietnam. Flying Nuclear Alert, his Thunderchiefs lacked armor plating, backup flight-control systems, X-band beacons, radar altimeters, gunsights, bomb racks, and a 20mm rotary cannon, all this and more equipment that had been retrofitted onto the jets in Southeast Asia for hard service in a shooting war. Though the 105 was a bat out of hell at low altitudes, it wasn't highly maneuverable. It could take a beating, and there were plenty of them, so the Thunderchief had become a workhorse in Vietnam. The nickname "Thud" arose and stuck because this was the sound the plane made when it hit the ground.

Sol had been trained to streak deep inside enemy territory, evade detection, open his bomb-bay doors, pull up at 4Gs, then fling a nuclear device forward to destroy the target city, airfield, or ICBM site. He'd carried a poison pill in his flight packet. He'd been ready to immolate several hundred thousand people at a time, and was fully prepared that his flights, if ever one had gone Code Red, would be one-way.

But he was in Vietnam now. Shunted here, an ill fit, like the Thuds.

An engineer knew the shortest path between two points was always a straight line. Sol lifted his beer and said the simple, straight thing. "Hell, yeah."

His gesture and deep swallow of beer reset the fraternal tone of the table. The pilots grew chatty, included him in jests and news of local girls hired as maids who did extra duty if requested. Beach turned out not to be the spokesman for the men, just their clown. Little Friedman, intense and sculpted, raised a hand for quiet and got it.

"Sol." This was the first time his name had been used since he'd arrived in Takhli three days ago. "I want to know something."

"You mean more than how well I fly?"

"Yeah."

"All right."

"What's your attitude about the war?"

Sol rolled the dewy bottle in his fingers. It was empty, he couldn't raise it for a swallow to buy a moment. The pilots folded hands across their belts.

"Not quite sure how to answer that."

"Look, you're a good pilot, you know what you're doing. That's not in question. But every one of us at some point is going to be flying off your wing tips. We're going to be relying on each other. We ought to know what's on your mind."

Daniels, the brawniest of the bunch and with non-regulation-length sideburns, piped up.

"They're shutting down Rolling Thunder. You know that, right?"

In March, President Johnson had announced that, starting in November of this year, the U.S. would halt all bombing on Hanoi, an offering to bring the North Vietnamese to negotiations.

"Isn't that good news?"

Friedman picked up the thread. "Not if you think about it. There's a couple ten thousand anti-air pieces and SAMs around Hanoi right now. What's going to happen to them in three months when they're not needed there anymore? Where are they going to be?"

Though the question was aimed at Sol, when he hesitated, all the pilots answered.

"Over the Trail."

Beach, apparently a one-trick pony, pressed his finger again onto the table. "Over the fucking Trail."

"And that's where we're going to be, count on it." Friedman pointed at Sol. "Into the shit. Day in and day out. And it's going to be worse than it is now by a hundred percent."

None of the pilots' flight suits had patches, nothing that could identify them in enemy territory. In his wallet, Sol kept a photo of the new sailboat his father had bought for the Chesapeake Bay. He couldn't carry his wallet with him on missions. Sol wanted to get home to see that boat. He knew nothing about sailing, and his dad would enjoy being Sol's mentor again.

"So you want to know if I'm gung ho."

As one, the table paused. Daniels, the weight lifter, spoke first.

"We want to know if you're gung ho, Sol."

"Again, I'm not sure how to answer that. You first."

Beside Sol, Friedman patted the air, seeing to it that calm prevailed.

"Listen, okay? We've been laying our asses on the line, some of us for most of a year. We've lost some good pilots, and every one of us has had the crap scared out of him over Indian country. Now they tell us we got to fight with one hand behind our backs. No more Hanoi runs. On top of that, we're supposed to start turning the war over to the South Vietnamese. Good luck with that. My wife sends me pictures out of the *New York Times*. I got one of some asshole general shooting a Viet Cong kid on the street in Saigon during Tet. There's riots back home. Bullshit in the news every day about the war. So it's a good question, Sol. Are you gung ho about this? Because I'll tell you the truth. I'm not."

Sol put his elbow on the table and his chin in his hand. He'd wait Friedman and the rest of them out. He wasn't going to push any button, drop anything, until he was sure.

Little Friedman wasn't finished anyway.

"We're not winning this war, that's over. So the war, frankly, can go fuck itself. What I *do* care about is these guys ten feet off my wing. I'm going to fly my butt off on every mission, for them. And I'll tell you what else. For some goddam revenge. Then I'm going home. Hero or no hero, I'm going home."

Friedman sat back with the rest of the pilots, who seemed to agree through their silence, hands knit in their laps like pictures of old soldiers. They were made stony by their ugly memories of this war, their bad dreams of it, and what they'd paid for both. Beach shrugged.

"Everybody makes up his own mind."

This wasn't true. Anyone with a differing opinion would not be at this table. As an FNG, Sol had one chance to get this right. That would be nice, to have friends. He'd largely kept to himself in Germany, Japan, and Nevada. All the nuke pilots did. A bomb that big will make you think a lot.

Sol raised his chin from his palm, taller than the rest at the table. He was older than them, outranked them. He didn't see himself as part of this bunch. But there was no sense making enemies. Vietnam held enough of those.

"I'm going to do my job, gentlemen. Nothing less."

The pilots greeted this with more flinty winces, as if they'd been outfoxed.

Sol rose. "And I believe that starts with buying the next round."

Slowly, Friedman shifted in his chair, the first to animate. "That'll work."

The others followed, relieved to have their afternoon returned to the familiar.

Sol retrieved six beers. The pilots talked of nothing important, sports and politics back home, nothing of their families, nothing that touched them here. The assassination of Martin Luther King, the shooting of Andy Warhol, followed three nights later by Bobby Kennedy's murder.

"Jesus," said Friedman between sips, "can't tell who we're losing faster. Pilots or celebrities."

With his second beer finished, Sol stood from the table. The fare-wells were all in his name rather than "Major." That was something, but Sol wasn't versed enough in the camaraderie of combat to figure where he stood on his third day in Vietnam with a full year left.

Stocky Daniels rose to walk Sol out of the Officers Club. He looked into the brilliant daylight without narrowing his eyes. He surveyed the blue, not looking for anything in it but simply at it, the way a farmer might view his fields from his porch, a man who knew how to plow.

"Where you from, Sol?"

"Maryland."

"Yeah? I'm from Virginia."

Back home, a few hundred miles separated these men. In Southeast Asia, so far from those homes, the adjacent states made them neighbors.

Daniels didn't pull his gaze from the perfect and limitless firmament. "Tomorrow, I'll go up with you."

"Okay."

The sky remained empty while Sol stood beside Daniels, both gazing up now. The base around them had no part in the vast quiet. Takhli thumped and echoed, baying with revving engines, the sibilance of fast-burning fuel, the grinding whir of rotors and wheels, and, beneath it all, the shouts of men.

Suddenly the base, like a spooked tree, released birds into the air. A flight of four bomb-laden Thuds rocketed off the runway, shaking the Officers Club windows. A big B-66 radio jammer lit out after them. Two Army Huey choppers elevated in tandem, ungainly things to a jet pilot's eye. Sol tasted their fumes. The rattle and power of their departure made him feel secure, that he was an American and he had all this. Daniels never looked anywhere but up.

In the heart of the din, Daniels called out, "Those guys are okay. Beach has the jitters, but the rest are good."

"What about Friedman?"

"He's short."

This was not a reference to Friedman's height but his time of service. "When's his DEROS?"

"Next week. No one wants to fly with him anymore."

Friedman's Date of Eligible Return from Overseas was coming up in days. He had what military pilots called "shortitis." Sometimes this made a pilot reckless, more often it made them overly careful. Somehow, Friedman had become both.

When the last aircraft had taken to the sky and the base returned to a steadier racket, Daniels knocked Sol in the arm.

"I'll show you the ropes tomorrow. We'll go after more than fucking trees."

Sol sat alone in his hooch, listening to the rain. He'd not had a roommate assigned yet. Whoever it was would be the next FNG.

The hut was a hastily constructed thing, not intended to be permanent. Plywood walls and floor, tar paper roof, a couple of cots, a steel chair, a metal desk rived by penknife graffiti, and a woven bamboo carpet would be the shape of his home for the next twelve months.

Sol pushed the chair up to the desk to try to write a letter to his father. The many carvings on the desktop from former residents of the hooch had made him lay the plain sheet of stationery on a comic book so he'd have a flat surface. Sol slid the comic and empty page aside to read some of the dozens of etched messages. Most were names of pilots or their girls, some idle musings like *War sux*, clumsy hearts, and initials. A few Christian crosses and Bible citations, one Star of David. A penis that someone had tried to scratch out before someone else had deepened it and added definition. Hometowns, most of which Sol had not heard of, small American places that had coughed up a pilot for the war. He started to add his town, Towson in Maryland, then changed his mind. He'd been in Southeast Asia for three days. No sense already acting like a prisoner in a dungeon. That day had come for all the names cut into the desk, pilots who'd whiled away their time fashioning this little memorial to themselves, their sweethearts, and their homes. What message were they sending down the line to Sol? Your day is coming. War sux.

In the gusts, the shack leaned. The window air conditioner and the drumming downpour lulled him into lying on the cot, hands under his head. He was unable to write his dad, a Marine pilot who'd been at Pearl Harbor, who'd strafed the beaches and hills of Iwo and Okinawa. The rain came in pulses, but the tar paper roof didn't leak. Sol had nothing to write about but burning trees and this rain. He could say he was sorry his mother had died, sorry he'd been away so much, sorry his father was alone, too. It was the hard rain and the rocking walls making him melancholy. No one flew in this weather. No one should write letters home in it, either.

When Sol sat up, the rain had stopped, or perhaps it was the ending of the deluge that woke him. A silent wash had replaced the storm, a dripping kind of quiet. No jets or choppers thrummed, not a voice, as if the rain had pummeled the base and left it woozy. Sol rolled his legs off the cot, smacked his lips, wanting something.

He laced on his boots, grabbed his soft cap, and stepped outside. He'd slept until dusk. The earth was baked and packed so hard that the rainwater made no mud, just puddles that evaporated even as he walked in them. At sunset the Southeast Asian heat remained a shock to the system. Sol wondered that it alone did not kill.

He strolled nowhere, down the long row of teakwood hooches. Window units droned into each shack; the collective hum added to the post-rain somnolence of the base like a snore. Sol passed squadron headquarters, the officers' mess, the laundry. He heard and saw only one splashing jeep. In the east, the dusk darkened to cobalt over Thailand, Laos, and Vietnam; to the west, the sky pinked above the jungles of Burma and the Bay of Bengal. Sol pronounced these alien names aloud, tried them on his tongue. The grate of his own voice, the faraway sound of these dangerous places that were so close, made him stop walking. When his boots quit sloshing and the lone jeep rolled out of sight, Sol heard laughter.

He'd forgotten about tonight's USO show. It had been mentioned around the table this afternoon. The show was being held in the enlisted men's mess hall. When the subject came up, Sol's first thought was that he wouldn't go. It didn't seem suitable to seek relief after just arriving at Takhli, after doing nothing of note yet in the war. At Nellis he'd been stationed a few miles from the Vegas Strip and hadn't gone to the shows there, either. Those entertainments were for the hoot-and-holler crowd. He was an officer and a pilot, son of an officer and a pilot. Sol had been among the last men to carry a nuclear bomb; his war had been the Cold War. That was over for him now, but he still sensed the cold, the isolation of those years. The laughter from the enlisted men's mess explained why the base felt so vacant. Sol strode out of the puddle he'd been standing in and stepped into another, toward the sounds of warmth.

Music, applause, and more cheers drew him through the screen door at the rear of the mess hall. Inside, sixty folding tables had been stowed so three hundred airmen and soldiers could sit facing a makeshift stage. On the riser, a brass band played. A dozen shining instruments belted a Dixieland melody along with a drum kit and a stand-up bass. The sound bounced off the corrugated steel roof, making the music even brasher. The song slurred, both trombone players curving their notes to make it sound like a striptease, because in front of them, off the stage, a Filipina girl was wearing an Army sergeant's glasses astride one of her tasseled breasts.

Sol found a blank spot against the wall to ease his back. Onstage, the trumpeters and trombone players raised the bells of their instruments and blared like rearing elephants. The drummer crashed around his drums. All this helped stoke the crowd yelling for the soldier to pull down the USO girl's American-flag panties.

Three other pretty women, also in tassels and red-white-and-blue underwear, worked the crowd. But the one with the sergeant's eyeglasses on her chest was bolder than they, brown like them, and the most buxom of the four. The soldier's black glasses fit on one of her breasts, which was apparently the size of his head. In time with the lurching music, she wiggled in front of him in the front row. The other three girls retreated to the safety of the stage as soldiers reached for their hips. The fourth, perhaps as charged by the music as the crowd, stayed behind to move the young man's glasses from her bosom to hang from her panties.

A cry went up in the mess hall for the soldier to retrieve his glasses. Sol didn't cup his hands to his mouth to join in. He imagined himself a younger man, one who could fall into these antics, just one anonymous serviceman hugging the fellow next to him without pulling his eyes off the Filipina, egging on that sergeant in the front row along with the other three hundred in the mess hall. Sol fashioned this different self as he watched the frenzy gather, the Filipina's waist sway, and the other three semi-naked girls ogle their partner's moxie. He let the imagined Sol clomp his feet and roar with the rest, while the real Sol leaned against the wall, hands behind his back.

The sergeant stood from his seat. Then he sank to his knees. Sol had to come off the wall to catch what he was doing. The soldier snatched his glasses out of the dancer's U.S. flag panties with his teeth. Then he leaped to his feet, arms wide, to show all three hundred what he had done. The crowd, standing, almost fell down.

The sergeant slid his glasses over his eyes. Sol wondered about the feel of those glasses, heated by the girl's bare skin. The crowd congratulated itself on the sergeant's feat, hundreds of hands and boots in unison. Sol clapped, not the imagined self, but Sol.

The sergeant acted like a boxer in triumph, arms in the air. He put his back to the crowd and dropped, disappeared from Sol's view behind the hundreds of backs and heads. Sol took another step away from the wall.

The sergeant popped back up, arms thrust high as before. This time, he had the Filipina's panties in his teeth.

The girl, too, waved her arms and bounced on her toes like a woman greeting a lover from a great distance. Her breasts wiggled, the tassels just tiny pompoms. The sergeant did not take the red-white-and-blue panties from his lips, but walked a circle like a matador around the Filipina with them dangling over his chin. The crowd stumbled into each other's arms to keep standing. The sergeant had done this, stripped a USO girl down to her bare ass and tasseled nipples, for all of them, the fighters, fliers, and workmen of the war. The band ratcheted up the volume while the sergeant paraded and the Filipina did a grinding dance. All was right for a loud, vulgar minute, except with Sol and one regulation.

Sol surveyed the big room with the scanning eyes of a fighter pilot. He searched for someone, anyone of rank, to move to the front of the room and take this responsibility off him. All the movement in the room was boisterous, all the voices music and guffaws. No one took a stride toward order. Sol did not ask himself if he wanted to do this, because neither engineering nor duty required a man's want.

"Everyone!" Sol lifted his own hands high as he made his way along the rows of chairs. He repeated himself twice until someone in the band saw him coming and signaled the song to quit. The music died raggedly. Three hundred servicemen stopped leaning against one another and came upright while Sol edged to the front of the mess hall. The men's cries curdled into hustling questions; a major shutting down their USO act was not good news. When he reached the stage, the Filipina looked aghast at herself in the uncomfortable hush; she covered up. In a flash, she grabbed her panties from the sergeant's mouth, stepped into them with a scalded sort of alacrity, and marched herself and the other girls away, turning their raw, muscled backs on Sol. The sergeant's hands flew back up where they'd been moments before, now in raw aggravation.

Sol set his jaw before the sergeant and cocked his head. The soldier lowered his arms but did not soften his glare, even at Sol's rank.

The crowd allowed Sol space to speak. No one of the three hundred sat, as though the order might come for them to evacuate the mess hall immediately. A few in the back rows anticipated this and slipped out the screen door into the humid night. Those fleeing few were behaving as if they'd done something wrong, like they were drunk or high, and didn't want to get caught.

Sol peered across the faces, many needing a shave, some with grease still on them, all young warriors away from home and girls and breasts. Nothing was wrong with breasts. But Sol didn't make the rules. He didn't keep his voice down or try to speak privately with the soldier.

"Sergeant, do you know this is against Air Force regulations?"

"What is? Sir."

"You can't have a dancer naked below the waist."

"I'm not in the Air Force. Sir. So I can."

"I'm not going to argue this with you. Have a seat."

Sol couldn't figure who the leader of the band was, so he made clumsy gestures like a conductor to get them playing again. This didn't work. The band, like a balky machine, stared back at him.

"No, sir."

Sol brought his attention back to the sergeant. Someone in the crowd, because he could do so anonymously, booed. That, just like the sergeant's glasses draped over the girl's boob, unleashed a torrent from the three hundred.

Sol's hands began to rise from his sides to signal for calm and quiet. He would explain himself, the regulation was plain. He was not a fool, he knew this would be unpopular, but structure meant survival, and the rules were structure.

He'd flown alone, far and fast above the earth, for years. Over that time the nuclear bomb had become his colleague. He'd talked to it on starry flights, traded philosophies with it about obligation and death.

The bomb was capable of such power. Sol had been in awe always when he was near it. The bomb steered much of his thinking, made him more respectful of order, rules. Without rules, look at the peril, the horror.

Sol dropped his hands. The instinct to explain himself had passed. He wheeled on the sergeant.

"No, sir, what?"

"No, sir, I will not take a seat."

With this, the soldier brushed past Sol, making contact—an offense, but Sol let him go. The soldier stormed off out of sight under a chorus of catcalls and boos that rose to the steel roof then bounced down over Sol. He stood in the roar, something he was accustomed to.

Sol aimed a finger at one of the band's saxophones. "Play. Right now."

The band, civilians, did not want more trouble. The sax player called out a tune, counted it off, and the group launched into a fast-paced number. One of the trumpet players approached a mic stand on stage and sang. The crowd was not assuaged easily, even those in the front rows close to Sol. They shouted for titties and girls, as if these were very separate things. Sol held his ground at the front, implacable. Slowly, in the face of his refusal to bend, a few men took their seats, then more, then band and singer drowned out the last shouts from the mess hall. Sol stepped away from the stage to let the show go on.

No one took the sergeant's front-row seat, a quiet form of protest. The men in the mess hall were in enough need of entertainment, deflection from the war and heat, labor, and danger, to let loose a rousing bellow when the Filipina girls came back onstage to the music, this time properly if scantily clad. The zealous girl shot Sol a withering brown look while she shook her red-white-and-blue panties and swung her tassels like golden propellers. Sol smiled back because her scold did not undo the facts that he was away from home, too, and she was pretty and mostly naked.

The show continued. Silently satisfied, Sol slipped away from the front of the hall to his spot in the rear, against the wall. He wanted to leave. The less time he stayed, the less chance he'd be identified with the mishap. But leaving would look like retreating, and that wasn't leadership. Sol watched the show, not the faces, and was glad he could not hear the grumbles.

The girls did a Motown song in harmony before the single microphone, pressing hips and shoulders together to make a soft wall of skin, four belly buttons, eight tassels. Swaying like church, the three hundred servicemen sang along. The missing Army sergeant seemed forgotten. Sol sensed the opportunity to go.

As if on that thought, the screen door beside him swung inward, inviting the steamy Vietnam night into the hall. Sol alone noticed that no one entered through the door; all other eyes and ears were fixed forward. He pushed off the wall to sneak out of the mess hall and return to his hooch. Before he could head for the open door, through it came not a man but a rumble.

The round green bore of a big artillery piece inched into the hall. Like the snout of a dinosaur, it pushed its way in, tilted to the ceiling as if to test the air. With several feet of its length through the door, the great gun stopped advancing.

The four Filipinas, facing the crowd, saw it with Sol. Over the heads of the singing three hundred, the girls pointed bare arms and stopped singing. The band, also looking rearward, yanked to a halt, this time everyone on the same note.

Every serviceman pivoted where he sat. The 155mm howitzer was aimed not at them but at the roof. This was little solace; they fell as silent as the band, so quiet that Sol heard the idling jeep outside the mess hall that had backed this cannon into the USO show.

The missing sergeant ducked around the cannon, through the door. Following his return, two Army colonels strode into the mess hall. Both appeared dangerously casual.

One stayed by the cannon, the other put his hands to his hips and leaned back, taking a gander at the mess hall's roof. The sergeant kept tight by his side. This colonel called out.

"Who's the officer in charge here?"

Before Sol, slowed by amazement, could respond, the sergeant pinpointed him.

"Him, Colonel."

The Army officer did not make a move toward Sol. That signaled Sol to walk to him. Within range, neither shook hands. The sergeant nodded with his lips tucked in. Behind them, the howitzer stood sentinel. The three hundred made not a peep.

"I am, sir. Major Rall."

"Major Rall." The colonel did not introduce himself. He did not need to. He had rank and a cannon. "Major, our young friend here"—he gestured to the sergeant—"flies a rescue chopper. He's a brave boy and a credit to his country and the United States Army. Which, by the way, does not have a regulation about a naked gal at a USO show."

The colonel had a nice twang to his voice, a plainsman's sort of unruffled elocution. His gaze was direct and unwavering. Here was an artillery officer who, like Sol with his bomb, commanded great clout. Fire shells here, now there, for how long, with what intensity, and destroy everything. This Army colonel did not brook disagreement, he did not expect things to survive him.

Though he and Sol were opposites—power had made the colonel flout the rules, not respect them—Sol knew this kind of man, believed and hoped he himself might be this kind of man. Forceful, undeterred.

"The Air Force does, Colonel. Half these men are Air Force."

To himself, Sol sounded unflappable. The great howitzer in the mess hall, the stunned silence of the room, did not stop him from being a jet pilot and a fellow officer.

The colonel picked up on Sol's confident, cooperative tone. He moved closer to speak conspiratorially, an arm lapped across Sol's tall shoulder. His breath was warm and menthol.

"Major."

"Sir."

"I want to help you out here."

"That would be appreciated, Colonel."

"I can see you've got yourself in a tight spot. And that's what we do in the artillery: help folks out of tight spots. So I'm going to give you a way out. You can put my sergeant back in his front-row seat. You can let one of them girly girls set her bare ass in his lap. And you can look the other goddam way for a few minutes. Can you do that, Major?"

"Sir, I've got regulations."

"And I have a cannon."

Sol leaned his head in a few more inches, almost touching foreheads with the colonel.

"Sir, would you really do that?"

"What, shoot a hole in this mess hall? Son, that would be a stupid thing to do. All that for one little sergeant rescue pilot."

Sol nodded sagely, appreciating the candor and insider whisper of the colonel. He brought his voice down to the same private level.

"Sir, I can't do it."

The colonel winced into Sol's eyes as though he were straining into a bright light. He smacked his lips.

"Yeah."

The colonel's hand on Sol's shoulder rose and fell, once.

"I tried it your way, Major. I tried to be a pussy. I just don't have it in me."

The hand, the arm, the menthol breath, withdrew.

The colonel took several long strides backward from Sol. This was how he worked, firing from a distance.

He dropped his jaw so wide that Sol saw all his back teeth.

"Major, you will put my sergeant back in his seat and a naked gal in his goddam lap, some titties in his face, or I will blow the fucking roof off this place! Colonel!"

The officer's silent counterpart, the other colonel who'd stayed watchman of the howitzer, spun to disappear out the door. That's where the trigger was.

Half the three hundred airmen and soldiers in the audience raised a howl for the colonel to do it. Dozens scrambled for the exits. The rest gaped in stupefied glee at the mayhem they had not expected at a USO show.

The colonel eased his voice, again just for Sol's ears, like the cooling of a fired gun.

"Major. Your call."

Sol was the FNG. He'd blown up trees. Made himself the least-liked man in a room of hundreds. Now he had to choose between being the loser in a confrontation with the Army and getting the mess hall roof blasted off because of him. On his third day in Vietnam.

Sol had never thought of it before, but he missed his bomb.

Onstage, a trombone player tripped over one of the girls, both trying to evacuate. They lay tangled, the musician holding his trombone high to keep it from harm. The Filipina screeched and slapped the musician when he grabbed one of her tassels, just one scene in the pandemonium.

The colonel returned his hand to Sol's shoulder.

"It's okay. You can do it."

He was saying Sol could back down. Could bail out. He had it in him.

Was this what Sol's year was going to be like? If so, he'd start carving into the desk in his hooch tonight. *War sux.*

This was all over one regulation about one girl in one lap. This was not a hill to die on, especially facing a man who'd already killed thousands on hills.

Before Sol could call for order and restart the show one more time, the colonel gave his shoulder a squeeze.

"And apologize to the sergeant."

The colonel had seen Sol's capitulation the same moment Sol had. He grinned and backed away more to give Sol room to burn.

Sol gestured to the sergeant. "If you'll come with me."

He led the rescue pilot to the front of the frantic room, where the sergeant joined him in waving his arms, calling for calm. The servicemen settled faster when the colonel, from the back of the mess hall, unleashed an immensely loud "Shut the fuck up!"

With fifty freshly empty seats, the room quieted. The Filipina and trombone player had both gotten to their feet; she snatched her gold tassel from him, denying the civilian his souvenir. The sergeant turned expectantly to Sol, wordlessly shaming him more.

"I apologize, Sergeant. I was mistaken. Please take your seat." Sol turned on the band. "Gentlemen. I'm sorry to you, too. Please continue."

The band, relieved and well-practiced, wasted little time before striking up another bouncy tune. The Filipina girl, on her own and in a defiant way, tugged down her American flag panties. She could not get the tassel to stick. A bare nipple violated another rule.

The screen door did not slam when the howitzer disappeared from the mess hall. It did when Sol left.

CHAPTER 3

July 15
Nakhon Phanom Royal Thai Air Force Base
40th Aerospace Rescue and Recovery Service
Tactical Unit Operations Center

The coin flipped up, ringing, then fell into the captain's palm. He slapped it onto the back of his forearm behind his big watch.

"Heads."

The other pilot, Bo's pilot, shook a pleased fist at the result. Jolly Green 22, Bo's chopper, would be the low bird on today's rescue. They'd go in first and perform the pickup. The second HH-3, Jolly Green 23, the high bird, would stay above in support with the mission to rescue the low bird if it got shot down.

Bo had been clutching a five-baht coin. In the rear of the small briefing room, away from the chalkboard, behind the folding chairs with air crew in them, in front of a map of Laos, he flipped his own coin. While the baht piece was in the air, Lee called it. Tails.

Bo fumbled the catch.

Lee stamped his boot on the coin before it could roll away on the plywood floor. Bo didn't know which side faced up.

Creases fanned Lee's eyes like they would on an older man, but he was twenty-six, four years older than Bo. He had a chest scar that Bo had seen for the first time in the squadron's showers yesterday, a four-inch keloid that Lee said was from a helo crash two years ago, when a flying piece of the rotor blades got him. Lee had the voice that New York City, cigarettes, and screaming had left him.

Lee stood on the coin with his toe tip, as if he were holding down something that might get up if he let it. "You sure you're ready for this?"

Bo shook his head no.

"Then let me pick the coin up. I'll take this one. We'll flip when you're ready."

Bo licked his tongue around the inside of his mouth. Dry as corn in drought.

When Bo was a kid, not that long ago, his father had hit ground balls to him in the backyard. It had not been so much a yard as merely that part of the five hundred acres not under crops. His father had a master's touch with the fields but no desire to maintain grass. The yard was weedy and uneven; the balls never rolled smoothly or predictably. As a youngster, Bo took a few busted lips trying to field them, which scared him. His father told him many times that the safest thing to do if you're afraid of the ball is to catch it.

Bo shoved Lee in the stomach to push him off the coin. Bo was too small, and Lee, a six-footer, brawny and the son of an Irish fireman, did not move.

"Okay, kiddo."

Lee stepped back.

Heads.

Bo was to be PJ 1 on the rescue. If someone on the ground needed help, he'd be the one to bring it.

The coffeepot had been neglected, so the briefing started without coffee.

The pilot of Bo's Jolly Green 22 stepped to the front of the ops room. He was today's AMC, airborne mission commander, a broad-shouldered Army major. His blond handlebar mustache drooped in the predawn hour. Heavy-lidded, he stood in front of both five-man crews: each Jolly Green carried a pilot, copilot, flight engineer/gunner, and two pararescue jumpers, the PJs. The major made Bo think of a classic English explorer, the kind who tut-tutted at dangers and wild men. He emanated an urbane, weary calm. The major was the old man in the room, maybe thirty. He took a deep breath, blew it out, and changed his mind.

"Someone get us some coffee."

One of the flight engineers rose to the chore. The major selected a folding chair in the front row, sat with hands and ankles crossed, and waited. He sucked his teeth, making little noises as if he were leaking.

The engineer returned quickly bearing a misting coffeepot. This led Bo to believe he'd stolen someone else's coffee.

Bo moved first, even before the major, to the pot. The major eased beside him, jumping the line. The man poured for himself into a Styrofoam cup. His name tape read Crebbs. Then he poured into Bo's cup, speaking through the rising steam and black aroma.

"You my new PJ?"

"Yes, sir."

"Where you from?"

"Kansas, sir."

"Farm boy?"

"Yes, sir. Good guess."

"I'm from Missouri. You got the look. Like you could kill a pig. Wring a chicken."

"Did a few, yes, sir."

"Okay. You got this?"

"Yes, sir."

Crebbs blinked, and his smile came and went that fast.

"Go sit down, Airman."

Coffee in hand, Crebbs addressed the room again.

"Joker sent us a dandy last night." Joker was the call sign for the Joint Rescue Coordination Center. Crebbs shook his head before taking a sip. "Just after sunset yesterday, a C-123 Provider cargo hauler running empty back to Takhli took antiaircraft fire over the Ho Chi Minh Trail in Laos. A couple 37-mil rounds hit the starboard engine, which caught fire. At two thousand feet, the pilot told the crew to prepare to bail out."

Crebbs pulled his lips into a round kiss. He held this while peering down again into the coffee. He seemed to be stopping himself from cussing or chuckling. This added to his aura of bravura, an intolerance for nonsense.

Looking up, Crebbs released his lips with the actual smack of a kiss. This seemed to suffice for a curse. "So, here's what we've been able to piece together. As soon as the pilot gave the order to get ready, the load-master in the cargo bay grabbed a chute and bailed. By his lonesome. When he didn't answer the intercom, the navigator went back to look for him. The navigator took one look at the starboard engine burning like hell, figured out what the engineer did, and joined him outside. Then the copilot went looking for both of them. This sumbitch tripped down the steps coming out of the cockpit and knocked himself cold. When he came to, he had no idea how long he'd been out. He guessed everybody else was gone. So he jumped."

Beside Bo, Lee chortled into his hand. The others in the ops room showed more restraint. Major Crebbs didn't glance at Lee to reprimand him; when Lee's snickers were allowed, the others snorted.

"Meanwhile, the pilot is doing his job, which is to keep the damn thing flying as long as he can to get away from the fuckers who'd shot him. When he's gone as far he can go, he bails. So. We got four crew from the same plane scattered about thirty miles apart."

All four had good beepers, and their locations in Laos had been plotted. Crebbs went on to describe the terrain where the four crewmen had hunkered down for the night, all jungle and forested hillsides. Each crew member had made contact with a Candlestick flight, a C-130 radio plane circling high over their heads during the night. All four had been authenticated. Three reported no serious injuries, the loadmaster thought he might have sprained his elbow. None had seen any enemy forces. Crebbs said the mission was a grab and go, then chugged his cooled coffee.

"We got four men who spent the night on the ground. They're going to be glad to see us." Crebbs turned on his boots. "Wheels up in one hour. First light."

Both Jolly Greens surged at treetop level. Any unfriendly guns they zoomed over would get only a fast glimpse. The top and sides of the HH-3s had been painted in jungle camouflage. The bottom was tinted a hazy blue to replicate the sky, just enough to buy perhaps a second from an enemy trying to spot it soaring past.

In the low bird Jolly 22, Bo sat in the rear on the vibrating floor, secured by a fifteen-foot-long gunner's belt. His survival vest weighed him down, festooned with grenades, canteens, radios, plus a .45 pistol in a shoulder harness. His M16 hung at his chest. Freighted like this, he felt the steel floor shuddering under him, and it made his fanny itch where he'd gotten his only tattoo, a pair of Jolly Green Giant footprints bought two weeks ago in Bangkok. The hot dawn air gushed past the chain guns in the open portals and did little to cool the cabin. On the way to his first rescue, Bo's main urge was to scratch. Beside him, Lee sat on a flak jacket to put more armor under him, to keep a shell from hitting him on his own Jolly Green Giant tattoo. The floorboards were also the fuel tanks. Lee must have read Bo's fidgeting as nerves, for he fed Bo a stream of chat to distract him.

Living on the farm, Bo had spent hours, often days, seeing no one but his folks and his brother. Tractors, silos, livestock, clouds, and corn did not draw out conversation. His family lived twenty miles from Pawnee Rock, the nearest town. He and his kin didn't feel their isolation unless someone pointed it out. Like the traveling salesmen who mopped their brows and said, "Whooee, y'all live a far piece out here," or the Bible ladies who came with pamphlets and notions that people who lived apart needed God even more than townsfolk. Bo had grown up with the fields, every year straight and quiet like them. He was never lost in the stalks when all he could see was sky, for if he was inside the corn, he was, in a way, home. The land ran so flat and treeless he watched from the porch while gray storms formed over Colorado, to creep toward Kansas over an afternoon. His dogs, too, didn't whine at coons or snakes, only when strangers came around. So Bo wished Lee would stop talking and let him ride.

Bo got to his feet to stop itching and to peek out the right-side portal. The flight engineer who manned the 7.62 six-barreled minigun stepped aside to let him look out. Emerald jungle whipped past under the Jolly's belly. Giant fronds and tree peaks waved when the chopper roared past, a rotor wash that could knock a man down. Bo saw nothing of the ground, the Lao cover was so thick. Under the low-slung sun the landscape rolled gently, the valleys cupped mist like cotton in a box. Jolly Green 23, the high bird, thundered beside him, flying in formation just fifty feet away. Another PJ doing the same as Bo, gazing out at the rushing morning, waved. Bo waved back and wondered how many rescues this other young pararescueman had, and no matter the number, was he scared?

Three thousand feet overhead, a pair of A-1 Skyraiders flew escort. Their mission, under the call sign Sandy, was to protect the Jolly Greens to and from the downed airmen and, if need be, engage enemy ground forces to keep them away from the rescue site.

The Sandys' job was, in effect, to get shot at, see who did it, and shoot back. The A-1s were the only propeller-driven fighter planes in the U.S. inventory in Vietnam, holdovers from Korea. The planes were bulky and slow compared to a jet. But they bristled with weapons, carrying more than an old B-17. Bo hadn't yet witnessed the Sandys in action, but the word was these two sentinels overhead could handle themselves in a fight. He hoped not to see it today.

The flight engineer nudged Bo aside. That was enough touristing; he needed to put his hands back on the gun. Bo returned to the floor. Lee napped. This was something the military prized, the ability to snatch sleep in shreds, then try to stitch it together into enough rest. Lee stirred when Bo settled beside him. Lee poked him in the arm to tell Bo to move over and give him more room. Lee's fingertips dug into the patch on Bo's camo tunic, a guardian angel's wings enfolding the world, the logo of the PJs. Beneath the angel unfurled the pararescueman's vow: That Others May Live. Bo ran his own fingers over the patch, admiring it not for the first time, proud of earning it.

Lee, again mistaken, thought Bo wanted to talk about the motto for reassurance as they sped low through Laos. He sat up, abandoning his nap.

"Don't think."

Bo said, "Okay."

Lee tapped his own PJ patch. "This isn't for thinking men. You understand?"

Bo opened his eyes because he was not rude. "Yes."

"You're a farm kid, right?"

"Right."

"I heard you tell Crebbs you killed pigs."

"Yes."

"You didn't think before you did that, right? You just, what, fucking hit it on the head or something."

"Pretty hard."

"So this is like that. Just hit it, man."

Lee nodded, as if he'd just said something profound and conclusive. He let this lay and said no more when Bo answered "okay." This bought Bo fifteen minutes of listening to the thrumming rotors as they whisked the tips of trees. In that span he closed his eyes and visited his Kansas home, the old house standing in the only shade on the property.

In Bo's helmet, Major Crebbs's voice sizzled over the Jolly's intercom. Two minutes out.

Bo and Lee got to their feet. Bo checked his medical ruck a last time, patting the pockets for tourniquets, syringes, and morphine vials, field dressings, suture kit, blades, bandages. He ran through the list as his fingers read the contours of the pack, imagining the need for each. As PJ 2, Lee squatted behind the rear minigun, now that Crebbs had lowered the cargo gate. The chopper blasted across the treetops at 140 knots, then leaped up in a steep-pitched climb before banking hard against its cyclone of air. The chopper descended out of the turn, slip-sliding back the way it had come. Bo held on hard, glad of his gunner's belt.

The morning's first rescue was the last man out of the downed C-123, the pilot. Jolly 22's flight engineer swung his mounted machine gun away from the right-side window to lean far out and peer across the thick overgrowth, so dense it seemed you could walk on it. Orange smoke purled up through the green crown of jungle. Bo stood close behind the FE, watching past his shoulder. Over the chopper's intercom, the FE and the pilot volleyed back and forth, guiding the Jolly to the smoke marker. Bo stayed poised, waiting for the word to send him into action. He caught himself tensing and could do nothing about it. He eased closer behind the FE, the clipped language of the rescue hot in his ears.

"Twenty meters. Ten."

"Roger."

"Five. Okay, hover."

"Roger."

Bo stuck his head out beside the FE. The Jolly hung barely five feet above the highest limbs, bending them in its downdraft, making the leaves shiver in ripples. Even with the trees pushed apart, Bo saw nothing of the ground or the pilot through the smoke.

"Hold hover."

"Roger."

The FE released the jungle penetrator, shaped like a large plumb bob with three paddle seats that folded down. The engineer leaned so far out that Bo grabbed the back of his vest.

"Hold hover."

With that, the penetrator was sent downward, blind into the jungle, fishing for the downed pilot. The winch played out steel cord to let the heavy penetrator shoulder through the branches. The line went down and down, reeling out more than Bo would have thought, testimony to the height of the jungle.

"Hold hover."

"Roger."

Bo shifted to the left-hand portal; the M60 mounted there just behind the cockpit would be his station if enemies showed up. Three thousand feet above, the high bird Jolly 23 and the two Sandy A-1s circled in a racetrack pattern. Bo rested a hand on the cool gun, thinking how fast and red-hot it could become. He patted the long barrel and asked it to stay quiet this day of his first rescue. Bo returned to the winch. It kept unspooling, the cord stayed taut, the penetrator on its way down.

The FE sensed the nearness of the ground and slowed the line just before it went slack. The penetrator had to touch the earth to get rid of static electricity that could spark, a danger around so much fuel and exhaust.

"Penetrator is down. Hold hover."

Bo glanced back at Lee to see if he was excited, too, but Lee stared down the barrels of his gun, hands on the grips.

The engineer waited long enough for the frightened pilot to peel down one of the paddles on the penetrator, loop the harness under his arms, and climb aboard. The FE tested the winch, hauling in twelve inches of line through a gloved fist. Somehow he felt the pilot's weight.

"Hold hover. Penetrator up."

The line reeled in, fattening around the winch. Instead of pushing Bo away from the door, the FE laid a hand on his back, letting Bo appreciate along with him what they were doing.

The winch reeled a long time, dragging the pilot up through the branches. The FE kept his gloved fist knotted around the spooling cable, sensing, nodding to himself. Then into the maelstrom from the downblast, the pilot surfaced, clinging. Branches whipped at him, he rose with his flight helmet ducked against the switching and the rotor wash. The FE worked the hoist to raise him level with the door.

"Package is up. Hold hover."

"Roger. Get him in."

The rescued pilot bore no smile, and his eyes darted below him as though he feared he might fall back into the jungle. He didn't yet know he was safe.

Bo yelled, though the pilot surely could not hear him, "We've got you, sir."

The FE stopped the winch. The pilot dangled facing the door, wide-eyed, a pleading look. How frightened was he after leaping from a burning and dying plane, then spending the night on the ground in Laos? The FE pivoted the dangling pilot to face away from the chopper. Bo lent a hand to swing him backward through the portal; the instant the pilot's boots were on the deck, the FE hit the winch to slack the penetrator.

"Package is onboard."

The Jolly pilot answered with immediate distance from the jungle roof. Lee came away from his minigun and, with Bo, helped the pilot out of the harness. With the chopper rising, they lowered him to the floor. The FE shifted his machine gun into the open door through which seconds before they had saved a man.

With hands crosshatched in scratches, the pilot removed his helmet. Sweat matted his thin brown hair, dirt lined the furrows of his brow and neck. In the darkness overnight, he'd smeared mud on his face to mask his paleness. He wasn't wearing his flight vest, and mud caked his boots. He sat head down, empty hands collapsed between his spread knees, like a man who'd just finished something terrible. Bo popped the lid on a bottle of water to hand it down. The pilot gulped it in one long tip. Lee stepped up with a small silver flask. He rattled it like bait in front of the pilot's face until the man took it for a gulp. The booze woke him from his torpor, the wildness in his eyes returned.

Lee took a knee. "You got any injuries, Captain?"

The pilot shook his head as if he could understand but not speak. Lee helped him to his feet. The chopper jostled as it drove onward. Jolly 23 came back to formation. The Sandys overhead kept their vigil.

Standing, the haggard, reviving pilot was a marvel to Bo. He extended a hand to shake. He shouted above the rotors, "Welcome aboard, sir."

The pilot took Bo's hand but in a distracted fashion. He shook it listlessly, with his focus out the gun door. "Where are we going?"

These were the first words from a pilot Bo had helped rescue.

Bo had no reply when the pilot repeated, "Where are we going?" The man yanked his hand from Bo's. He shoved his head out the portal, swiveled his gaze all around at the jungle, at Jolly 23 beating the air a stone's throw away, up at the Sandy A-1s. He whirled on Bo.

"We're headed east!"

Before Bo could agree, the pilot took a step toward the cockpit. The flight engineer barred his path. Lee sidled next to him, silver flask still in hand, offering it again.

The pilot backed away, to slump once more on the quivering floor, the same sapped posture as before, hands fallen between his knees. He ignored Lee's flask.

Bo left the pilot in his heap. With Lee, he moved to the rear of the big HH-3, to sit flanking the minigun. Lee didn't offer Bo a swig, nor take one, and stowed the flask.

"What's the matter with him?"

Lee gestured the back of his hand at the pilot, being watched over now by the FE. "He's pissed."

"At what? Us?"

"Yeah."

"Why?"

"'Cause he wants to get out of Laos. Not go further in."

"But that's where the rest of the crew is."

"I know."

Lee laughed openly, a good sardonic laugh that said he'd seen much, and this was among the memorable bits.

"He doesn't want to go pick the motherfuckers up. They jumped out on him, man. He was left alone."

Lee shook his head at the jungle flashing beneath the lowered cargo bay door.

"That's some scary shit down there."

Twenty miles deeper into Laos, the trash hauler's copilot waited for rescue. A forward air controller in a Cessna O-1 flew lazy rings directly above him in the slanting early light. The terrain ran to hills, some with sloping forested faces. The sky loomed crystal clear; the heat was rising quickly.

Both Jollys held a mile back in a wide-turning orbit while the pair of Sandys circled the downed copilot. The A-1s banked hard a few hundred feet off the ground, wings straight up and down, wheeling like vultures. They were panning for trouble, to see if they drew ground fire. They did not; the morning stayed blue, green, and motionless except for the American planes looping around. Bo's chopper was cleared in for the pickup. The high-bird chopper stayed at a distance.

Crebbs surged across the treetops. Again Bo watched over the FE's shoulder. Bo liked the way the branches parted as the copter raced over them. Lee took his station at the rear gun, fixed behind the six Gatling barrels. Near Lee, the rescued C-123 pilot curled into himself, sour on the whole enterprise.

The Jolly slowed its approach. The trees thinned and the land flattened. Morning mist along the ground fled the chopper's downward gust; a patch of ten-foot-high elephant grass bent over and shivered in pulses.

In the middle of the juddering field stood the copilot, waving both arms either in welcome or panic that he might not have been spotted. He wore no helmet, only sunglasses, and he looked cool and clean. The FE guided Crebbs until the chopper was straight above him. The copilot took a knee to keep from being blown over with the grass.

The pickup went smoothly. Crebbs hovered at fifty feet. The copilot was nimble climbing onto the penetrator. A big grin split his face while the FE hoisted him; the man kept beaming as Bo wrangled him and the penetrator through the helo door. With the copilot's boots on the floorboards, freed from the harness, he hugged Bo first, then the flight engineer. Crebbs wasted no time at the throttle and raced away from open ground, keeping low again in the cover of the treetops, forging east.

Bo was quick to sit the copilot on the deck. He knelt with a water bottle. The copilot grinned in thanks and sipped. Lee arrived with his flask. From this, the copilot took a deep slug.

Above the flier's left eye, a pink bump rose around a small split in the skin. Bo turned for his med kit, but the copilot waved this off. Instead, the man reached as far as he could across the deck to bat the knee of his muddy pilot, gleeful that both were safe. The pilot turned away, flipping the copilot a raised middle finger. Bo wondered which of these two had actually fallen on his head.

The two Jollys and two Sandys forged deeper into Laos across thickly forested hillsides and the last wraiths of morning haze. The formation cut across a bend in a river where water buffalo lounged. A native longboat poled in the shallows, three men in coolie hats standing with fishing nets piled around them. The three caught only a fast glimpse of Bo and he of them, but Bo got a bad feeling. Lee must have sensed the same, for he left Bo's side and went to his aft gun.

Bo watched a little more of the enmity between the pilot and copilot. The pilot had tugged his helmet back on and pulled his knees to his chest. He looked as small as his spirit. The copilot wore no helmet. He must have removed it in the Provider's cockpit; that was how he'd managed to conk himself out tumbling down the steps. He was lanky and breezy. He seemed curious about the fate of his crew, ignored the pilot, and crawled beside Lee to watch the jungle gush behind them.

After more minutes of shaving the treetops, Jolly 22 reared back and climbed fast, up to four thousand feet to join Jolly 23 in a wide, gradual circle. Both helos were now beyond the range of small-arms fire from the jungle. The circle pattern meant they were loitering, not positioning for a rescue. No word came from Crebbs as to why he'd taken them up so far.

Bo stepped behind the left-side M60. He had nothing to shoot at through the feathery trees. The ominous sense in the chopper moved him to be ready.

Miles ahead, the pair of Sandys traced the terrain. They flew figure eights, combing the field like hunting dogs. They shuttled from spot to spot, helter-skelter, sniffing. From his high perch, Bo watched out for smoke, a parachute hung in the trees, the sparkling arc of a pen flare, any sign of the downed navigator. Neither the searching A-1s nor Bo caught sight of anything.

When Crebbs's voice surged over the intercom, Bo's hands had grown sweaty on the gun's stock.

"The package is not there. No voice contact, no smoke. We're moving on."

Not there? Just last night the navigator had been authenticated, answered questions only he'd known the answers to. He'd been in touch with Candlestick through the night. He was in hiding, he was going to make it. Now, an hour after dawn, with rescue a mile away, he was gone.

Jolly 22 broke out of its gradual bank, with Jolly 23 alongside. Both choppers kept their altitude as they headed east.

The copilot gestured out the open gate, beseeching Lee, pointing down at the jungle. Lee shook his head.

This failure to retrieve the C-123's navigator did nothing to break the plane's pilot out of the hard grip he had on himself on the floor. Standing by his gun, Bo felt his own stomach rise as if the chopper had taken a nosedive. He moved to the ramp to kneel close to Lee. He paid no attention to the copilot, an officer, and interrupted him to shout.

"What's going on?"

"Might be a SAR trap." Lee gestured to the copilot. "That's what I'm telling him."

A search-and-rescue trap, a nasty tactic of the North Vietnamese. After capturing an American flier, they'd fix his emergency radio to a tree and leave the tracking beeper on. The trick was meant to draw in rescue planes and choppers, then to shoot them down. Fliers were taught to wreck their emergency radios before capture to keep them out of enemy hands. The navigator had either forgotten, been caught too quickly, was badly wounded or dead.

The copilot seemed slow to accept that his crewmate was missing. He cast hurt eyes around the chopper's bay as if to grab something to throw at the ground. He glared at Lee's gun like he wanted to fire it, looked wildly over the cargo ramp as if to jump out himself. Lee pointed away, for the man to go sit with the bad news.

Lee patted Bo's shoulder in condolence. Together they watched the Lao wilderness slide beneath them, leaving behind the spot where the navigator had gone missing. The place was nothing special, no different from the rest, just emerald and crowded, then gone behind a hill.

The Sandys came level to fly escort beside the pair of choppers. The search for the navigator was over. Bo didn't know how to grieve for the man, how much to let go. The navigator wasn't a face or even a name, but Bo had been sent to bring him home and did not. He looked to Lee for his cue. Lee had saved men and left then behind, too; the navigator wasn't his first. The older PJ stared out at the hot, rushing world.

The copilot sat against the fuselage opposite the pilot. He had his head down, arms folded.

Across from him, the pilot caught Bo eyeballing him. Bo mouthed the word *Sorry.* The pilot called out, "Serves him right."

The copilot pushed off the wall. Bo leaped to intercept him.

"No, sir, no!"

Bo corralled the copilot around the waist before the man could reach the pilot. He held on until the copilot stopped reaching for the pilot, who scrabbled away on the floorboards, kicking his muddy boots.

Bo forced the flushed copilot down to his backside. He sat between him and the pilot for long, tense minutes. The copilot finally shook out his hands like a boxer after the wraps came off, dumping the last of his anger. He looked calm enough to talk to.

"You good, sir?"

The copilot bit his lower lip, then released it. "Yeah."

Bo lowered his hands from the man's shoulders. "Mind if I talk to you for a minute?"

With a distracted shrug, the copilot motioned for him to go ahead.

"They say these things skip generations."

The copilot stroked fingers beside his mouth as if he had a beard, a gesture to calm himself and his ire. "What things?"

"My grandpa was a quiet sort. Like most everyone else where we come from. All farmers." Bo leaned in to be heard clearly over the chopper's throbbing and the whooshing wind. "But my daddy, now, he can talk. He talks about crops and such, church gossip, weather. Folks say he talks like a preacher, like a man paid to do it."

"How about your mother?"

"She's from an old Kansas family. Her people been quiet for a hundred years. But me and my brother, we're like Grandpa. Not much for gab."

"Your brother older?"

"Three years. When he took off for Vietnam, Daddy lost half his audience."

"What's your brother do?"

"Backseater in a Marine F-4."

The copilot nodded. He didn't say, "Good for him." Nobody congratulated anybody for being in Vietnam. "So, where is he?"

Outside, past Lee and the six-barreled gun, the blue sky glowed endlessly empty. It seemed wrong to be up here in it, marring it.

"His plane got shot down. Two years ago. No word. Don't know if he's dead or POW."

The copilot covered his mouth, wincing above the back of his hand. "I'm sorry."

Bo bobbed his head. "My folks said I couldn't go. But I was, no matter what."

"That why you're a PJ?"

"It's what made them let me join." Bo tapped the pararescue patch, the promise on his sleeve to save others. Other sons. "This here."

The copilot reached for another handshake, this time without the adrenaline of being pulled out of Laos. "Thank you, Airman."

Bo gripped the hand. "Thanks for listening."

"It's okay."

"It's just that I haven't told anybody else that."

"Why tell me?"

"I swore I'd tell the first man I rescued."

The copilot let go Bo's hand to gesture at the pilot across from him. "What about him?"

Bo rose to his feet. He looked down on the copilot, memorizing him. Then he considered the pilot. That man was weedy ground, not a proper place for a marker, for what might end up being a gravestone.

"No, sir."

Bo moved again beside the flight engineer. Together they watched the jungle speed by as the Jolly drove deeper into Laos to fetch the last downed flier.

The terrain climbed and the choppers climbed with it. The morning haze that had burned off in the lower elevations stayed dense nearing the highland border with Vietnam. Banners of fog snagged on the spines of rocky outcrops and peaks. The poor visibility forced both Jollys above the clouds. They leveled off in sunshine at seven thousand feet, skirting a solid cloud cover. The helos were unescorted because both Sandys had stayed at treetop level to spot the downed loadmaster, who was in voice contact with Crown, an airborne rescue command post.

From the cockpit, Crebbs kept the crew of Jolly 22 informed of what was happening. He told them the rescue site was socked in by a ceiling at one thousand feet.

"The package says he's in a secure hiding place. Doesn't know if he has enemies in the immediate area, but he hears ground fire across a road to his south. Says he's in some pain from a busted elbow. PJ 1?"

Bo startled. Lee poked him to answer. Bo pushed his talk button.

"PJ 1 up."

"Be ready to go down the hoist to assist."

The words burst in his gut like a flock of birds.

"Copy."

Lee and the flight engineer both turned to Bo; neither the surly C-123 pilot nor the copilot were plugged into the intercom, but they picked up on the nods sent Bo's way, so they stared at him, too.

Bo stepped away to squat against the fuselage. He gathered himself, made himself and his thoughts quiet, coiled, and ready.

Crebbs continued. "We've got a good fix on the package. We're looking for a hole through this crap to drop down into the valley. Sandy high's come up to help. Stand by."

Bo peered out a gun portal. The clouds looked thick, like snow-drifts. One of the Sandys buzzed in the sunny distance, circling and searching for a break in the clouds. It looked like no hole was going to present itself to fetch the loadmaster in the next few hours. With gunfire near his position, how long could the man stay undetected on the ground? He'd already spent one night in the jungle with a bad arm, was he headed for another?

Crebbs came back on the intercom:

"Listen up, here's the plan. I've asked Sandy low to fly into the middle of the valley. He's going to give me a long radio count. We'll direction-find on his signal. Then we'll drop under the clouds. Jolly high's going to stay up here."

This seemed logical, and Crebbs sounded steady. But Lee's tight-lipped look, the clenched posture of the flight engineer, both more experienced fliers, gave Bo cause to rethink. The rescued C-123 pilot, without even knowing what Crebbs had said, threw up his hands as if decreeing he knew what was going on and didn't like it. He hunkered even tighter into himself.

Their chopper was going to drop five thousand feet, white-blind. Crebbs was hoping not to hit anything on the way down, like a mountain.

Bo stood in the gun portal, watching Jolly 23 soaring alongside, framed by the spectacular clear blue and a puffy pale carpet. The flight engineer in Jolly 23's doorway shot him a thumbs-up signal. Before Bo could return it, his own chopper dipped into the mist, and Jolly 23 disappeared in a silvery blink.

The world was washed out on every side of Jolly 22. Through the racing, ghostly mist, Bo watched for sudden looming shapes. The white-ness of the clouds grew murkier the farther the chopper dove away from the sunshine up top. Crebbs read out altitudes.

"Five thousand feet, five hundred feet per minute. Four thousand feet, five hundred fpm. Three thousand feet."

Bo held on to the sill of the gun portal as if that might protect him. The rescued pilot dourly shook his helmeted head; Bo was tempted to slap him upside it to make him stop. The copilot had slid next to Lee in the rear, Lee's flask in hand.

Bo unplugged from the intercom. The pilot's countdown, meant to be calming, stretched his nerves, already strung tight because he would be going down the hoist. He stuck his head out the portal, into the wind and rotor wash. The cloud was so thick it wet his cheeks. Bo watched for the haze to part and the dark green ground to rise out of it.

The first glimpse was elusive, like a fish it darted then was eclipsed. Something was seconds away, the jungle, a mountainside? Bo spread his boots for impact and tightened his hands on the sill beside the machine gun.

Jolly 22's rotor wash blew away the final wisps. The earth spread out directly beneath the chopper, rising to steep mountains left and right. The clouds blocked the sun and stole much of the valley's beauty. Crebbs slowed his descent just a couple hundred feet off the ground, too close for comfort. Bo could sense his pilot's relief, how he let the helo float above the world as though to admire their survival. Bo released the windowsill.

The chopper tilted violently, heaving Bo off his feet. Before he could grab hold, he was thrown to the hard floor, sliding on his rump past the copilot's ankles. Skidding across the floorboards, his stomach churned even as he fought to hang on with everything tipping, accelerating. The copilot grabbed one of his arms while Lee snagged Bo's gunner's belt to keep him from sliding off the open cargo ramp. One of Bo's legs made it that far, dangling out. Bo yelled, crazy frightened. The copilot and Lee couldn't drag him inboard, not while the chopper was listing so badly against centrifugal force. Bo yelled for them to haul him in, clawing at them, the floor, anything. Lee shouted back for him to shut up and hang on. Though he was harnessed in, Bo saw too much jungle under him, not enough floor. In the open air, barely ten yards behind Jolly 22's tail, a set of wings flashed past, running upward, banking hard. The A-1's engine wailed as it scorched past, zooming close enough to stun Lee and the copilot, who stopped hauling Bo in while they watched Sandy low's camo belly streak away over the jungle. Bo hollered for their attention.

Crebbs leveled out not so fast, because that would upset the chopper. Hand over hand, Lee and the copilot grappled Bo in from the ledge.

They'd popped out of the clouds right on top of Sandy low. Crebbs had done too good a job tracking the A-1's signal and almost collided with him. Bo scrambled to his feet and backed away from the open gate like from a snapping dog. The copilot took another snort from Lee's flask.

The Lao valley lay cupped inside a ringing ridgeline of steep hills. A small river wound through it, though the water didn't glint on this dull morning. Crebbs followed the stream north, whipping the shallow waters with his rotors. Sandy low stayed to one side, escorting the Jolly low bird.

After a few miles skimming the skinny river, Crebbs banked away above the dark treetops. Bo moved behind the FE to plug into the intercom next to the hoist-side door. Crebbs stayed mute. The jungle slipped past; Jolly 22 skipped across more tree peaks. The pilot crackled in Bo's ears.

"PJ 1, ready?"

"PJ 1 ready."

The chopper leaned back to bleed off speed. Sandy low pulled ahead to take up a wide, circling turn, bodyguard for the Jolly. Ahead another two miles, carrot-colored smoke drifted through the overgrowth. Crebbs throttled up and headed for it.

The flight engineer shook his head at Bo. "Too fucking soon, man."

Bo had no time to ask what this meant because the FE pointed him back to his station at the left-side M60. Bo scrambled over to it. With Lee manning the rear and Bo and the FE stationed on the left and right guns, Jolly 22 raced toward the rising smoke.

Crebbs approached from the south, keeping away from the enemies reported to the north. While the chopper covered the distance to the orange marker, Bo spotted nothing on the ground through the trees and brush, not a trail or any open space. Crebbs shed altitude, dropping the bottom of the HH-3 ten feet over drooping palm fronds and sprawling branches. This time on the intercom, Bo noted the first strains of urgency in his pilot's voice.

"Be aware. Sandy says we're taking heavy ground fire."

Bo still found nothing on the closeted ground to turn the minigun on. A bus-sized chopper framed against the sky made a much better target than a North Vietnamese soldier on the ground under all those leaves.

That's what the FE meant when he said too soon. The downed loadmaster had been overly excited: he'd popped his smoke as soon as he heard the Jolly and Sandy drop into the valley. The drifting orange marker had been spotted by enemy troops looking for him, and he'd given them a head start. Now they were racing Jolly 22 to get to him.

The first bullet struck the chopper. The sound was solid and mean like a hammer against an anvil. The HH-3's armor held. Bo made himself ease his touch on the machine gun's trigger, to stay loose. Jolly 22 was going to fight its way in and out of this rescue.

Crebbs surged over the treetops to the smoke. Halfway there, Lee unleashed a blast out of the rear. Bo saw nothing to shoot at and wasn't sure Lee had either. He was tempted to squeeze off a hundred rounds, too; it would take an instant, so fast was the gun. Before he could, the copilot appeared beside him, arms out and waggling his fingers, wanting something. Tension and wind blocked Bo's ears against the copilot's shouts, but the man made it clear he wanted Bo's rifle. Bo unslung the M-16 and handed it over. The copilot slid to his knees near Lee and aimed out the back with him. The C-123 pilot pulled his knees tighter to his chest, pitching in by staying out of the way.

The closer Crebbs flew to the loadmaster's smoke, the more Bo became aware of bullets flying around him. Sparks struck in the whirling rotors, deflecting rounds. Another clunk sounded under his boots, where the armor held again. Bo wanted to answer with the gun but held back without a clear target. He'd settle for anything, a muzzle flash through the fronds, a tracer round, a glimpse of running uniforms or black pajamas, but if he fired recklessly he might endanger the package.

North of the package's smoke, close, inside a hundred yards, Sandy low was in a frenzy. The A-1 swooped over the forest, unleashing its full arsenal. Rocket trails spurted from under both wings, gun pods blinked, and the jungle exploded beneath it. Burning trees keeled over, earth was flung high, and a body cartwheeled in the blasted air.

"PJ 1."

"One up."

"We're taking some hits. Not a lot of hover time. Saddle up. Get down, get the package on the hoist, and get back up here fast."

"Copy."

Bo left the machine gun. He took his M-16 back from the copilot and slung it on. Lee squeezed another short burst from his weapon, adding to the rising ruckus in the chopper. Lee tossed Bo a curt nod for confidence, then returned his attention to the gun and the enemies he saw that Bo had not.

With bullets in the air, Crebbs didn't move the Jolly gently but flung it ahead, wheels and external fuel tanks skimming the dense trees. The chopper coursed forward, the orange smoke was blown down and away. The wounded loadmaster was down there, under the canopy looking up, with enemies creeping his way. Bo was desperate for a glimpse of him before riding the penetrator down.

Sandy low blistered the jungle even closer. Crebbs slowed the Jolly, approaching a hover. On every side of Bo, trees were on fire, guns chattered, propellers howled. The copilot had manned the left-hand M60 and was working over some threat on his side. A bullet hole opened in the fuselage over the doorway Bo was stepping toward.

The flight engineer hauled the hoist inside the chopper. Quickly he unfolded one of the paddle seats and motioned for Bo to climb on and strap in. Bo unplugged from the intercom. In seconds he was seated on the penetrator and swung outside the giant Jolly into an immense wind, boots only a few feet above the wavering forest tops.

Crebbs goosed the chopper forward. Bo hung on tight while one more time Sandy low zoomed in to thrash the bushes and trees. Outside the chopper, Bo had a powerful view of the A-1 slashing at the emerald jungle, casting up columns of smoke and gouts of fire.

Crebbs slowed to a crawl. Beneath Bo's feet, the whipping trees thinned out, then the forest gave way to an opening no bigger than a backyard. The loadmaster stood in the short grass there, madly waving his good arm at Jolly 22.

Bo motioned for the FE to hit the hoist and lower him. The engineer wagged this off, pointing instead to the ground, into the ring of swaying trees and scrub. There on three sides, emerging from cover not thirty yards from the loadmaster, small men in black pajamas slipped through the overgrowth. They were too close to the loadmaster for Sandy low to take them out. Lee and the copilot were on the wrong sides of the chopper, facing away from the clearing. Bo's hands were busy holding on to the cable, and the FE had shoved his M60 aside to put Bo on the penetrator.

In ten more seconds, the loadmaster was going to be captured. Right there, under Bo's hanging feet.

Crebbs didn't know what was going on under him or he would have pivoted the Jolly to bring his gun stations to bear. So excited was the loadmaster that he didn't see the enemies advancing on him, or he would have stopped waving at Bo and run for his life. Bo kicked at the FE to get the man's attention. He pointed at the clearing, insistent: *Send me down.* Bo had an M-16, he could get on the ground, hold the VC off long enough for Crebbs to bring the chopper's guns into play.

"Send me down!" Bo yelled. "Let's go!"

The FE shook his helmeted head. He mouthed, "No way." He reached for the steel cable to pull the penetrator and Bo back inside.

Bo spread his legs, planting both boots against the chopper's frame. "Send me fucking down!"

The FE held out his hands, stymied. He couldn't leave Bo outside and unprotected, couldn't lower him, and Bo wouldn't come in. With bullets flying, enemies closing in on the loadmaster, the FE didn't have the seconds to consult Crebbs.

The FE did what he could do fastest, and did it probably by instinct. He pointed at the Viet Cong, six of them coming through the woods. To the loadmaster, the FE shouted, "Look, look!" with no chance of being heard on the ground, but he jerked his arm hard enough for the man to shift his attention to the jungle around him.

One of the pajamaed soldiers stopped creeping forward long enough to take a potshot up at Bo. Stuck in the open on the penetrator, Bo flinched, but nothing hit him. He yelled again at the flight engineer to lower him. Bo did not remove his boots from the fuselage.

The FE didn't register that Bo was screaming at him. He fixed his eyes on the clearing as if he were seeing something remarkable.

The loadmaster had drawn his .38 pistol. With the VC only twenty yards from him, moving in to capture or kill him, he began to run around the clearing, firing his gun into the air. The man dashed into the woods, shooting not at the Vietnamese but into the trees, all the while screaming, darting around with no pattern, just random and madcap.

The loadmaster's reaction was so startling, even fearsome, that the little soldiers started to run, too, away from the large crazed American flier chasing them, shooting at nothing. The loadmaster zigzagged through the trees, his enemies fleeing out of his way. The clearing below was empty.

The cable shuddered. The paddle seat under Bo dropped, making him tighten his grip. In the chopper doorway, Lee had pushed the flight engineer aside. Lee shook a balled fist at Bo while his other hand worked the hoist.

Bo rode the penetrator down through Jolly 22's hurricane wind, a hundred feet to the blowing grass. The bottoms of his feet prickled, reaching for the ground. He felt naked sliding through open air, vulnerable on the cable. He closed his eyes, just long enough to will himself back to his training. He made himself ready to do what he'd been drilled to do, what he'd accepted and sworn to do. He opened his eyes, still scared, and the ground rose up under his boots.

Touching down, he ducked out of the harness, pushed off the seat, and put his rifle in his hands. Bo took a knee, scanning for his next move. He'd lost sight of the loadmaster; the man had run out of the small clearing chasing away the VC. Bo still didn't know what to make of that, it was either the bravest or insanest thing he'd ever seen. Either way, the loadmaster burst from the scrub, running pell-mell for Bo, mouth wide open. One arm stayed in the air but without the pistol; he must have thrown that away. The other arm hung at his side, plainly injured. He didn't run like a man in pain but one frightened and witless.

Bo took aim into the jungle and fired a few rounds to slow whoever was chasing the loadmaster. The next second, the trees and bushes behind the running man began to molt, their leaves, bark, branches, everything that made them plants got chewed and flung in the air. Then the same happened on the opposite side. Above, Crebbs had finally rotated the Jolly. Lee and the copilot rained bullets, a couple hundred per second, spitting fire from their miniguns.

Bo had to catch the loadmaster, who almost galloped past him. The man had eyes like a rodeo bull, bucking and pained. He was breathing really hard, gulping air, and shouting, "Go, go, go . . ."

The chopper's guns kept tearing up the jungle. Bo had never stood in so much sound, except maybe once as a boy when a Kansas twister spun close to the farm. That wind was worse, but this was louder. He turned the loadmaster to the penetrator, pushed him onto the lowered seat, then worked the harness around the man's shoulders. The loadmaster stiffened having to raise his bad left arm, Bo couldn't hear the cry on the man's oval lips. He couldn't take time to be gentle either; he yanked the harness into place. The loadmaster's face turned crimson.

Bo folded down the second of the paddle seats. His place on the penetrator was opposite the package, facing him, legs around him. The penetrator bounced up several inches; Crebbs was doing his best to hold the chopper motionless, but he was still taking ground fire. Bo would have to jump to make the seat.

A flash made him wheel around. Thirty yards away, bursting out of the jungle, untouched by the chopper's bullets, a black-pajamaed VC sprinted at him. The small man fired an AK-47 from the waist. Bo had no sense of the rounds missing him, but they weren't all going to miss.

His training told him to answer fire first. But the chopper overhead was still taking hits, the navigator wanted to get off the ground and so did Bo. The VC was running through the trees, Bo had no clear shot at him and no idea if this was the only enemy running and firing into the small clearing, even with the miniguns above blazing away. Bo's choices were to get into a gunfight or get onboard the penetrator.

Had it been just Bo and the VC, he would have shot back. But it wasn't.

He leaped, not onto the open paddle seat but up onto the loadmaster. Bo grabbed hold of the cable above him with both hands, wrapped both legs around the loadmaster, and hugged his chest to the man's back. The penetrator tilted under the unbalanced weight, but the harness would hold the loadmaster on. The man yelled this time loud enough for Bo to hear him.

The hoist began to reel them up, not fast enough. Bo didn't look down to see where the VC was or if he was shooting at them. He clung to the cable and enveloped the loadmaster, who shivered like he was cold. Bo waited for a round in the back, steeled himself for the jolt. He tightened his grip even more, so if a bullet came, he wouldn't let go. At best, he was going to get yelled at by Lee.

CHAPTER 4

July 16
Binh tram 16
Fifty kilometers southeast of Tchepone on the Trường Sơn Road
Laos

The others backed away from her. The child, the frightened old crone, the enemy soldier from the South, all withdrew in awe. Minh could not act as if she saw them, because her role was that of a blind woman. Nor could she take note of the setting sun tipping the peaks of the hills. The light set her character ablaze in hues of orange; Minh fought the urge to wince, it shined so bright on her face.

She stood alone in the center of a stage made from slats. Minh turned a full circle, keeping her face dull for the audience. She was not supposed to see them, either, the ranks lining the clearing and in the trees on every side of the stage, hundreds of soldiers in black pajamas, a great round shadow. As she pivoted, Minh did not deliver the final lines of *The Flag*, did not bring the play home as she ought, but lingered in the last moments of being admired. She could not do this as herself, that would be out of step with the revolution. She could only stand on a stage and be prized as someone else.

Minh let the whole watching battalion see her bask in the sun's gold. Then she raised her hands like a sleepwalker. Drama called for large gestures; heroes were not the same size as regular people. She pretended to stumble forward and use her hands as feelers, searching for the box on the plank floor of the stage. Minh milked the moment, a woman sightless but determined. Thi, portraying the child, slid the box into her path, impatient to be done with the play and the heat of the costumes. The sun was in her face, too.

"Come on," Thi hissed below the hearing of the audience. "I'm hungry."

Minh reached clumsily for the box, laying hands first on Thi. She pinched the girl as if she were an actual child. Thi squealed, overreacting and annoyed, drawing laughter from the crowd, wrong for the patriotic finale. The soldier and the crone, both younger girls, shot Minh thin-lipped glares. Minh was the leader of their troupe, she could guide the play as she saw fit. But she accepted that she'd gotten carried away in the gilded light for the moments it had shined on her.

Minh rummaged inside the box. When she righted, she pulled forth a brilliant banner, a bright yellow star against a red field. This was the flag of the North, though she played a woman blinded by the war living in the South. The woman of the play had been hiding the flag in her hut at great risk, waiting for the moment to display it when the forces of the revolution finally came to liberate her village. Standing before the flag, Thi straightened her spine to give a child's salute, a nice blend of softness and fervor. Nhu, acting the crone, saluted with a quaking hand. Yen, the enemy soldier, recoiled as if in the presence of a dragon when Minh thrust the flag at her.

"I am no one's slave," Minh intoned for the crowd. "I am not alone. I am many. I will not die. I will live always in the revolution."

At the final line, in the first gray tints of dusk, Yen, the enemy soldier, regained herself. Changed by the courage of the blind woman, she saluted, too.

The men and boys of the battalion shot to their feet. Their applause eased the steamy dusk; under their claps and shouts, Minh did not mind the sweltering heat. Her troupe did not bow. Minh held the red standard high, turning its yellow star a last circle.

Beside her, Thi did not smile for the clapping soldiers. She said again, "I'm hungry."

The elephant carcass had been dragged behind a truck into binh tram 16. Its hunters had left the dreary mound in the shade so the sun wouldn't spoil it so fast.

Even as the soldiers lined up for the sunset meal, meat was carved out of the great corpse. A man stood inside the body, in the red cave of the elephant's gut. With a hatchet he shaved strips straight off the ribs. The butchering had to be done this way because the elephant's skin was too thick to cut it up from the outside.

In the food lines stood a hundred young soldiers passing south through binh tram 16. Behind them came dozens of workers and local farmers stationed here to maintain their share of the Ten Thousand Mile Road. Minh and her troupe were escorted to the head of one line to be served first. The men bowed as the girls passed. The black pajama–clad fighters were polite, every one of them. On the Road, in the binh trams, Minh did not let her girls flirt. If she saw evidence of it, she would hold a self-criticism session before bed. The soldiers were without their wives, mothers, girls, and sisters, some for years, and most would be for more years. Flirting was cruel because it would make them think of home. The men were with the war only, and there they must stay. The Trường Sơn was a one-way road; none of them, not the fighters, not Minh or her girls, would go home until the revolution was over. Not even death would send them home.

The girls accepted plates of meat and a square of manioc cake. Sitting alone at a rough-hewn table under a camouflage screen, they talked about the performance. Nhu and Yen, both eighteen, were chatty and brimming, ideas came out as the food went in. Minh was glad to see them eat well on this last of four nights at binh tram 16; at dawn they would set out for their home base, Tchepone. The walk would take twelve hours, nothing out of the ordinary.

Like Minh, Nhu and Yen had joined the war a year ago, and like her, they'd been marked by the Road. On their way south, both had taken bouts of malaria, not enough to knock them down but sufficient to pit and sallow their skin, cost them weight and strength. They were not yet fully recovered; Minh had walked, sung, and acted with the two girls when neither of them could raise an arm afterward.

Nhu and Yen also shared backgrounds similar to Minh's. All three had been *bui doi*, dust of life; Minh and Nhu were orphans in Hanoi, Yen an orphan from Hue. All three had lost their parents to disease or French bombs. They'd been recruited out of the alleys and into the war by the communists, who promised a part in the revolution and a better life after it. Separately, the three girls had walked south a thousand kilometers. None could recall the wholeness of the journey, just a steep hill here, a swollen river there, a rest stop and kindnesses, brilliant quiet evenings, disease, hunger, bugs, bombs, fatigue. Each had walked with countless men and women streaming south on the Road. Strapped on all their backs were supplies: Nhu had carried steel bars for concrete, Minh and Yen had each borne two antiaircraft shells.

A year ago, in a paddy northwest of Saigon, Minh had given her twin shells to soldiers who would fire them at American airplanes that very day. For the next week, she rested at a binh tram, a depot and staging area. Minh earned food there by singing to passing soldiers. Another communist brought her to his tent, Minh thought for private entertainment. He introduced her to two other girls he'd caught singing. Because Minh was the oldest, he put her in charge of her own FEG, a front-entertainment group. The troupe was given flags, texts, songs, and a circuit, a one-hundred-kilometer stretch; they were to move between three different binh trams, entertaining troops passing through each.

Two weeks ago, Thi had been assigned to Minh's FEG. The girl was nineteen, beautiful, and a wonderful singer. She came from a family of innkeepers in Sam Sun, a northern beach town. Thi complained about the Road, slept through political sessions, giggled at the soldiers. Thi was childish, not a patriot but a romantic; she'd joined the war for the adventure. She'd not walked but ridden south in a truck.

A thin soldier joined them at their table. The man was an officer; Minh judged this not by rank—none was worn in the camp—but by the gray in his hair and his gentle manner. He was genteel in his bow and request to join them. He had little on his plate, he seemed severe, without hunger.

"Your performance was stirring. Thank you."

Minh spoke for the girls. "The credit belongs to the revolution. We only say the words."

"My name is Danh. Chief surgeon at the hospital."

Minh introduced the girls, then herself.

The doctor smiled with crinkles from long sun and wind. His hands rested beside his plate. To Minh they seemed as strong as the elephant's skin. His hair was cut flat, brushy, like a rice field.

Danh pointed at the man inside the elephant hacking at the innards.

"That is one of my doctors. When he is done, we will grind the bones for medicinal teas. We do the same with tiger. Have you eaten tiger?"

Yen said she had.

"Did you like it?"

"Yes."

Danh shook this off, kindly, not to dispute but to continue the conversation. "Tiger tastes even worse than elephant."

Nhu remarked that her favorites were wild pig and monkey.

Thi, bold and simple, asked the doctor if he was going to finish his meat and root cake. Danh scraped his meager portions onto her plate. Thi tucked in.

The doctor grinned widely at the girls, pleased. He seemed to be selecting.

He settled on Minh.

"Would you like to see my hospital? It's underground."

Minh wondered at the criteria for being picked. Had she sent some signal?

"Thank you, doctor. But no. My girls and I need to rest. We leave at dawn."

"The sun may not come up tomorrow. What will you do if there is no dawn?"

The surgeon Danh fancied himself a poet. Minh could have thought him anti-revolutionary, playing on the fatalisms of war, saying that the next day was promised to none of them. So if today was all you might have, then have as much as you might. That was his line. She did not judge the surgeon, he seemed to want only some attention for his sacrifices, and who did not? He saved lives with his underground knives, and he was asking Minh what that might buy him. A stroll through his wards, a touch?

She shook her head. Unfazed, the doctor smiled again, this time as if he'd just jumped up from the ground, unhurt. He glanced between Nhu, Yen, and Thi. "One of you, then?"

Following Minh's example, Nhu and Yen lowered their countenances, answering with their dark curtains of hair across their faces. Thi shoveled in the last bite from her plate.

"I'd love to."

Thi did not seek Minh's permission; Minh was not sure she had it to grant. The troupe was hers to direct, but they were not in the military.

Thi, younger than Doctor Danh, got to her feet before him.

The two walked past the eviscerated elephant, away across the station into the jungle. Minh watched them go longer than did Nhu or Yen; the younger girls seemed unaffected, unaware of what they'd just witnessed. Minh pivoted back to the table with the relief of someone who had dodged something, with sad gratitude for the one who went missing instead of her.

She removed Thi's abandoned plate, which had held twice the girl's portion. She carried both platters to the kitchen, then led her remaining two girls to their hut. In the early night, Minh lay awake on her bamboo mat with shuffling and voices outside, and vehicles arriving in the dark.

When a rap came on the hut's woven door, Minh sat up, surprised. She'd slept with her thoughts. Yen and Nhu did not stir. Minh stepped on Thi's empty mat. To the rumbles of trucks entering the camp, Minh tiptoed to the door.

A teenager stood on the trampled grass. The headlights of a truck washed over him but did little to brighten his black pajamas and weathered skin, a farm boy. He was a courier holding a little box. "You are the FEG?"

"Yes."

Minh accepted the carton, a battered and taped-up thing. The courier turned on his sandals without thanks. He'd arrived in the night with the mail, and like his letters and parcels he stayed nowhere long.

Minh's name had been handwritten on the outside of the box, addressed to binh tram 16. She shook it gently and caught her breath. Her nails tore into a seam of the cardboard.

Inside, a lotus blossom reached to her in petals pink even in the night, edges flushed red as if with shame or love or both.

"Wait."

The courier stopped. Minh ran into the open to speak to the boy without waking Nhu and Yen.

"Are you going on tonight?"

"Yes."

"Where?"

"Back to 17."

Binh tram 17 was the first station at the northern tip of the Road into Laos. Tchepone.

"May we ride with you?"

"In the back. With the mail."

"Of course."

"We leave in ten minutes."

"We'll be right there."

"We won't wait."

Minh squeezed his arm for delivering the lotus.

She ran back to the hut to rouse Nhu and Yen. The girls sat up logy and greedy for more sleep. Rest and food were their only payments and they wanted their share.

"We're going."

"In the morning?"

"Now. We have a truck to ride."

Knuckling eyes, both looked to Thi's blank mat.

"Are you punishing her?" Nhu asked.

"No. I'm rewarding her. Let Thi stay. Let her become a nurse."

Let her become, and let her have, what she will. The surgeon was right, there may be no dawn.

In the bed of the mail truck, seated on cartons under a canvas roof, Minh and her two girls sweltered. The Road was as much a tunnel through the jungle as it was a pathway, and the jungle seethed heat deep in the night. The girls bounced as the truck struck ruts, flipping beads of sweat off their noses. Thi was spoken of only once, with hope for her. Oddly, it was not as if she had been abandoned or died, but had somehow been found or born.

Minh sat near the tailgate of the truck to breathe what unfettered air she could. Dust clouds curled up from the tires and drifted into the truck bed whenever the driver slowed for traffic, wrecks, or craters. The vehicle behind them and the trucks bunched behind it used cat's eyes over their headlights to mask their lamps from the midnight sky. Many more trucks, beyond counting, coursed the opposite direction, south.

The Americans had turned the Trường Sơn Road into a nocturnal highway. They bombed it beginning at sunup every day, circling like hawks watching for movement, attacking everything from convoys to single trucks to bicycles. In her year on the Road, walking it as a singer and an actor, Minh had witnessed marvels of life and death, things she could never have invented. Men torn in half, sitting upright as if their missing lower halves were only buried. Oxen and water buffalo flying through the air mooing in wonder at themselves. An American bomber that zoomed in low to dump a thousand empty beer bottles on the Road. Bombs that bounced, bombs that divided into hundreds of smaller bombs. Bombs that charred the rain forest or killed it with chemicals. The binh trams defended the Road when and where they could with antiaircraft guns and rockets from Russia. They fired relentlessly. The Americans attacked with an unlimited arsenal of planes and helicopters and a godlike anger. Minh had seen a sky filled, literally, filled, with metal. But because the war in the South required an endless flow of men and materials from the North, many continued to brave it, even under the sun. To be caught out in the open on the Road was to die unlucky or careless.

Nhu and Yen left their places by the gate to arrange boxes as cots. Bumping along on their knees to keep from being thrown off-balance, they made a flat surface of mail cartons and lay down together. While they curled up, Minh stayed in place, not ready to sleep. From her backpack she opened the small box to breathe in the lotus blossom. She closed her eyes and saw herself as small enough to lie on the petals.

With a jolt of the truck, Minh was tossed off her cardboard pedestal onto the legs of Nhu and Yen. The three scrambled in the shifting mail and cartons. Minh could not protect the lotus; it tumbled out of the box and fell apart, gone dry in the mail. In the jumble of girls and boxes, the pink petals were lost. Minh let them go without wistfulness, for she'd had them to lose and that was something.

The truck stopped and cut its engine. Minh climbed over the gate down to the Road. The hooded headlamps of the truck behind crept closer. It, too, shut down, and the trucks behind it did the same, crowding tight. No traffic came from the other direction. The Trường Sơn Road settled and, when it did, the jungle's hot silence, which had always been there, filled the void.

Minh walked to the front of the truck. The mail courier and a dozen others came from their own stopped vehicles. Yen and Nhu stayed behind, opting for more sleep on their cartons. Beside the halted trucks, a crush of bicycles flowed to the head of the line. The men and women pushing them wore coolie hats even at night. Their bicycles were not meant to be ridden but to be used like oxen, yoked with long sticks and hung with supplies. The bicycles were so freighted with munitions, oil, food, cloth, caged fowl, and firewood that their frames were invisible inside the mass. All the walkers beside the bicycles were old, not fighters but peasant farmers and widows, wiry as any soldier. Many bikes rolled on worn rubber tires; the rest had cloths tied around the rims.

Minh and the crowd worked their way alongside resting trucks and cooling, pinging engines. A few drivers carried lanterns forward to see what the stoppage was.

An explosion waffled through the trees like a gust, shaking the branches. The jungle canopy flashed orange, the courier and the men around Minh recoiled, then quickened their sandals to get a look at what they'd just heard. Minh hurried with them, unafraid like them, accustomed to blasts on the Road.

They hurried past twenty stopped trucks; each slumbering vehicle sloughed off heat. At the head of the convoy, Minh and the clutch of drivers were stopped by regular North Vietnamese Army soldiers in uniforms and round green helmets who made a picket of their rifles and outstretched arms. They held at bay all those rushing forward. Many shouted to the soldiers, "What's going on?"

"Mines," they answered. "Clearing mines."

Minh had seen this, too. American bombs that dug into the earth to wait.

Beside the road, a steep bank rose. Bamboo and palms grew out of it. A few younger men and boys kicked off their sandals to hoist each other up the curvy palm trunks. Minh joined them—she was not as good a climber, but the courier helped her to a perch. She clung to the rough bark, legs wrapped about the trunk, with the courier just beneath her.

Ahead fifty meters, behind the soldiers stopping the traffic, the Road burned. Flames sparkled in a ring and in the drooping branches above it, in the dense undergrowth left and right. In the center of the Road stood the inferno of a ruined truck. All four tires were popped and melting, the canvas over the bed a flaming torch. If the mail carrier had struck the mine that did this, Minh and her girls would have been incinerated.

Even as the truck blazed, two big vehicles bashed at it with their bumpers to shove it off the Road, ram the fire into the jungle, and let the damp smother it.

A hundred meters beyond the fire, the halted headlamps of several southbound trucks beamed from atop a minor hill. They lit the labor of a dozen men wrangling fifty-gallon drums into place at the crest of the rise. The men tipped the steel barrels onto their sides, then rolled them downhill one at a time. The drums joggled down the uneven track, hitting ruts and roots. Most careened off the Road into the bush; a few made it to the bottom. Minh's legs tired around the palm trunk and she considered going down. The courier slid higher to let her rest against his shoulders.

The barrel-rolling looked like a game until, halfway down the hill, one big drum detonated with a flash. It launched high off the Road, out of sight, riding a furious blast and an empty, thwarted boom that did nothing but blow up a barrel. The watchers in the trees cheered as if a point had been scored. Minh, her grip on the palm fading, could not take her hands away to clap, so she only shouted. Then, satisfied, she asked the courier to let her climb down past him.

On the ground, Minh approached the only NVA soldier left blocking the road; the drivers understood now what had stopped traffic and most had gone back to their cabs to sleep. The bike pushers had leaned their loads against trees then lay on the ground beside them, arms for pillows, still in their straw hats.

The light of the fires came from behind the soldier, to give him an orange, jittery halo. His face lay recessed in the shadow of his wide-brimmed helmet, but his stance and hands showed him to be a young man. He might live, he might die. Minh walked up with hands clasped at her waist, brow tipped down and mild. She needed no confirmation that this soldier thought the same of her as he lowered his rifle. It was the hello and good-bye of every passing encounter in war. This one might survive. This one might not.

"Where are you from?" she asked.

"Vinh." The voice was youthful out of his murky features.

"I'm from Hanoi. Do you have a cigarette?"

"Sorry. No."

"Would you like one? I can get one for you."

"No. I thought you wanted one."

"I could never smoke. I'm a singer."

"You're pretty."

Minh was stringy, even gaunt, her toes were gnarled. Her skin lacked softness and felt foreign to her sometimes. He was a boy from a small city carrying a gun into a jungle. It was all right to say she was pretty when she was not. It was fair for her to rise on her toes, dip into his darkness, and kiss his cheek. He thanked her. He'd wanted just that.

"Do you know how long we will be stopped here?"

"The trucks won't go until all the mines are cleared. That could take until morning."

If it did, the convoy would not move until the following dusk. The drivers would pull off the Road, find as much cover as they could, then wait until night again to travel on.

Minh had lost the boxed lotus blossom. She'd let that go. But she would not release her claim on another day, on the chance she might tomorrow take a fresh flower from his hands.

"Let me go through."

The soldier, blocking the light, also blocked the way.

She expected him to say no, or at best ask her why. He pivoted his shaded face left, then right, too slowly to be a refusal. He looked to see who might be watching. Minh turned to scan with him. A few drivers remained in the trees, keen on the next barrel tumbling down the Road. The rest of the crowd had dispersed or lay asleep. Five soldiers sat in a circle passing a bottle of something, perhaps rice wine, and a cigarette.

Minh did not ask the young soldier again or go to the edge of the Road to sneak around him. She walked plainly past. He turned not even his head. She touched the boy's wrist as she slid by, to give him faith that he existed and to tell him he, too, should find a reason to live through the war years.

Weighing very little, she did not fear the minefield. The buried American mines were set to blow up vehicles or bounding fifty-gallon drums, not small women. She moved in the flickering darkness to the bottom of the hill, lit by flames from the blown-up truck, the waning fire in the leaves, and the hooded headlamps on the top of the hill.

Minh passed the wreckage slowly, trying to see bodies in the cab or bed. Nothing human-shaped smoldered inside. Minh walked on.

Behind her, on the other side of the guard, Yen and Nhu slept on boxes. They were safe there. She'd see them in binh tram 17 in two days when they finally arrived. They'd be on their own for a while and perhaps afraid for her because she would be missing. That would be good for them, to imagine what they'd do without Minh. She imagined their reunion, and it pleased her to think of her reappearing before them alive.

When another barrel skipped down, Minh stepped aside to watch it go, thinking it somehow a merry thing. The men pushing them down the Road did not see her in the firelight and truck lights. This invisibility added to her sense of rightness and drove her steps up the long hill.

At last, near the top of the hill, someone shouted at her, "What are you doing?"

Minh strolled past the gathered drivers and the drum rollers into the headlights and on. She owed them a song, perhaps, but no explanation.

Minh walked north on the Road. Because of the mine blockage behind her, traffic flowed only to the South. Sometimes minutes passed between diesel trucks rumbling out of the dark, scratchy and squeaking on old springs, lamps downcast. Each truck was so burdened that even in the starlight they seemed swaybacked, bearing the machinery and supplies of war, and the true fuel, men. No one noticed Minh against the jungle.

Never in her time on the Road had she been this solitary. Between trucks, the rain forest crackled with insects' songs, echoed with hoots, the woods ticked the way the cooling engines had. Always before, she'd moved with a troupe of women or with soldiers, with trucks or bikes or a hundred others on foot plodding along. By herself, the hours until dawn and more to binh tram 17 seemed weighty and trudging. Among the jungle voices, a tiger roared. Was the big cat yawning before sleep, thundering after a kill? Was it close, or did that bellow run far through the jungle? Minh's steps sped. Though she was alone with the Road, it was not alone with her.

She tried walking passages of the black path with eyelids closed, playing a game to see if she would go straight or sense the jungle before she put her face into it. She did not sit to rest, for that would be to sit near an unseen snake or on sharp ants. Even empty, the Road at night was not a place to be motionless. Minh slogged on. When she tired, with no one to talk to or follow, she walked in her heart.

She pulled up memories of him, though she had so few. Flowers left for her in the binh tram, notes after performances or mailed in secret without his name on the box. Glances, or the feel of his trailing fingertips, when no one was looking. He could not declare himself openly for her; the revolution wouldn't permit that. He was a political officer, he belonged to discipline. He was an example. He could not love her.

At sunrise, the sky lightened before the dark jungle. Minh walked up a hill toward a blue heaven that beckoned. In the forest on both sides, first light pierced the branches to make sharp baubles on the ground.

In the rising dawn, Minh did not yet recognize where she was on the Road. Though she'd come this way many times, always she'd traveled alongside others to chat with, she'd taken less notice than she did alone. The Road was scarred and dirty, great swaths of it had been torn up and repaired; it showed the marks and damage. But it rolled on. Minh sang songs to the Road as she walked it, songs of itself.

The heat rose faster than the sun until her private night on the Road had ended. Bicycles, oxen, goats, sheep, and soldiers appeared around her, bustling obliviously, like daytime ghosts. A dark-skinned peasant carried a box of dynamite on his shoulder; the traffic ignored him as much as it did Minh.

She hummed to herself as she went. Midmorning, she stopped to accept a ladle of water from a Lao woman squatting on bare feet. The woman must have lived nearby, for a teen boy emerged from the brush lugging a fresh sloshing bucket. Unless he was simple, and he did not seem to be, the lean boy would receive a visit soon in his village, either from the government to join the Lao Army against the communists or from the communists themselves to become a Pathet Lao, a guerrilla. No matter that his mother loved him or that he hauled water to the Road, or that he lived deep in the countryside. Minh from the city had no mother, and she drank the water the boy brought. No matter. The war was like a mouse, it could get in anywhere.

Minh trod on her shadow, noon. She'd walked for ten hours. Her appetite seemed to have its own eyes, too, for her hunger swelled at a familiar bend in the river. Three more kilometers lay between her and binh tram 17. Minh had one more walking hour between her and a meal, a cot, the sight of his white shirt, perhaps a word.

The Road ran to this spot because the river flowed narrow here. Seventy meters wide, the water was broad and deep enough to make traffic on the shore pile up until dark, when it was safer to cross. For livestock, bicycles, and the walkers of the Road, a ferry had been rigged up; a wooden platform floating on pontoons made of empty diesel barrels crisscrossed the river on a rope pulley driven by a truck motor. The ferryman, an elderly farmer with three sons fighting for the communists, ran back and forth across the river during the day. Minh didn't know the river man's name, but one year ago when she first crossed, the old man asked her for a song when he noticed her singing to herself. Since then, like a toll, while the engine huffed, Minh sang for the old man every few weeks when she came this way, sometimes blending her voice with bleating sheep and lowing cattle.

The big trucks could not go on the raft, they might sink it. At night, the canvas-backed, lumbering giants drove across the river itself, a miraculous thing to see. Just below the surface, engineers had laid great stone blocks to fashion an underwater bridge. The bridge would never wash away and was difficult to spot from the air.

The raft chugged toward her from the north bank, bearing only the ferryman. When it reached her shore, Minh stepped aboard, followed by six loaded-up bikes and the small man carrying dynamite on his shoulder. Water lapped at the empty drums, sun gleamed in the ripples flowing over the submerged bridge. The ferryman winced into the glare and the afternoon heat when Minh sat beside him. She had seen him two weeks ago as she headed south with her girls. He asked after them. She replied they'd be along soon.

Before the old man could put the raft's engine in gear to ride the tugging line out over the water, one of the truck drivers on shore lost his patience. Under the bright sun, he drove his large eight-wheeled rig openly into the river, tiptoeing onto the unseen stones. The ferryman tensed at this.

"He should not do that. He should wait until dark."

The ferryman idled his engine to bob against the shoreline, reluctant to cross while the trucks were doing so. What if they were seen? The vehicle crept forty meters onto the river, and for those minutes all seemed safe in the blue sky. The next truck in line crept out from under the jungle cover to cross, too. A third truck inched from under the trees to prepare for its turn.

On the raft, the little dynamite man sat on his case, the bike pushers dangled their feet in the river to cool their feet. No one seemed nervous, only the ferryman. He said, "I don't like this."

Minh didn't either, but she was hungry and lonely and wanted to reach binh tram 17.

The ferryman said, "I'm not lucky."

He had three boys in the war, the bicycle pushers in their straw hats were away from their farms, Minh was an orphan, and dynamite rode the river with them. The ribs of the bicycle pushers showed through their shirts. The dynamite carrier closed his eyes, asleep inside his leathery skin. None of them were lucky.

Two weeks ago on the river, Minh had stood away from the engine to fold her hands and sing for the passengers, livestock, and her girls. She performed "The Mat Song," about soldiers who marched far from home to fight with machetes and mats on their backs. The ferryman had requested it. On this noon, he did not ask for a song. The scent of lotus flowers reached Minh from the far shore, and she wanted to go on.

She scooted closer to the ferryman and took one of his old hands in hers. She put her chin on his shoulder, to croon only into the folds of his ear, a quiet song without lyrics, just a melody. She sang to the ferryman like she had to the Road the night before, as if they were alone. When the old man smiled, the ruts beside his eyes were deep enough to have shadows.

In the torpor of the heat, Minh closed her own eyes. She invented the tune as she went, listening to her voice in the ferryman's ear, hearing the river slap the pontoons and the idling motor. The ferryman shifted into gear and the raft bumped forward, onto the water.

The ferryman guided the raft out onto the river. After a slow minute, Minh lost the smell of lotus flowers in the diesel fumes spitting from the trucks nearby. She kept humming to the ferryman, to calm him and keep him fording the river.

The old man pulled his hand from Minh's. She raised her head off his shoulder, still humming. The creases in his face remained near her opened eyes, but his old smile was gone. She quieted. They were halfway across the river. He stopped the motor to listen.

Minh keened her ears with the ferryman and the bicycle pushers. They all pointed above the water. The dynamite carrier had awakened and he pointed, too. They aimed their arms and fingers like little guns at the American spotter plane flying low over the water, wings below the treetops, straight at them.

CHAPTER 5

20,000 feet over central Laos

At this altitude, the world's curve allowed Sol to conjure the rest of the earth in his head. Only at tremendous heights could he do this, understand the entire sapphire globe. Up here, immensity became finite. Distances turned into nothingness, great features of the earth were reduced to mere shapes, the colors of man and his stacked works were expressed in a limited palette. On the ground, the too-much complexity, the politics of sea-level people, muddied the view. Sol felt sometimes lost in that smaller, infinite world.

To the west, the rumpled greenery of Laos and Thailand slipped by on the hiss of jet fuel and pressurized oxygen. Eastward, Da Nang Harbor sparkled at the foot of a mountain range. Beyond the coastline, the earth turned blue, an oceanic ball. Out on that blue floated one of the world's great warships, the carrier USS *America*. Two destroyers sailed at her flanks, a third in her wake.

Daniels's voice fluted in his helmet: "We call that the Tonkin Gulf Yacht Club."

Whitecaps rippled to the shore north of Da Nang. This was Sol's first clear look at the DMZ. The unseen line that separated warring North from South wasn't lit up with explosions and tracers, wasn't pyrotechnics or a tombstone, just more serene planet. Sol put North Vietnam to his back and brought his Thud into formation, just below and to the left of Daniels.

The undercarriage of Daniels's jet bristled with bombs, napalm canisters, two Sidewinder air-to-air missiles, and external fuel tanks, just like Sol's. Flying in tandem was something he'd done very little of in his nuclear years over gray Europe. Jetting through this perfect firmament far above Southeast Asia, Daniels's Thud was a powerful mirror for Sol. Silver winks glinted off his wings, flame shot from his tail. Streaking across the shapely world, they were both heavily armed, looking for something to strike. Sol wished for a photograph of himself like this, miles up behind his oxygen mask, all blue fire and silver light.

"Ready to go to work?" With this clipped transmission, Daniels in his cockpit pulled down his visor.

Sol did the same, then thumbed the transmission button on his stick. "Roger. No trees."

"No trees."

On the UHF channel, Daniels hailed Cricket. This was the airborne command and control center, a C-130 flying high and safe over South Vietnam carrying a battery of radios and traffic controllers. Cricket was in charge of the day's bombing missions over Laos and Vietnam.

"Cricket, Dash flight checking in. Over."

"Good afternoon, Dash flight. Got nothing for you right now. Stand by."

"Dash flight standing by."

The earth rolled slowly toward Sol. Beside him, Daniels went into an easy rightward turn, banking to stay over their assigned sector in Laos, southwest of the village of Tchepone, along the Xe Banghiang River.

Sol maintained formation off Daniels's left wing. In midturn, Daniels crackled in his helmet.

"Want to see a trick?"

Daniels sounded impatient. Sol never had that issue in a jet fighter. For years, he and his nuke flew far above the earth, supersonic and alone with each other near the borders of belligerent nations. Impatience had no role in vigilance.

Sol shrugged to no one. "Sure."

"Follow me."

Daniels banked harder across the azure morning. Sol pushed the stick and toed the rudder pedals to keep pace and position.

"Where we going?"

Daniels answered by throttling back and bleeding altitude. Sol tagged along, turning east with him toward Vietnam. There, crossing into Laos, a C-130 transport winged in their direction at fifteen thousand feet. Daniels hailed.

"Westbound C-130, this is Dash flight. Two Thuds hanging around looking for work. Could you use an escort?"

"Dash leader, this is Hillsboro 8. Come alongside."

"Roger, Hillsboro."

Daniels cast Sol a thumbs-up, nodded his visored helmet sharply, then split away to race past the transport. He did a hot turn, contrails zipping off his wings. Sol stuck to him. They must have looked beautiful from the C-130's cockpit. Daniels settled off the transport's starboard wing. Sol nosed up on port.

Daniels called, "Switch to Fox mike." He wanted a private word on the FM channel, outside the hearing of the C-130 pilot.

Sol toggled to change frequencies. "Go."

"You a good shot?"

Inside his oxygen mask, Sol licked his lips, scanning for the right answer. This brought to mind the conversation at the Officers Club, where Sol was asked questions that might have been traps for the wrong reply.

He flew a Mach 2 jet loaded with a pair of air-to-air missiles, a 20mm six-barrel Gatling cannon, sixteen 500-pound bombs, and two 450-gallon drop tanks. No one was given the keys to that without being a good shot. Some pilots were better than others, that was all. Sol had been in the middle of the pack in training.

"Good enough. Why?"

"I'm going to ask you for a fuel check."

"Okay."

"You tell me you're bingo." This was pilot's lingo for low on fuel.

"But I'm not."

"Play along."

"Okay."

"I'm going to chew you out. Then I'm going to radio the transport to tell them we're off station because you screwed up."

Sol hesitated to agree. They'd just got here. Why would the transport care if they left? And why did he have to be the screwup?

Daniels laughed into the radio, anticipating. "It's my idea. You can be the good guy next time."

Sol had no visual on Daniels on the other side of the big C-130. He envisioned a large grin between Daniels's non-regulation sideburns. Whatever Daniels had in mind was also not by the book. Sol's choices were to say yes or no and be branded by either.

"Okay."

"Then we're going to drop altitude and head toward base."

"What are we doing?"

"It's not a trick if I tell you. Back to Uniform."

Sol returned to the UHF channel, where anyone could hear that he was about to be called a bad pilot.

"Dash 2, Dash lead."

"Go, lead."

"Give me a fuel check."

Sol was no fan of tricks. No engineer liked them. Structure, facts, sums, these were the building blocks of the world.

"Lead, I'm bingo fuel."

"Dash 2, repeat."

Sol sighed before thumbing the transmit button. "Dash lead, I am bingo."

"Copy, Dash 2. How the fuck did that happen?"

Sol didn't know what to say. He hadn't been told to make up a story.

Again, Daniels got out front. "Don't fucking answer. In the future, keep your foot off the gas and don't showboat so much. This isn't how we do our jobs, understood?" Whatever dodge Daniels was pulling, this felt a little personal. Sol had said in the Officers Club, indeed, that he would do the job. The showboat thing stung, too, since that was something he never did.

The C-130 pilot was listening, the worst part.

"Hillsboro 8, Dash lead."

"Go, Dash."

"Sorry, Hillsboro. We've got to RTB. Dash 2 is bingo. You're on your own."

The transport pilot had been on his own to begin with. He said, simply, "Copy."

Daniels moved first. He peeled down and away from the C-130's side. At two hundred miles per hour, the Thunderchief, capable of far greater speeds, seemed to be sleepwalking. Sol followed.

Who cared if they abandoned a transport that hadn't asked for them? Sol considered asking Daniels. But whatever game they were playing was already afoot, so Sol tucked in his lip, feeling once again put in a position to be judged: Was he a good sport, was he gung ho, was he a good shot? He nudged the stick to close in on Daniels, take up a perfect formation, and demonstrate he was a gifted and experienced pilot.

If the C-130 was watching them go, they'd see no screwup. Sol locked his wing on Daniels, headed for the deck, southwest toward Takhli.

Daniels transmitted nothing while they flew through ten thousand feet, down to eight, then six. Sol waited to be let in on the plan, growing more concerned with every moment that this was no trick but a joke on him. After his mistake in the de-arming area yesterday, followed by that public debacle in the mess hall last night, he feared a trend taking shape for his time in Vietnam, a yearlong lurch between fuckups and blunders. The Thai border approached, only minutes away. Was Sol going to land again with his ordnance unspent, the unmistakable badge to the ground crew of a mission without action? He laid his thumb over the transmit button, just about fed up.

The UHF band clicked in Sol's helmet. He expected a laugh from Daniels, maybe a gotcha.

"All flights, all flights, Red Crown."

This wasn't Daniels's voice but Red Crown, a Navy ship stationed in the Gulf monitoring all the airfields of North Vietnam.

"Alert. A pair of MiGs has scrambled out of Dong Hoi. Repeat, two Bandits out of Dong Hoi. Tracking southwest two-one-zero degrees, at twenty-two thousand feet."

Daniels jumped on the transmission. Even as he answered, he throttled up and began gaining altitude. Sol kept pace.

"Red Crown, Dash flight leader. We are turning to intercept."

"Copy, Dash flight. We have you on radar. Expect intercept on your location in four."

"Copy. In four."

Daniels carved a sharp, climbing bank. Sol's wing tips wept mist, pulling three Gs in the turn beside Daniels. This was why Daniels had asked if Sol was a good shot. MiGs incoming.

And this was the trick. The North Vietnamese had been monitoring their transmissions. Daniels sought out a transport, a meaty, unprotected target to sucker them in once the two 105s left as Sol was pretending to be bingo.

"Dash flight, Dash flight. Hillsboro 8. Do you copy?"

"Go, Hillsboro."

"Bogeys on the way. We're hung out to dry here."

"We're on it, Hillsboro."

"What about your fuel?"

"We found some more. No problem."

Daniels had pushed his throttle to the stops, riding a fiery spike out of his tailpipe. With Sol on his shoulder, he zoomed past the westbound transport, racing to slam into the MiGs and engage.

Sol had never been in a real dogfight, only exercises, and the last one was three years ago over Japan. He'd not fared so well then, but his recall was hazy with adrenaline spreading into his fingertips. Daniels surged over the radio.

"Weapons hot."

Sol's gut fluttered, wanting to pause and ask questions. He had no time to figure out what all this meant, drawing out MiGs into aerial combat, using a C-130 as bait, playing games on open radio channels. With no warning he was charging into a lethal fight on a morning that had been clear and wide-open blue, all because of a ruse. Was Daniels a good shot? Should Sol ask? Hurriedly, he set switches for weapons delivery, two sight controls, activated the pair of Sidewinders, and adjusted his radar for air-to-air. Lastly, he changed the targeting sight for air gunnery. Sol slid a forefinger over the trigger for his 20mm Vulcan cannon and took a practice peek through the reticle on the gunsight into the empty sky that was minutes away from becoming a battlefield.

Sol cleared his throat to open his voice, keep it from betraying how unprepared he felt. "Copy. Weapons hot."

"Level off at fifteen thousand. We'll jump them from below."

"Copy."

Sol located the afterburner switch, ready to use it in the fight. The Thud wasn't the most nimble of fighters, so speed was everything.

"Dash 2."

"Go, Dash lead."

"You got this."

Uncannily, Daniels again knew what was rummaging inside Sol's head. Maybe Daniels had played this gambit with other new pilots over the past year. More likely, he just knew the ropes. Sol lessened his grip on the stick, eased the tension in his gloves, ready to reach for a range of switches and toggles. Sol was beginning to trust Daniels and, in doing so, trusted himself a little more.

"Roger."

Red Crown narrated for them the location, route, and speed of the oncoming MiGs. Sol chewed his lip and thought of his father scrapping with Japanese Zeros twenty-five years ago over the Pacific. Sol was going twice the speed of his dad at double the altitude, in a plane not designed for this kind of combat. Sol imagined himself swapping dogfight stories with his old man, then rid himself of everything that was not here and right now. Sol nodded and accepted that he, like his father, would be judged by these next minutes. Alongside Daniels, he scorched eastward just under six hundred knots, ready to jettison his drop tanks and take up a fight.

Sol soared beside Daniels, scanning the firmament and spoiling for his oncoming enemies, two Soviet-made North Vietnamese–flown MiGs. The sky gave up nothing to the pair of Thuds hurtling through it. Tension mounted in Sol's palm, thumb, and index finger, each in charge of something different, flight, missiles, the Gatling cannon.

"Dash lead, Red Crown."

Daniels answered. "Go, Red Crown."

"The bogeys bugged out. Ten miles downrange."

"Copy. Next time."

"Next time, Dash. Out."

Daniels backed off the throttle and turned lazily. Sol stayed in formation, buffeted in Daniels's ruffled wake. He wrestled to marry his relief at the avoided battle with the burning urge that had built in him to fire his weapons in battle. The two emotions didn't settle well with each other. Sol took his hand from the stick to let the Thud fly itself for a few moments, to work his fingers and get the tingle out of them.

"Dash 2."

"Go, lead."

"They decided to *didi*."

"How many times have you done this?"

"A bunch."

"Have they ever showed up?"

"Not once."

"What about Hillsboro 8?"

"What about him?"

"Won't he be pissed at being used for bait?"

Daniels pressed his talk button so Sol could hear him laugh while he snapped his Thunderchief into a perfect barrel roll. The maneuver, stunning and so fast, said to Sol: Fuck 'em. We're in jets.

"Dash flight, Cricket."

Daniels took the call. "Cricket, Dash lead. Go."

"Dash flight, proceed two-five-five degrees for one hundred miles from the channel one-zero-three Tacan." Tacan was a tactical air navigation transmitter on the ground that allowed pilots to determine direction and distance from it.

"Copy." Daniels repeated the instructions.

"Dash flight, make contact with your FAC. Nail 34. He's on 299.3."

"Dash lead switching to 299.3."

"Get there quick, Dash. He's got a good target for you."

Sol switched frequencies, too. He thumbed his mic twice, clicking to let Daniels know he was on the new channel. Sol would monitor Daniels's conversation with the forward air controller.

"Nail 34, this is Dash flight of two checking in for targets. Over."

"Copy, Dash flight. I've got a winner for you this morning. How far are you from me?"

"Six zero miles. Be there in eight."

"Copy. Let's go over the target brief and you can ADF me." Nail 34 was going to give them the intel for the bombing run. While he talked, Daniels and Sol would use their automatic direction finders to home in on the FAC's radio signal and location.

"Nail, go."

"Weather is CAVU." Clear and visibility unlimited. Sol flicked on his direction finder as Nail transmitted. "I've spotted a ferry working a bend in a river."

"Copy."

"Next to it, there's a couple trucks crossing a submerged stone bridge. Pretty clever. You'll hit the bridge and anything that's on it. The ferry is primary, bridge is secondary."

"Copy. Ferry is primary target."

"Elevation is five hundred feet. I've been working this area for the last few days. I saw the ferry before, it stays pretty busy. The trucks on the water caught my eye today. I haven't seen any antiaircraft fire. I think the area's clean."

"Copy, Nail. Good news."

Daniels wagged his wings at Sol, as if to say, "Yippee."

"Dash flight, what's your ordnance load?"

"A flight of two Fox 105s. We both have two Sidewinders, sixteen Mark 82 bombs, and six hundred pounds of twenty mike-mike. We have twenty minutes of playtime."

"Copy."

Nail 34's location popped up on Sol's ADF scope. Daniels adjusted five degrees south, Sol eased with him. Off to the east, just across the border in Vietnam, the landing strip for the Khe Sanh air base looked like a bandage on a field of scars. North Vietnam's massive Tet siege of Khe Sanh had ended only a week ago, after six months. From the air, the fury of American bombs dropped on the surrounding plain and hills and the attackers was clear. Great scoops of bare earth and blackened forest told of an epic battle with a determined enemy.

After girding himself for a tussle with airborne MiGs, targeting a ferry on a river in a valley with no reported hostile gunfire seemed a letdown. This wasn't going to be Khe Sanh. Sol kept that to himself. Like yesterday, this looked to be just more target practice.

CHAPTER 6

Xe Banghiang River
Near Tchepone
Laos

The American plane breezed down the river, blatant and slow. No one on the ferry had a gun, only bicycles and dynamite. The first truck forging across the underwater stone bridge hurried to the far shore to duck into the jungle and hide. The two big trucks behind, caught in the open, honked their horns and waved stupidly at the American pilot who, in sunglasses, waved back. On the raft, the man sitting on his dynamite stood, then sat back down as if he saw no threat greater than his box. If Minh had had a gun she would have shot at the plane, the first gun she would have ever fired. This was war, and all the songs and plays told of fighting and killing the Americans, not waving and honking. The truck drivers and bicycle pushers, they must be locals. They didn't yet know the dangers that came with the little puttering plane into their quiet valley.

The plane filled the river valley with echoes of its engine. The pilot flew past the idling ferry and the pair of exposed trucks, then followed the water around the bend, out of sight behind the trees. He swept his American noise away with him.

The ferryman put his engine back in gear. The rope pulley engaged and the raft putt-putted over the river. Three minutes were left to reach the opposite bank.

The trucks in the middle of the water revved to resume crossing. Minh sat again beside the ferryman. Nestled against him on the bench seat, she felt him shaking, badly frightened.

The ferryman blinked upstream after the vanished American plane. Minh reached for his hand again. He pulled it away.

"You sang in my ear. You bewitched me."

He raised the hand between them, a barrier, and would not look at Minh.

"I blame you."

CHAPTER 7

Nail 34 was a twin-tailed Air Force O-2 with two props, one facing forward, the other pushing from behind. From a mile above, the top of Nail's white wing made him look like a great gull circling the river bend. Daniels hailed.

"Nail, Dash lead. We tally your position. Smoke the target when ready."

"Dash flight, copy."

The O-2 sheared away left, dipped his nose at three thousand feet, and drove straight for the river. Sol admired how low and slow the FAC pilot flew to do his job, although those were probably his best protections; he could hide in the treetops, slip in, and power out before the enemy gunners got a fix.

Nail 34 made a beeline for the ground on such a severe angle that he almost stood his plane on its front propeller. At one thousand feet, inside small-arms range, a puff appeared below the O-2's wing. Nail had fired a willy pete rocket, white phosphorous, before pulling up hard out of his dive. The rocket slammed into the bank of the river bend. Where it struck, a column of smoke rose above the jungle and shining water.

"Dash flight, do you tally my smoke?"

Daniels didn't answer the FAC but hailed Sol instead. "Dash 2, you want to be low bird? Take the first shot?"

This took Sol by surprise. He liked the notion, felt ready for it, but Daniels had made himself hard to trust after the gambit with the MiGs. Was this one more trick?

"Dash 2, you copy?"

Another yes or no answer, another defining moment. Sol thumbed his mic.

"Dash lead, affirmative."

"Get some."

Sol nodded to himself. He tightened both shoulder harnesses and gave his lap belt a quick tug.

His gauges said his Thud was on a 12,000-foot perch. He'd climb to 14,000, then roll into a 45-degree nose-down dive. Release bombs at 6,000 feet. Bottom out no lower than 4,000 feet. Break left from the target and climb. Sol radioed all this to Daniels, who clicked his mic twice to affirm.

The FAC broke in. "Dash 2, Nail."

"Go, Nail."

"My smoke is on the north bank. Drop two Mark 82s fifty yards south of that. There's the ferry, in the middle of the river."

Sol picked up Nail's position at his two o'clock, still scribing a lazy arc over the jungle.

"Copy, Nail, have you in sight."

"Dash 2, your approach is good. You are cleared in hot."

"Dash 2 is in hot." Sol checked the sound of his own voice. He told himself to remember it and to tell this later, the words of his first real combat run, as cool. "Dash 2 is lighting burner now."

Sol lit the afterburner, the Thud surged, pressing him back into his seat. He pulled the stick to climb up to his perch of 14,000, using the afterburner so he wouldn't lose any of his 560 knots during the climb.

Hitting his altitude, Sol cooled the afterburner. He nodded to himself; he had this. With a flick, he rolled the Thud over 135 degrees, almost inverted, into the bombing run.

He located Nail's rising smoke, then jinked to bring the mark of it to the center of his windshield. His bombsight pipper settled just below the rising white pillar. Still two miles over the target, Sol couldn't make out the ferry, only the meandering bend of the river through the dense Lao valley and the wisps of phosphorous smoke. With his throttle at 90 percent, Sol accelerated downhill at a 45-degree angle.

The ferry emerged on the river, just a small gray square by the north shore near the FAC's smoke. To its right, a pair of trucks seemed to be skating across the water itself; this was the submerged bridge. Sol drove the Thud down the chute, steep and swift, streaking to 600 knots at 6,500 feet. The pipper rested dead center on the ferry, now big enough to recognize people and supplies crowding it. Sol wondered about the people, the notion of killing them, then dismissed this as an abstraction, a luxury not afforded in combat. He limited his curiosity to only whether or not the people on the river saw or heard him coming. With his thumb on the stick, Sol depressed the red pickle button.

The ejector racks under his wings thumped as two Mark 82s released into the air to sail ten seconds and two miles to the target.

Smoothly, satisfied he'd lined up his run as well as he could, Sol pulled back for a wings-level climb. Against the building gravity, he was pressed deeper into the ejection seat as the Gs mounted. He lost sight of the river while the jet's nose nudged up ten degrees out of the dive.

The altimeter showed that he'd bottomed out at thirty-five hundred feet. The Thud's powerful engine took over from gravity and accelerated into a fierce climb. When the unbroken sky filled Sol's windshield, he shoved the stick over to break left.

Still pulling Gs, he radioed Nail and Daniels: "Dash 2 is clear and off target."

Turning and climbing fast, Sol rolled the Thud on its side to get a view of what his bombs were about to do.

CHAPTER 8

The rope pulley creaked, the engine chugged, and the old ferryman sitting beside it all could not hear the whistling bombs. The bicycle pushers soaked their feet in the river, resting and pacific. They wore wide-brimmed coolie hats to shade their faces, and the dynamite carrier had closed his eyes again. None of them saw the jet. Only Minh heard the bombs, saw the plane, and dove off the raft.

She did not have even moments to scream a warning. Her breath was needed for the water and the seconds for getting away.

Minh hit the river kicking and stroking. She always knew she would die alone, an orphan's instinct, but had never foreseen this. She was not a strong swimmer and used every muscle to claw at the water. The moments ticked in her windmilling arms and thrashing feet; she flapped toward the center of the river, away from shore and the moving ferry. Minh whimpered as she swam, hearing her own panic when her mouth rounded up for breath.

The seconds dragged longer than she believed they would, expecting the blast in every one of them.

Minh's feet dragged the muddy bottom. She'd reached a bar in the river, too shallow to swim across. She began to run, knees high, foaming the water. She'd not gone far enough and didn't believe she could anyway. Across her shoulder, she looked back at the raft. Even trying to escape, Minh wanted to see it, the explosion that was her end. She'd watched a man do this on the Road, a thief who'd stolen food. He was to be shot and had asked to remove his blindfold. She'd stolen nothing, not even love, and did not deserve this. But she could face it if a thief could.

Twenty meters away, still plugging for shore, the ferryman hadn't stood on the raft, but he looked at Minh. The bicycle pushers sat in a row facing away from her, their hats like paper lanterns. The dynamite carrier was on his feet watching her go, but he stood beside a box of dynamite with his back to the climbing jet.

The bombs plummeted too fast to be more than black whirs in the air. The first splashed ten meters beyond the ferry; a heartbeat later, the water fountained again, closer to shore. Minh sniffled, and this told her she'd been crying in the water.

The first bomb blew. A concussion ring knocked away her feet, chopping her facedown into a raging swell of white water. Minh was dragged backward as if chained by the ankles, both hands plowing through mud. Her head went under and she lost all orientation except for the roar that swallowed, squeezed, and flung her.

She floated in a black realm that was more than water. She could not find surface or bottom to it, up or down; it held her limp and seemed to be turning her in its hands, examining her.

She needed a breath and opened her mouth to take one. Solid, cool, and killing water went down her windpipe. Minh choked and jerked awake, eyes already open. She saw only daylight in the churning brown water, so muddy that her own thrashing hands were hidden. Her lungs groaned on their own. Minh kicked as she floundered, adding to the burning need for air. She sensed her final seconds and struggled to think how to save herself, but only water and light touched her, nothing else.

Minh could not keep her mouth shut against her lungs any longer. She parted her lips to breathe the river in.

Her toe scraped a rock. Her heel sank into muck.

Minh's mouth gaped and closed like a fish. Her rib cage was on fire. She closed her throat against the water, dropped her other foot. She was dulled but knew this was her last act. Minh pushed off into what she prayed was up.

CHAPTER 9

The first of Sol's five-hundred-pound bombs erupted in a great cannonball of water. The second, closer to shore, geysered a moment after. The first explosion flashed again, a secondary detonation. Something on the ferry had been incendiary and went up with a gratifying bang, probably munitions. In his cockpit, Sol balled a fist.

He swooped into the last of his turn, scanning the river bend. The remains of mist ghosted across the water. The ferry was gone, no trace of the trucks. Sol finished off his turn, throttled back, and leveled wings to wait for Nail 34 to give him his bomb damage assessment.

"Dash 2, looks like a direct hit."

Sol's first combat run had been a bull's-eye.

Daniels chipped in. "Good shooting."

Sol waggled his wings to acknowledge.

"Dash lead, copy?"

"Go, Nail."

"The two trucks made it to shore. I want four Mark 82s one hundred yards north of Dash 2's smoke. They can't be far from the river. Let's take a shot at the Trail."

Daniels repeated the specifics of the FAC's request.

"Dash lead, you are cleared in hot."

"Copy, Nail, Dash lead is in hot."

Daniels rolled in from Sol's one o'clock high. Bits of the ferry still smoldered on the river, so Nail didn't need another willy pete to pin the target. Daniels's Thunderchief put its nose down and knifed for the earth like a hunting hawk. Against the blue backdrop, the swooping jet was all power and modernity, an electrifying sight. Sol wanted to go in again.

At sixty-five hundred feet, a pair of Mark 82s catapulted from under Daniels's wings. The Thud powered out of its dive, then into a climbing snap turn to the right. Sol lost sight of the bombs but locked eyes on the rim of the river bend where he expected them to hit. He counted to ten before the first, then second, third, and fourth bombs blew apart the jungle; limbs and fronds catapulted out of the twirling, fiery blasts. Sol imagined he could hear the crumps over his own jet engine across the open sky. He throttled back more, easing the stick and ailerons to lay his F-105 over on its side, shedding altitude. He wanted a clear view of Daniels's strike, to see this little part of Laos burn and maybe catch sight of a ruined enemy truck or two. An hour from now he'd describe to Daniels and the pilots in the Officers Club what he'd seen, what he'd done, he'd laugh along with them at that crazy bit Daniels tried to pull with the MiGs.

He soared lower, slower, panning the river for that underwater bridge. Sol was going to ask the FAC to send him in on a second run to rubblize it.

Daniels's voice cut across the radio, shouting *yahoo* like a cowboy. The man was enjoying this.

Sol thumbed the mic to tell his wing mate: *Nice shooting, too, buddy.*

Before he could speak, Nail 34 broke in, also shouting, but frantic. "Dash 2, break left, break left! You're getting hosed!"

Daniels squawked, "Get out of there, right now. You're taking fire."

Even as he yanked the stick sideways and slammed the throttle forward, Sol swiveled his head, searching for tracers. His Thud accelerated immediately, taking on instant speed and altitude that slammed him against the seat. Damn it, he'd gotten careless, drove his jet like a rocking chair because Nail had seen no gunfire in this area for a few days, and because Sol's first run had been like fish in a barrel, Daniels's run, too. Now Sol was corkscrewing out of the way of red streaks, a hundred glowing dashes in the air zipping up at him. All he could move were his chin and his eyes, enough to see more burning rounds off his port wing. He jinked the stick right, the Thud jolted that direction, then yanked the stick straight back to gain altitude. The sun flared across his windshield. Dials and gauges measured his climb while Nail's excited radio voice described what Sol could not see, scarlet tracers fading behind and below him.

At ten thousand feet, Sol backed off the throttle. The golden blobs of blood light in his vision eased as the G forces decreased and the G-suit deflated around his legs. Sol growled all kinds of things without thumbing the mic for Daniels or Nail to hear, muttering *holy shit* and *Jesus* until he was calm enough to breathe through his nose.

Leveling off, Sol peered down at the river. The smoke from his and Daniels's bombs had dissipated to resemble only a morning mist among the trees and on the river. Except for a denuded patch of forest north of the bend, with no ferry or trucks on the water, the Lao morning glowed untrammeled. The pounding of Sol's heart seemed without cause.

Again, Daniels did that thing where he appeared to know what Sol was thinking. "Dash 2, take a peek at your four o'clock low."

Sol pivoted in the cockpit to gaze down and behind him. A mile from the river bend, from the side of a hill cloistered in jungle, a pair of small spotlights blinked at him.

Daniels arrived off Sol's starboard wing. "Those are zeeps. Remember it. That's what they look like."

ZPUs. Sol had been briefed about them, about all the flak the North Vietnamese would throw at him. ZPUs were four-barrel 14.5mm antiaircraft guns that could fire 2,400 rounds a minute. They were very effective up to 5,000 feet; at that rate of fire they could chew a jet's wing off. A pair of zeeps had picked Sol up at 4,000 feet while he was grazing in the greenery, admiring his and Daniels's firepower. But why were they still firing, shooting up a shower of useless sparks that ran out of steam halfway to the Thuds cruising at 10,000? Sol asked Daniels. Nail 34, laying low somewhere in the weeds, answered.

"Dash flight, look across the river."

Sol peered down past his swept-back wings. Another light, a single one but amber, slower and angrier than the zeeps, winked at them from the emerald depths of the jungle.

"You guys woke up a 37. The zeeps are just marking you for their big brother."

This bigger gun fired eighty rounds per minute and was lethal to 10,000 feet. Sol hadn't seen any tracers from this weapon, so the gunners hadn't tracked him yet. He checked his altimeter. Daniels nudged higher another thousand feet. Wordlessly, Sol rose with him.

He searched far below for Nail 34's white wing top and figure-eight pattern. Nail worked his little O-2 down there in the crevices, scuttling across treetops, poking up his head then ducking out of sight into the natural undulations of the valley. Sol couldn't see him, but if the zeep gunners did, if they drew a bead, Nail would disappear in a cloud of shards and spinning propellers. Both guns had quit firing.

The FAC radioed Daniels his bomb damage assessment, a little long of the target but okay. No enemy trucks had been hit, but they might be somewhere close by, still viable targets. Nail was zooming around looking for them on the Trail.

Sol wanted a try at those guns. They'd missed him when he hadn't even known they were there. Now, with both the ZPUs and the 37 pinpointed, he and Daniels could take them on with eyes open and plenty of ordnance left to blow them to pieces. Nail could go back to telling jet pilots this area was safe from antiaircraft artillery.

It wasn't up to Sol to make the request. Daniels was Dash flight leader, and they were both working Nail 34's mission. Sol flew straight, high, and quiet. The cockpit of the F-105, his office for the past eight years, had become intrinsic to him while escorting a nuke around the world. Today, he rode one decked out with guns, rockets, and bombs above a far brighter, hotter battlefield than any he'd flown over in the Cold War. Sol had enemies who weren't just looking for him but right at him with guns of their own. His confidence in the Thud was expanding; the plane he'd claimed wasn't right for this shooting war had swept him safely in and out of enemy fire after delivering a bull's-eye.

Daniels started the conversation with the FAC. "Nail, Dash lead."

"Go, Dash."

"We've got about ten minutes of playtime left. Plenty of ordnance. We'll put it where you want it."

Daniels initiated a slow turn to the east, to stay in Nail's playground a little longer.

The FAC didn't answer. Sol flew with both eyes on the ground. Daniels began to straighten out of the turn, apparently resolved to head back to Takhli and the Officers Club with enough of a tale under their belts for one day.

Two miles below, a cotton ball of smoke puffed. There, just behind it, sailed the pale fixed wing of Nail 34. A rocket trail threaded almost straight down, a very steep and short distance. This showed how close in Nail 34 had flown to smoke the North Vietnamese 37mm gun.

His willy pete detonated on a hillside above the river bend. The jungle valley seemed to exhale steam, maddened.

"Dash lead, Nail 34."

"Go, Nail."

"Fifty meters right of my smoke, on the hillside."

"Copy. Five oh right."

"Have at it. Nail out."

CHAPTER 10

Minh was too far from the bank she'd left. She had no choice but to swim for the burning shore.

Bits of the ferry drifted by as she paddled under a thin pall of smoke. The river, so violent moments before, had calmed quickly to an eerie flatness, forgetful that it had just tried to drown her, and ignorant of what was spattered over it. Busted planks, bales of wool, a warped bicycle, a coolie hat, Minh pushed these aside and was afraid with every kick and pull that she might bump into a floating body or a piece of one. She saw no corpses. Reaching the shallows, she ran out of the water in a panic.

Dripping, Minh shivered on the riverbank. She wasn't cold; the fire in the jungle blew heat her way. She was suddenly alone with no thought or sight of anything but death. The river current drifted away all the awful evidence; Minh felt this keenly, watching her terror and the killing of the ferry swept off around a bend, no monument to them. In minutes there would be nothing left but the river, a fire crackling beside the Road, and Minh standing, shaking, between them.

She wrapped her arms around herself, and this helped with the quaking. While the water rid itself of grief, the air filled with it. Minh looked up through the smoke to the sound over the valley. There in the air was the memory and the monument to the destruction, in the distant thunder of jets and the constant war.

Minh turned her back to the river.

The first American pilot had been deadly, blowing the raft and the people on it to splinters. The second one had gone after the trucks and the underwater bridge but hit only jungle. Scattered fires burned in the cut-down trees and scrub, much of which was green and only smoked. Haze rose from the craters, and the wind wafted it across the Trail where Minh walked north.

She'd not gone far from the water when the last film of mist curled away. The jungle arched its roof over the Road, and the afternoon reminded her of its heat. In the brush, bugs cricked with the same grinding sounds as the fire in the woods. The afternoon remained quiet, shed of the explosions. Minh could no longer hear the American jets ripping above the hills. She could make out only the faint engine noise of the other American plane, the smaller, slower spotter, puttering on the other side of the river valley.

For minutes, Minh walked blankly, nothing on her back or in her hands, surprised only that she'd kept her sandals on. Binh tram 17 still lay an hour away. There she would eat and sleep, then after dark tell the girls what happened. The bombing of the ferry had been the second time she'd come very close to being killed; the first was the machine-gunning of the Chinaman six months ago. When she thought of them both together, her knees buckled.

A truck trundled toward her in a great hurry, not wise with American jets about. Minh struggled to her feet to step to the shoulder of the Road. The truck passed, then slammed on brakes, raising dust as it skidded to a stop. The passenger door flew open. Minh held her ground. A hand extended, waving her to come fast. The hand became an arm in a white sleeve. Minh ran to the open truck door.

She leaped up behind her heart into the cab. She did not fall across the seat to Loi, still unsure she was alive. Then he opened his arms and she was inside them.

His whisper in her ear could not hide how frantic he was. "What are you doing here?"

It was Loi, really him. They were by themselves, something that had never happened before. Only minutes after she was nearly killed, Minh was alone with him. What was this day?

She had to raise her lips off his shoulder to speak.

"I nearly died."

This was not the answer to his question. Minh gripped him close, though she was wet. Loi held her tight, too.

She put her nose against the skin of his neck, into his hair that was longer than a soldier's. Before he could release her, Minh let him go. She closed the passenger door. That said *I am with you, let's go.* From his smile, this pleased him.

Loi shifted the big truck into gear, urgency in his movements. The truck lunged into the smoke of the burning jungle, headed to the river.

"The ferry is gone," she said.

Loi took in her damp, clinging clothes, then turned his attention back to his driving. "Are you all right?"

"Everyone is dead."

He nodded. The simplicity of the gesture told her that everyone is at war. Everyone, Minh. And what can we do for the dead but drive this truck forward until we join them or win the war?

She stopped her mouth with both hands. This was the second time he'd found her like this, shaken, surviving, stumbling into his arms. She straightened her spine against the bouncing seat and laid both palms on her thighs. Minh pulled her eyes from Loi and put them where he'd put his, on the Road.

"Where are we going?"

"Across the river."

"Can you tell me why?"

"I have a gun crew there."

"Yes."

"I need to stop them from shooting at the Americans."

She fidgeted at his answer. What kind of sense did that make? Of course the Americans should be shot at, torn out of the sky the same way they'd torn the ferryman, the dynamite carrier, and the bicycle pushers out of their lives, and almost Minh.

She didn't ask. Loi did not have to clarify himself to a singer. Her fidget drew a glance.

"You don't understand?"

"No. But it's all right."

"The 325th. My division."

"Yes?"

"We were at Khe Sanh for so long."

Back in January, only days after he'd found Minh running through his camp covered in the Chinaman's blood, Loi had disappeared with his division. Three weeks ago, after six months of murderous fighting for the American Marine base at Khe Sanh, he'd returned to Laos and Tchepone without half of his men.

She watched his face for any sign, any flinch of that battle. Loi let out a long exhale, that was all. He breathed out five thousand dead. He was not a lyric in a song or a warrior on a stage. Loi was the man the songs and plays were about. He was a patriot and handsome and he sent her secret flowers. Minh bit her lip to keep from saying aloud that she loved him.

"The division isn't ready to be found. We're still healing." He reached across the bench seat for her hand. She gave it to him. "That's what you do. You sing for us. Did you get the lotus?"

The day he'd left for the battle in Vietnam, she'd given him a lotus blossom for luck. During the six months he was gone, Loi sent back six lotus flowers in unmarked packages.

"It came last night. It's why I hurried back." Minh's laugh felt good in her chest where the weight was. "You almost got me killed."

"Let's see how I do on the bridge." Loi took back his hand to shift into another gear. He fought the clutch until it caught, and the truck surged ahead. "I've never driven over it. I'm not much of a driver anyway."

"You're doing very well."

Loi grunted, leaning over the wheel. He did look uncomfortable.

The truck punched through the waning smoke from the craters. The jungle opened onto the riverbank where Loi braked and idled. The only trace of the ferry was a pulley wheel bolted to a tree, trailing an empty length of rope.

Minh climbed down out of the truck to walk in front of Loi, guiding him over the underwater stones. The water rose to her knees. She kept him on the bridge, though sometimes he edged too close and nearly bumped her into the water. Minh focused on her steps and the warm radiator at her backside, not the river bend and what had happened here minutes ago.

Before she stepped onto the south bank, the American spotter plane reappeared. It bobbed above a ridgeline in the hills. Diving and slip-sliding, the plane fired a rocket into a hillside three kilometers away. The rocket burst with tendrils of white sparks, leaving a tower of smoke. Behind her, Loi spurred the engine to pull onto the shore. He stopped but didn't open the door for Minh. He shouted out the open window.

"One of my guns has been marked. You stay here."

"I want to go." The truck inched forward. Minh leaped for the door handle, wrangled it open, and jogged beside the truck. She shouted at Loi through the opened door, "I want to go with you."

He braked.

Minh climbed onto the seat and slammed the door. A pistol that had not been there before sat on the bench between them. She was not mad that he'd tried to leave her. He was sheltering her.

Loi drove fast off the riverbank. On the Road, he sped with both forearms on the wheel to help steady it over the ruts. After a kilometer, he turned from the wider path onto nothing more than an uphill trail, then crushed through the weeds and stalks. Loi fought the truck up the slope, bouncing Minh so badly she braced her hands against the roof of the cab. The American spotter plane zoomed by on its way out of the valley but did not notice Loi's truck or did not care.

White smoke from the rocket filtered down the hillside, a chemical stench that choked Minh and Loi, but he powered on. When the truck could go no farther, when the trees became too thick to bend under the bumper, Loi snatched the pistol off the seat, flung open his door, and ran ahead. Minh jumped down and followed.

Loi crashed up the hill, carrying the pistol openly. He was perhaps ten years older than her, ropy and dynamic; she forced herself to keep up. The smoke spoiled each breath and watered her eyes, branches whipped at her. Loi did not look back.

He followed the trail fifty meters through the smoke, then another fifty where the slope leveled off and the smoke had thinned. The sound of the spotter plane had ebbed from the hills when Loi stomped across a patch of low grasses to a small open-roofed vehicle. Behind it, standing where it had been towed to have a view of the valley, was a long-barreled artillery gun on wheels. Four men in black pajamas served it. Two sat on either side of the gun's breech. They had handwheels to aim the gun left or right, up or down, over the valley. The other two Viet Cong waited by crates of 37mm ammunition. Even before he reached the gun crew, Loi shouted:

"Who ordered you to shoot?"

None of the men noted Loi's arrival. Their eyes were riveted above the valley and the sliding smoke. Loi stomped up to the artillery piece. Minh stayed back.

The oldest man answered only with his voice, not even lowering his weathered face from the sky. He was seated on the gun platform, hands on a wheel. Far off and unseen, a jet rumbled.

"Who are you?"

Loi jiggled the pistol in his hand. Still no one looked at him. "All artillery batteries in the regiment were ordered not to fire without instructions. Do you know this?"

The old man was probably a peasant, a village elder given this gun and a crew. Loi's demand came off as too formal, too military; the old man ran things up here on this hillside. He was careless with his sneer when he replied to the young fellow who had arrived with a much smaller gun and a woman.

"Again. Who are you?" After speaking, the old man focused once more above the valley, scanning for the American jet.

Loi took the few steps to bring him within arm's reach from the old man. He raised the pistol to the elder's temple.

"I'm the cadre who issued the order."

This brought the old man's eyes down from the sky. His face went wild trying to see the short barrel beside his ear. He blinked at Loi, silently shocked and appeasing. His hands came off the wheel, conjuring in the air but producing nothing.

The old man pointed across the valley.

"They fired first."

Through the smoke, Loi looked with him.

"I'll visit them next."

The pistol, pressed against the elder's temple, made only a pop when Loi fired. The man's head whipped away, tumbling him against the mechanism of the steel gun. He did not fall out of the seat but sat askew, hands fallen to his lap. The other seated Viet Cong leaped from the chair, sprayed with his comrade's blood and probably brains. He raised his arms high, surrendering as if Loi were a robber. The two ammo loaders held their hands away from their bodies, too. Minh recoiled but caught herself; she dropped one foot behind the other, not to retreat from Loi but to steady herself for him.

Loi lowered the pistol and turned his chin to the sky. Minh turned her head also. The coming American plane was too high and fast to be seen, but the valley whispered of it, a low whine, a warning. In the next few moments, like the tip of a knife, the jet would appear in the blue, a dot that would widen into a blade so quickly there would be no time to warn anyone who did not hear and see it for themselves.

Loi addressed the gory Viet Cong, the one who'd been seated next to the old man. "Put your hands down. You have a bunker?"

"Yes."

"We need to get in it. Now."

The man moved as though his legs might fail him. He scrambled into the bushes, followed by the two ammo loaders. No effort was made to save the corpse still in the 37's steel chair.

Loi snapped his fingers at Minh to come. He held out an arm to her, putting her in front of him. Twenty strides away through the bush, hidden under a mound of cut tree limbs, a hole had been dug then topped with logs. Minh crawled into the dirt hole, a sloped burrow, into a small chamber with barely room to sit. Behind her slid Loi. At his rear, by two seconds, landed the bombs.

CHAPTER 11

Daniels took the first run at the 37. He set up his approach from a 14,000-foot perch, rolled over, and hurled his Thud down at Nail's smoke.

Sol circled high and out of the way. Clearing 10,000 feet, Daniels entered the range of the Vietnamese gun, but no tracers sailed up to meet him. The Thud honed in, piercing 9,000 feet. The hillside stayed green and still. Daniels flew right down the big gun's bore until at 7,000 feet he pickled his bombs, then hauled back on the stick. He'd cut his bombing run short, discharging the Mark 82s high to thwart the zeeps across the valley. Daniels drew no fire as he turned, wings level, waiting for his Thunderchief to unload the Gs from the dive and start to climb.

On the ground, four hammershots pounded the green slope. The jungle rose and flared. There was something stolid about the way the hillside accepted the explosions, with no resistance from the 37mm. It seemed almost belligerent that the North Vietnamese didn't fire at him. At 6,000 feet, Daniels broke right.

Sol knew the look of blasted trees. Again, Daniels's bombs had landed long.

Nail 34 didn't wait before he radioed in. He made no mention of Dash lead's miss, sparing him the embarrassment of a poor BDA. Nail said only "Dash 2. You're cleared in hot."

Sol got a visual on Daniels climbing past 10,000. He flicked the weapons-selection toggles for station, sequence, and number, four Mark 82s. Sol savored the quiet on the radio, no cussing or yahoos from Daniels, nothing more from Nail, just his own hand nudging the stick, the balls of his feet on the pedals, and the smooth acceleration of his F-105 in afterburner up to 14,000. From there, he cut the burner, then rolled into his dive at 560 knots. He eased the bombsight pipper a hundred yards short of the clouds from Daniels's bombs on the hill. Sol radioed nothing yet, letting Daniels and Nail watch him drill through the brilliant day like a dart, pick up speed, silent and on the mark, a few moments of flair.

He thumbed the mic. "Dash 2 is in, weapons hot."

The Thud powered for the earth riding a 45-degree downward slope. The pipper settled squarely where Sol wanted it, on target for another good run. The 37 did him the same favor of staying mute while the broad expanse of the valley spread itself for him, too, showing the smoking pocks of Daniels's inaccuracy. Sol would come in lower than Daniels, drop his bombs at 4,500, and stick it down the 37's throat. If they didn't want to shoot back, that was their problem.

Rocketing through 8,000 feet, Sol swiveled his head to check for tracers anywhere near him, from either side of the river. He made one last pipper adjustment. Like Dash lead, he was getting a free run. Unlike Daniels, he wasn't going to screw it up.

Sol brought his focus inside the cockpit to his gauges. Instantly, a pang of dismay coursed through his hands. In a blink, he'd lost too much altitude; the Thud's speed had climbed to 600 knots. Before he could ease the throttle, he'd already flashed through 7,000 feet. The bombsight hadn't wavered, he could still pull off another bull's-eye, but he had to act fast. The rolling Lao landscape filled his windshield. The fires from Daniels's blasts and the last of Nail's phosphorous smoke made perfect guides. Sol held the pipper tight on the mark for a long moment, then waited one more beat to be sure. At 4,000 feet he pressed the pickle button, felt the releasing bombs shiver in the fuselage, then pulled back the stick fluidly. The Thud's nose began to rise, still well below the green horizon. The wait began, endless-seeming time, for the Thud to shed the momentum of its hurtling descent, level off, and jet Sol away from the rising ground and the guns.

He glued his eyes to the G-meter, airspeed, and altimeter. Too eager to show up Daniels, too cool without taking fire, he'd busted through his minimum altitude. The Thud roared past 3,500 feet, then 3,000. If the ZPUs' eight barrels wanted to open up on him, Sol had flown well inside their range. He whirled to look back at the rocky mountain, saw no sparking lights, then locked again on his gauges.

Sol pulled back harder on the stick. At 2,700 feet, he muttered into his mask, "Climb, you fucker, climb."

Below and behind him, his four bombs exploded, but Sol paid no mind.

He shoved on the throttle, already at the stops. At 2,500 feet, his altimeter paused, then reversed directions—*2,800, 3,000, 3,200* feet, Sol whispered the rising numbers.

With the Thud finally on the climb, he relaxed his squeeze on the controls. He became aware of how badly he was sweating and bracing himself.

"Dash 2 is clear of the target."

The Thunderchief arced into a sheer climb. For the next ten seconds, the plane would have little forward movement as it needled upward. Its big belly was at its most exposed in this frame against the sky. Sol took on 4.5 Gs; air gushed into the G suit, squeezing around his legs.

The vertical gyro told him his nose attitude was 10 degrees up. The emerald sill of the world retreated below his field of vision, replaced by open blue. Sol sensed the Thud unloading, beginning to get its power back and accelerate into the climb. In another few seconds, he could make his break. The altimeter read good news, closing in on 4,000 feet.

Sol backed off on the stick to slacken the G forces and encourage the gaining speed. He'd dived so low, his bombs couldn't have missed that gun. He was almost away and began to congratulate himself, to imagine his place at the table in the Officers Club. Nail's radio voice was the first step toward that, another perfect BDA.

"Dash 2, Dash 2!"

That was all Nail could transmit before the first flaming ball zipped past Sol's cockpit. Startled, he jinked away to the right, still without full control of the Thud's forward momentum. One of the ZPU gunners had guessed correctly. Like the edge of a sawblade, a line of red fireballs waited for him there.

On instinct Sol dodged back to the left. He scanned the ground for the source of the tracers, to the base of the karst mountain. The two zeeps blinked in a circular pattern, and with each white flicker another red-hot tracer scorched up at him, like roman candles, with six or seven unseen rounds in between. The guns had him bracketed, moving his Thud back and forth into their twin lines of fire. The altimeter read 4,400 feet.

Damn it, the gunners had him in their sights for the second time. Daniels might be crazy and a piss-poor bomber, but he was cautious and still alive. Sol got himself into this; he'd been too aggressive and careless. Now he had to get himself out.

There were only two ways: lean back and climb as furiously as he could out of the guns' range, or try to evade the tracers closing in on him.

Speed and altitude. These were the Thunderchief's hallmarks. Not nimbleness.

With both hands, Sol yanked the stick back.

One more time, the enemy gunners guessed right.

CHAPTER 12

Loi shielded Minh with his body, pushing her to the dirt bunker floor. Explosions rattled the earth under her, while against her chest Loi's heart raced. The three Viet Cong gunners hunkered in their own corner, pressed into the shadows in their dark pajamas.

The first round of bombs did not land close. The logs over their heads shuddered, but no smoke or heat coursed between them. Only dust rained into the bunker. Minh's ears did not pop from a pressure burst. Loi eased his weight on her.

She whispered, "That must have been terrible. Shooting that man."

Loi considered her, their faces close. His white shirt seemed to catch all the thin light that slipped into the bunker. "Do you disagree?"

"No. I mean it must have been a terrible thing for you to have to do."

Loi seemed surprised to find the pistol still in his hand. "He disobeyed."

They were lying like lovers. Loi straightened his arms to push himself up, to behold her. He ignored the others in the bunker. "I've never done anything like that before."

He seemed to want an answer from her, Minh the orphan. She could not smile, nor stroke his back, nor reply.

Loi cocked his head. "I wonder." He paused and his mind traveled elsewhere.

She dared a touch to his white shirt, to his ribs. "What do you wonder?"

Loi's focus stayed away. Minh's heart sank a bit that she could not summon him. Then he returned to her. He adjusted his hands in the dirt to lift his face higher, to see more of Minh under him.

"I wonder if I did that for you."

Minh stiffened in the dirt. Loi's eyes flitted over her face as though something were written on her brow. She lay still, looking past Loi to the log ceiling as if they had indeed been lovers.

Had he actually killed someone because she was watching him? Or did he shoot the old gunner solely to defend his division and for discipline? Was Loi in love with her? Was the killing a new kind of gift, a war gift, some leap beyond unsigned boxes and lotus blossoms?

When Loi had put the gun against the old man's head, Minh hadn't seen anger. Not madness. He was declaring that he could shoot a man outright for defying him, asserting that he had the authority.

If so, he had enough power to claim her, didn't he?

She lay between his arms on the bunker floor. Minh eased the tension in her muscles so Loi would not sense her marveling and think it disapproval. He hovered over her, with the light behind his face.

The whistles of another round of bombs cut through the log roof. Loi lay across Minh again, chin burrowed in her neck and hair, chest against her chest.

CHAPTER 13

Sol's right wing took a wallop.

The whole plane bounced, then nothing more out of order. The Thunderchief continued to climb; no red lights, all of Sol's gauges showed him gaining speed and altitude. He scanned the right wing for damage, and as he did, the world outside tilted.

The jet listed to the right, the nose sank toward the horizon. Automatically, Sol jiggled the stick and kicked the rudders to adjust. He came out of the climb to level flight; his airspeed checked in at 500 knots, altimeter just under 5,000 feet. Sol goosed the throttle and pedals for more altitude. The Thud trembled. Maybe his wing had taken a round in a stabilizer or a fluid line, but his hydraulic gauges looked good. Whatever it was, he lost confidence that he could push for more altitude. The Thud was done climbing. A new line of tracers stitched to his right, jerking him against the chest straps. Sol jinked away to the left and felt how sluggish his jet had become. He wanted a snap turn but the Thud banked slowly, the injured right wing barely coming up.

He slipped the tracers by a tight margin and stayed with the left-hand turn. If he couldn't get above the zeeps' range, Sol hoped to put some distance between him and the twin guns. The turn kept him over the river, but he wasn't worried about the 37mm on the other side; Sol was certain he'd knocked that one out.

A mile overhead, Daniels kept pace, locked against the blue. Somewhere below, Nail was probably scooting out the back door. Sol limped between the spines of the green Lao valley, trying to get away, too.

"Dash 2, Nail."

The FAC was still in the neighborhood.

"Go, Nail."

"Dash, you're way too low."

"I took a round in the right wing. This is all I got."

"I count maybe ten triple As zeroing in on you."

What? Ten antiaircraft artillery guns! Sol whipped his head around to look behind him.

Nail continued to narrate. "There's five 37s, and a couple 57s. You kicked a hornets' nest, man."

Streams of triple A were going off left and right; red and white tracers crisscrossed, waving and feeling for him like antennae. Streaks of burning rounds arced through the air while enemy gunners swung their barrels. They were trying to raise a curtain of shells for Sol to fly through. These bigger guns were radar controlled and wouldn't miss him for long. The valley was thick with artillery. What had he flown into?

Sol needed altitude, but that wasn't going to happen. He couldn't dodge the triple As, the plane wasn't responding, and he was afraid of stressing the wounded wing. The only thing left to him was speed.

He had the afterburner. And he could dive.

He'd grab all the speed he could on the way down, pull up at 1,500 feet, trying for 650 knots to see if the enemy gunners could hit a blur over the hilltops. He'd see, too, if the right-side wing would hold up.

Sol didn't have time to radio Nail and Daniels a Mayday to tell them what he was going to do. Low and go was his best chance; he had just seconds to execute before the guns had him in their crosshairs.

He nudged the stick to tip the nose below the horizon. He lit the afterburner, slamming himself into the seat. Another stripe of fiery orange orbs came zipping up for him; they nicked the air where Sol would have been had he not sped and ducked. The airframe buffeted, rocketing for the deck. The right wing shimmied. His altimeter bled out the numbers, 4,500, 4,000, 3,500 feet. His airspeed ramped up, past 550 knots. On the right side of the instrument panel, an amber caution light lit up, but Sol couldn't link that to any specific reading of his gauges. The antiaircraft fire increased around him as he dropped lower, getting larger in his enemies' gunsights.

Swords of multicolored fireballs crossed in front of Sol; the gunners were leading him. He skipped right and left, defying the Thud to stay with him. Sol ignored his gauges, focused on the light show slashing on every side. These Soviet-made guns could put over a thousand rounds into a box of airspace in less than five seconds. A new orange round, like a flaming beach ball, reared directly in his path, with another chasing it. This was the biggest gun of them all, maybe a 100mm. Along with all the other antiaircraft aiming at him, it was plain that this river valley was incredibly well defended. Why?

The question in Sol's head went unanswered. In his right wing, the tremors mounted as the speed built. In seconds, the vibrations enveloped the whole plane until Sol's dashboard, all his gauges, became impossible to read. He shut down the afterburner, returning to military power when the stick began to over-oscillate between his legs; he gripped it with both hands, trying to corral the jet out of the dive, to pull up before the speed that might save him could also shake the plane to pieces and kill him. But the Thud wouldn't respond. The stick jerked out of Sol's hands to swing wildly with more force than he could control.

The nose yawed to the right, then whipped back to the left, over and again in a violent rattle. Sol's helmet banged between the canopy and his headrest. Under his boots, the rudder pedals bucked so fast they threw his feet off. The horizon flipped up and down as the jet's attitude rocking-horsed.

Battered back and forth inside the cockpit, Sol could not slow his vision. He tried a last time to collar the stick bouncing between his knees, managing to grab it only for a moment before it wrenched free. In a fleeting glimpse, the vertical gyro instrument came into focus; the gauge was erratic, spinning madly between inverted flight and upright.

A dark flutter pitched past his cockpit, gone and dooming the Thud. Sol's right wing had wrenched off and flown away. The jet engine with the throttle wide open was thrusting his uncontrollable plane at the ground, spinning and pitching.

Sol stopped grasping for the stick and pulled in his feet to let the Thud have its death. Inside his bashing helmet, Nail's shouts of "Eject, Dash, eject! Eject!" mixed with the banshee of wind tearing more metal away from his disintegrating plane. Sol took one moment inside the maelstrom to say good-bye and accept defeat. Dodging the guns and fighting the wounded plane had left him no time to be frightened. He dropped his hands to the grips on both sides of his ejection seat. Sol needed to leave the lurching Thud before it finished him. The image of ejecting over Laos, becoming a POW of the Viet Cong or the Pathet Lao, even being seriously injured or killed in the exit from this cart-wheeling plane, made his gut prickle.

"Fuck."

The ejection seat had handles left and right beside his thighs. Sol yanked the right one, squeezing the trigger at the same time. Instantly, the clamshell canopy blew away. This exposed him to a wind that crushed him against the seat, then flung him against the restraints as the Thud spun on its axis. The seat belts popped and, before Sol could sense it as a separate action from the jet spinning, the rocket catapult fired. A delay shocked him and seemed to stretch far too long, though it was just a fraction of a second; the emerald ground seemed to be everywhere at once, washing around and around while the Thud tumbled toward it. Then the rocket lit, banging his teeth together. The ejection seat surged under his rear. With a swoosh, grunting under 17 Gs of thrust, Sol jolted out of the Thud into the open, streaming air.

The fuselage had been hurtling backward when Sol left the cockpit; the rear of his ejector seat took the brunt of the wind's initial blast. He was knocked facedown to see his whirling dervish of a plane beneath him, missing its right wing all the way to the root. Sol grew weightless as he lost upward momentum. The Thud plummeted away, growing smaller, sadder, and more abandoned. Under his rump, a pair of "butt snapper" bands tightened, ejecting him out of the steel-frame seat. Sol fell freely.

Before he could panic, the container strapped to his back shivered and opened, unspooling an expanse of pale nylon and riser lines. The chute flapped, then blossomed and filled, the lines playing out without tangle. Instantly, his descent was arrested. Sol's innards felt like an accordion. Then, in the sudden manner of everything that had happened in the last several seconds, he was floating.

He had to look up to find his empty Thud, flipping around itself, jet engine still firing and spiraling it into mad somersaults. Sol had punched out around 2,000 feet. His plane corkscrewed the last of that distance, into the side of a hill one mile downrange. The jungle absorbed the crash. Jet fuel sprayed an especially bright flame.

CHAPTER 14

Walking the Road, she had never been so close to an explosion of this size. If she had, she wouldn't have been alive to describe it. As a young beggar in Hanoi, Minh watched old men in the alleys gamble at *Cho-Han Bakuchi*. They'd rolled dice or polished bones in a cup and bet even or odd on the numbers. Sometimes they gave her coins or chased her off; nasty ones tried to buy her for an hour. In the shaking bunker, because she thought she might die, Minh recalled the game, the rattled bones and dice in the cups, and the gamblers in the alleys.

The shelter was in ruins in the aftermath of the explosions. In the stilled, spilled earth and logs, Loi seemed to have blacked out on top of her. All his weight pushed her into the strewn floor. Rubble and dust smoked behind his white shirt. Pressed flat on her spine, Minh turned her head to see the Viet Cong gunners in the corner; they were gone beneath a part of the roof that had collapsed.

Her ears felt crammed, her tongue lay in her mouth, wrung and dry. Both eyeballs were sore as if they'd been poked. Minh squirmed under Loi; she believed she'd spoken but couldn't hear herself. Loi stirred, his chest expanded against hers. Slowly he pushed up to his elbows, shrugging dirt and debris. He blinked. Bark from the logs crowned his black hair.

He wheezed, "Are you all right?" A shaft of light that had not been there before beamed through the haze in the bunker. She had to read Loi's lips because of the whine in her ears.

She touched a button on his shirt. "Are you?"

He nodded. They were alive. The three Viet Cong in the corner were probably not.

Loi took in their condition. He winced at the fallen timbers around them and the jumble of earth and wood where the VC gunners had cowered. The short tunnel leading out of the bunker had collapsed. One of the logs in the roof had cracked and splintered like bone. Loi smoothed a palm across Minh's forehead, pushing her hair from her face. She wished they could stay like this for a while, though for Loi and her to be fully alone, the Viet Cong would need to be dead, and they were not. In the corner one filthy leg kicked out of the wreckage, then another. A peasant gunner in black pajamas crawled out coughing.

Loi smiled, sorry also that they could not linger.

"Cover your face."

With that, he buttressed his arms on the floor beside Minh. He shoved backward, heaving himself against the ceiling. Strain stretched his face. Dirt cascaded around Loi to splash on Minh. She brought up her hands as Loi had instructed, warding off the falling litter of the explosions. She did this only for a moment, then put both hands to his chest to add her own strength to their escape. Loi grunted with his effort, Minh with hers. The bunker's logs began to lift and separate until they fell aside. Fresh air and clean light broke into the hole.

Loi stood into the day, sun on his filthy shirt. He lifted himself out, then reached down to bring Minh up beside him. The VC was left to fend for himself, and for his comrades, too, if they also lived.

The hillside had been skinned by the blasts. A hundred trees were snipped away at the ground, leaving smoldering stumps; other trunks were bent over in half. Fronds and branches were scattered over the ground. Minh had seen tsunamis do this on the Trường Sơn Road. The 37mm gun had only been tipped off its wheels but did not look bashed or melted. Loi patted the barrel and smiled at it the same way he'd smiled at Minh for surviving. The elder's corpse was nowhere to be seen, likely lofted off into the jungle. His crew could find him or leave him, as they saw fit. Loi stepped down the slope with Minh following, brushing at the back of his white shirt. He said nothing while she cleaned him.

Over the river, an American jet tried to flee the valley. The pilot dove sharply for the green hills, hoping to hide in their creases. He hadn't yet come down from the sky but remained framed against the day's spotless blue. From every slope of the valley, from the outskirts of Tchepone to the bend in the river where Minh had almost died for the first time today, the jet was followed, led, and flanked by tracers; red, white, and hot orange threads danced around him. It was amazing that the American could fly through such a barrage. She set a hand to Loi's back, to tell him she saw this.

He answered her unasked question.

"I'm to blame."

Minh left her hand on his back. Loi did not shirk it. Behind them, the jungle sizzled; two dirty gunners heaved their way, cursing, out of the bunker. Over the river valley, the American plane broke apart.

CHAPTER 15

Nakhon Phanom Royal Thai Air Force Base
Air Rescue Alert Shack
Nakhon Phanom, Thailand

Across from Bo, Lee lay on his cot, ankles crossed, staring into a *Playboy*. Bo watched the older PJ intently, deciphering if Lee was actually reading or pretending to read the magazine. Lee's eyes flitted back and forth, but Bo couldn't be sure if that was back and forth over words or pictures.

On his own cot, absentmindedly, Bo rubbed the small bump on his forehead. The ready shack's little fridge made no ice, so since last night Bo and Lee both had to make do with cold-water compresses to nurse their lumps. The flight engineer lay asleep on his cot, and Major Crebbs smoked outside the hut on one of the cheap plastic chairs.

Bo spoke quietly, not to wake the FE. This was only Bo's second three-day cycle through the alert shack, but he'd learned that sleep helped pass the time better than the *Playboys*.

"You just knew the guy was a sumbitch."

Lee didn't shift on his cot to answer. "Get off it."

"He should've just gone along. Like he was supposed to."

"You've said that. A few times now. I thought you didn't talk much."

"I like it." Bo meant that he liked the tradition. He saw it yesterday for the first time. When a pilot was rescued, on his return to base he went straight to the Officers Club. There, he bought rounds for all the men who'd saved him, even the enlisted men, who were allowed in for this sole purpose. Afterward, the rescuers threw that pilot over the bar; no one explained why. The flier would erase the number of successful rescues counted on a chalkboard that was held in the arms of a stuffed Jolly Green Giant and increase the number by one. Bo thought it a manly and raucous celebration, and kind of warlike.

Yesterday afternoon, when Jolly 22 touched wheels down at NKP, the rescued copilot and loadmaster led the way to the Officers Club. The pilot wandered off to make some report. The copilot bought rounds somberly at first, raising glasses to his lost navigator. The mood shifted when the loadmaster, still wearing the sling Bo had put on him in the chopper, raised his good arm to make a new toast to Major Crebbs and Jolly 22's crazy, fearless crew, Bo in particular. Nobody mentioned that the loadmaster's behavior on the ground had been far crazier than anything Bo had done. When it came time to be heaved across the bar, both fliers submitted; Major Crebbs and the FE handled them with merriment. The copilot and the loadmaster, in their turns, added their numbers to the 40th Aerospace Rescue and Recovery Squadron's rescue total, at 144 and 145 for the year.

Bo was surprised to see the Provider pilot enter the O Club. Maybe the man had no idea of the rescue unit's tradition, maybe he was contrite. With his negative attitude toward his crewmates and the rotten thing he'd said about his navigator being lost, Bo had reckoned it unlikely he'd see the pilot again. But there he was, drinking alone. He bought nothing for anyone and took no part in the ceremony. Bo and Lee labeled that more of the man's poor judgment. He was there only because Jolly 22 had plucked him out of the jungle, so it seemed only correct that Jolly 22 toss him over the bar like the others, where he would damn well add his number to the total.

Lee approached the pilot about buying a round for the rescue crew. The pilot declined.

"I just want a quiet drink, Sergeant. It was a hell of a day."

"It was a hell of a day for all of us."

"Captain. You mean it was a hell of a day for all of us, Captain."

Lee, an experienced sergeant and not an unintelligent man, appealed to a higher authority. He turned for Major Crebbs across the room. Crebbs set down his free beer and said, "Toss him."

Lee was a gangly fellow with a scar across his chest and had had more than one brush with trouble. Bo lacked Lee's strength but knew how to wrangle a calf or a pig when it came time to eat one. The Provider pilot landed one shot against Bo's temple until Bo wrapped his arms. Lee tugged the pilot's feet out from under him and took a boot in the chin for it. No one else in the club pitched in; even Crebbs and the flight engineer stood aside. The pilot went over the bar struggling like a catfish in a net. He landed on his behind, and everyone in the Officers Club, a few dozen Air Force and Army aviators, applauded. The pilot stormed out without paying for the bourbon he left on his table. Lee hopped the bar to raise the chalkboard number to 146 while Bo paid for the pilot's bourbon.

Back in the alert shack later on, sitting outside in the crinkle of insects and the purple evening heat, Lee had asked Bo why it mattered so much to him, to get in a fight just to throw the pilot over the bar. Bo shrugged. Lee wanted an answer between them, so he gave his own.

"Me, I'm Italian Catholic. You don't shit on tradition."

Bo thought this well said; he admired short answers. He wished his own answer could be so compact and romantic. His would have to be about his brother, the plains of Kansas, and how much he wanted to be away from them and honor them at the same time. His talkative father who believed in doing things the right way, and his selfless mother. The continuity of good conduct. The Provider pilot had offended all of it, insulted places in Bo he didn't know much about but believed the Vietnam War would take him to, places such as honor and sacrifice and the patch on his sleeve.

"He was a sumbitch."

Lying on his cot, Bo concluded that Lee's eyes were bouncing between breasts, not words. He put the Provider pilot out of his head, let the sumbitch bail out. Bo would fly on without him, the ingrate, and would not recall that man as his first rescue.

The red phone in the alert shack was hung beside the door so that whoever answered it could get going as fast as possible. Day after day, every flier and PJ who lay in these cots wished the scramble phone would ring and feared it ringing. Bo listened to the sunlight in the rafters of the shed crackle the beams and stretch the corrugated steel roof. The heat in Southeast Asia made everything twitchy, so when the phone rang, he jumped on his cot. Lee and the flight engineer sat bolt upright, Lee stowed the *Playboy* under the pillow for the next guy. At the other end of the shack, the crew of Jolly 23 all heaved to their feet as if the bell had unleashed something in them. On the porch, Crebbs knocked over the plastic chair getting out of it. He snatched the scramble phone off the hook, listened, then intoned, "Roger." The major set the receiver in the cradle while circling one finger beside his head, the signal for "spin-up."

Lee and the FE were already on their feet. Lee tapped Bo on the head as he passed. "Let's go, Kansas."

With speedy hands, every man donned his vest packed with survival radio and smoke flares. Bo secured his vest, then slipped on the black shoulder holster holding his .38 automatic. Crebbs and Jolly 23's pilot were already out of the hut and onboard their big choppers by the time Bo grabbed his M-16 from the weapons locker and broke into a jog, last in line, to the runway.

Both rescue helos had been left cocked on alert status; each crew had only to jump onboard, the pilot to punch the start button, and the FE to pull the chocks. Crebbs held the unit record for getting airborne in 27 seconds after the scramble call.

CHAPTER 16

Above the Xe Banghiang River Valley
Near Tchepone
Laos

Floating under his parachute fifteen hundred feet in the air, Sol had a little time to think about his life.

He was squarely among the living, firm in his living, and had believed every day until now that it would go on. Gliding toward his demise in Laos, he shook his head and said aloud, "It's a shame." He wanted someone to talk to, not to repent anything in particular, just to mark his remaining moments. He thought about being brave somehow, but dangling under a sinking chute gave him no bravery to perform. He had little to do but hang there, sad and disappointed, and wait for a bullet.

Seventy yards away, a bareheaded man in black pajamas ran toward him down a trail. Sol's chute was about to drift too low to be seen past the treetops so the soldier stopped, raised his weapon, and squeezed off a few rounds. The rifle popped, but no bullets buzzed past Sol; the guy was a crappy shot and for that Sol was grateful. Behind the pajama man, a half dozen others galloped down the trail, shouting excitedly and pointing at him descending. The running bad guys looked to be Viet Cong or, worse, Pathet Lao guerrillas; neither bunch was renowned for their hospitality to American pilots. Sol's worries about death sharpened into a fear of capture, torture, and then death.

With the last gliding seconds before he hit the ground, he wished he were married. The thought of widowing somebody was better than having no one, having no children to leave behind for his folks to remember him by, to see him imprinted in those kids. In the jungle the pop of another rifle made Sol seize up. Again nothing hit him, and he began to begrudge how long this was taking.

His jet had plunged into the jungle a mile west, where it burned like a fallen star. The antiaircraft guns had gone silent. Sol heard nothing of Daniels's Thud overhead, no rocketing about, only the distant thrum of Nail's O-2 somewhere in the notches of the hills. Daniels was following protocol, flying high to alert Crown, the airborne C-130 communications platform, to activate the rescue force and come save his downed wingmate, while Nail kept an eye on where he landed.

Sol's fears rose with the ground welling up at him now that the moment was at hand. His teeth chattered, almost drowning out the far-off rumble of Nail's propellers. With a hundred feet left to drop, he reached behind him to release the forty-five-pound survival kit strapped there. The kit fell away to hang by its ten-foot tether; this reduced Sol's weight to ease his landing.

He sailed straight toward a grove of bamboo trees, eighty-foot-high shoots. These might snare his canopy and leave him exposed far off the ground, a white ornament. Sol jerked hard on the left risers to slip the chute sideways toward a small opening. He lifted his boots to avoid clipping the green tips of the bamboo, then plummeted through some smaller shafts, shearing off branches. He bent at the knees, did a forward roll, and he was down.

No injuries, that was his first thought. He'd broken nothing on ejecting, twisted nothing on landing. His second was to get control over himself; all those thoughts about torture and death had to be left behind, up in the air. He was on the ground now. He was alive still. His third thought was to fucking run.

Flipping the shoulder, chest, and crotch fittings on his container, Sol dropped the chute off his back. He popped the bayonet clips that held the mask to his helmet, tossed away the mask, then tore off his helmet. He threw it in the opposite direction that he intended to go.

Sol dug into his survival kit; he mined the life raft for two bottles of water and a box of .38 ammo. With a last glance at the kit and his chute, and no time to hide them, he lit out into the pickets of the bamboo grove. Another rifle clapped in the jungle behind him. The VC were shooting at glimpses of him through the brush and skinny trunks.

Sol dashed into the bamboo, throwing elbows and hips to wedge his way into the stalks. He needed to buy time to radio Nail and Daniels that he was on the move. If he got desperate, he could draw the .38 to make a stand and buy time that way, but a gunfight was at the bottom of Sol's short list of options.

He hadn't done much physical training in the past few years. Nuclear Alert didn't call for it; since he wouldn't have survived a real mission anyway, there wasn't much need for physical conditioning. He'd been in the jungle for thirty seconds, running for ten of them, and already his heart felt like it wanted to leap through his rib cage and surrender without him. He throttled up, ramming aside the stalks, unable to let his lungs catch up. Behind him, the VC crashed through the foliage, smaller and quicker men in jungle shape. Sol considered whirling with the pistol, firing a few rounds just to let the pajama boys know they were chasing an armed man. That might slow them.

Then he was out of the bamboo, staggering onto a trail. A well-packed ten-foot-wide lane running north and south, covered by overgrowth. The path looked like a tunnel, as though it had been bored out of solid jungle. The day was late, and the slanting light barely made it to the smooth red-dirt way. The trail ran for a few hundred yards before it curved; pastel flowers, variegated leaves, gnarly trunks, and birdsong made it quietly idyllic. The temperature felt milder under so much shade. Was this the Ho Chi Minh Trail? For an American pilot trying to hide in Laos, beautiful or not, this was absolutely not the place to be.

Earlier in the year, during one week in the Philippines for JEST, jungle environment survival training, Sol's handlers had been clear about avoiding trails. He'd shown little instinct for the woods then and had the same lack now. Sol was a jet pilot, in the Philippines with other jet pilots in a pretend scenario, and he shared the fliers' hubris that he wouldn't be shot down in the first place. At JEST, Sol had heard from another Thud jockey that he could bribe the local tribesmen to bring him food in the bush and then look the other way. Sol tried this; they took his money, brought him food, then turned him in. The experience shortened Sol's stay in the course and left a bad taste in his mouth for jungle-survival training. He fought to control his breathing and to recall what else they had said about trails, since he was standing on one.

Another rifle round drilled through the leaves, striking a bamboo trunk, spraying white splinters. The VC didn't know where he was and were shooting at guesses. Though he was on the ground, Sol stuck with his pilot's intuitions: What would he do in the air? He needed distance from his pursuers. That meant speed.

He made up his mind to bolt down the trail. If he could reach the bend in the path before the VC burst out of the bamboo behind him, he'd be out of sight. Then he could find a lair or some hidden place to get on the radio and call for close air support.

Another rifle report provided the starting gun for his sprint. Sol churned his arms and legs, gulping at the cooler air. Weighed down by his survival vest, the G suit, his parachute torso harness, and the handgun in his armpit, he pushed through the fire in his lungs. Like a sprinter, Sol took the inside lane around the dense green curve. His breathing came out as a wheeze.

He scampered under a solid emerald canopy. Nail's propellers yowled directly over Sol's head; the FAC would never see him through the arching branches of the Trail.

Sol rounded the bend, almost bingo on stamina. He risked a look over his shoulder, no one was chasing him. Fifty feet off the road through a tangle of vines, a big tree rotted on its side. The trunk was fat, four feet thick. Sol had to choose between slowing to a fatigued trot or stopping to hide. His legs made the decision; they were done.

He angled off the path into a green tangle that snatched at his G suit. Sol waded in, kicking with his last dregs of energy. He worried about the noise he was making, adding to the sounds welling up in his throat, the moans of fear he could not stop.

Bashing his way to the great trunk, finally exhausted, Sol bellied up and over. Too beat to catch himself, he fell to the hidden side, where he lay on his back, heaving for breath. Sol sprawled in the dampness of the jungle as if on a soggy mattress, in the thickness of decay, on spongy earth that never fully dried out, atop the crawling tininess of its creatures. Worried about the bellows of his lungs, he cupped a hand over his mouth. Sol blinked up through the few gaps in the trees to the sky he'd been cast out of.

He filled his lungs as much and as fast as he could so he might control himself enough to work the radio. This felt like it took a long time. Sol couldn't prevent a whine from staining his exhales; he didn't want Nail or Daniels to hear his plain fright. Sol waited himself out, listening through his throes for the sound of Viet Cong fighters beating the bushes for him. When he could breathe normally and sound like a pilot, he sat up against the tree.

The green survival radio wasn't big, maybe the size of two packs of cigarettes. It had a foot-long rubber antenna and only a few switches, on and off, two frequencies, beacon, and a push-to-talk on the side. Sol turned it on to send the beeper beacon out over the guard channel, the emergency freq that all pilots monitored, and Nail was surely keeping an ear to. The beacon would communicate that he was alive, or at least his radio was. If Sol was about to be captured or killed, the last act he had to perform was to destroy this radio.

He needed to send out his voice so Nail would know the signal was him and not a VC ruse. Sol dialed the radio to transmit.

The radio shouted in his hand, ". . . just got a good beeper signal."

Sol almost dropped the radio. He'd screwed up; he'd put the radio on receive instead of talk. The volume was all the way up, and Nail's voice shot out of Sol's hiding place like a startled parrot. He clamped a hand over the speaker as if it might continue, scared even more out of his wits, then turned down the volume.

He whispered to himself, "Settle down, boy. Settle down."

An explosion rocked the jungle, coming out of the direction he'd run from. What was that? Sol shook with the questioning, every bit of him way too alert. The radio slipped from his hands into the loamy dirt. One of the Sidewinders from his burning Thud must have cooked off, that's what it was. Sol puffed his cheeks and blew out. He made a patting motion with both palms to tell himself again to calm down, way down, or he'd never get out of this alive.

With the back of his hand he swiped a cascade of sweat out of his eyebrows. It was just after six p.m., the sun wouldn't set for another two hours. For the first time since he'd hit the ground, maybe three minutes ago, Sol noted the stifling humidity. He had to get rid of some gear, lighten up, if he was going to stay nimble and moving. *Good,* he nodded, *good. You're thinking.*

Working quickly, he slid out of his survival vest and holster so he could shed the parachute harness beneath. Next he unzipped the G suit and wriggled out of that, careful to make as little noise as possible. For something so thick and looming, the jungle had an odd ability to carry sound. Wearing only his lightweight olive-drab flight suit, Sol crammed the abandoned gear under the tree trunk and pushed leaves over it. The bulky survival vest went back on, pockets bulging with the small first aid kit, .38 ammo, signal mirror and flares, spare battery, pocketknife, stuff to slow him down or save his life. A coin toss.

Sol brought the radio close to his lips. He drew a deep breath, ready to speak no louder than a murmur, then pressed the push-to-talk.

He slid his thumb off the switch.

The valley erupted with the echoes of jackhammering and clouting, like a giant construction zone back in Baltimore. The repetitive thumps were antiaircraft artillery, the dozen or more guns spread over the wooded slopes and along the winding riverbank, the guns that had appeared out of nowhere to shoot him down. Why the hell was this valley so heavily fortified?

All around, the artillery rang enough to shake the jungle floor. Or Sol believed it did; this may have been more of his nerves. Through the din, a hiss like a fire hose, then a roar like a fire, streaked down from above. The sound scorched low just above Sol's hiding place. The branches shuddered, the air shattered on the other side of the unbroken green canopy. Someone in a fast mover, maybe Daniels, had just zipped by at five hundred feet and six hundred knots to take a look at Sol's chute, see if there was a body attached; if not, the pilot had to determine what situation Sol was in and what help he needed. Sol reproached himself for not transmitting sooner, to save whoever that was from having to dive down into this defended valley. But he'd been busy running for his life.

The shrill whoosh of the wings and jet engine swept away with incredible speed. Left behind were voices on the trail, Vietnamese or Lao. Sol didn't know which and didn't care.

He was too frightened to raise his head above the rotting trunk for a look, and too scared not to. He couldn't just sit back and get nabbed. Sol slid the .38 from its holster; the handgun felt far too heavy and real, the possibility of a shoot-out welded in its weight.

Holding his breath, Sol inched his eyes above the mushy bark of the dead tree. Through fifty yards of creepers and twigs, five VC stood on the trail, all with AK-47s strapped around their necks. One black-pajamaed man spit harsh orders at them. Sol fingered the trigger on the .38, in case those orders were "Go get him, boys."

The big guns in the valley quit firing.

The VC dashed off, not into the vines to surround and capture Sol, but back down the Trail toward the bamboo grove. *What were they doing?* Sol slumped behind the trunk, relieved a little, mostly dumbfounded.

The distant and distinct rumble of a Thud's water-injected afterburner told Sol what was happening.

Daniels was in a tight, climbing bank. That had been him coming in low and hot; he'd seen Sol's collapsed chute. After Nail reported the good beeper, Daniels flashed down to confirm that Sol was alive and evading. He'd tried for a look at any VC, but at that speed and with this foliage, it was unlikely Daniels saw anything but jungle. Daniels had ordnance left; he and Nail were setting one more run for Daniels to use it and take some heat off Sol.

The VC were rushing back to the bamboo where they could see the open sky. They wanted to turn those AK-47s up at Daniels's return.

Sol lay on the damp jungle floor, just beyond the bamboo.

Daniels tended to drop his bombs long.

Sol had to get out of there, fast.

He holstered the .38, freeing both hands, then hoisted himself over the tree trunk. In the unseen sky, the thrust of Daniels's engine disappeared; he'd climbed to his perch. Sol lifted his knees like running in the ocean; vines and composting leaves sucked at his strides, slowing him, sapping his speed trying to get back on the Trail. Sweat drizzled down his neck, but he was lighter without the flight gear. Careless of the noise he made with his choppy strides, Sol no longer sniveled as he ran.

Approaching the Trail, he ducked to be sure no one else was on it. Left and right, the way was empty. As Sol stepped on the hardened dirt, the valley resounded again with antiaircraft fire. Daniels was closing in, barreling down the slope of his dive; the zeeps, 37s and 57s, maybe that big 100mm, were sending up fireworks for him to fly through. Two hundred yards behind Sol in the bamboo field, a racket of AK-47s tore up the rest of the late simmering day.

Sol ran faster than he thought he ever had in his life. His heart flooded his temples and ears. He swung his shoulders into the sprint, not knowing how to go this fast, not much of an athlete. Daniels was ramming his Thud in low, knifing in deep, deeper than he had against the ferry or the guns; the guy was crazy with those sideburns and batshit out of his mind to be slicing through the tracers of all those wide-awake guns. With a fellow pilot on the ground, Daniels had to be accurate, and he had to know he rarely was. So he was going to stomp on the VC to try and be sure. Sol was not sure, so he ran hard.

Under the canopy of trees, the din of Daniels's closing jet intensified. The guns of the valley roared at the invading Thud. As Daniels accelerated down, Sol hurtled through the pounding anvil of his heart and his gusting breaths, the caws of frantic birds beside the Trail, the yelp of a monkey in the great jungle shadows. The shriek of the Thunderchief swelled as Daniels pulled back on the stick, nosed up out of his dive, throttle to the stops, wings straining against the thickest air on the planet, bombs on their way.

Sol leaped off the Trail. He slid feetfirst into a thicket to come in low under the twigs and thorns. He shielded his face as he skidded. He crawled on his belly and elbows to a murky depression, a sunken sodden spot. Arms behind his head, eyes closed against the jungle floor, he listened to the falling Mk82 five-hundred-pound bombs. They really did whistle on the way down.

He crammed both hands over his ears just as the first concussion rippled across his shoulders and the seat of his flight suit. Heat baked the back of his head. The earth trembled. Sol bit on his lip and squeezed his ears and sphincter, balled up on his side like a bug.

He wasn't fried or mutilated. He tried to swallow but couldn't. He waited for the air to clear of clamor and heat before he opened his eyes. The ground cooled his cheek and he sighed at this little comfort.

The valley went silent. Slowly, skittishly, Sol rolled onto his back. Nail's propellers were gone, Daniels's jet, too—his speed had been so swift that he'd vanished even before the black mushrooms of his bombs were done, and the trees and bamboo were split. The VCs' guns had either gotten to him or not, but they'd settled into their corner to wait for another round. In the scoured quiet, gazing up at the underside of a bush, Sol unclenched. In the hush, the immense jungle reasserted itself; the place was unafraid of bombs, perhaps even used to them. Birds piped up and insects twiddled as if Sol were not there at all. A breeze riffled only the highest boughs, shifting the sunlight, making the canopy spangle.

Sol sat up enough to peer in the direction he'd come from. Sure enough, the whole acre where he'd hidden behind the downed tree was a smoking crater, everything shaved to the ground and white with ash. The entire bamboo stand was obliterated, too. Daniels' first two bombs had taken out every VC chasing Sol. The third and fourth flew long. There'd be more VC coming soon. But for now, Sol liked his hidey-hole. He decided to wait for rescue here.

Sol turned on the radio and pushed talk twice, to signal Daniels and Nail that he'd not been killed by the bombing run. He lay back, looking for calm.

He figured now was a good time to be frank with himself. This was no time for posturing, no professorial monologues alone at thirty thousand feet. He confessed to the jungle, which seemed to have ears and eyes everywhere. He'd come to Vietnam begrudgingly, fair enough. The only silver lining he'd been able to identify in this place was that here, after years of mastering the macabre loneliness of Nuclear Alert, he might truly find out what sort of man he was. The same way the other Thud pilots at the Officers Club had asked him his character—was he gung ho?—Vietnam might ask him, what are you made of? So far, he'd been shot down on his first combat mission, then been unmanned by raw fear, reduced to a running, chattering, frightened mess. Sol was thankful they'd been private moments, but he sensed the branding of them, the realization that these moments were going to harden into memories he'd never outlive.

He let these admissions flow past him. He asked if he were a coward, and demanded an honest answer because he had to rely on himself to get out of this. No, he didn't think he was a coward. This day was a hell of a thing. Anyone's teeth would have clacked. Still, the question lingered.

He'd wait and see. The day was far from over.

CHAPTER 17

Valley near Xe Banghiang River
Laos

Loi drove madly down the hill. He had no regard for safety and none
certainly for Minh's comfort. He made no conversation. Earlier, on their
way up the slope, she might have taken this bumpy, silent ride for a lack
of concern or attention to her. But they'd survived the American bombs
in each other's arms, and he'd said nothing when she climbed into the
cab next to him as if that was where she belonged. Minh braced herself
and figured this was what loving Loi was.

The valley throbbed with the sounds of artillery, so loud it seemed
to Minh not a great green expanse on the earth but just a small crack
in a sidewalk, the constant guns like the scraping of shoes. The smaller-
caliber weapons fired so quickly that they grumbled with the constancy
and hurly-burly of traffic; the bigger guns could be horns. The reports
bounced among the hills and fed on themselves. The shredding of the
air above the river was like nothing Minh had ever seen, not even during
the worst air raids on the Road.

Loi had thrown his pistol onto the bench seat between them. She gathered it into her lap. In the lurching cab she clutched the handgun very tightly, so much so that she was afraid she might squeeze too hard and it could go off. She tried to feel for Loi's wrath and dignity in the steel and kept her fingers far from the trigger in the bounding truck.

Several times down the hillside, Loi swerved to keep from getting stuck in ruts or dense bushes. He fought to control the wheel and gearshift, but never cursed. Minh projected she would learn to drive for him and take this chore to herself so he could hold the gun, as was proper. She tried not to pull her eyes off him while she imagined more but took too much of a battering in the wild swings of his steering, so she put her eyes back on the path.

The trail emerged from the trees onto the wider road. Loi stepped on the accelerator to barrel to the river. He drove with such haste that, reaching the bank, he slammed on the brakes to keep the truck out of the water. Again Minh walked in front of the truck over the submerged bridge.

Once across the river, she climbed into the cab. Loi took off with a pop of the clutch; his skills were improving. For the first time since leaving the hillside where they watched the American plane go down, Loi spoke. He glanced over as though to make sure she was still there, then back to the road.

"I don't know how to do this."

Minh motioned to his hands on the wheel and the shifter. "You're doing much better."

"I mean I don't know how to say something."

"What?"

"I'm going to headquarters."

"Do you want me to get out?"

"No. No. I want you to go with me."

She liked the way he put it. Not a request or a command, as he had the authority to do. A want. Why was this difficult? "As you wish."

"And then."

The road had smoothed enough for Minh to set the pistol down on the seat between them, but she did not. She did not want it or anything there. She kept the gun in her lap, held it with both hands. This helped her not to reach to him.

"Then?"

"I want you to stay."

"What do you mean? At headquarters?"

Loi twisted his head at her like an owl, blinking. "No. No."

"Where?"

"With me."

"With you."

"Tonight."

One of Minh's hands came off the pistol to cover her heart.

She fixed on the Road speeding by as fast as the moments. She needed to manage her thoughts. She wanted to say yes, but saying that would begin it, and this was a dangerous thing. Loi had much power. A thousand men obeyed him; she'd watched one die for not doing it well enough. Lying in Loi's bed would be playing with fire. What if she displeased him, what if he discarded her? But she thought she might love him and that, too, was flame. She held his gun and his gaze as they hurtled over the Road.

Out of the distance, from the direction of the downed jet, an explosion shook the valley. Loi drove through it, and Minh did not answer while the blast echoed and faded.

"Do you understand what I'm asking?"

She nodded, avoiding words. She thought words somehow more binding.

"If you stay with me, others will know. I have a cot, in a tent to myself. But little else. Do you know what that means?"

She did know, of course. Tomorrow and onward, when she sang the revolution's songs and acted the roles for the soldiers of the Road and the war, her lips would hold more for them than the melodies, her body would be more than the roles she played. To all who whispered, she would be the woman who slept with the cadre.

There would be a cost for Loi to have what he was asking. He would not be the one to pay it.

Minh nodded again.

Loi pinched his lower lip, then rubbed the fingers as if testing the feel of his next question.

"How old are you?"

"Twenty. And you?"

"Twenty-six. Minh."

The sound of her name caused her to realize how rarely he used it. "Yes."

"When I first saw you. Running into the camp, six months ago. Carrying the papers you'd saved from the Americans. You were covered in blood. I caught you."

"I was so scared. I would have run all the way back to Hanoi."

"I thought you were heroic."

"I was weeping like a child."

"You took a long time to let me go. You didn't look me in the face, just held on."

"I remember. Your white shirt. I ruined it, I'm sure."

"At Khe Sanh. I never forgot. What holding you felt like."

"You're very kind to me."

"I can be kind. I'm sorry what you saw, up on the hill."

"I understand."

"I want to ask something. I don't know how."

"You barely know how to drive, either. Do it the same, fast."

"Clumsy."

"All right, that too."

Loi stiffened. "Are you a virgin?"

Even awkward, even gently, here was the command, his expectation of her agreement. As she'd learned on Hanoi's streets, the order of things asserts itself.

"No."

Loi changed again, he laughed openly and marveling. "Why didn't you lie to me?"

This was too mercurial; he was silent, then grim, then bumbling. She spoke the truth, it was the easiest to keep track of.

"Because I would have to act like a virgin. Do you want that? A silly thing?"

For the speed Loi drove, he spent too many moments looking at Minh. What must she look like, for him to stare? He was not so good a driver to do this. She motioned for him to put his eyes back on the Road. He did, shrugging. "I don't know what I want."

"Why not?"

"I suppose I should lie to you, then."

"Are you a virgin?" She meant this as a joke.

"Yes."

He was not looking at her, so she was able to gape quickly before closing her mouth. The surprise was pleasant. Minh viewed his inexperience the same way she'd imagined learning to drive for Loi: how she could be of use. She set the gun on the seat. She wanted her hands free; the urge to touch him rose.

Before she could move or lean his way, the hills erupted again with artillery fire. Minh saw nothing of it, no flashes or streaks beyond the green cap of the jungle. The thrashing noises of battle on every side, then the shriek and streak of another jet tearing low through it all over their heads made the truck seem very small and her own heart very raw. Something delicate that might have been between them had flown out of the truck into the reverberating, terrible valley.

The draw of him remained. Minh sat upright. To keep herself from reaching for him, she joined both hands again around the gun in her lap.

CHAPTER 18

Aboard Jolly Green 22
Thirty miles southwest of Tchepone
Laos

Every second in the air, Bo saw more trees than all the ones added up in his lifetime in Kansas. His chopper cruised at five thousand feet, above small-arms range, and the Lao countryside rolled past rumpled and steady green, thick as any cornfield but impenetrable. The humidity that his Jolly flew through smelled damp as a plains rain.

Friday night football had been like this. He and his high school team got so amped up they'd ram into each other before the games, just to start hitting. Bo played cornerback and receiver. He grunted inside his helmet with every collision because, though he lacked the size of some others, he hit hard. Only two years ago he was wearing pads, not forty pounds of gun and gear. He had boys around him, not men, and they did not rely on one another for their lives. But this chopper and that green field below felt like game day.

They were thirty minutes out of Nakhon Phanom and Bo hadn't moved from the window. Over the barrel of the M60 he watched Laos spool by. He wasn't idle, he spent the time pepping himself up, while Lee and the flight engineer catnapped. In the air alongside, Jolly 23 flew with the sun at its back, too.

Just before takeoff, Major Crebbs and the pilot of Jolly 23 had flipped a coin. Bo and Lee had also flipped. Again, Bo was PJ 1 on the rescue low bird.

From the cockpit, Major Crebbs announced over the intercom the arrival of two flights of Skyraider escorts; these were four A-1s, call signs Sandy 1, 2, 7, and 8. The Sandys dropped down from above to slip into a diamond formation around the pair of Jollys. To Bo's way of thinking, they resembled football linemen, burly and looking for contact.

In echelon they flew deeper into Laos. Bo checked his survival vest, radios, and ammo, and tightened his bootlaces. When the chopper banked, Lee and the FE didn't revive but stayed on the floor, resting their heads on flak jackets.

With no word from Crebbs, two of the four Sandys bolted off on their own. They rushed east toward a winding and wooded valley ten miles off. The other pair of Sandys stayed with the orbiting Jollys.

High above the valley ahead, lit in the clarity of a sinking sun, eight attack jets circled. Bo didn't notice Lee standing beside him until he spoke.

"That's a shitload of fast movers up there."

"What's happening? Why are we stopping here?"

"Keeping a safe distance."

"Aren't we going in?"

Lee pointed. "You see that many jets in one place? Tells you one thing. That valley's hot." He held up the coin he'd tossed to win Bo his PJ 1 position. "Two out of three?"

Bo riveted his attention on the valley minutes away. Eight jet bomb-ers and two loaded Skyraiders represented a lot of firepower rotating over one downed pilot.

The flight engineer joined Bo and Lee to look out the portal. He pursed his lips and shook his head. "I don't want to go in there." The FE rapped Lee in the vest. "You want to go in there?"

"No, I do not."

The FE tapped Bo's chest. "You do not want to go in there."

As one, the three shifted to the opposite window while the Jolly continued to orbit. In this fresh view, one of the jet bombers peeled away from the circling cohort, nosing into a steep turn to take a run at the valley. Bo had never seen this before, one jet diving alone, so exposed. It seemed daring and risky. But there was no other way to do it; they couldn't just roll in together and blow the hell out of everything, not with an American pilot on the ground under them. Their bombs had to be surgical.

In a blink, every hill in the valley reached up to the speeding jet with colored arms, slicing and swatting at it. On either side of Bo, the two experienced airmen flinched.

The flight engineer repeated himself, drawing out the words so they sounded almost musical. He spoke not to Bo or Lee but to the valley. "No, I do not want to go in there."

CHAPTER 19

Xe Banghiang River valley
Laos

The antiaircraft guns boomed again; this time Sol was certain he felt it in the ground. He rolled onto his stomach to scrabble deeper into the soft humus of the jungle floor.

The guns sawed so hard they covered up the roar of the oncoming jet. Their different calibers made distinctive noises: the bray of ZPUs and 23s spitting thousands of angry rounds per minute, the larger 37s going off like strings of firecrackers, the jackhammer of a 57, and the slower 100mm like a booming bell. The artillery piece nearest to Sol was maybe a hundred yards farther along the road, a 57 above him on a slope.

Suddenly, that 57 quit firing; another went quiet, too, maybe a zeep. With an American jet whooshing down on them, the VC up in the woods had taken their fingers off the triggers and bugged out for cover.

In the lull, the hills funneled to Sol the strain and might of a jet bottoming out.

The bombs whined, shrill and loud. Whatever they were—five-hundred-, seven-hundred-pounders—they were going to land close to Sol, or right on top of him.

He clenched every muscle, jaws to toes. Sol grabbed handfuls of leaves and hung on, and judged himself again for trembling.

The jet muscled out of its dive. In the falling seconds, Sol wished himself up into the jet's cockpit, to be the one flying away, looking down for the crump of his bombs, not the poor bastard burrowed into this humid thicket under them. He covered his head with the leaves and cursed.

The first blew to his right; the earth jittered like a snare drum. Sol shouted into the ground to release pressure in his lungs. The second bomb missed the road to land up the slope; there might have been third and fourth blasts, but Sol didn't hear them in the cacophony and his own yelling into the leaves. The explosions threw vines, dirt, bark, and splinters high to patter down over his back and neck.

The bombs left him alive and panting, lying on the lumps of his balled hands. His ears felt pushed in. He rolled onto his back, smelling scorched grass, and blinked at the mosaic of sky showing through the leaves. He caught no sight of the fleeing bomber.

That pilot hadn't been Dash lead; Daniels was surely out of ordnance by now. Besides, the bombs had been too accurate to be Daniels. Whoever it was had been vectored in by Nail for gun suppression over the valley. That was the good news: It meant a force had gathered. Sol's rescue was under way. A gray mist from the explosions blew over his thicket, a low, floating haze like ghosts crawling over the ground. Sol lay still until his breathing slowed.

He sat up to do a ground-level BDA. Seventy yards to his north, the jungle had been excoriated, flayed down to skinned trunks and pale smoking stumps of brush. Around the valley, the artillery slowed. The gun on the hillside above him stayed quiet.

He whispered to the departed pilot, "Nice shooting." Even so, Sol wouldn't live through many more runs this close to him. To keep the bombs off him, he had to let Nail know exactly where he was and, following that, to guide the Jollys and pararescuemen in for his pickup.

In jungle survival training, the JEST instructors had shown the pilots a film clip depicting Viet Cong and Pathet Lao troops moving through the trees with old science fiction–looking crates on their backs, spikey with antennae—gizmos supposed to be directional finders that could home in on ground transmissions—to make the point that if you got chatty on the radio while evading, the bad guys could find you. The film had bad Asian actors. Sol hadn't taken it seriously. None of the pilots had.

He tugged the radio from his vest, wondering if that film was just scare tactics or real. He wished he'd paid closer attention. With relief, he noted that his hands weren't shaking. Others were coming to get him, and this buoyed his morale. Jet jockeys, Nail, A-1 Skyraiders, chopper pilots, and PJs, all taking chances to save him, maybe risks worse than the ones that had got him shot down. Sol owed it to them to stay calm. He'd been on the ground for forty minutes and, with a hint of shame, realized this was his first thought of anyone besides himself. But he'd never been so afraid for this long. He was on a journey around the fringes of his own character—a lot of what he was seeing in his reactions was for the first time.

"Okay." The word spoken out loud made some kind of handshake with himself. "Time to get out of here."

Before he turned on the radio, Sol checked the volume knob. He emitted a four-second beeper to alert Nail or Crown, whoever was monitoring, that he was about to broadcast. Holding the speaker to his ear, he heard no one talking on the guard channel. Sol stole quick glances up and down the Trail, deep into the jungle, away to the smoldering acres around him, and up the hillside where the 57 crew was likely dead.

Pressing talk, Sol spoke as hushed as he could to be heard.

"Nail 34, this is Dash 2. Over."

Seconds passed with no response. Away over the valley, the VC guns continued to yap. Was it Nail they were firing at? Had he been shot down, too? Was someone else coming?

"Dash 2. Great to hear your voice, man!"

Even with the volume turned low, Nail sounded excited. Sol pulled his thumb off the receive switch, silencing the radio. Again, he listened into the jungle, up the trail, to see if any VC had heard Nail's outburst. A few fires still crackled in the craters, some hardcore birds had recovered enough from being stunned to resume their calls. Sol set the volume dial to its minimum and pressed receive. Nail was still talking, but not to Sol.

"All rescue aircraft. Dash 2 is up on this frequency. Stay off the air while we make contact."

Sol stepped back in, whispering. Every word he formed felt like a separate act of courage. Far off, through the potshots, smoke, and birds, the hopeful buzz of Nail's twin-prop O-2 reached his thicket. "Nail, Dash 2."

"Go, Dash. What's your status?"

"I'm good. Not hurt. In a secure hiding spot for now, but VC are nearby."

"Copy. What's your location?"

"Too close to the last bomb run."

"Copy that. No more bombs 'til we have a fix on you."

"I'm three hundred yards northwest of my chute. Who dropped those bombs? He's good."

"Gunfighter 1, an Air Force Fox 4. I've got eight fast movers stacked up, ready to tear this valley a new one."

Sol made a mental note to find Gunfighter 1, Nail 34, all the fliers on this rescue mission, and get them very drunk. "I'm flattered."

"We're going to get you out."

"Good news."

"Dash 2. Ready a smoke to mark your position."

"Roger."

"I've got two Jollys on orbit ten miles west. Sandy 1 is descending inbound. Stand by for his call. Stay with it, buddy. You're on your way home. Out."

Sol sat up in the leaves to fumble in his survival vest. He removed one flare. The day end of the Popsicle-size tube would release a bright-orange smoke cloud; the night end produced a burning white phosphorus glimmer. Enough daylight was left to use the smoke. With the flare in one hand, the radio to his ear like a teenager, Sol lay back to wait.

Once he arrived, Sandy 1 would take over as on-scene commander. It was going to be his call to decide whether or not to bring in the Jollys, to determine if the rescue was safe enough to proceed.

Sol surveyed the green canopy overhead. The density of those leaves was going to hinder visuals. Sandy 1 would have to zero in on Sol's orange smoke signal.

But if Sol popped the smoke, the VC would see his hiding place, too.

"Dash 2, this is Sandy 1. You copy?"

On cue to the muted voice, the guns in the valley cranked up. Underlying the rising artillery was the bass growl of the coming A-1's big engine. Sol rose to his knees to face the direction of Sandy 1's approach down the course of the river.

"Lima Charlie, Sandy." Loud and clear.

"Dash 2, I'm going to ask for authentication." These were the answers to private questions every pilot provided to guarantee the enemy wasn't faking with an English speaker to draw in rescue flights. "Name your elementary school. Over."

"Cromwell Valley."

"Your first dog?"

"Moose."

"Your first car."

"Red VW bug."

"Roger. Authenticated, Dash 2. I'm heading in low for an ID pass. Pop your smoke when you see me, over."

The guns on all sides of Sol began to intensify from the bracketing hills. Sandy wasn't a sleek jet bomber flashing down at speeds just below Mach 1, but a broadside target flapping in at 230 knots, 300 feet over the trees, looking for a friend. It sounded like every artillery piece in the valley opened up on Sandy following the river. Small-arms fire kicked in, too, every Viet Cong with a rifle or pistol took a crack at the A-1 blaring past. The snaps of these smaller guns revealed something awful that Sol hadn't fully realized, or he hadn't let himself admit.

He'd been shot down in the middle of a damn lot of VC. They were everywhere.

"Sandy 1, negative on the smoke. Too many bad guys, too close. I'll give you a hack when you fly past. Over."

In his cockpit, surely dicing through bright threads of tracers, Sandy 1 put his thumb on the transmit button too fast; Sol caught the opening curses of his radioed response. After a pause, the A-1 pilot said, "Copy."

Sol tracked Sandy 1's progress by the rising volume of artillery and ground fire. How was the A-1 going to make it through the same guns that had shot down Sol's Thud, going a lot higher and faster?

"Sandy 1."

"Go, Dash."

"Sounds like you're getting hosed. Maybe you should abort."

"Maybe you should pop a fucking smoke."

This startled Sol. His gallantry had been met with a surly rebuke. Another self-centered snapshot went off in his head: Okay, pal. It was my job to attack, now it's yours to come get me. So do it. Sol readied the smoke in case either he or Sandy 1 lost his nerve.

The A-1 pressed on through the barrage. For the next few moments, every VC in range would keep his eyes and gun barrels glued upward while Sandy 1 shoved through their bullets. The roar of the A-1's engine swelled, with seconds before the plane reached Sol. The foliage blocked him from seeing enough of the sky. He needed eyes on Sandy if this was going to go right.

The rim of the nearest crater lay seventy yards away through the forest. Sol gulped and made a decision. He had to take a gamble, the way Sandy 1 was.

He took off sprinting.

Sol crashed through a webwork of creepers and grabby brambles, jumped over downed and rotting trunks, righted himself from stumbles as he galloped across the soft and uneven ground. The noise he made was barely audible under the drumbeat of cannons and the cracks of small arms.

Sandy 1 called on the radio in Sol's swinging fist but Sol couldn't slow to answer. The crater lay just ahead while behind him Sandy 1 astounded both him and the VC; somehow, Sandy kept coming. Nearing the crater's rim, Sol stopped short; he wouldn't stand in the open, not without a rescue chopper directly over his head. Every VC on every hill in the area could look down on him in the soot of that crater. Best to stay back in the trees where the branches and leaves had been thinned by the blast just enough for him to get a mottled view over the jungle at the flak and at Sandy 1 boring in low a half mile off. Sol held the radio tight to his ear.

The plane looked slow and heavy, jinking in ponderous swerves. How much fire was Sandy taking? Streaming behind his tail and wings, arching above his canopy, dots and dashes of tracers flew in the hundreds every torturous second. Sol could only imagine the unseen rounds. From ground level, it looked to be an impossible thing to fly through so much gunnery.

"Sandy 1, I have you in sight."

"Copy, Dash."

"I'm off your right wing. You'll pass me by in a hundred yards. I'm in the woods near the first crater."

"Copy."

The Sandy drilled onward. The colors around him gave the valley a surreal feel, some kind of evil ticker-tape parade. Sol kept the radio to his mouth.

"Sandy, you're almost on me. On your right." The A-1 was a big target, growing bigger. Sol would buy this son of a bitch pilot as many beers as it took. "Off your right wing . . . on your right . . . hack, hack, hack! Now you're past me. Copy?"

Sandy flashed past, banking out of sight. The red tendril of a ZPU skated behind him.

Sol ducked and flung himself under a bush. The guns farther along the valley leaned on their triggers, holding the racket at a nerve-racking level while Sandy 1 climbed out of the hills. None of this stained Sandy's voice. Whoever he was, he was made of ice.

"Dash, I'm not sure I got your location. Hold where you are. I want to make another pass for a positive ID."

"You took a lot of ground fire. You sure?"

"It's going to take a bunch of gun suppression to get you out of there. If you don't want your ass blown off, I need to know exactly where you are."

"I don't like it."

"I don't, either. Pop a fucking smoke." This time Sandy 1 left his thumb on transmit so Sol could hear him laugh.

Sol bit his lip while considering what to do. He could spare this unbelievable pilot another nail-biting pass. Or he could stay hidden and let Sandy gut out another low-level run.

"Dash. It's getting dark. You want to go home?"

"Yeah."

"No smoke?"

"No."

"Then I'm coming around again."

CHAPTER 20

Aboard Jolly Green 22
Thirty miles southwest of Tchepone
Laos

Neither Lee nor the flight engineer commented. If they had been watching anything else, sports or some other kind of match, they might have said that the Sandy pilot was crazy or stupid, they might have gone "Wow" or "I can't believe this." But they said nothing when the A-1 came around for a second run. They crossed their arms and barely blinked. Standing next to scarred Lee, who knew what it took, Bo adopted his silence. When you are seeing immense courage, you shut up.

The Sandy's first run through the gauntlet of the valley had been a spectacle of smoke and brilliant light. From a safe distance, the action took place in slow motion. Scarlet fireballs and white bolts clawed at the A-1; the Sandy was invisible so low over the treetops, but Bo tracked him by the tracers lighting up his route. The sound was like thunder far away, like those mean rumbles that made Bo's father bring in the horses.

Bo had gasped when the low bird A-1 popped up out of the valley unscathed. He, Lee, and the FE scooted across the steel floor when the Jolly's orbit turned their door away, to keep watching the scene, to see the incredible A-1 banking around for another pass.

With the sun sinking lower and daylight waning, the antiaircraft fire seemed even brighter. The ridges cast long shadows over the valley; the burning of the downed jet and the low-slung tracers glittered on the darkening jungle. The Sandy pilot leveled his wings and lanced in across the treetops. Again, Bo lost sight of the plane but the spewing flak traced its path. The valley boomed, sounding like giants in battle.

This time, when the low-bird Sandy emerged from the valley, he trailed oily billows from his engine. Tracers stretched out for him, straining to pull him back, but he broke free and climbed. His high-bird wingmate looped around him, checking for damage. The Jollys and their two A-1 escorts did nothing but continue to circle while the wounded Sandy emerged from the valley, streaming oil smoke. The plane flew away west in silhouette against the pinking horizon, followed by his wingmate. Bo asked Lee what this meant.

"It's late. They're calling it for the day."

Lee turned from the open door. He swung his gunner's belt out of the way to keep it from tangling with Bo's and the FE's belts, also attached to the floor. Then he stopped and shook his head. Lee came back beside Bo in the doorway. Some intuition, or fear, told Lee to keep watching the departing Sandys.

The hills had gone quiet and the long shadows began to mask their tops. The rescue, the valley, the day seemed in limbo.

Suddenly Jolly 23 turned sharply, as if dodging something in the air. The helo showed Bo its underside leaving the holding pattern beside his chopper. Jolly 23 split away to the west, to hustle after the injured Sandy limping back to NKP. Major Crebbs did not follow but held Jolly 22 in its slow bank, maintaining the holding pattern alone. Lee spit out the door, into the wind.

"Damn it."

Before Bo could ask for an explanation, the pair of Sandys that had been protecting the choppers left their stations overhead. Wing to wing, they did not go after their smoking A-1 comrade, did not guard him on his limping flight home to the west. Instead, they carved away to the east.

Lee, the FE, and Bo shifted to the other side to keep the planes in sight. After a minute, one Skyraider climbed into the brassy sunlight. The other, the next low bird, launched into a dive, knifing for the twilit valley.

CHAPTER 21

Xe Banghiang River valley
Laos

Standing at the rim of the trees near the crater, Sol waved to make himself as visible as he could without popping a flare. This was all the bravado he thought he should be asked for.

Sandy 1 powered in lower than his first run, picking his teeth with the treetops and bamboo stalks. Sol got on his tiptoes, hand held in the air, radio to his mouth and ear. Flak arched over the charging A-1's cockpit, beautiful. The great din of the valley shook in the leaves and against his flight suit.

When it was two hundred yards and two seconds from passing his position, Sol keyed the push-to-talk button. He shouted into the clamor of guns and the low-passing plane, "Hack, hack, hack!" The A-1 flashed even with him. For an instant, Sol and the pilot exchanged a glance. Sandy waggled his wings as he roared past.

"Dash, I've got a lock on you. Over."

The first round that hit Sandy 1 came from a small-caliber zeep, a red Roman candle on the hillside opposite Sol. It struck the left wing, making the A-1 shudder as it coursed over the valley. The plane was a muscular old platform, built to take a beating as well as give one. Sandy 1 kept to his climb, howling to get out of reach. Sol crawled back under his bush. He stuck the radio to his lips, thinking he might call encouragement to the pilot and plane.

The second bullet must have been small-arms fire, for it struck Sandy with no fireball or skinny tracer, likely a lucky shot from one of the hundred AK-47s spitting lead straight up. Sandy coughed like it had been punched in the gut. A gout of gray smoke belched from the engine. The plane ran rough as it flew out of sight. Behind it, around Sol, the rifles and pistols shut down first, then the big guns. The last noise in the valley was Sandy 1, laboring into the distance on the cusp of night until it went quiet.

Lying in cool leaves, Sol's gut seized. Had Sandy taken a round in his fuel line, or hydraulics? Either one meant he wasn't coming back. But he'd seen Sol. He'd done it. Now he was leaving?

In the resounding hush, Sol's spirits felt like they, too, had taken a hit. With the valley quieted, it dawned on him again just how many guns there were packed around him. Even if Sandy had made it out of the valley in one piece, could he really have brought back a Jolly to pick Sol up? A big hovering HH-3 would probably get cut to ribbons in the first minute it dallied over Sol's head. Could he expect a Jolly crew and a PJ team to pierce that amount of triple A for him? Would he have the stones to do it? No, he wouldn't. They probably didn't either.

The JEST teachers had made it clear: the longer a pilot stays on the ground, the worse his chances. Staring down the barrel of spending the night in Laos, Sol wrestled with what to do. Should he put distance between himself and the hulk of his crashed jet, try to get out of this heavily armed valley? Or go back to his thicket and hunker down to stay close to where Sandy 1 had spotted him?

The daylight grew delicate. The vibrant greens of the jungle drained to a blue-black, the sky bruised to violet. The forest clung to its heat, not letting it go with the light. Sol had little faith that he had the instincts or training to slip out of the valley through the jungle with a very large VC force on the lookout. The Ho Chi Minh Trail would become a highway at night, he'd need to stay off that. If he opted to move, where would he go? He had no maps. He could wander into a worse situation.

No. He couldn't.

But he couldn't stay here on the rim of the bomb craters. The cover was too sparse, too burned out. Anyone seriously looking for him or driving slowly down the road might see him curled up under the bushes. Sol's only chance was to creep back to his thicket and ride out the night. Dawn would bring more bombs and a rescue bird. All he had to do was be alive and at large when they showed up.

He cast his senses out into the hillsides and the empty road nearby. When should he make his move? The light dimmed by the minute, the shadows yawned. Should Sol move now while he could still see, or wait for full dark when he'd be harder to spot but night-blind?

He liked none of his alternatives and brought the radio to his lips. His broadcast would be low power; anyone in range of his voice would need to be close by, though the hills were soundless. Sol put his thumb over the transmit button. Just to see, maybe, before nightfall.

"This is Dash 2. Anyone on guard channel? Over."

Sol moved the radio to his ear. He listened to the sad whisper of hissing. Then came a voice.

"Dash 2, this is Sandy 5. Copy?"

Sol almost dropped the radio. "Sandy 5. Where are you?"

"Coming around on final. I got a good idea where you are. I was watching Sandy 1 pretty close. Near the first crater."

"Affirmative. Fifty yards east of the rim."

"Copy. You got me and one Jolly left."

"Sandy, there's guns all over these hills."

"Copy. It's getting dark. Everyone else returned to base. But maybe we can slip in and out. You game for one more try?"

"Hell yes."

"If I need a flare, will you give it to me?"

Sol had little belief he'd survive the night. But he figured he had no shot at all if he waved a white phosphorous flag in front of the VC on all sides of him. "Negative. Sorry."

"I understand. I don't like Asian food either. Let's see what we can do. Making my turn now."

Sol lowered the radio. Out in the void of the valley, a deep hum rolled across the slopes framing the river. Sandy 5's approach was his last chance to get out of Laos tonight.

The radio crackled, easy to hear because the guns had not begun.

"Get ready, Dash. I think I can pull this thing off."

CHAPTER 22

The late day sun slipped amber light through the treetops in winks and pieces. Screened by the trees, the Trường Sơn Road was too murky, rough, and swervy to be driven so fast, especially by Loi. He must have realized this because he slowed the truck, looking disappointed at his own downshifting hands.

He surprised Minh when he pulled off the track and braked to a stop. She followed when he climbed down, stayed with him when he stomped off into the bushes. He did not speak as he batted at the jungle, kicking aside vines and stickers with a sort of disgust. She stored away his sullenness, put it with his bad driving, the news of his virginity, the upwelling of violence, the lotus blossoms, and the weight of him on top of her. Minh knew little about how to be a man's woman. She'd done what was needed in Hanoi and that never included love. Changing to suit Loi seemed the best way to proceed, but she couldn't be certain. Minh had no other woman to ask, she was the eldest in her entertainment group. She thought back to the old Lao woman this morning, giving water from a bucket to passersby. Perhaps Minh ought to ask someone else's mother for advice when next she walked the Road.

Ahead, Loi quit stamping through the brush, grasses, and thorns. He'd found a clearing where he stood hands on his hips, white shirt needing a wash. Minh arrived with such small experience of what Loi might want that she lingered back, unsure whether to stand beside or behind him. He waved her forward, next to him.

From a slight rise, they overlooked the valley. The river meandered and glistened below. Left and right of the water, the hills made a canyon of shade. High above, where the ebbing sun still shined, a ringlet of jets circled, too far up to hear, but they glinted the way American things did. Scattered in the jungle, spots smoldered where bombs had fallen and the jet plane had crashed. The muscular growl of another propeller plane filtered down the contours of the river.

The Americans were coming back for their downed pilot. With not much daylight left, and so many guns in the hands of Loi's thousand men fixed on the darkening swells of the valley, they were coming back.

Loi loosed a long exhale. He jutted his chin in the direction of the engine as the plane grew louder. The first of his artillery sparkled. Loi pulled his hands off his hips, folded his arms over the white shirt, and stared off into the valley as if he were alone. Minh asked and received nothing. Perhaps loving a man wasn't too different from being an orphan: you took what little came your way and waited for kindness.

The American plane flew into the valley from the same direction as before. All of Loi's gunners were already sighted along that path and the pilot flew right into them. This seemed foolhardy. The big motor brought it prowling just above the gray-green jungle, trying to sneak through the dusk. So many vivid tracers buzzed around him, firing so low across the plane's trajectory, that Minh feared the gunners might shoot each other on their hills facing across the river.

One blazing stream of red intersected the plane, then another of yellow. The pilot didn't eject when flames flared from his engine; chunks of metal catapulted from his wings that turned sideways to the earth.

The plane did not explode in the air but did so magnificently when it cartwheeled into the jungle. Orange and black fire boiled out of the trees on immense whumps. The American's bombs and rockets were cooking off; the blows came separately, one after another, like a colossus pounding the ground in pain.

Loi remained stoic, arms folded. Across the sunset hills, his guns all ceased. The valley gave no breeze to disperse the smoke, so the gray plumes rose high. Beyond reach, the American jets continued to circle. One pilot was dead, another was hiding in the forest. The distant jets could help neither, so two at a time they peeled out of their orbits and flitted away.

Loi extended a hand to Minh. She took it. He did not pull his eyes off the valley; everything he needed from Minh lay in her touch. She wanted to give him more but didn't let herself consider what that might be. She didn't want to be dissatisfied with these moments of holding his hand above a river as the day grew faint.

His fingers held hers with pressure; they were present and grateful. When he let her loose, the dark had taken hold and he'd decided something.

Loi walked away for the truck. Again she stayed behind to observe, the way he moved thoughtfully, with little haste now. She began to understand how lonely he was.

She caught up to him in the brush. Together they climbed into the vehicle. Loi drove slowly, properly in the final light. Others had started to take to the Road headed south, walkers and laden bicycles. Loi continued north. Minh felt she could speak first; even such a small thing seemed daring.

"Are we still going to headquarters?"

Like a bait, she'd said *we*.

"Yes."

"What are you going to do there?"

Minh said *you*; she released him now that she'd caught him. This was how to be sure the fish would always be there.

"I'll call a meeting of the division's officers."

"Why?"

"To tell them I'm responsible."

"For what? You did nothing wrong."

Minh stopped herself, fearing she'd said too much, that she'd walked in front of him and not behind. Loi inclined his head, granting that she had indeed questioned him, but she might speak on.

"Your gunners acted on their own." She measured her next phrase. "You corrected it."

He smiled broadly and reached for her hand again. She gave it.

"We're communists. No one acts on his own."

He drove with one hand. When he had to shift, he took his hand back and spoke.

"It's why I asked you to stay tonight. Just tonight."

She tried to stop herself, but her body asked the question, turning on him, perhaps too hard. One night. Why?

Loi spoke to the Road, slow beneath them. "The Americans know where we are now. We'll have to go."

The division's underground bunkers, sleeping quarters, storage, the complex of tunnels and trenches, months of work above and below the ground to fashion a jungle base for two thousand men, everything was going to be abandoned, all because one of Loi's gunners fired first at the jet that had bombed the ferry.

"You understand, Minh. This means I'll have to go."

More lotus flowers in the mail? Maybe after tonight, he might sign the packages.

No. Minh would not be left behind again. She lifted the pistol off the seat between them, into her lap. She would not let it go. She'd call Loi on his words that communists don't act alone. She and the gun together were a new thing, not just a singer.

Loi saw her actions; he might have seen her resolve.

"But first," he said. "Before we leave."

167

Tonight. He was talking about tonight. And tomorrow she would tell him she was going with him. He said *we*.

"Yes?"

"I'm going to issue one more order. For the whole division."

The road bumped and this drew Minh's attention to the windshield. They had entered the camp; she'd not noticed. Loi stopped the truck.

He did what she wanted; he reached for her.

His hand was out for the gun. She handed it over.

"What are you going to do?"

She meant *with me?* But Loi was in the momentum of his plan, the one he'd hatched holding her hand in the heart of the valley.

"I'm going to tell them not to capture the downed American."

"You're going to let him go?"

Loi shook his head. No.

The division wasn't leaving, not yet. Loi had a plan for tomorrow. If Minh wanted a place with him past tonight, beyond lotus blossoms, she would have to find a place in that.

He leaped out of his opened door, then slammed it. Loi called over his shoulder.

"Wait here."

He strode off with long steps, eager.

Minh threw open her door to land like a cat. She ran around the truck's grille.

"I almost died twice today."

Before he could reply, she took hold of his wrist above his gun hand.

"You and I make the beginning. The ending will come on its own."

She slid her hand down to take the pistol from him. Minh would enter the headquarters with Loi, one step behind but carrying his weapon.

CHAPTER 23

Sol could not rise off his knees. He ignored the damp that soaked through his flight suit and the strong urge to run. He couldn't lift his eyes, either.

In the soft brown earth, Sandy 5's exploding bombs and rockets rumbled. The last purple light slipped from the valley. The emergency radio dropped from Sol's hand, and he did not pick it up with Nail calling.

Sol was to blame for Sandy 5's death. No he wasn't and yes he was, and this went around in his head, stuck on his knees as the A-1 burned and blew apart. The pilot had flown in from the same direction as Sandy 1, too low to eject. He came in knowing the number of guns in the valley. Sol tried to warn him off. But Sol had got shot down in the first place and Sandy had to come in to find him. Sol wouldn't pop a flare. What was Sandy 5's name, did he have a family, was he dead before impact? Sol measured and weighed as the earth under him trembled to the A-1's obliteration. Beside Sol's bent knees the radio whispered, Nail 34 saying good night and good luck, he was returning to base, bingo fuel. Sol peered up through a break in the foliage; the stacked jets were all gone.

Night fell on him fast.

He felt like he was waiting, but uncertain for what. For rescue. For the VC to find him, capture, or kill him. For Sandy's ordnance to stop going off and damning him.

Sol became aware of the radio again. This time a new voice, older and more gravelly than Nail's, was hailing him.

"Dash 2, Dash 2, this is Crown. Do you copy?"

The dark had hardened under the jungle canopy. The sky was slightly lighter, a starless charcoal. Sol brought the radio to his lips, wanting to describe what he'd seen of Sandy's death. He felt the urge for memorial.

Sandy 5 was out of the game. Sol couldn't mourn him now; he'd do it in the years to come if he had years left to him. In the fresh night, with Crown calling, Sol abandoned his guilt with the same sense of ejecting that he'd had from his Thud. Sol could not go down with his own plane or Sandy's.

"Crown. Dash 2. I copy, over."

"Dash, it's getting too dark, so all rescue planes are returning to base."

Not all planes. Not Sandy 5. It wasn't darkness shutting down the rescue, but flak and two American planes burning on hillsides.

"Copy."

"We'll have a Spooky orbiting your position all night. If you need help, just call." This was an AC-47 night-vision gunship. Each of its three miniguns could fire a hundred rounds per second. If Sol needed that kind of help, he was already in deep trouble.

"Copy. When's the rescue force coming back?"

"Sunrise is 0557. I'd say 0558. Set your alarm, Dash."

"Will do."

"If you want to improve your chances, be advised it's best if you try to move to a location better suited for pickup. There's some activity in your vicinity."

"Copy."

"Also, you should know. Word just came down from Seventh Air Force. Turns out you've been shot down by an NVA division they've been on the lookout for."

"Crown, explain."

"The NVA 325th. Bigtime at Khe Sanh. About a month ago, they retreated into Laos. Haven't been heard from since. Some dumbass Charlie shot you down. And now we know where they are."

That explained why no one had fired at Sol or Daniels on their first runs at the ferry and the underwater bridge. The 325th had been hiding, licking its wounds. Sol's shoot-down was a mistake.

Now he was on the ground evading in the middle of an entire enemy division. A couple thousand men, all hiding, too. They were going to be pissed, even more than normal, if they caught him. Sol's heart—which he'd thought had sunk as far as it could—dug a hole.

"Dash, Seventh Air Force is calling them the Lost Division."

"Crown, what's that mean?"

"Good news for you."

"How?"

"Seventh Air has let it be known. We got twenty-four hours to get you back. After that, they're going to Arc Light the whole valley."

B-52 carpet bombing. Nothing, not a tree, not a VC, not Sol if he was still on the ground, would be left standing in the moonscape after an Arc Light.

The price to bring Sol home had already been high. Seventh Air Force had just upped the ante.

Sol had flown one combat bombing mission, one, and had his jet shot out from under him. How many more pilots and planes were they willing to risk for him, a rookie? What if the butcher's bill got too high?

Would some impatient general just call in the B-52s and be done with it, no matter if Sol was under them?

Would they let an entire enemy division, the Lost Division, slip away?

"Dash copies."

Sol stowed the radio. He fumbled for one of his two water bottles. He sipped two swallows. His knees were soaked. He'd been on them too long.

Sol climbed to his feet in the blackness. He stepped into the creepers and hilly brush. With two thousand armed men looking for him, fueled on his own sweat and fright, it was time to get moving. The clock had already started.

CHAPTER 24

Nakhon Phanom Royal Thai Air Force Base
40th Air Rescue and Recovery Service
Alert shed

Lee wasn't supposed to have his hip flask with him in the alert shed. He sat outside on the cheap plastic furniture burning through cigarettes, washing the smoke down with swigs. When Bo sat beside him, Lee held out the flask.

"You drink some, I'll drink less."

"You shouldn't be drinking at all."

"True."

Lee accepted and ignored responsibility in one word. Something about that capsulized the war. Bo took a pull from the flask. The Scotch went down full and peaty; there were stories inside the flavor of it. He figured a few shots might help him sleep, get past the images of the A-1 pinwheeling into the ground. Probably Lee was doing the same, trying to take his mind off the Lao valley, or at least dull himself enough to get some rest. He required more Scotch than Bo did.

Bo handed the flask back. Lee lit another smoke. The humidity draped them; Lee's gray exhales floated upward, amazing to Bo they could rise in such heavy air.

Bo said, "We got twenty-four hours to get him out of there."

"We can do it."

Bo dug into his pocket for an American quarter. "Let's flip for PJ 1 tomorrow."

"No. I'm taking it. You stay in the bird."

"That's not fair."

Lee spit past his crossed ankles. "I give a rat's ass. And don't give me some Kansas lecture about cornfields and barns and shit. About fair. You stay in the bird tomorrow."

Bo stuffed the quarter away. That wasn't the Scotch talking. A grimness had settled over Lee while he'd been outside, smoking and sipping alone. Lee had broken another rule by not flipping with Bo.

"Tell me about your scar."

Lee cast Bo a glance, quick like a swig, short and meaningful. When he looked away, past the chain-link fence that surrounded the hut, the lights of the base had stolen all but the brightest stars. Lee didn't gaze up, just out, searching through distance or years.

He seemed to be choosing to speak to Bo or not. Maybe it was because Bo had done once what Lee had done many times, yet still he had done it—ridden the penetrator down into the jungle. Maybe because they'd both sworn their lives to save others, and Lee himself felt like an other right then, needing help, something, from Bo. Maybe it was the flask. Lee rapped Bo on the thigh.

"My mother married an Italian off the boat. They were both young, she didn't know any different. He was okay. Then he joined up. Marines. Went off to the Pacific. Tarawa, Okinawa. He came back and did a little too much of this." Lee rattled the half-full flask. "She threw him out when I was six. I didn't see him for a while."

Lee fired another cigarette. Was he talking about his scar? Or could he not? If he couldn't, that too was powerful. While more tobacco smoke rose on the heat, Lee mulled in silence. Bo was about to apologize for bringing the scar up. Lee surprised him and continued.

"See, someone can do something like be your father. Bring you into the world. What's bigger than that? Then they can disappear. And the only thing they mean is what you make them mean. It's up to you. You understand me?"

Bo believed he did. His brother was missing. Bo tried every day to give him meaning.

"The old man came back when I was seventeen. I wasn't too pleased. I threw a punch at him, he threw one at me. Knocked me through a plate glass window. Even so, my mom took him back. I went and joined the PJs."

Lee tapped his tunic, near his heart where the scar ran.

"These pilots that get shot down. We don't know these guys. They don't mean nothing to you and me unless we make it so. What's that say about us? That we would put our lives down for them. What's that tell you about what we need?"

Bending the plastic chair, Lee rose.

"You stay in the bird tomorrow, Kansas. You selfish little shithead."

Lee tossed the flask into Bo's lap, then went inside to sleep for the few hours they had.

CHAPTER 25

NVA 325th Division
Outside Tchepone
Laos

In the underground bunker, only Loi stood.

A dozen men had gathered from around the camp, called together by Loi. Because there had been a battle today, the fighters seated on the dirt floor were long-faced, weary, and quiet. Some were dirty like Loi and Minh, they'd been in the thick of things. The rest had plainly known other battles; their manner was expedient. They understood that nothing could be done for the dead but to lay out a plan for tomorrow, to make sure they'd been well spent.

The men sat cross-legged. In their center, a colonel, the ranking officer in the bunker, smoked a French cigarette. His uniform fit very loosely, as if he'd been ill. The colonel could have chosen to take the lone chair beside the radio table; no one would have spoken against it, for he looked poorly. But he settled on the bare ground with the others, as was the custom for a self-criticism session.

Minh squatted along one of the earthen walls beneath a pinned-up map of the Lao valley and the meandering river. She did not belong in the bunker; she was neither military nor political branch, though she could claim that the equality of the revolution implied she did belong. She openly bore Loi's pistol in her hands; her presence was more a display of his authority than the men's tolerance.

Wisps of the colonel's smoke wreathed Loi's head. The shafts to vent the air sipped slowly and did more to drip the night's humidity into the bunker than to relieve it. Ten men on the floor dressed in the olive drab uniforms of the People's Army. Two others, cadres like Loi, wore black pajamas and sandals.

Alone on his feet, Loi did not talk at first. He portrayed shame convincingly, seemed to struggle for words. A pair of lanterns lit him, casting two shadows on a wall. The only electricity in the bunker ran the radio, and that was done by a hand crank.

Loi looked his audience in the eye. Minh admired his poise and style. His white shirt stood out, and to stand out in war was courageous. His initial words were what he'd said to Minh on the hillside. *I am to blame.* He admitted that he'd not properly instructed the antiaircraft crews of his regiment. By firing first, his guns became the reason the division was now endangered. From Khe Sanh, they'd retreated to this valley to regroup and resupply before heading south. Now they would have to leave before they were ready. Loi raised both hands to his breast, as if gathering fault to himself.

The colonel nodded; the lesser officers followed his lead. Loi had told Minh not to worry, this was how it would go. Even so, she fidgeted against the wall, making the map behind her crinkle. No one paid attention. She was not comfortable in the close quarters of the bunker, not so accustomed to a roof over her head.

Because the colonel didn't speak, none of his soldiers did. One of Loi's counterparts, a regimental cadre, piped up. He was an older man, gruff like a shopkeeper. Gray hair bristled his scalp. He said Loi's antiaircraft battery had fired first, yes, but his regiment had fired on the American planes, too. His guns had hit the second plane. He disguised his pride badly. The third regiment's cadre, a firebrand and perhaps the youngest man in the bunker, claimed that he, too, deserved fault for shooting down the third plane, the one that crashed. He said the word *fault* but he meant *credit*.

Loi did not stop there, as Minh would have, since his fellow political officers were trying to let him off the hook. Next he told them of shooting the old gunner on the hillside. Loi admitted to anger.

The colonel nodded at this as well. Minh could read nothing into the old man's nods.

Loi asked to be demoted in rank and responsibilities. He'd warned her he would do this. It was a dramatic offer and not to be taken seriously. The colonel waved the request away. Loi inclined his brow in humility.

She wanted him to leave, be finished with his performance. She wanted him to be eager to start their own evening. But Loi bent to his knees among the men, leaving the smoke to cling to the ceiling beams without him. He cast no glance back at Minh, ignoring her as he smoothed a palm through the space between him and his listeners. The colonel lowered his cigarette and did not raise it to his lips again while Loi spoke.

"We are all tired. I know. Of the rain and heat. The jungle. Hunger. Of the years being away from our homes."

Loi indicated the colonel.

"Of hiding."

The officer's narrow eyes closed at this, away to some memory, some anger, for when he opened his eyes, his teeth showed. "Yes," he said to Loi.

"The Americans know we're here. Soon they'll attack us in force. I suspect they'll bomb the entire valley. We can't do anything about that now. We'll have to leave. Every tunnel, every bunker, trench, and gun emplacement we've dug here, we'll have to dig somewhere else."

The soldiers and the two regimental cadres bobbed their heads.

"What's keeping them from attacking us in the morning? One thing. One American pilot on the ground. At dawn they'll try another rescue mission. They've seen our artillery, they'll come back in strength. If we turn our guns loose, they'll bomb us. If we hide, they'll take their pilot and go. Then they'll return with ten times the bombs to kill us. Either way, it'll be an impressive display. We know what the Americans can do. We saw it at Khe Sanh."

Every man's eye faded back to the long, violent clash for the American Marine base. Minh recalled the Chinaman absorbing her bullets there. In the span of Loi's pause, she counted the number of times she should be dead.

"Soon after they get their pilot back, or once he's dead or captured, this valley will become a volcano. But not until. I say we have two choices. We can spend tonight getting ready to leave, and in the morning let them have their pilot."

The colonel's brow rose and fell, somberly like the branches of a rainy tree. He dropped his smoldering cigarette in the dirt. Loi continued.

"Or, tonight we can resupply every gun on every hill. We can tell the division the Americans are coming with the sun. We know where and we know when. We can tell our fighters that before we leave this valley, before we go back into hiding, we'll let them fight."

Loi stood, to show he would be the first to go outside this bunker to do whatever these men decided. Minh rose also, with Loi's pistol. The soldiers and the two cadres seemed to shed their exhaustion under his voice.

"My regiment will locate the pilot. We won't capture him and we won't kill him. We'll bottle him up in the valley, under the artillery. The rest of you carry more ammunition and men into the hills. When the Americans come back at dawn, we won't be hiding. We'll fight. Then we'll slip away before they can destroy the valley."

The colonel stared down at the fading smolder of his cigarette. Thin smoke trellised from it. He picked the butt from the dirt, put it to his lips, and drew deeply. The cigarette came alive, glowing red like a tracer once more between his fingertips. He drained the last of the tobacco; this seemed an act of finality, closure on his time in the river valley. The sickly colonel cleaned his lips with a sweep of his tongue and nodded.

For two hours, Minh rode with Loi in the truck. He crisscrossed to the bounds of his regiment, issuing orders to his commanders and their companies. She did not stay in the truck but got out where Loi did. She stood behind him in the night, always carrying his pistol. The men who gathered around him gathered around her. No one said anything negative but dipped their heads at her alongside Loi. Some may have recognized her from the entertainments. On the eve of battle, the cadre had a woman; this seemed an acceptable notion. Like the division itself, she and Loi were done hiding. Most of the fighters were rural peasants; Minh was a peasant of the city. Listening to Loi, she felt the same as they did, freed and excited, on the cusp.

If the American pilot was seen, he was not to be captured. He was not to be shot at. Every man not posted to a gun crew or carrying ammunition must walk the jungle in his area. They must guard the river so the American did not float away, guard the hills so he did not climb out. The point was to spot the pilot, then make him know that his enemy was searching for him, to keep him in whatever hiding place he was found in. Once the pilot was located and trapped, the division could focus their firepower over his head. Then let the Americans come for him.

At Loi's final stop, the American's parachute was brought to him, a great swath of white material. Minh had never touched anything

American. She walked up from the dark to handle it. The cloth was smooth and sturdy, like the dress of a rich woman. Minh wanted it, to wear it or sleep in it, to have it because it was white and quality. For the first time since they'd left headquarters Loi took her hand. He pursed his mouth in sadness, seeing her want. He could not give her the parachute and could give her so little. In front of the men, he led her away.

In the truck, she wanted to keep his hand in hers, but Loi needed both arms to start and run the vehicle. The Trường Sơn Road bustled in the dark. Soldiers crossed it searching for the pilot. Other trucks swayed into the hills, carrying ammunition and extra gun crews. A convoy rolled up from the south, walkers and bicycles too. Maybe Nhu and Yen had arrived. Minh was eager to see her girls but would be afraid for them if they were still here in the morning when the American jets returned. She felt disloyal, not seeking them out, not warning them. But she would not leave Loi.

If she couldn't touch him while he was driving, she would test her freedom another way.

"What more can you do?"

"What do you mean?"

"I'm only asking what else you can do. You, personally."

"We have to find the pilot."

"You won't find him yourself." Minh put out her hand but stopped short of him, again to show her want. "I'm here."

He drove slowly behind others on the black Road, with nowhere left to hurry. The moon had not come out yet.

He said, "This feels fast."

She set the handgun down for the first time in hours, on the seat between them to show that it connected them but was not a barrier.

"And that is how we may die. Tomorrow. The next day. If that's so, then why not live fast?"

Loi may have been looking for this logic, this permission, because he honked the horn and drove around a clutch of bicycles lit by candle lanterns, with loads as big as oxen. Suddenly he drove well, boldly, making Minh giggle behind her hand. He laughed, too. Loi did the unthinkable and turned on his headlamps, drawing shouts from the walkers and more mirth from Minh.

The truck rumbled into a vast camp of tents. Scattered among the trees and rising up a slope, half a hundred cook fires blazed beneath canvas covers that masked them from the air. The jungle glowed with the flames as if sequined. Pots boiled on coals; wild meats braised and dripped into the ashes. The camp was busy with soldiers making food or bolting it before going to their nighttime tasks or into the hundred dull tents that dimpled the dark, or their bedrolls clustered around tree trunks for when it rained. To Minh, war had always seemed a wounded beast, something hurt and vicious. She'd witnessed enough war—it had lunged at her many times—for her to think of it as madness. But this hour, this tiny bit of the war, felt sane. The camp was busy and tranquil, it lay distracted enough for Minh and Loi to believe they might lie down beside it.

He stopped the truck. Nothing about his tent stood out from the others, another canvas rectangle around a center pole. Loi shut down the motor. He didn't climb out of the cab, unable yet to take the lead with her. Minh opened her door; Loi followed, looking anxious.

She couldn't tell him that she, too, was a virgin in this. In Hanoi she'd not taken a hand that did not have coins in it. He followed her; she was led by her heart, which had nothing to follow. He held the flap open to invite her in. The tent smelled nothing of him.

She asked, "Do you have a candle?"

"I'll get it."

Practiced in the darkness of his own space, Loi struck a match. A wick drank the flame and Minh's first look at his quarters was yellow and jittery. A cot and tick mattress, a small trunk, a table without papers, a chair with no arms, these were his private world. No food or books. Loi was privileged as a cadre, but he did not take advantage. The last bit of her that needed to fall tumbled. She stepped out of her thongs, leaving them side-by-side on the dirt floor as though the girl who wore them, who came into this tent, was still there and invisible, so Minh could return to her when she left. She pushed down her pajama trousers to her ankles, then tugged the black cotton tunic over her head, dropping it, too.

Minh glanced at the bare table; she'd never been naked in front of a man before without money out or somewhere nearby. She was aware of giving herself instead of selling. Her ribs showed from hunger and malaria, nipples as small and brown as her eyes. Calloused feet and strong legs from the Road. Her sun-dark arms and face. The space between her legs was wild and washed by the river. Minh didn't worry that her body would be rejected, because her body wasn't the gift.

She asked, "May I undress you?"

Without a clue how to answer, Loi raised his arms like a child. Minh lowered them, then unbuttoned his white shirt, wishing she could wash it. She pushed it off him and dropped it on her own clothes, to keep it out of the dirt. She lay a hand between the small mounds of his chest muscles to read his own hunger and dangers, the costs, in his broad breastbone. Though she was naked and he half so, she let this moment exist forever as the place they stopped before they crossed a border and did not come back. She undid the drawstring on his pants. Before they could fall, he stepped sideways out of his sandals.

He had a purposeful body, slender and hairless except, like her, between his legs. She sat on the cot and he stood; at her eye level he was uncircumcised. She put out her hand for his, he took it and strode closer, but he did not sit with her.

"Can I tell you who I am?"

"Yes."

"I studied with the French in Hanoi. To be a priest. My family is from Hội An in the south. They're tailors. My mother made my shirt."

Without his mother's shirt or a priest's gown, Loi did not know what was expected of him. He floundered, needing to find words first, his history, and an explanation. Minh pressed his hand and let him proceed. She was here for his need. Loi wasn't nervous. He was emptying himself, a young warrior, and this was how he put the war down. By talking and telling, by making himself raw and open. He meant to step from behind all cover, his clothes, his past.

But his wet eyes glistened, and that was enough for Minh. She pulled him down to the cot.

CHAPTER 26

Sol waggled his fingers in front of his face and couldn't see them. The murk of the jungle was rich and the silence was just as deep. Not a bug or bird rustled in the night. The bombs must have scattered or killed all the life near him. The only sounds were his, the crouched half steps, about ten per minute. The roof of trees sealed out any trace of a breeze; the humidity was a veil, soaked, draped over Sol's every move.

In an hour he'd traveled just fifty yards. He crept into the dark, inched over roots, squatted until his hips ached, sweating far more fluid than he could replace, sticking his face into unseen lattices of twigs and thorns. The tension wore at his muscles and gnawed on his nerves, made him hyper attentive and worn down.

Sol stopped. The low-slung fronds of a stunted palm brushed his hands. He felt the spanning leaves in front of him; they formed a sort of cave that might hide him on four sides.

He'd been moving just to move, to convince himself he was engaged in his rescue and to keep his spirits up. But his progress was so slow and draining. Where was he going? He needed a strategy, and he'd not formed one. He needed to rest and think.

Sol slid inside the shelter of the little palm. Motionless, he was instantly alarmed at how badly he was sucking air. Pulling in his knees, he wondered what they were saying about him back at Takhli. Dash 2's first combat mission, and he got shot down. He got a rescue pilot shot up and another one killed. Hopefully, around the Officers Club, Daniels was sticking up for him, describing the volume of antiaircraft fire they'd faced over this damn valley. Sol had never stood out before. In the Air Force, he'd always done his job, flown his nukes, drawn his pay. He'd never thought twice of his reputation, because he'd done nothing to earn or damage one. Until today. Maybe yesterday when he'd made that stupid decision to run the Army sergeant out of the USO show. But that was a regulation. He could have chosen to ignore it. Where were the regulations out here? The book ordered Sol to evade and survive; to everyone else, the book said *Go get Sol,* and no way did he want them to ignore it. Regulations cut both ways. Now he saw that.

He went through his options, figuring he had only three.

He could keep struggling forward. Even short distances at a time would add up. But Crown had said he was smack in the middle of a division. That meant thousands of NVA and Viet Cong in every direction, guns and crews on every hill.

What if he made it back to the river? He might float out of the valley, away from the troops. But they were surely keeping an eye on the water, an easy thing to patrol with flashlights in the dark. Besides, at the rate he was going, he stood no chance of reaching the riverbank before sunrise, even if he could find it.

Or he could stand pat. Locate a good hole, crawl in deep, and wait for rescue. But the debacle of the day made it plain that if he stayed in the middle of the valley, his chances of being picked up without more planes getting chewed to pieces were slim and none.

Sol fumbled for his drinking water, affording himself a few sips. He took from his vest a roll of Charms candy, holding ten pieces. He chewed one, feeling pitiful and disillusioned that he'd not been able to talk himself out of blundering onward into the dark. With a quiet sigh, he admitted the need to keep going.

Shielding the bulb of his pencil light, Sol checked his watch. A little after 2100 hours. He'd found a good spot under this short palm tree; best to wait until midnight to move out. The NVA should be asleep, and his lousy odds might become slightly less awful.

A rifle shot made him jump, stirring the fronds touching his head. Sol crammed the candy and small light back into his vest, then rolled to his knees. He swallowed a bilious taste; he'd almost puked at the suddenness of his fright. He took a deep breath, held it, and eased out his face.

Through the undergrowth, two hundred feet away, four flashlights like fireflies swung back and forth. The beams were articulate, bright tunnels in the black. Sol had heard nothing, the NVA moved through the bush natively. This scared him even more, to realize just how foreign he was here, an American pilot in the jungle, and they were not.

The lights came his way in a line, sweeping left, right, forward, back. Every few moments one VC would brighten another and a small black-pajama-clad, bareheaded man with a rifle would be illuminated, then fade behind his own flashlight. At one end of the line, a VC fired his rifle again into the air of the teeming forest.

"Captain."

The English word chilled Sol worse than the shots.

"Captain. Hey, Captain."

The searching beams marched straight at him. Sol's brain raced, too fast to remember anything he'd been taught at JEST school. He'd not been in this war long enough to have spoken with any other pilots who'd been shot down and rescued. He had no idea what to do and had to figure it out, fast.

He wished he'd thought of this scenario in advance, his hands might shake a little less. He recoiled back inside the fronds dripping over him. One flashlight shined on a suddenly green spot five feet away.

Again the rifle fired, trying to make him bolt into the open.

With no time or any other idea, Sol tugged the .38 from under his armpit; he lay on his belly. There, through the shrubs, the four flashlights panned for him. Behind them on higher ground, appearing and vanishing among the trees, shined four more.

"GI Joe, you hungry?"

The lights closed in, relentlessly straight at him. What should he do? Before he'd considered it fully, he centered the barrel of his .38 on one of the flashlight bearers. Sol's arms lay in the sodden earth; this kept the gun from quaking too much, his aim was good. If they walked too close, if a beam shined right in his face, he'd shoot the flashlight VC, knock him down, then haul ass the other direction.

Sol glanced over his shoulder in the direction he planned to sprint. A situation that he figured couldn't get worse did; he gawped at more lights, not flashlights but candles, dozens of tiny flames drifting along inside lanterns. A truck threaded slowly among them, headlamps masked downward. In the darkness, beyond his notice, during that grueling hour while he'd been casting his senses no farther than inches, Sol had skulked within a hundred yards of the Ho Chi Minh Trail.

He couldn't run that way.

His index finger tightened over the trigger. The lights advanced. Two beams rose into the trees to check if he might be clinging up there. The third beam swept wide, toward the other flashlights on the far hillside. The last light coursed over the ground, right at the VC's shuffling sandals. The little man pressed forward enough for Sol to see his brown toes. Like a lighthouse, this beam rotated a full circle, away from Sol, around, then toward him, past and across him. Then back. Then stopped.

"Captain? Where are you?"

The macabre query was crooned in a measured voice, one that seemed to know where its audience lay. It was the most disturbing thing Sol had ever heard.

Sol was going to shoot him. Then run straight at him, jump over the body, firing left and right, and go full speed through the woods. Into a tree, a ditch, a hole, another bunch of VC.

Here it was. That first moment when he earned his own rescue. If he was going to expect more A-1s, more jets, Jollys, and PJs to fly into a boatload of danger in this asshole of a valley, he was going to have to man up to some serious peril himself.

The flashlight had quit weaving; its bearer stood rock still. The round beam feathered at the edges, aimed straight at Sol's green nook from fifteen yards away. Sol lowered his eyes so they wouldn't sparkle, but he kept the pistol trained into the beacon. The rifle fired again in the air; Sol tensed against the ground, stirring the leaves. Did they hear him?

This moment was millennia old: enemies a stone's throw apart. Sol saw him; did he see Sol? What to do? Make the first move or wait for the VC's move? Clamp down his own terror, stay cool, choose wrong and die, or throw up his hands in surrender? There'd been no training specific for this confrontation; for pilots, the clashes from the cockpit were not so ancient and near. Was that why Daniels had tried to summon the MiGs, some warriors' ages-old desire for proximity, to close the fight? If Sol lived through this, he knew in his bones that right now were seconds he'd replay forever, these chilling moments not when he stared at his enemy but lowered his eyes not to be seen.

His tongue was sandpaper on his lips; he couldn't hold his breath. Sol listened for the swish of leaves under a sandaled foot, a snapped twig, any hint that the VC holding his light, so level at Sol's little palm tree, might be stepping one inch closer.

"Captain?"

The call retained its singsong quality. An appeal. But a little less sure.

"Where are you?"

Sol bit his lip, succeeding in stilling his lungs to let him hear only the Viet Cong right in front of him.

A string of indecipherable words was exchanged between the four searchers. The beam didn't waver off Sol's hiding place. Footsteps in the leaves dared him to glance up.

Three of the four VC had turned away. The one, the skeptic, the clairvoyant perhaps, lingered his light over the umbrella of Sol's fronds. Then the white shaft swung up into the trees directly above him. Finding nothing, the English-speaking fighter joined the others to move on into the jungle. He called ahead of himself, "Captain."

Sol sagged into the moist ground, sensing the damp in his hips, hoping he hadn't pissed himself. The tide of adrenaline ebbed and left him headachy. One more rifle report rocked the humidity. The flashlights drifted out of view; the night closed around Sol except for the spectral candles on the Trail.

Sitting up, he holstered the .38 then mopped his brow. He wished he could dig this young palm up, put it in a pot, plant it in his yard back home, and tell folks how it had saved his life. He didn't want to leave it; he felt safe here and began to rethink his plan to move from this spot.

Over the next two hours, another three teams of searchers came panning his way out of the south with flashlights and rifle shots. They stayed at enough distance that Sol didn't draw his revolver. At one point, a huge lightning bug, ten times the size of the ones in Maryland, blinked almost on top of him, so brightly, Sol nearly bounded to his feet in surprise, shocked that some VC had gotten so close. He braced, hand on the pistol grip, then laughed a little manically at himself when the insect lumbered past, oblivious and massive. Another surge of adrenaline withdrew. Sol sucked on a second Charm candy, feeling wrung out.

Approaching midnight, the gleams on the Trail slowed, then snuffed as the traffic passed on. Sol climbed to his feet, standing at his full height for the first time in hours. He stretched out the kinks and turned a circle to get his bearings. The time had come to decide if he should move, and if he did, which way to go.

So far, he'd headed north, following the terrain of the river valley, tracing the Ho Chi Minh Trail. Deep in the forest, from the direction he'd come, where his plane had fallen and Sandy had crashed, another round of tiny lights shined, floaters against the gargantuan darkness. They flashed, then disappeared and blinked again. Sol waited to make sure he wasn't being fooled a second time by more bird-size lightning bugs. These were flashlights in lines, fifty VC sweeping the ground and branches, more scary calls for Captain.

A quarter mile off, west through the trees and across the Trail, an eerie wine-colored luminance lit the jungle, a glimmer he'd missed while the road had been busy. Sol didn't recall any bombs landing that direction. What was making this glow? He stepped away from his hiding spot, careful but confident that he was unseen, for a better look. The glow was fire—not a single one but many dozens. Cook fires.

Sol sank to a crouch, marveling. How the hell could this be a Lost Division when the VC seemed to care so little about staying lost? How did Seventh Air Force manage to miss this, a ten-acre-wide barbecue at night? The jungle here was thick, okay. But come on. A spark, a gleam, some sliver of light or smoke or movement had to be spotted from the air at some point if someone was even halfway looking for them. Sol had been vectored into this Lao valley, which, unbeknownst to *anyone*, was festooned with guns and jammed with Viet Cong. All so he could take out a damn ferry.

He didn't bother checking if midnight had arrived. The great swath of cook fires didn't look like they were going to fade anytime soon. Besides, he had a good ration of indignation going. Might as well ride that as fuel.

Before moving, he radioed Spooky that he was still in the game and intending to gain some distance from his current location. He'd search for a good pickup spot for the morning rescue, maybe some high ground. Spooky said he'd pass this on, and "hang in there, Dash 2."

Sol patted a frond of his little palm tree before turning from it.

He took his first dark step north toward the Trail and the distant, glinting camp. The ground, littered with sticks and leaves, crunched under his foot. Sol waited, then took another stride, walking upright. With no lights between him and the cook fires, and the fifty VC hunting him still a long way back in the jungle, he hurried his strides, feeling bold and under way again. Sol moved like this for fifty yards, arms out, feeling like a blindfolded man for trees and branches, ready to dive to the ground at any noise other than his own.

He took a knee at the edge of the dirt road, panting in a heat that was unconscionable for this time of night. Not far up the Trail, a gaggle of loaded-up bicycles were walking his way, stacked with supplies, pushed by men and women in coolie hats and long black pajamas. Many of the bikes were lit by candles in lanterns dangling off the handlebars. Two hundred yards behind, the wave of flashlights swept the jungle, headed his way. Sol shrugged, with no choice. Like the hunted rabbit he was, he listened carefully, then dashed across the road and dove into the bushes.

He waited facedown in the soft earth until all the bicycle pushers had passed. When he came up off his chest, sure that no one had seen him, Sol stood again on straightened legs. The camp lay slightly closer, but was still a long, hazardous hike away. The campfires were scattered like sparks on the ground, too far off to shed any light on his path. As he walked straight at the glows, some of the trees and obstacles in his path blotted out one tiny red light or another; this gave him silhouettes to guide him. The straighter Sol made for the camp, the larger the lights would grow, and the faster he might wend his way forward.

He kept his stance erect and his gait slow, with only short pauses between strides. If he were seen by a sentry in the night, an upright posture instead of a furtive crouch might look less suspicious. The more Sol walked, because every step felt defiant, the better his morale firmed up.

He pushed through small trees and low branches, making swishes and crackles as he surged north. He kicked aside ferns from his knees down, keeping the camp in sight as a bearing. The flickering fire pits multiplied and spread out even more than he'd guessed. Seventh Air Force was going to have a field day pulverizing this valley; the carpet bombing was going to be a major score against a concentrated VC location, a division they'd bloodied but let slip away at Khe Sanh. Sol imagined the valley and hills being blasted and fried, all this old growth burned to black chips, the oil-thick darkness opened to the stars and for rain to fall on bare, cremated ground. The Lao forest was impressive and Sol held no grudge against it; he felt bad for his little palm. But the inevitable result of his being shot down wasn't his fault, and it wasn't under his control. Seventh Air Force was going to do what it had to. This was war, and war was misfortune, even for trees.

Sol inched his way toward the glowing sprawl, making dark and wary progress until he came within range of the camp's gossamer light and sounds. The snapping and popping of fires resembled his own foot-steps. This let him increase his pace a bit; he stopped only every third step to listen for voices or other footfalls. Once he came within seventy yards of the nearest fire, holding the camp on his right, Sol halted.

He kneeled in the bushes to take a sip of water. He'd already put a goodly distance between him and his parachute; that might be enough for the VC to lose his trail. Maybe he ought to pivot away from the camp, strike out again into the murky jungle. He'd find his way up a hill, then climb a ridge and get out of the arena of the valley floor before dawn. That would mean more torturous creeping through pitch-black wilderness, enduring more sweaty and nerve-racking single steps over uncertain terrain, up a slope that might turn treacherous even faster than level ground. Artillery dotted the hillsides; Sol had no idea where the big guns were. The last place he wanted to be at sunrise when the gun suppression started was near an enemy battery.

Or he could press on around the camp's perimeter; he was making good time. The VC didn't seem to be trolling for him here, in the flimsy firelight under their thousand noses. If he was lucky, he might make it all the way around the camp by morning, covering at least another half mile.

Hooding his penlight, Sol checked the time: 0045. The odors of hot coals and meat wafted past, even some chatty conversations, though he saw no one through the trees. Another smell, rotten like waste, made Sol duck into the thigh-high ferns. That was all he needed, to wander into some VC taking a crap out here away from the camp. But if he stayed veiled in the trees, if he haunted only the thin rim of the fires' glow, he stood a chance. A better chance than stumbling up a hillside without a star or a spark to guide him.

Sol sucked on another Charms candy to answer the saliva rising in his mouth from the cook fires. He cast his ears forward and narrowed his eyes. Though he couldn't see the ground, he could make out the broader contours of the jungle, letting him ease around trees and avoid wandering into thorns. The world was just dark enough. Sol rose and strode into it, keeping the camp to his right. He followed one stride with another, then paused to make sure the night stayed closed. The stink of filth drifted past.

Detecting no reason not to continue, Sol stepped again, then again, then into nothing. The ferns disappeared.

He tumbled after his unplanted foot. Unbalanced in open air, suddenly panicked, he threw his arms wide in a chance he might grab hold of something. He clamped his teeth against shouting, even as he fell. Prone in midair, facedown into blackness, Sol plunged.

Eyes wide in shock, he saw no bottom. On instinct, he drew in his arms and legs, falling sideways in a ball, blind, terrified, and senseless.

He landed not as hard as he'd feared. His left shoulder and hip struck first, then the side of his head splashed. His left eye and cheek buried into a cool, sticky mass. Sol had only a moment to be amazed he was alive before a terrific pain burst inside his left shoulder. Like a blacksmith's blow, the ache rang through his body. He tried to sit up but couldn't push off the ground. Sol clamped his teeth hard to swallow a scream.

Though he was certain he'd not shouted, he heard one anyway. A squeal, a raging manic caterwaul, raced around him.

A pig. Sol had fallen into a pit dug for a pig. He wasn't lying in mud.

He struggled upright, cradling his left arm so the pain wouldn't black him out. The pig ran in circles, hysterical; Sol was in too much agony to shush it. The animal's screech was sure to draw someone to this hole if he didn't shut it up or climb out fast. Sol thought about shooting the pig but that was the pain and terror thinking.

He shook his head to clear it; a clump of mud flew off. The pain in his shoulder was excruciating but not his worst problem. The pig, an inconsolable, bloodcurdling, and unseen little siren, ran loops around him with a Viet Cong division in earshot.

The beast's shrieks gave Sol a sense of the dimensions of the pit; it wasn't vast, just a pen. He staggered to his feet, not hearing himself groan as the pig galloped past. Its haunches brushed him, nearly bowling him over. Sol wasn't sure he could drag himself to his feet twice.

With his good hand, he reached to find the wall. The pain in his left arm folded his knees but the dirt wall was close; he caught himself. Sol leaned against it while he probed his shoulder through his flight suit, feeling the knobs of bones out of socket below his clavicle. He panted, fighting off nausea and the urge to faint.

The riled-up pig kept circling. Sol kicked at it weakly, missing when it flew by. He had to get out of this hole. Wincing, he raised his right arm to measure the height of the wall; it stopped just above his head, six feet. Sol's left shoulder threatened to unhinge him from his senses with every move, but he had to climb out. The other choice was to be captured by the VC after collapsing in pig manure.

He tucked the wounded arm inside his vest to stabilize his shoulder as much as he could. Measuring the wall without seeing it, Sol waited for the shrieking pig's circuit to take him to the other side of the pit, then strode into a one-armed jump. He misjudged the leap and slammed his face and chest against the dirt, knocking himself backward. The pain in his shoulder spiked, crossing his eyes. The pig scampered between him and the wall. Sol spit into the stinking sludge, sick and scared that he might end here.

He stepped back again, the last escape effort he believed he could endure. Drawing deep breaths, steeling himself, Sol planted both boots in the muck. He flung his right hand as high as it could go and jumped, snarling between clamped teeth. His right arm cleared the wall up to the armpit, then he slammed down his hand like a grappling hook. Clutching for purchase on the jungle floor, Sol dug in his nails. He grabbed hold barely enough to bring his boots into play against the pit wall. He scrambled to drive himself up and out, pulling with his right arm while his left felt like it was being torn out of him. Tears welled in his eyes as he shut his mouth against the pain. His boots scrabbled at the wall, his right hand held. Sol pulled with everything he had.

It wasn't enough. With only one hand, he lacked the strength to haul himself up past his armpit, out of the hole. His fingers clawed deeper into the loam, but the soil wouldn't hold. He began to slide backward. The pig squealed its loudest, frantic.

Sol grunted, the loudest noise he'd made since being shot down. He thought nothing of being heard and everything of hanging on, scrambling out of this fetid pit, staying conscious against the rising dark tide in his vision. The ground crumbled through his clutching fingers; he slid backward.

The animal wanted out, too, for it threw itself at the wall, nipping and nosing at Sol's boot heels, hoping he, too, might climb out. Without thinking, Sol landed one of his boots on the pig's broad bawling face; he stepped on it. With the foot on his head, the strong and desperate pig lurched upward. Sol gained the inches he needed to re-sink the anchor of his hand into the jungle floor, to pull with his last reserves and edge his chest above the hole, then his belly and legs.

Out of the pit, he rolled to his back, seeing spots. Nerves and pain made him woozy; he came close to passing out. The pig continued to squall. If Sol was going to lose consciousness, he'd best do it in the bushes. He forced himself to his knees and scuttled away on them, blind in the darkness, white floaters popping in his vision. He wriggled under cover of the ferns and pushed deeper into the foliage until he could crawl no longer. Sol fell over, face up, gasping. Gingerly he tugged his bad arm out of the vest to let it lie flat beside him, trying for some relief.

Gradually, the pig calmed while Sol heaved for breath and battled to stay conscious. No one came from the camp. He lay moaning until he could think straight and stop himself.

Sol needed to take stock of how badly he was hurt. He was done moving for a while, even with Seventh Air Force's deadline bearing down on him.

CHAPTER 27

July 17
Nakhon Phanom Royal Thai Air Force Base
40th Air Rescue and Recovery Service alert shack
Thailand

In the early morning, Bo awoke on the porch to cigarette smoke and the small weight of Lee's flask being lifted from his lap.

Lee rattled the silver container. He sucked on his cigarette, heating the tip tracer red.

"You don't like my Scotch?"

Bo rubbed his eyes. "I don't drink before missions."

"All right." Lee pocketed the flask. "After. Come on."

"What time is it?"

"0300. We got a briefing in the TUOC."

Bo jumped from the plastic chair to glance into the empty alert shack. "Everyone else already gone?"

"We're the last."

"Oh, no."

Major Crebbs, the flight engineer, the commander, and crew of Jolly 23, all had filed past Bo passed out in a chair with a flask in his lap. Like a dragon, Lee chuckled with smoke puffing out of his nose as he walked away.

The tactical unit operations center didn't have enough seats to accommodate the size of that day's rescue team. Bo and Lee leaned on a wall opposite a blackboard, crammed shoulder to shoulder between two Sandy pilots. The briefing room was a windowless plywood box with one hardworking air conditioner, a dozen folding chairs, and a coffeemaker on a card table. The air was edgy with the smells of twenty pilots and airmen, their sweat, caffeine, and nicotine. No one in the chairs or against the walls yawned or betrayed the early hour while a redheaded Air Force lieutenant colonel delivered the briefing.

The first pilot the briefing officer addressed was the forward air controller, Nail 34, seated down front. The FAC was a good-looking captain, a few years older than Bo, lanky and linen-skinned with matted dark hair.

Nail's orders were to make contact at sunup with Dash 2 on the ground, then notify Crown. After that, once Nail determined the weather was clear, the rest of the rescue force would scramble.

Nail looked up from scribbling his notes. "How big a force?"

"Twenty-four jets with every kind of ordnance we got. You want it—napalm, cluster bombs, rockets, seven-hundred-fifty-pounders—just say where. You'll get it."

Nail raised his eyebrows and kept scribbling.

Most of the fliers in the room had been over that valley yesterday. Intelligence had confirmed that the river valley and hills around Dash 2 held numerous enemy troops, estimated at two thousand. At least a dozen antiaircraft sites had already been spotted; there were likely more. Lee elbowed Bo to whisper, "You fucking think?"

The briefing wrapped up with a repeat of Seventh Air Force's order to get the downed Thud pilot off the ground today. Period. The briefer finished by rapping a knuckle repeatedly against a topo map of the river valley.

"Gentlemen. Be clear. You are going to attack that valley until every antiaircraft gun is silenced. When that's done, and only when that's done, you go get Dash 2. Dismissed."

CHAPTER 28

Outside Tchepone
Laos

Minh opened her eyes into darkness. The lantern had been blown out hours ago. She drew a breath spicy with the smells of two people, both sharing the narrow cot inside the warm canvas walls.

She was surprised to find Loi still beside her. When she'd drifted off, Minh had the notion that she'd awake alone, that he would have been drawn away into the night by some detail or problem of the coming battle. But he lay breathing lightly with his back to her, naked and touching her with his heels.

In Hanoi, Minh had been with more than a dozen men; she'd given herself to none and had awakened next to none. She didn't find this awakening beside Loi pleasant; the cot felt crowded and the tent too hot. She imagined a bigger bed, open windows, and a basin of water to wash herself.

He'd snuffed the lantern too soon in their entanglement. She'd wanted to leave it burning, to help guide him. In the dark, they became an unorchestrated grapple. The end came and Loi had no soothing words for her. He fell asleep and the tent grew stuffier, but he didn't leave and he didn't ask Minh to go.

Loi stirred. Was he a light sleeper? Or had he been waiting for her to rouse first? That would be sweet and she preferred to think this.

She searched for his hand. He moved it where she could take it.

"Hello," he said.

"Hello."

"What will you do today?"

She would shop and make him a fine meal, though she was an inexperienced cook. She would tend the children and the house. The question was so easy to float away on, far away from the tent and cot and the war to a bigger bed and a future of open windows.

"I'll stay with you."

"All right."

"Do you know where the American pilot is?"

"He was seen."

"Where?"

"Half kilometer south of here. He's moved closer to the camp."

"Close to here?"

"Yes."

"How do you know?"

"Where the American planes fly. They go over his head. We don't know exactly where he is. But no matter. He's where I want him."

"Why?"

"Many of the guns are focused over our heads. He's right under them." Loi shifted onto his back to face the dark pinnacle of the tent. She did not know if his eyes were open. "I want you to know. It's going to be dangerous."

"In this valley, where is it not going to be?" Minh squeezed his hand. She rolled to her side to layer herself against him; she flattened a hand across his ribs and quiet heart.

When he finally spoke, his voice was a monotone. "I want to tell you about Khe Sanh."

He was saying to her, *If you want to know me, know my nightmares, too.*

"All right."

"Two thousand were killed there. Fifteen thousand wounded. In six months the Americans dropped a hundred thousand tons of bombs."

His flesh was warm, like the ground must have been at Khe Sanh.

"We were a ruse. A fake. Hanoi didn't want us to take Khe Sanh. We fought for six months so the Americans would bring forces north against us, away from Tet in the south."

Minh knew only her tiny part of the war. All she could do for Loi was listen, say nothing, imagine his misery, and let his heart beat under her touch.

"We were sent there to die as slowly as we could."

He sat up. Minh's hand fell away.

Loi was ready to leave the bed. To stop him she wrapped him in her arms and legs, and he allowed it.

"No," she said against the battle calling him.

He lay in the circlet of her arms, not as long as she wanted. When he rose from the cot, Minh stood with him. They dressed in the dark. By feel alone, she buttoned his white shirt.

CHAPTER 29

Sol hadn't meant to fall asleep. While he lay trying to get accustomed to the pain in his shoulder, staying motionless so it wouldn't jab him, he lost his keenness and drifted off.

His eyelids shot open as if to clanging noises, though nothing had startled him. He became instantly aware of his circumstances and half-expected to find himself staring into the bore of an AK-47. When no one stood straddling him in the dawn, Sol exhaled long and hard. When he inhaled, he smelled the pig and the pit drying on him.

The first tints of daylight gave shape to the trees and the lake of low-lying ferns he'd dozed under. Before sitting up, Sol listened. Far-off birdsong heralded the morning. The chill of an early mist laced the ground. He gathered his left arm across his waist, prepared himself for the stab from it, and sat up.

He sucked his teeth; the hurt had barely lessened in the night. The VC camp was dim, all their fires had cooled into a brooding hush. The trees were more spaced out here than where he'd landed, giving him a restricted view in all directions. Sol pivoted to peer behind him, toward the pig pit.

His breath froze in his chest. Two shapes loomed two hundred feet past the hole. A pair of matching conical structures, like teepees, stood on guard, thirty feet between them. Each was eight feet tall.

Both pointed shelters had been made from nylon parachutes, probably from downed American pilots. They stood in a patch of open grass with a view of the sky to the east, above the valley floor. If Sol hadn't stumbled into the pit, he might have walked right into one of these. What were they?

In the mounting light, he barely made out the muzzles, four of them protruding from the peak of each teepee. The tents were camouflage for antiaircraft guns, a pair of multibarreled ZPUs.

Each artillery piece would have a crew of four or five. If they were bunked inside, they'd rouse soon. If they spent the night in the camp, they'd walk to their gun stations after breakfast, right past him. Either way, Sol was going to have company.

He had to decide what to do: Stay or move again? He felt secure under the ferns and the morning bed of fog, though the haze would burn off within the hour. His dilemma was that he didn't want to be this close to twin zeeps once the rescue started. This area was going to get savaged.

His best plan, and the toughest, was to start hiking before the camp ramped up. Sol had no idea how well he might travel with his bum shoulder. He sipped some water, lamented his hunger, then drew his legs under him to lift his head out of the mist. He paused with the early emerald beauty of the place, picking his direction. Sol disliked the notion of tramping up a rocky, uneven slope with a separated shoulder. The best way to put distance between him and the VC base camp was to keep forging north, stay on the valley floor. He tucked his left wrist inside the vest. He'd find a way to make a sling later.

Before Sol could put both soles to the damp ground, the drone of distant propellers filtered through the canopy. That would be Nail reporting to work. Sol tugged the radio from his vest; he clicked the talk button twice to tell the FAC that sunrise had found him still alive. He tucked the radio to his ear to hear the wonder of two answering clicks. The big show was about to start. Sol had to get moving.

He stood, rising to a half crouch.

Seventy yards on the other side of the pig pit, a shirtless Viet Cong in black pajama bottoms lifted the flap of the teepee. Sol dove for the ground. He grunted at the wrench in his shoulder; he lay flat, biting his lower lip, petrified that he'd been seen or heard.

Prostrate below the ferns, Sol held his breath to catch the sounds of steps. The VC was walking in his direction. The shirtless fighter stopped not ten paces from where Sol lay strangling his panic. He couldn't draw the pistol lying flat on his chest, he'd rustle the fronds if he twitched. Sol listened to a trickle and a man's morning moan. Two more voices emerged from the teepees. They came just as close to Sol to pee.

As they took their leaks, a bugle blew.

The oddly American sound issued from the camp, the wake-up call of reveille. Sol dug his chin into the soft ground as activity heightened all around him. The pissers walked off to the tinny rattle of pots and pans, the smells of resurgent cook fires, sizzling fish and hot oil, and laughter and shouted orders. The clarity of the noises told Sol he'd come closer to the camp than he'd known last night.

Beside the teepees, a delicate bell tinkled. The sound had a magical quality among the trees and fog. Sol eased his good right elbow under him, daring to raise his head to see what was happening.

The crews of the two artillery pieces had emerged from their nylon shelters, ten men total. They sat on their folded legs with fog blanketing their laps. The bare-chested VC presided at their front; he tapped a stick against a metal bowl to make a peaceful tolling ring. The men droned in unison, a deep, ancient tone. The same rose from the camp, more light bells and the throaty hum of hundreds of soldiers.

Sol closed his eyes, trying to piggyback somehow on the prayers of the Viet Cong. It didn't work, and he opened his eyes to the jungle.

These were his enemies. He would never shake the sight of Sandy tumbling in flames into the valley, or the rifles firing at him as he parachuted down. The blazing tracer that took off his wing, the misery in his shoulder right now, the humiliating chatter of his teeth. This was war. So what if it was war with men who prayed?

The bells stopped, the chanting with it. The day lurched on. A truck rumbled into the camp, then two more. Hatless men in black pajamas and regular soldiers in khakis and round helmets walked off in droves, all armed, many close to where Sol lay hiding. On his back, sore and hissing at every surge from his shoulder, Sol had power over these hundreds of men. As soon as they killed him, captured him, or he got away, they were good as dead. Seventh Air Force was the giant grenade that was going to go off in this valley. Sol might be hiding and scared shitless, but he was the grenade's pin. His freedom, his life, would determine how long the Lost Division lived. He wished they knew it, if only to see some of his own fear on their faces.

A hundred and fifty feet overhead, a light rain tattooed on the treetops. The dampness returned to the jungle floor and more vapor congealed out of the air to tuft around the trunks, thickening Sol's cover. He was thankful on the one hand, but the sound of Nail's propellers came no closer. The dawn valley was without the bass thrum of a Sandy or the thunder of a jet. The rescue hadn't started and might not while the weather was socked in. Sol couldn't even consider making a move without the distraction of the battle. He was stuck in place until it started, next to the teepees and the pig pit.

Under the dripping rain, it was time to call Nail for the morning's news, good or bad.

Sol keyed the transmit button twice. When he got the answering clicks, he whispered, "Nail, this is Dash 2. Do you copy?"

"Copy, Dash 2. Good morning. Long night?"

"You don't want to know."

"Hang in. We'll have you out of there in a few minutes. What's your condition?"

"Injured. Separated shoulder. Hurts."

"Copy. We'll make sure a PJ comes down to assist on the pickup. What's your position?"

"I moved. Half a kilometer north from where I was last night."

"Copy. What's your situation?"

"I've got a triple A site seventy-five yards east from me. And a major VC camp east at two hundred yards."

"Dash, you understand you're supposed to move away from the enemy."

"Don't start."

"Copy. Here's the deal. There's a big push to get you off the ground today. Weather's moved in, scattered rain, five-hundred-foot ceiling. We'll wait for it to clear. Once it does, find a hole and get in it. We've got a lot of firepower lined up for gun suppression."

"Roger."

"Let me know if the bombs get too close. You willing to pop me a smoke today, Dash?"

"You get close enough. Yes."

"Deal. I'm going to fly north up the valley. When I get near, click twice."

"Roger."

"You're doing great. See you in a few."

"Out."

Sol could have done without the optimism. He didn't need cheerleading, he needed a rescue chopper. The sound of Nail's engines over the river valley did more for him than anything the FAC had said. The O-2 was a pretty-sounding plane, its two rotors making a classic high-pitched thrum. Nail drew no fire yet from the valley's many guns. The VC either didn't see the O-2 as a threat, or they were inviting him in. Either way, the morning stayed quiet, and the camp continued to clatter with breakfast. Sol imagined being in the cockpit with Nail, what the spectacle of the Lao jungle looked like from a slow and low top-wing Skymaster sliding across wet treetops, green slopes on every side, mist dressing the earth. From the altitude and speed of his Thud, Sol never saw more than a rounded horizon of green and blue, or stars and tiny lights, a place to bomb.

He'd been in Vietnam less than a week, but the only real cheerfulness he'd encountered belonged to Nail flying over enemy positions. Among the jet pilots in the Officers Club, Sol had met none of the FAC's geniality or high spirits, only braggarts, gung ho, and crazy sons of bitches like Daniels. Nail wasn't out here this morning risking his neck over Laos to kill anyone, just to save a downed American pilot. Sol considered again the Army sergeant he'd run out of the USO show. A rescue chopper pilot. So good a kid that two bird colonels came back with him threatening to blow the roof off the mess hall if Sol didn't put titties back in the boy's lap.

Sol readied to click his talk button as the whine of Nail's engine drew nearer. He wondered if he might rather fly an O-2.

CHAPTER 30

The sun had been up for two hours, and Bo with it, circling a mountaintop called the Rooster Tail. At seven thousand feet, basking and bright above the morning's overcast, Jolly 22 rendezvoused with a C-130 tanker to fill up.

From the cockpit, Major Crebbs kept his crew informed. The package, Dash 2, had checked in; he'd survived the night. He was in a new location half a klick north of yesterday's spot. Dash 2 had gotten injured somehow and would need help on the ground to be evacuated. Crebbs asked who PJ 1 was today. Lee jumped on that. As soon as the weather broke, Nail would okay the fast movers to start their gun-suppression runs. Until then, the three Jollys and their half-dozen Sandys would orbit the Rooster Tail.

Lee napped against the fuselage, hands twined in his lap as if in thought. The FE opened a paperback. Bo stood in the door to take the warm wind on his face. He enjoyed the aerial ballet of the refueling, the chopper pilots' expertise in playing darts with the fuel drogue. Far below, a gray cap of clouds rested on the river valley, and daylight crawled across steamy Laos.

At 0820 the rain stopped, and at 0850 the blanket of fog began to tatter. Stripes of green emerged, along with the knolls and rocky spires. The haze burned off the woody slopes of the Rooster Tail. Five thousand feet over Bo's head, a flight of two F-4s rocketed into formation. Four more F-4s flashed in from the south to churn high over the valley. A minute later, four Thud 105s came in hot, trailing their own mist when they banked onto the scene, for a total of ten jets waiting for the word to roll in.

The chopper's intercom stayed silent. The flight engineer paid no attention to anything outside his book. Lee slept, so only Bo watched the force gathering high above the river. This rescue mission, his second, was going to be big. The drama was rising, and Bo would have a role in it. He wanted to dive in just like the Sandys and the jets were going to. Then he wanted to have done it, his heroism behind him, so he could be indifferent like Lee.

The first Thud rolled over at twelve thousand feet to power dive into the valley. No ground fire rose to confront it. The day's first bombs struck against a slope, dazzling. The second Thud swung into position, swooped down, and was met by tracers so thick they looked like strung-up Christmas lights. The Thud pulled up short, let its bombs go high, and banked away sharply.

These first bombing runs signaled the A-1 Sandys to enter the fight. Four of them banked away with a racket that shook Bo's chest, showing their bomb-laden bellies. Two stayed behind to guard the Jollys. Ten miles away, deep in the hips and swales of the valley, Nail stayed busy marking more VC gun sites so the fast movers could pummel them. Skirting the treetops, the Sandys would hunt down Dash 2. Once they had a fix on his location, the word would go out for the low bird, Jolly 22.

The third Thud, then the fourth, plunged into the valley. They keyed on the smoke from Nail's rockets and the fires set by the already dropped bombs. The antiaircraft fire they stirred up was withering, more dense and brilliant than yesterday. The Thuds released their bombs high, keeping their distance from the artillery. When their first passes were completed, all four Thuds raced around the southern end of the valley before rocketing in for a second run. They dropped another round of ordnance, blitzing a hillside south of the river, then bugged out for home. The next sortie belonged to a flight of Fox 4s.

For the next hour, the pounding on the valley went uninterrupted. Lee snoozed through it all, and the FE stayed engrossed in his paperback. The Sandys prowled the valley floor, blowing up trails and trees, going one-on-one with the VC in the jungle. All four Sandys drew barrages of smaller-caliber fire, white and gold strings from the zeeps, while the jets got sprayed with bigger stuff, the red fireballs. Hillsides and ledges on both sides of the river erupted in flames and pillars of smoke, but Crebbs did not announce "We're going in."

The guns of the valley wouldn't be silenced. There seemed a bottomless supply of ammo and desire to battle. The sun climbed to its peak and the morning mist was forgotten.

Bo and the three choppers kept their distance.

CHAPTER 31

With the skinny gunner beside one shoulder, the man's plump son on the other, Minh planted her feet and heaved. The two burly loaders and Loi pulled on a rope tied to the gun's barrel. Loi shouted for greater effort, but the artillery piece did not tip upright. Minh lowered her head, the gunner and son did the same. Loi hauled so hard on the rope that his back almost touched the ground, leading by how hard he was trying.

The 37mm's wheels inched off the ground. Minh grunted, putting her back into it, driving against the warm metal. The gunner's son cursed as he pushed, making the gunner take one hand off the knocked-over cannon to swat his boy in the back of the head. The weapon began to tilt up, then over. The gunners, loaders, Loi, and Minh, all groaned; the weight of the artillery piece shifted across its centerline. Minh and the two gunners let go, jumped back, and the big 37 jostled upright.

Minh and the gunners dropped to their knees, Loi and the loaders to their backsides. The six of them panted, but the rumbling of the valley put Loi on his feet first. He inspected the 37. The old gunner joined him and Minh followed. The others lay in the grass, taking this as a break. They'd not been happy to see Loi drive up in the truck. They'd thought they were lucky that their gun had been knocked out of commission and they weren't killed in the bargain, then here came the cadre to make them shoot more.

Two glass-covered gauges had been shattered, the steel platform was warped, the gun's mint green paint was chipped, but the barrel was straight and the aiming wheels spun and worked. None of the ammo crates had exploded. Loi and the thin old gunner hauled a fresh case over, loaded a magazine of gleaming rounds, and the gunner fired off ten in a single burst. Minh shoved Loi's pistol into her waistband so she could put both hands over her ears.

Loi had nothing to give the crew, no medals, no more ammunition. He said to Minh that he wanted to speak to them, thank them, and keep them in the fight, but they only had eyes for her. Loi asked her to sing for the crew as their reward.

The valley rang and echoed with the battle. She used to make a sound like that in Hanoi as a girl, running her tin bowl across the pickets of a fence in the rich neighborhoods. She didn't want to sing over the battle in the valley; the hillsides tossed the screeches of the Americans' jets and the throbs of their fat propellers back at them, ten thousand artillery rounds ripped the air every minute, bombs thundered and clashed with Loi's many guns. Minh took pride in her singing, and to perform for this crew she'd have to shout.

Her reluctance made Loi lean close. She expected a rebuke.

Another jet sliced down through a shattered rainbow of colors. Loi raised a hand to this.

"Where is it not dangerous?" Her own words, mirrored back at her. "Where in this valley do we not give everything?"

If Minh stepped under his raised arm, would he lay it across her shoulders like a veil? Loi could be so gentle about life and death, as if it were indeed just a veil. He had a streak of fury in him, too. These together made him remarkable. Had she ever seen him as a young priest, had she ever begged him? She would have wanted him if she had, if he'd spoken to her. Loi would have made a wonderful priest, or beggar; he had the knack for asking.

The old gunner and Loi joined the crew on the grass. Minh waited for another bomb blast to fade, using it as a gong to begin. She sang a revolutionary ditty, "The Riddle of the People":

> *It is the riddle of the people*
> *that they cannot die,*
> *so long as one man lives.*
> *It is the riddle of the man*
> *That he cannot die,*
> *so long as the people live.*

> *It is the wonder of an idea*
> *that it cannot die*
> *so long as one flag waves.*
> *It is the riddle of the flag*
> *that it needs no man*
> *but can wave on the wind.*

When she was done, Minh didn't think she'd sung it well. The clash in the valley had surged; a mile to the north, another jet slanted out of the sky, Loi's guns answered, bombs drummed another slope. The crew applauded but not as she'd wished.

Minh expected Loi to climb back into the truck. Since dawn he'd chased the Americans around his regiment. He rushed back and forth with an abandon that frightened Minh worse than the chances of being blown up. He'd crossed the river in the open with planes in the air, but they showed no interest in a single truck. They were after bigger targets, the barking guns. In the pitching cab, Minh held on while Loi swerved and sped. They hardly spoke and she didn't touch him, but with blasts in the hills and smoke drifting across the Trail she felt she'd gone to war with him, and this was another bond to add to the lotus flowers and last night in his cot.

Loi didn't turn for the truck but stayed to watch the crew load and ready their 37. He told the old gunner to keep the gun quiet until he ordered them to shoot; the Americans thought it was ruined and out of the fight and they could use that to their advantage.

He found a plot of shade. Without an invitation to join him, Minh went to sit beside him. This was pleasant because it felt expected; of course she should come sit with him. Together, with the gun at their backs, they watched the sweeping and swooping battle.

Eight jets circled miles above the earth, like children waiting their turn to go down a slide. One at a time, a bomber would peel away from the pack, turn its nose down, and rocket at the guns. The pilots juked left and right before they released their bombs and pulled up; here their engines worked the loudest. The *budda budda budda* of artillery, the colors and bending shapes of tracers, explosions, and their echoes, then another jet howled and another steep charge into the guns; all this made the fight for the valley a sight for a lifetime.

The gun crew stayed out of the fray as Loi commanded. No planes flew close enough to their hill for the 37 to have a worthy shot. Loi pointed to the valley floor below the slope where he and Minh sat, a flat span patchy with impenetrable jungle and some sparse places. This area, he said, was where his men had driven the downed American. He knew this because his guns in that section had not been attacked. The jets were staying away to keep their fellow pilot safe.

Minh wanted to take Loi's hand, but that would have broken the spell of them being warriors together. She hoped for another night in his cot, with all this to talk about. She envisioned the musty tent, leaving the lantern on.

A jet peeled out of its plunge early. Smoke barreled from its tail. It banked hard to escape the reaching guns, chasing it closer to the quiet 37. The crew spun the aiming wheels. Loi called for them to wait, this jet was already wounded and not worth revealing themselves. Let it go.

The plane departed the fray, leaving a contrail of smoke. It might have been mortally wounded, or it might limp home. Either way, this was the first trophy of the day's battle. The Americans seemed stunned by it, like a bloody nose, and the dive-bombing stopped. The guns rested.

The only motion and sound over the valley came from one of the hulking propeller-driven planes that had been stalking the treetops. This plane soared alone, straight and unaware at Loi's silent 37. Stubby with rockets and bombs, the plane looked thuggish, something bad-tempered in its flight.

Intently, leaning forward, Loi watched the American come. This seemed like a match, Loi seated across from the advancing pilot. Will the American see us, will he turn, will he fire first?

"What do you think?"

Loi was letting Minh choose the target, giving her the trigger. They were at war together. She pointed at the approaching American.

"Shoot that one."

Loi shouted her words to the crew.

CHAPTER 32

In the morning when the weather cleared, the parachute tarps came off. The guns came out blazing.

Both were zeeps, four-barreled, low-caliber, high-volume artillery. Together they spit five thousand rounds per minute. When they opened up, the tumult shook the branches around Sol, even his flight suit; the constant woof of the ZPUs, the ring of brass casings ejected onto growing piles, the streams of sound, all were deafening and wicked. Maybe these were the twin sons of bitches that had shot him down. Sol considered calling Nail down on them, but figured it was best to stay put and quiet.

A crew of five tended each weapon. They fired for four hours straight, until both cannons stood on their own shadows in their little plot of grass. The sky, once it turned blue, stayed that way. Through the trees, Sol caught glimpses of streaking jets or trolling Sandy A-1s. No one had taken on the pair of ZPUs close to him.

The noise in the valley was so great it sounded like the place was being created on day one, thrust out of the earth in volcanoes. The ferns above Sol shook; he lay pasted to the ground by the heat. The zeeps near the camp halted only when a truck arrived with fresh crates of ammo. At midmorning, one vehicle rolled up with only a tall white-shirted man and a small woman; the man patted the black pajama backs of the gunners while the woman strolled close to Sol. He flattened even more, spurring the pain in his shoulder while she peered into the pig pit. Sol followed her down the snub barrel of his revolver. When she walked away, she had a pistol of her own jammed in the black waistband at her back.

The air versus ground battle raged past noon. Sol worried about his radio, with only one spare battery. If he wore them down, he was finished. He tried to stay off the guard channel but every time the zeeps cranked up, he tucked the speaker against his ear, hoping to hear who they might be shooting at, a bomber, a Sandy, Nail, maybe a Jolly finally coming to pick him up. Because Sol couldn't hear the planes over the thumping artillery, he followed the fight this way.

He listened to a menagerie of flight names—Cobra, Eagle, Bat, Panda, Locust, Barracuda, Viper, Lobo—all of them Thuds and F-4s, plus a handful of Navy A-7s from a carrier in the Gulf. Each jet rolled in to take on one gun battery after another, guided by a succession of Nails who crisscrossed the valley until their O-2s flew on fumes, before they bingoed back to base.

At 1300, the zeeps took a break. Everywhere in the valley and above it, the combat paused to catch its breath. Maybe it was because the heat of the day had reached its peak, or it was just that men and steel had breaking points and needed to back away. Sol sat up among the ferns to scan his vicinity, the camp, the artillery, and the pit.

In the small field, the gunners drank from ladles and buckets. Through the trees, the camp lay smokeless and emptied. The pig had shut up. To the south, among the foliage, another squad of VC searchers fanned out, looking for Sol. Through the quiet jungle, without booms and echoes, a rifle shot cracked, then the reedy call, "Captain." While the battle in the valley had been crashing around him, Sol forgot that he was being hunted.

Two hundred yards away, the VC progressed slowly, twenty in a line abreast. They were going to sweep right over him unless he moved. He had no way to do that; he couldn't run with the zeeps not firing, and he couldn't crawl away with his shoulder wrecked. Sol called Nail.

"Nail, this is Dash 2. Copy?"

He listened for the O-2's drone over the valley but caught only a tweeting bird and another far-off call for Captain.

"Nail, Dash 2. I have a problem down here. Copy?"

Sol waited, the radio pressed to his ear, volume low. He snagged a peek at the VC. They progressed slowly, combing the brush, calling into the bushes, shooting in the air. Maybe he had ten minutes until they were on top of him. The zeep gunners were breaking for lunch. The jungle had gone breathless and hot, the insects making the only noise beside the searchers.

Through the buzz of bugs and the crackle of rising heat, Sol caught the distant hum of engines.

"Dash, this is Nail 32. I copy. I need you to verify."

This was a new Nail in the fight. The FAC wanted to make sure Dash 2 was still a free man and not talking with a Vietnamese gun to his head.

"Go ahead, Nail."

"What's your mother's maiden name?"

"Jacobson."

A wrong answer would have signaled that Sol had been captured, or it wasn't Sol.

"Roger, Dash. What's up?"

"I've got a visual on twenty bad guys moving up on me. I'm not able to evade. I don't have much time until they reach me. Do you have a tally on my position?"

"Dash, I have a general idea but not an exact location. Can you pop a smoke?"

Was he kidding? With a squad of armed VC bearing down on him, Nail wanted Sol to light a smoke flare? Again, Sol considered switching to the FAC corps if he got out of this mess. How valuable could he be to a downed pilot with his own experiences on the run?

"Negative. Listen, I'm still close to where I was last night. A half kilometer north from my chute. There's a pair of zeeps seventy yards away. They're in a small grassy opening. Find them. I'll walk you to me from there."

"Copy, Dash. Stand by."

Sol snuck another glance at the VC inching his way through the trees; every move of his shoulder stabbed him. He didn't have time to stand by. He needed bombs falling on his hunters in the next few minutes, he needed the zeep gunners paying attention to the sky. Just below his need, Sol relished the notion of going on the offensive, of telling the VC that chasing him, shooting in the air, calling out "Captain," came at a fucking cost.

"Dash 2, Nail."

"Nail, go."

"Sandy 3 is headed your way. When you hear him, give him a long count. He'll home in on you."

This wasn't what Sol was expecting. He figured Nail would wend his way down the river, hustle through the treetops, fire a willy pete at the zeeps, then bug out while a jet flashed in, weapons hot. Sending a Sandy without knowing exactly where the guns were, or where Sol was in relation to them, was dicey. If Sandy took ground fire and returned it, if he started strafing or bombing too soon, Sol might get in the way. In effect, Nail was saying, "It's too hot for me, buddy. I'm sending in a big dog to find you."

"Copy, Nail. Sooner the better."

"Sandy 3 is turning your way now."

Gritting his teeth, Sol rolled into position under the ferns where he might keep an eye on the searchers. Another rifle shot accompanied promises of "We won't hurt you." Sol held the radio to his ear, making no such promise to the VC.

"Dash 2, this is Sandy 3, copy?"

Sol whispered, "Go, Sandy."

"Start your count."

From the south, across the bowl of the valley, the rumble of the A-1's big motor swelled quickly. Sandy 3 was squeezing every bit of speed he could out of his Skyraider. The searchers heard him, too; they turned that way, heads tipped to the canopy that hid them.

Sol whispered into the radio, "One. Two. Three."

While Sol counted, Sandy's motor grew louder. At *eight*, Sandy 3 radioed, "Got you."

The zeeps opened up. Sol jumped, jarring his shoulder. The VC searchers froze, sensing they'd walked into the middle of something they hadn't bargained for. A few took a knee as if that might help. Half took off running back where they had come from, to get away from whatever action was brewing over their heads. Four ran right at Sol, swinging their AK-47s, sprinting toward the hammering artillery and the clearing. They wanted to get in their shots at the closing American plane.

Rolling onto his belly, Sol didn't bother squelching his gasp; he couldn't hear it, so no one else could. He propped his chin on the brown humus and had to pick between holding his pistol or the radio. Sol chose the radio.

Four sets of brown feet and sandals raced by, one of them a few strides from where Sol lay. Had the VC not been so excited to join the fight, had they just looked down to their left, they'd have their prize. But the growing churn of Sandy 3's engine had the VC in thrall, and they hurried past. Sol's stomach unknotted. He raised his head, listening hard into the radio.

The ZPU crews had waited all morning and into the afternoon for this: at last, an American plane came their way. A different attitude suffused the gunners. This plane was theirs. In the pit, the pig went nuts. Even the VC on foot, the ones who ran into the clearing, felt the change. They lifted their rifles, adding their bullets to the storm of ZPU shells that Sandy 3 was flying through to find Sol.

Sol wanted to cover his head but couldn't let go of the radio. Sandy 3 zoomed closer; the zeeps made the trees tremble. Sol couldn't tell if Sandy was firing back or not. Head down, he closed his eyes and lived the fight through the pandemonium, the shuddering ground, and the radio.

He hadn't known how raw his nerves had grown. Sol struggled against the urge to scream into the earth. Desperately, he needed Sandy to come get him, and at the same time he wanted the A-1 to get the hell out of there, he was getting hosed. A tear rolled off Sol's cheek into the loam; with no free hand he couldn't wipe it away. He puffed into the soil, tamping down the panic that returned as Sandy 3 went toe-to-toe with the zeeps.

Sandy 3 spoke calmly into the radio: "I've taken a hit."

As though the guns could hear the transmission, they seemed to fire faster and harder. Sol's head could not sink lower into the dirt. The radio peeped again in his ear.

"Losing oil. I'm not bringing this one back."

The thrum of Sandy's big engine became irregular, a spurting rasp. The power of the motor was leaking out; Sandy pulled away from the fight. His engine strained to gain distance. The VC didn't let him go quietly.

First the rifle fire stopped, then the artillery. The jungle echoed for moments, before giving over to the halting sputters of Sandy 3 trying to escape.

The crash sounded like another bomb in the valley.

CHAPTER 33

The 37 crew fired three quick bursts at the drifting parachute. Even kilometers away, Minh could see the American pilot kicking under his parachute with the 37's red tracers flashing past.

Loi bounded up the hill, waving and shouting for them to stop. Minh followed.

When she reached the ridge, the gunners were talking all at once. They were frustrated that the American plane had been taken down by another battery, a crew on the valley floor, a smaller caliber than theirs. The 37 had good shots, clean shots, and missed. The skinny old gunner wondered if his big gun's targeting had been put off by being toppled over. He told Loi he was calibrating his artillery piece's aim by firing at the parachute. He was sorry, too, for disappointing Loi and his friend.

Loi told the crew to wait, more American planes would come now that they had two pilots on the ground. The 37 wouldn't lack for targets.

Four kilometers off, the white chute floated toward the valley floor. Wind blew the pilot to the north, away from the ridge where Loi intently watched it descend. The white half-moon of the chute sailed out of sight, disappearing behind one of the knolls rimming the valley. Loi asked the crew if any of them had a rifle. One of the loaders fetched a battered AK-47 with two ammo magazines. Loi traded his pistol from Minh's waistband. He grabbed the rifle, Minh the ammo. He wished the crew luck and discipline, then jogged with Minh for the truck.

Loi wound the truck down the wooded slope, then onto the Road, not driving hell-bent like before. He apologized to Minh for not shooting down the American plane, as if doing so would have been a gift from him. This seemed odd, but she'd never been a warrior before and didn't know what warriors promised each other.

She told Loi they could still get one.

It was easier to sing songs about killing men than to watch it. War was Loi's world, and two people cannot love each other in different worlds. So while the truck jounced under the archway of trees, Minh clung to the heavy rifle and kept the extra magazines in her lap. She didn't ask Loi where they were going, because she knew. They were going to do exactly what she'd said.

At the main base camp, Loi commandeered a squad of a dozen Viet Cong. They were all veterans of Khe Sanh and, like the rest of the men in the river valley, glad to have Americans to shoot at. Loi loaded them onto the bed of the truck and took off. He didn't explain Minh to them.

He motored four kilometers north along the road, then pulled over. The VC fighters jumped down off the bed, Minh and Loi from the cab. She strapped his AK-47 across her back and gripped one cartridge in each hand. She filed alongside the VC. Loi tilted his head, smiling, glad of her in the line. He made no move to relieve Minh from carrying the rifle but led the troop into the jungle at a jog. Minh fit into the middle of the pack. She had no problem keeping up.

They high-stepped through tall grasses, serpentined around trees and bamboo stalks. Minh sweated and wished for water, but no one had any, Loi had loaded the men on the truck so quickly. They hustled after him; she caught only glimpses of his white shirt dodging through the brush and shadows, in and out of patches of light. They were not quiet at all but snapped branches in their path and joggled with their guns.

At last, the squad slowed to a walk, then Loi allowed them to squat and catch their breath. They were on no path here but forging through thick foliage, airless, humid, and dark. Some leaves were gargantuan, many plants flowered, the splendors of the jungle here were untrammeled. Loi walked down the line checking on the men. He passed Minh with the same nod he gave the VC. She kneeled among them, and when a bag of dried elephant meat was passed, Minh was offered some.

Loi let them rest for only minutes. They pressed on into an even murkier patch of forest where the soil softened under Minh's sandals. The undergrowth thinned and Loi could lead them faster through the fewer, fatter trees. Keeping the gold shafts of light slanting from his left, he let the sun guide them north.

The jaunt through this green cavern lasted not long enough; Minh enjoyed the quick pace and cooler air. Finally, bright light drew them to the forest's edge. Loi sped the pace, emerging at the base of a thinly wooded hill. He told the dozen men to wait there. He turned away, then stopped and reached for the AK-47 from Minh.

"Come on."

Without the weight of the rifle, she could have handily beaten him to the top of the knoll. She didn't, but stayed close behind him to make the point.

They encountered no thorns, and the lush passage to the crest went easily. Neither labored to breathe; they were alone, so she could talk to him.

"Will you leave tonight?"

"The division?"

"Yes."

"I don't know."

"What about what you said? The Americans are going to bomb the valley. You can't stay here."

Loi replied with longer strides to the top, where they had a full view of the valley floor, even to the river. The battle was at rest; no guns rang in the hills and no planes dove on them. The sun perched high and the heat could get no worse.

Loi answered now. "If they keep coming, we'll stand. So far, we've shot down three planes and damaged one. I know them, the Americans won't back off."

"You're saying you'll fight as long as they do."

Loi nodded patiently, as if she didn't know. "That is war."

"When you go, will I go with you?"

"Binh tram 17 is on the other side of the hills. You'll be safe there."

"You know that's not what I'm asking."

Though both of Minh's hands were filled with ammo, Loi took them in his.

"This isn't helping the war. Carrying my guns, my ammunition. You're a singer. An actor. You walk the Road. You give the men heart."

She almost dropped the cartridges. "Are you leaving me?"

"Did you ever think it could be otherwise? Did you ever think we could matter more than all this?"

"What about the flowers?"

"I've been selfish."

"What about last night?"

Deep in the warm distance, above the western rim of the valley, a dot emerged against the perfect sky, balanced on the green horizon. It arrived too far off for sound; that would be next.

Loi took the two ammo magazines from her, leaving her empty-handed, bearing nothing of his world.

Though he stood beside her on the hilltop, Loi spoke as if he was already gone from the valley. Or she was.

"You gave me heart."

She had no ready words and Loi didn't wait. He shifted his attention to the helicopter approaching out of the west. Two hundred meters from their hilltop, directly in the path of the coming helicopter, a tip of the white parachute showed in the trees, just a pale dot against the jungle.

CHAPTER 34

Without a word from the cockpit, Jolly 22 broke out of orbit to dive for the deck. The high bird, Jolly 23, peeled away and headed for altitude.

Had Bo missed an intercom transmission from Crebbs? He poked Lee and the flight engineer; both shook their heads. The chopper banked hard for the sunny valley. Ten miles away, Sandy 3's pillar of smoke rose above a forested ridge.

The trees came up fast and Jolly 22 leveled just above them. Crebbs blasted across the jungle at full speed, following the terrain, nap-of-the-earth flying.

The pilot made an announcement over the intercom.

"We've been called off the Dash rescue. You all saw Sandy 3 go down. We've been fragged to go get him. The pilot punched out, he's made contact, and we're homing on his beeper. The chute is caught in a tree along the west rim of the valley. We're going in fast before the guns can find us. PJ 1."

Lee answered, standing. "PJ 1 up."

"Get ready. The rest of you, we don't know if the zone's hot. Stay frosty."

Before moving to the rear minigun, Bo knocked Lee on the shoulder. He pulled out his five-baht coin to show Lee, in case he wanted to flip again. Lee raised his middle finger; they shook hands. Lee patted all his gear and guns, doing a checklist, then undid the latch of the gunner's belt at his waist. On the lowered cargo gate, Bo hunkered behind the Gatling gun. The view of Laos was expansive and green, windy and loud.

Bo gripped the minigun's handles as Crebbs raced the last miles to Sandy 3. Jolly 22 traced the rolling faces of the terrain, up and down, a roller coaster of green and brown. When they arrived in a crease between hills, out of sight from much of the valley and its artillery, Crebbs jettisoned the chopper's external fuel tanks into the jungle for better handling. He flew one speedy circle around a pale parachute snagged on the point of a tall tree. The forest ran dense and Bo had only glimpses of the jungle floor through waving boughs and fronds. The FE manhandled the penetrator inside for Lee to climb aboard, then, as Jolly 22 slowed, wrangled it outside for Lee to dangle and wait. The FE worked with the pilot to ease into position above the chute. Twenty meters, fifteen, ten. Five.

"Hover."

Crebbs settled the chopper so deeply into the trees that the tallest branches whipped against the edges of the cargo door. Bo swept his six barrels left and right, wishing he had better visibility. Before sending Lee down on the hoist, the FE narrated to the pilot the situation directly under them.

"The package isn't moving. He's hanging fifty feet off the ground. I'm going to drop the PJ right in front of him. Hold her real steady."

"Roger."

The FE punched the hoist button to lower Lee. Bo lost sight of him beneath the chopper, swallowed into the canopy.

On the ground a flash of black, something ducking from shadow to shadow, caught Bo's eye. He swept the minigun there but wasn't sure enough to pull the trigger; he might have seen just the shade of a wavering branch or nothing but his own nerves. He stayed off the intercom, leaving it for the FE and the pilot, and kept watch with his gut balling tight.

The hoist played out line slowly, sinking Lee and the penetrator deeper into the cover of the trees. Crebbs, too, must have seen something he didn't like. He asked over the intercom how it was going.

The FE said only "Hover."

The flight engineer leaned far out the door, gazing down the steel cable. He worked the hoist button, stopping and starting as Lee below guided him a few more feet, waited, then another few feet.

"Hover. Steady."

Above Bo's head, a spark struck against the doorway. The chopper jerked; something had jarred Crebbs's hand on the stick. Lee was headed down on the penetrator, the FE was working the hoist; Bo's gun remained the only defense for Jolly 22. Though he saw nothing to shoot at, he made a choice.

Bo tugged the trigger. The minigun flamed to life. The grips stayed eerily firm in his mitts while the six barrels spun and blazed. Brass casings cartwheeled out the open door, a hundred more spilled around Bo's boots as he swept the gun side to side and sprayed the shadows. The treetops that had been swaying in his way got shaved off. After a thousand rounds, Bo backed off, breathing hard, scanning the ground for movement. The minigun's barrels whirled emptily, slowing, smoking. In Bo's helmet the FE's voice had been droning the whole time, but Bo heard it only now.

"Hover. Hover."

The FE was raising the penetrator. Crebbs's voice belted in Bo's helmet.

"Get him in! We're taking hits."

"Steady."

The FE mashed one hand over the hoist button to keep the spool reeling the penetrator up to the chopper. His other hand, bloody, clutched his thigh.

Bo shouted, "You all right?"

The flight engineer didn't turn from his job, but thrust his reddened hand behind him, telling Bo to do his.

Another zing stuck the rotors, flinting more sparks. The chopper shivered again in Crebbs' hands, trying to hold Jolly 22 in place until the penetrator was onboard while enduring terrific ground fire. Bo's minigun faced the rear, where he had nothing to shoot at. Whoever was peppering the chopper was on the FE's side.

Bo jumped on the intercom. "PJ 2 to pilot."

"Make it quick."

"Pivot the tail gun ninety degrees right."

A pause was followed by "Roger, PJ. Light 'em up."

The big HH-3 rotated around the hoist line. The FE kept reeling the cable in; Lee and the pilot were dragged through branches on their way up. Bo leaned over his hot six barrels, scanning for anything on the ground that wasn't a plant. The tail rotor swung right, the hoist continued to grind; through the waving branches, Bo caught a flicker of movement down in the jungle, not a shadow, but a glimpse, a riffle through the leaves, of a soldier firing a gun from the shoulder, a soldier in a white shirt.

CHAPTER 35

Overhead, in the madly waving trees, the big American helicopter reeled in its rescuer. The man clung to the metal chair he'd ridden down through the branches, piercing the jungle through its roof. This rescuer rose alone, without the dangling, tangled pilot he'd been lowered to save; the pilot was dead. Just before the helicopter arrived, as the pilot fumbled for his pistol, Loi had loosed an entire magazine at him. The pilot hung a hundred feet in the air and was not easy to hit.

When the chopper began to hover, Loi's men scattered, looking for open lanes between the branches to fire at it. They shot poorly at first, having to hold their heavy AKs high. Some fired from the hip. None of the small men could stand directly under the helicopter; even through the trees, the wash pushed them around.

Loi had disappeared from Minh's side, running straight into the skirmish and flying bullets. She stayed back, not as far as he'd told her to; she stood close enough to be in danger if the helicopter spotted her. The noise of the battle ranked with anything in the valley between jets and artillery. In the closeting trees, a dozen semiautomatic rifles rang, firepower blistered from the helicopter, spinning blades whopped, and the branches whipped. Above, the dead pilot swung from long white lines under a deflated parachute. Though she could barely see the fighting through the trees and flying debris, it seemed a battle between men and an airborne monster, a monster that turned its back on the men to unleash another torrent of bullets with a horrible mechanical yowl.

Minh had never seen combat this intimately before. She'd been shot at blindly at Khe Sanh, bombed on the Road, almost blown up yesterday on the river and in a bunker with Loi, but this was the first time she'd witnessed men shooting at other men they could see. Everything happened so fast, so loud, men jumped and scrambled, they screamed through their weapons, some fell bloodied. Combat was nothing like her songs or plays. This was dreadful and simple, killing and dying in close.

The gunner in the helicopter had a powerful weapon, firing at a remarkable rate. A cascade of golden shells tumbled through the branches, little bells littering the jungle floor, macabre for their beauty. Two VC went down like shaken dolls, struck over and again in the blink of an eye. A third, wounded, tried to crawl toward Minh as though she might help. He was fifty meters away. She inched in his direction.

The helicopter's gun sprayed the forest without targeting, just random and horrifying sweeps of rounds, showering the fighters with bullets, torn leaves, and bark. Loi's men dashed about, shooting up through the whipping branches. The helicopter was massive, and many of the squad's bullets must have hit it, yet it continued to hover while their rescuer was raised through the highest branches. The American rescuer put his rifle in his hands, answering Loi's guns with downward fire of his own. Minh ran toward the wounded VC still dragging himself across the forest floor.

When she reached him, he raised a hand. She took it and rolled him over. Minh pulled his AK-47 from around his shoulders. He moaned and questioned her, "What are you doing?"

Minh strapped on the gun. A beggar, a singer, an actor could not go with Loi. A warrior might. She ran into the frenzy, looking up while she dodged trees and scrub. The American rescuer had risen into the last of the jungle crown, almost gone; the battle was nearly done. Minh sprinted until she was in the strongest wind, directly beneath the hanging pilot and the helicopter. She raised the barrel of the AK and held it above her head. Not knowing what else to do, no longer looking up, she squeezed the trigger.

The gun became instantly wild, but Minh clung hard and kept it pointed up into the trees. The muzzle leaped left and right while she deafened and terrified herself. The downblast of the helicopter, the shuddering of the gun's recoil, the fear in her legs, staggered her. She didn't want to die, only to be with Loi. Minh let off the trigger when the rifle clicked, out of bullets. Then she toppled over.

The shooting around her stopped. The helicopter's gust disappeared but in her stuffy ears, its throb sounded wrong, stuttering. It climbed, still coughing, then faded away over the valley.

Loi and his men emerged from the woods.

He reached for her gun. Still dazed, she held it back from him, a thing enmeshed to her now. Loi helped her stand.

He shouted orders for his remaining men to carry the wounded fighter and the two bodies back to the truck. They would leave the American pilot hanging in the tree, with no way to get him down.

The squad moved to obey, leaving Minh alone with Loi. She expected sharpness, but he was gentle.

"I told you to stay back."

She put both hands on the weapon hanging at her waist, to pose like a soldier.

"Give me the gun." He snapped his fingers. "Give it to me."

She pulled the strap over her head to hand the rifle over. "I want to go with you."

"I know what you're doing. This doesn't make you a fighter."

"There are women fighters. I've seen them."

"You could have been hurt. Or killed."

"What about you? You could have been hurt or killed."

Shouldering her AK, Loi lay a hand on her shoulder. He touched her throat with the pad of his thumb. "Yes, but I can't sing."

"Are you going to keep doing this? Running after the Americans? Jumping in front of them like this?"

"I can't lead from a bunker. Until we leave the valley."

The first of the corpses was carried past.

"You might not live long enough to leave."

"Then you have no worry about me going without you. And you? Are you going to keep disobeying me?"

"No."

"No?"

She shook her head this time when she answered. She was learning Loi. He desired certainty. "No."

"We'll see."

This was all done quietly, in the presence of the dead and a thousand brass casings on the jungle floor. Loi had said, "We'll see." That meant she might yet stay with him. As a singer, or a soldier, even a secret, Minh didn't care. She lowered her eyes the way she did after the last line of a play, the way he had in front of the headquarters officers.

The wounded fighter was carried piggyback through the jungle. Minh helped bear the two dead bodies. The heat of the day, the hills, the sad slack heft of the corpses, made this an awful task. Loi walked at the head of the line; he never once looked back at her. When they reached the truck, she climbed in front beside him. He looked then.

CHAPTER 36

The minigun yowled and Bo, too, yelled behind it, unintelligible battle things. He flicked the minigun's flaming barrels at anything that moved on the ground, certain only a few times that what he saw were men with guns aimed back at him. He witnessed one VC go down with a burning tracer in the chest, hit hard. Others darted in and out of his aim; he didn't see the one in the white shirt again.

Crebbs and the FE kept up a dialogue over the intercom, heated and clipped exchanges. Words like *fast* and *now* and *hits* flew through Bo's earphones, but he was charged up behind the minigun, barely listening to anything else. The chopper shuddered from the small-arms fire it was taking. When Jolly 22 began to climb out of the trees, Bo kept firing, flinging empty casings out the cargo door. Lee's hand came across his wrists to stop him.

Bo jerked around, still amped. Lee stood there flushed, every inch of his face red and stretched like he wanted to scream. Bullet holes showed in the fuselage. Far forward, the flight engineer sat on the floor beside the penetrator. Pain flattened his face while he clamped a crimson hand over his thigh.

Where was the pilot they'd come to rescue? Lee didn't wait for Bo's question, shouting.

"He was dead! Fuckers shot him, just hanging there. Fuckers!"

Bo came alert quickly, finished with the steaming minigun. Lee looked unhurt. The flight engineer needed attention. Bo unplugged from the intercom, grabbed his med kit, and scrambled forward, dragging the tail of his gunner's belt. Lee slid down the perforated wall.

Immediately Bo tightened a tourniquet around the flight engineer's upper leg, in the inguinal area, to stop the bleeding. He drew the long blade he kept sheathed above his boot to slice away the FE's pants leg. The AK round was a through and through, a neat tunnel in and out of the meaty part of the thigh. The FE could move his leg with discomfort, so the bullet had missed the femur and the major nerves. Bo packed the hole with sterile gauze, poured in antibiotic powder, and fast-wrapped the wound. Before he could give the FE a shot of morphine, Jolly 22 lurched so badly, Bo almost dropped the syringe out the open door. For the first time since leaving the minigun, he looked outside at Laos.

The jungle remained only a hundred feet below. Bo figured they ought to be coursing at cloud level by now. The chopper staggered again, making Bo hold on. The FE waggled urgent fingers to hook Bo's attention back to him, to the morphine. "Give it to me," he hollered.

Bo stuck him in the thigh and shouted, "You're gonna be okay. It's a clean wound. Straight through."

This did nothing to ease the FE's tension or his waving arms. He wanted something more from Bo, reaching to him, or past him. To what? Bo whirled.

The FE wanted his bailout parachute.

At the other end of the Jolly's bay, Lee was on his feet, strapping on his own emergency chute.

Bo unclipped the FE's parachute from the wall. Before he helped the flight engineer put it on, he needed to know what was happening. Bo plugged into the intercom.

Crebbs counted out altitude numbers, ". . . three-fifty, four hundred, four-fifty." The chopper chugged to stay airborne.

Bo thumbed his transmit button and cut in. "Captain, PJ 2."

"I'm busy, son."

"Sir, I've been off-line. What's going on?"

"We took a lot of ground fire. A hydraulic line got hit. We're leaking fluid. I've got maybe a minute or two of control before she's done. You got your chute on, Kansas?"

"No, sir."

"Put the goddam thing on. I'll get us up to fifteen hundred feet, then we bail. I'm aiming for the western rim of the valley. When you're out, try to clear the ridge. Stick together."

This left Bo speechless. The FE tugged on his leg. Crebbs didn't want anything more from Bo and went back to his count. "Six hundred." The chopper bounced again, struggling to stay airborne. Bo took another look outside; the ground was way too close.

The FE hit Bo in the butt with a fist. He'd skidded back against his parachute container and managed only to buckle the chest fittings, but stood no chance of securing the crotch straps. Bo bent to his knees to assist. The pilot intoned, "Eight hundred."

Lee, already in his jump gear, worked his way forward, hand over hand along the chopper's bucking airframe. He hooked a mitt under Bo's armpit to lift him to his feet. Pointing to the rear, he shouted, "Go, go."

While Lee tended to the flight engineer, Bo yanked out his intercom plug and careened to the rear of the chopper to dig out his own stowed emergency chute. He hefted the container across his shoulders, then with fast hands clipped into the chest, lap, and crotch belts.

He didn't plug back into the intercom to listen to Crebbs count. When Lee jumped, Bo would jump. He checked his rifle, the survival radio in his vest, the .38 at his armpit; he clipped on his med pack because the FE was going to require more attention on the ground.

Bo scanned the bay for anything else he might need. He checked his compass to know which way was west, to sail out of the valley like Crebbs said.

Jolly 22 gasped. Bo heard it through his helmet, a whine like a horse going down; he felt the mechanical demise through his boots. The chopper began to list, rolling onto its right side. The rotors kept spinning but all control had been lost. Crebbs couldn't keep the chopper flying anymore, it was flailing now.

Lee threw the flight engineer out the door.

Bo stood in the rear, at the cargo bay door; Lee shot him a thumbs-up down the length of the bay. The Jolly's floor tilted badly. Lee didn't jump so much as he was tilted out the door, and he was gone.

Bo faced open air. He had to jump now; once the chopper began its plummet, he'd be trapped inside. He ran one, two, three clomping strides across the tipping floor, almost stumbling, heart in his throat, and leaped.

In his first weightless moment, Bo recoiled in midair away from the Jolly's great propellers; they spun not over his head but, because the chopper was listing sideways, beat beside him dangerously, crazily close. They threw a gale at him, knocking him into a tumble. Bo twisted as the blades fell away and he lost sight of the ground, blown out of his bearings.

Reaching blindly to his chest, he clutched the D-ring. One yank would release the canopy.

A sudden, terrifying force folded him in half. Bo's arms and feet shot away from his torso, doubled over at the waist. He ought to be falling free, but something dragged him behind the dying chopper, facing his own boots. Helpless and mystified, he screamed.

His chute hadn't deployed. What was happening?

Against the force yanking him backward, he pulled in one of his hands to feel at his waist.

The gunner's belt. Bo hadn't unhooked it before bailing.

Jolly 22 rolled farther onto its side; Bo trailed it in midair at the end of a fifteen-foot tether buckled at his waist, clipped in at his back. The chopper towed him as it fell, ripping him through the sky, angling down toward the treetops.

Desperately, Bo clawed at his waist, trying to spring the quick-release lever of the belt, but the pressure of his belly against the buckle wouldn't let it budge. He dug at it again, breaking nails. It wouldn't give. He was stuck, and he was going to die.

Bo fought nausea that reared out of his fright, a throttling despair, and his own stupidity. He wanted to close his eyes against so much swirling shame, exhale one last pained breath, and let the squeezing in his midsection and the pulsing blades drag him down, careless and doomed, as though he deserved this. Bo tried it, shut his eyes to let the killed chopper and his guilt have their way. But in that instant, his missing brother didn't let him quit, nor his parents, nor his training, nor Lee.

Bo flung his eyes wide open like he'd touched a live wire. The ground lay twelve hundred feet below. Jolly 22 was doing a swan dive into the jungle, and Bo, still attached, had no idea what to do. In the frenzy of the mess he was in, he caught a momentary sight of parachutes blowing over a ridge and out of the valley.

The rotors of the failing Jolly still beat, and with that came a forceful wind. Bo's chin and chest jolted against his knees, the world wobbled in and out of focus. He struggled for what to do, how to get loose, some idea to slow his rising panic.

His forearm whacked against something hard on one of his legs, not for the first time, but Bo had ignored it while he'd been allowing himself to die.

He tucked his hands hard under his calves, trying to restrain his rippling torso and bouncing head, long enough for one motionless moment, one glimpse of clarity.

There. His knife. Sheathed at his left calf.

Bo reached for it, but the wash of the blades and the jarring backward ride shook him like a rug, his arms and legs shuddered of their own will. He tried again, managed to touch the black handle, but his leg whipped away from his fingers. With every fiber of strength he had, and with no other option, he drew in his legs to curl into a ball. The tether at the small of his back snapped him hard like he was on the end of a whiplash, but Bo clung to his ankles. Holding his boots tight against him, by feel alone and with seconds left to his life, he snatched out the blade.

Bo slashed at his back, frantic, only nicking the taut belt the first two passes. He had no time to pray, so he just said, "Please."

He reached behind him, his final effort. The sharp edge nipped the tether; then, on the downstroke, he sliced himself loose.

All motion stilled. Bo hung free in the air, feet down, head up, ready to vomit. He pulled the ripcord on his emergency bailout chute as he lost sideways momentum. The canopy opened perfectly, and Bo gently transitioned from falling to floating.

He had only seconds of peace while his heart left his throat. Not far below, big Jolly 22 shaved off the tops of a hundred trees, dug itself a green grave in the forest, clipped off its blades, then pranged without an explosion. To the west rose the ridgeline the others had cleared. Bo had been dragged a mile away and wasn't going to make that. He descended into the valley with the VC guns. The jungle came up fast.

CHAPTER 37

The bombing and the artillery rested.

At the risk of wearing down his battery, at very low volume Sol monitored the attempt to rescue Sandy 3.

He was thrilled to hear Red Crown relay Sandy's opened chute and good beeper. Minutes later, a Jolly agreed to zip in before the VC's guns could reposition themselves. Sol rubbed his forehead in frustration that one of the choppers was about to risk rescuing another pilot before him. But when Jolly 22 located and hovered over Sandy's chute, Sol rooted silently. He wanted Sandy 3 rescued, to show it could be done. Then came the report that Sandy 3 had been found shot dead in his harness, hanging from a tree. Sol sank under the weight of blame for that. The shoot-down of Jolly 22, then the terrible boom of another crash in the valley, broke his spirit. He considered standing up in the ferns, raising his one good arm to the zeep crews to put a stop to all this. He shut off the radio, unwilling and unable to listen to more, afraid if there were more, he might just surrender.

Sol wiped away sweat that was worsening his dehydration. He lay face up in a pool of remorse, betrayal, and abandonment. He couldn't move for the pain in his shoulder, for the VC looking for him, for a hundred reasons. He felt buried under the ferns and heat, incapable of doing anything in this jungle except cause the deaths of others or get himself captured.

On all sides of him, the Viet Cong were using the downtime well. They cleared fallen trees from their bunkers and around gun emplacements, they fixed a meal in the camp. An ammo truck arrived to resupply the twin ZPUs. Where were the bombers, where was Nail, to punish them, make them run for their lives? Sol wanted to strike; he had no other way to make all this square but to somehow get out of this valley alive, ball a fist, wrap it around the stick of a damned jet, and come back here. For Sandy 5, Sandy 3, Jolly 22. And who else before all this played out?

Sol checked his watch. Sundown lay only a few hours off. The VC broke the quiet of the valley, re-arming, digging in, eating. The hills echoed only with them, no hint of Nail's propellers, no thunder from Gunfighter, Viper, Gambler, Lobo, or Panda flights. No bombs, no guns, no rescue.

And what of Seventh Air Force's cutoff, the twenty-four hours they'd given the rescue force to fetch Sol off the ground? When the sun set, the bell would toll on that deadline. Were they actually going to carpet bomb the valley with Sol on the ground? He didn't want revenge on the VC bad enough for that.

Sol lowered the radio from his ear. No one had called him in hours.

CHAPTER 38

Bo drifted down on a scrubby knoll. He tugged the risers to avoid a dead tree, lifted his legs to clear a bush, then put boots down in waist-high weeds and rolled. Popping up, he felt visible on the hilltop. Quickly, he reeled in his parachute.

The sun beat on him miserably; the ridge lacked shade. The chute snagged in a prickly hedge, and Bo had to yank hard a few times to free it. Branches snapped, but he was more engaged with speed than stealth.

When he had the big chute gathered, he wrapped the riser lines around it, tucked the bundle under one arm, and took off running.

Bo raced downhill, not pausing for thorns or branches. He had no strategy beyond getting out of sight. He bulled through dry scrub and tall grasses, lowering his head, turning his shoulders, slowing for nothing. He headed for a copse of trees a hundred yards off, where the shade looked thick as tar.

Bo hit the jungle panting hard and rammed his way through the first hundred feet, the way he used to bust into the walls of corn, practicing for football. He ran until the undergrowth thinned and he could move forward without dodging trunks or knocking aside stalks. The darker the woods grew, the taller the trees reached, until Bo slowed to a walk, then a halt, under a vaulted ceiling of speckled light.

He dropped the chute, took his M-16 in hand, and, turning a slow circle, caught his breath.

Jolly 22 had gone down a mile east. When Bo's chute popped, he was under a thousand feet altitude, so he floated only for seconds. If he was lucky, none of the VC had seen him cut loose from the chopper. If they were looking for survivors, they were likely headed for the crash site.

His revved-up heart and lungs began to notch down. He stopped his breath to listen. The jungle creaked like an old barn, mice in the straw, heat in the rafters, but no humans nearby. Bo supposed he'd been pretty afraid two minutes ago when he landed, he could barely recall hitting the ground or hauling in his parachute. The sprint down the hill into these trees was a blur. He seemed to have run it out of himself; he wasn't scared, not jittery anyway. Just very aware and ready. Why didn't he feel more frightened? He ought to be. He wasn't being dragged backward behind a helicopter. His prospects were looking up. He was well armed. Bo took a knee.

He turned one more circuit, cautious and keen, peering and listening deep into the shadowy woods. Nothing stirred beyond bugs and a breeze in the high limbs. He tugged the radio from his survival vest. Turning down the volume, he clicked twice to announce himself.

"Crown, Crown, this is Hallmark. Do you copy?"

The airborne rescue command post answered as soon as Bo lifted his thumb off the transmit button. "Hallmark, Crown. Good to hear you. State your situation."

"I'm on the ground, somewhere in the valley. No injuries. I'm in a jungle area maybe a mile and a half east of Sandy 3's location."

"Copy. Are you secure?"

"Don't know. I think I got down without being seen."

"Copy. We heard you had a pretty wild ride."

"What about my crew?"

"Hallmark, choppers are inbound to pick them up."

"All of them?"

"Roger."

They made it over the ridge, out of the valley. Bo sensed something sharp plucked out of him, a grief for Lee and the rest that he was ready to bear and now didn't have to. He could focus on what he had to do.

"Hallmark, stay in place. As soon as Jolly's crew is picked up, we'll send rescue your way. Do you have smoke?"

"I do. But negative on the rescue."

"Say again?"

"Crown, I said no rescue. I want you to guide me to Dash 2."

CHAPTER 39

Loi drove the truck carrying the bodies, the wounded, and the soldiers back to camp. On the bench between him and Minh lay their two AK rifles, an escalation from the little pistol that had ridden there before. Loi's rifle had killed the American pilot; Minh's had shot down the helicopter. The two guns rode quietly, with weight and gravity, like heroes.

At the camp, the dead were unloaded, the wounded fighter was carted off to the headquarters bunker for care. Minh wondered about Thi with her doctor at binh tram 16. Was she safe? And her girls Yen and Nhu, did they think Minh was dead? Shouldn't she go find them? If she left the camp and the valley to do this, would she find Loi again before he left? Minh had to choose and, like Thi, she chose without hesitation to stay.

Loi stood over the two bodies. He muttered a silent prayer before motioning for them to be taken away. They'd be buried in plain wood boxes in unmarked graves near the camp. Their names, home province, and birth and death dates would be written on scrolls, stored in penicillin bottles, and buried with them. A record was kept of all gravesites. Families could come for them after the war.

Loi sent ten men to the helicopter crash site. They were to salvage what they could from the wreckage: weapons, ammunition, medical supplies, electric wiring, radios, flares, glass. Minh stood aside while Loi discharged his duties, but he seemed to be running out of them. The late sky stayed empty, the Americans had been turned back by the arrival of dusk. The camp clattered with preparations for the night. Firewood was stacked, fighters straggled in. Loi stood on the outskirts of the activity, near his own tent, with no orders to issue or skirmish to rush off to. Minh approached.

"Go in your tent," she said. "Take off your clothes."

Loi seemed abashed. She enjoyed his reaction.

"I'm going to wash them."

Loi folded his arms, not finding the humor. "I don't like being made fun of."

"Perhaps it hasn't happened enough. If I wash them now, they'll dry faster. And I'll bring you a basin of water. You smell like dirt."

He held his ground, but she shooed him into the tent. His good nature restored itself before he entered, telling her to stay outside. He'd hand out his clothes. She pretended to peek when he poked them through the slit in the tent.

She fetched water in a steel basin, leaving it outside and calling him to grab it naked, as her revenge, then walked off to wash his clothes at the camp cistern. While she scrubbed his white shirt and green khaki pants and socks, she sang to herself.

At the tent, Minh draped his clothes over branches. The waning day remained warm, they'd dry before dark. Without tapping on the tent or announcing herself, she entered.

The light through the canvas cast Loi in amber. He lay on the cot, facedown and asleep. The warmth in the tent vented too slowly, it hovered at her shoulders. She bent to her knees under it. Loi was clean; the water in the basin revealed the grime he'd washed away. His back and buttocks, calves and the bottoms of his feet drew her to him, but she held back.

"Loi."

She said his name twice more before he roused. Loi didn't roll over on the cot but stayed on his front when he lifted his head.

Kneeling, she said, "You were tired."

He lowered his head to his arms as though to go back to sleep. Minh had little time she could spend with him away from his obligations as cadre. She wanted this space where he was naked, and she felt she held some power to make him answer.

"You prayed over the bodies."

He spoke through the ring of his arms, into the thin mattress. "Yes."

"Did you pray like a priest?"

"Yes."

"What is that like?"

Loi didn't answer until he'd lifted his face out of his arms, raised his torso onto his elbows on the cot. He shook his head for a better question. She tried again.

"How do you find a place for God in the middle of a war? You stood over dead men and prayed. For what? For the war to be over? To kill more Americans? What?"

"For their souls. That's all."

Not for victory, not the revolution. Loi asked God for none of the things she sang about. Not the grand deaths of men, but their souls.

"Why did you stop being a priest?"

Loi rolled off his chest to sit up and put his feet on the bare floor, hands on his knees. He seemed not the young, bashful man now but older, perhaps a priest—she didn't know.

"I didn't lose God. I lost the church."

"What does God do for you?"

"Why do you want to know?"

"I want to know you. Everything."

"Why?"

"I've watched you. How you lead. How they follow. I can do more for the war than sing and dance. I can help you. You, Loi. I can fight through you. I want you to let me."

He ran a hand through his black hair. "When you begged, in Hanoi. What did you ask for?"

"Money."

"And with that, you bought food and clothes."

"Yes."

"That's what God does for me. I beg Him and He feeds me. Clothes me. He doesn't fight my battles or save my life. But my soul is never hungry." Loi glanced down at himself on the cot. "I am, however, naked."

His smile brought her to her feet into the heat of the tent.

"Tell me I can stay with you."

"You can stay with me."

In two long strides Minh stood between his spread brown knees. Laying both hands behind his head, she cradled his cheek into the black tunic over her belly. Loi didn't hold her in return but only received her embrace, a needful pose.

She let him loose, to look straight down on him. "Sleep."

"Where are you going?"

"To get you food, of course."

CHAPTER 40

Through the trees and brush, the first campfires of the evening began to burn. They glowed widely over the valley floor and dotted the hillside with flames and twirling sparks. Clanging pots and pans and the aromas of cooking drove Sol into his vest for three more Charms candies and the last swallows of water in one of his plastic bottles. He hadn't eaten more than this in a day and a half.

The pinpoints of early stars twinkled between the leaves. Sol had flown a thousand night missions with his nuke, and all of them together did not feel so lonely as this mounting darkness under the ferns, smelling his enemy's food. The pig must have caught a whiff, too, thinking he was next, because he started to go crazy. He squalled and ran circles in his pit. Hours ago the ache in Sol's left shoulder had peaked; now it felt numb. With his left hand tucked in his vest, Sol scooted to look behind him at the hole, in case the pig was right and someone was coming their way. His shoulder pained him enough to squeeze his eyes shut; he clamped his mouth to stifle a cry. With his good arm, Sol propped himself up to keep from falling back.

When he opened his eyes, he found them hard to believe. Sol blinked to be certain that what he saw peering down into the pit thirty feet away, licking its lips, was a tiger.

The great beast was orange and white, so vibrant it defied the dying light. The black stripes made its muscles vivid. It must have weighed six hundred pounds and stretched ten feet long. The tiger leaned over the hole, snuffling, deciding to jump down or not. The pig put up its only defense, which was panic. The great cat made a low, chesty growl, baring a palisade of teeth. It seemed annoyed at the pig's incessant squeals, as if eating it held the extra benefit of shutting it up.

Carefully, Sol unholstered the .38, grinding his molars to stop even a squeak from the pain of movement. He had no confidence the pistol could stop the tiger if the thing took an interest in him instead. Shooting the beast would probably do nothing but give away Sol's position, or what was left of him.

The big cat seemed of a mind to have pork for dinner.

It crouched beside the hole, ears laid back, ready to pounce. The tiger, sleek and coiled, waited, weighing something; its snout scribed a small circle as it followed the squealing, spinning pig below. Sol wished the tiger to jump into the hole, to have it fed and get some quiet.

The tiger's focus seemed to waver. It blinked extravagant lashes as though alerted to something else. Slowly, silently, the cat lifted its massive head and golden eyes from the pit. Both ears pricked forward. It lifted its nose in the air; black nostrils widened in a fearsome way. The tiger rotated his broad, whiskered face to stare dolefully, almost frowning, at Sol.

It stood.

Sol couldn't stop himself from whispering, "Oh, shit," and knew the tiger heard him, just from how it laid a paw his way.

He needed both hands to steady the .38 but had only one, and it shook badly. Sol extended the pistol at arm's length above the ferns, hoping the jungle cat might understand what a gun was, even a small one, and go away.

The tiger padded a second short stride. It stopped to loll a length of pink tongue while gazing at Sol's little pistol and one good arm.

With surprising speed, the tiger whipped around, pivoting his haunches and long striped tail to Sol. It crouched just as a rifle cracked.

The bullet missed and ripped away through the brush. With a snarl, the tiger flattened lower to the earth.

Three gunners from a zeep crew rushed through the bushes, around trees, shouting and leveling their rifles. One fired again, missing. Were they protecting their pig or trying to kill the tiger? The big cat didn't linger to find out; it bounded away, vanished into the jungle in two leaps. The VC slowed to watch the marvel of it going, complaint in their voices, less stunned than Sol at the cat's power and swiftness. They retreated to their teepees. The pig continued its manic grunts and circles, still scared out of its wits.

This explained the mystery of why no one had come out of the tee-pees last night when Sol fell into the pit. The gunners must have figured the noises meant the tiger was visiting; none of them were willing to confront that beast in the pitch-dark, and Sol could not blame them.

He lay back under the ferns, exhausted and pained. He wasn't sure how many more times he could withstand these acute bouts of fear, as wearying as hunger and thirst. He let the first sheets of night slip over him, unable to find comfort from his aching shoulder or rest for his thoughts. Sol added a roaming tiger to the list of things that might kill him in this valley.

He dozed, waking with a fright. His breathing shook, his palms sweated, though nothing but the light had changed; the camp still smelled of food, the zeeps were quiet, the pig had run itself out. Sol sat up to listen for the tiger that might come back for him or the enemies who might stumble over him. He scanned for flashlights to the south, where they always came from. His pulse had sped while he slept. He tuned his ears high in the new night sky for the sound of bombs falling on the valley, and on him, because Seventh Air Force's deadline had been sundown.

Sol's nerves were fraying. He needed to move far away from the VC camp, but where to, and with his bad shoulder, how? He couldn't climb, and if he tripped he'd probably scream. He needed more sleep but didn't trust it, needed food and water but had too little. The misery in his arm was unrelenting. He needed hope, but that broke apart with every crashing plane. He was alone and scared, but a pilot couldn't say that.

Sol plucked the radio from his vest, for someone to talk to.

Turning on the power, he set his thumb over the push-to-talk. Before he could click twice to announce himself on the guard channel, the radio muttered. Sol hurried the speaker to his ear.

"Dash 2, Dash 2, this is Crown. Do you copy?"

Sol composed himself, to let all the hardship settle out of his voice before responding.

"Crown, Dash 2 copies."

"Dash, where you been? I've been hailing for an hour."

Sol was in no state to be chastised by some sergeant at fifteen thousand feet with a coffee cup by his hand. "Saving my batteries. You got news?"

"Affirmative. A Jolly was shot down not far from you."

"I heard it."

"The crew bailed. They made it out over the hills. They got picked up before dark."

"Good for them."

"Except one. The PJ."

Another death on Sol's hands. He questioned how much more toll he could stand. Maybe Crown ought to let this kind of news wait. "Sorry to hear that."

"Negative, Dash. The kid's fine. He's on the ground. In the valley. He's looking for you."

The PJ wasn't dead? Sol felt lightened by that, if only a small bit.
"Dash 2."

"Go."

"We don't have your exact location. Can you give me a landmark, terrain, anything to home him in?"

"Negative. Tell the PJ to sit still. There's too many VC around me. He won't make it. Tell him to find a hole and get in it. Get him out of this valley in the morning."

"No can do, Dash. He's already turned down that offer. He's coming your way. Now give me something."

The PJ was going to walk right into the teeth of the VC camp, at night. "Crown, can he do it? How's he going to find me?"

"I spoke with the commander of his Jolly. Says this isn't the toughest thing the kid's done today. Besides, he's like twenty-one. And he's a PJ. He doesn't know he can't do shit."

"Copy."

"The PJ thinks the VC don't know he's on the ground. He's got that going for him."

"Where is he?"

"A mile and half southwest of your chute. On your side of the river."

"All right. Have him head west, stay on the valley floor. He'll cross the Trail, then go north. If he gets close to the hills, keep them on his left. At some point he'll see campfires, a lot of them. Head for the fires, keep them on his right."

Crown repeated the instructions, then said, "Copy."

"Tell him to keep it slow. I'm not going anywhere. Have him hail me every half hour after he sees the campfires."

The PJ had the same low-powered survival radio as Sol; both had limited range when talking to each other, especially through the dense jungle. He'd have to be close before Sol would hear him calling. Sol would try to guide him in. But how? He let that worry go—he'd figure it out if and when the PJ made it this far.

"What's his call sign?"

"Hallmark."

"Copy. Crown?"

"Go."

"What about Seventh Air Force?"

"You got another twenty-four hours. That chopper getting shot down might've saved your ass."

"They were going to bomb me?"

"Take it up with the brass, Dash. I just work here."

Crown's words felt like the breaking of some pact between Sol and the military, the promise that they would do everything possible to bring home their own. Of all classes, warriors hold promises most sacred.

"Crown, you coming back for me?"

"At sunrise. Big-time. Now there's two of you on the ground, the word came down."

"What word?"

"At all costs. Hang in there, Dash."

"Dash 2 out."

CHAPTER 41

Bo didn't know much about the woods. He hadn't grown up around them. Every square foot of black dirt within a hundred miles of his family's farm had been put under the plow a century before he was born. What they had in Kansas was sky.

In the stretches where the trees were few and far between, the underbrush grew dense and barbed, and the grasses rose taller than his head. Here the going was tough. Punching through was slow work. But he had starlight to reveal the terrain and obstacles, and he could maintain his direction west. Bo moved steadily and slowly, confident he was going undetected in the thickets because anyone in there with him was making the same noises, edging through the same leaves and switches.

When his path led him under the tallest trees where the triple canopy was solid, the stars became blocked and the darkness near absolute. Bo bumped into tree trunks and scraped his face on twigs he couldn't see. Without the constellations, he got turned around and had to check his compass with his penlight several times. If the VC were lying in wait for him, that was a risky thing.

In both terrains, he moved with hands on his M-16 to keep it ready, and to keep it from rattling on his back or against his chest. This prevented him from feeling his way through the jungle's many faces, frustrating him, hampering him. Bo sweated profusely; the jungle air was so thick with humidity it seemed he was walking through the lungs of the earth. Without stopping, he pressed on for two hours, a mile. Every step, a thousand of them, was taken on high alert, winding him tighter. His eyes were often useless and his hands were full. Bo didn't know where he was or who was looking for him, only what he needed to do.

Without expecting it, he stepped out of the forest into a small clearing without brush or tress. The clear sky twinkled, and under it Bo felt the first cooling breeze of the evening. He trod toward the middle of the open ground, down a short slope. The clearing was round. Bo bent to grab a fistful of grass but his fingers dug into crumbling powder. He was in a bomb crater.

He sat on the slope in the starry ashes, looking at a sky not too foreign from Kansas. He rested the rifle across his lap, out of his grasp for the first time in hours, and felt the tiredness of his hands. After a sip of water, Bo left the jungle night alone for a few minutes, enough to clear his head, ease his nerves. He listened to his own breathing instead of the jungle's, pulled off his soft cap to let some sweat evaporate. He thought of known things to brighten the dark unknown. His taciturn mother would enjoy sitting here quietly with him; she'd be stoic about the heat. His brother slipped out of sight into the cornfield, playing hide-and-go-seek. Bo swallowed the accustomed pang of his disappearance. Lee had survived the valley, the punch from his father, and the scar. Bo's own father had never struck him. The Big Dipper showed the way to the North Star, which pointed Bo through more jungle to Dash 2.

The bomb crater indicated he was headed in the right direction. Something had been targeted here, enemy guns or troops. They might still be close, but the clearing was walled in by trees, and Bo sensed he was still unseen. He put on his hat, walked through the dead bottom of the crater, and returned to the trees.

Bo stumbled out of the jungle. The almost impassable bush simply stopped in the tarry dark and he stepped right out of it.

He took one stride onto a flat dirt lane. The sky remained hidden. A hundred feet to his left and again to his right, the small lights of candles clustered, like the windows of farmhouses across a black prairie. Much closer to Bo, almost invisible, wheels squeaked and rubbed along the ground, along with the flops of sandals. The many murky figures were little more than shapeless, moving bits of the night.

This was the Ho Chi Minh Trail. What else could it be, this nocturnal highway, crowded and rolling? The bloodstream of North Vietnam's war in the south. Crown had said he would come to it, but not so suddenly.

Whatever number were walking the Trail right in front of him, no one and nothing reacted to Bo standing there. They followed the lanterns far ahead through the dark. Bo was as blind to them as they were to him. If he stood still, they would pass by. But another flight of floating lanterns headed his way; they would surely see him.

He let his rifle hang by the strap, to extend his hands and feel his way across the Trail.

Bo strode, and once he started had to continue; stopping in the middle of the path would create a collision. He waved his arms in small arcs in front of him, and in his third step brushed a shoulder, bony and short. Bo bit his lip not to say "Excuse me." A woman's voice uttered something gentle and tired, then the shoulder slid from his fingers.

He bumped into no more travelers but felt the presence of a hundred trudging south. Bo reached the other side, the wall of jungle there, but paused before stepping into it; he turned to remember this flow of people and metal by foot, cart, bicycles, all by night and candles. These folks were poor and their war was clearly desperate. They were slight, by the feel of the shoulder Bo had touched. These were men, likely old, and women, and from the sounds of their feet, dog-tired. Bo's enemies were common folk.

Slowly, he slogged a long way from the Trail, until he could no longer see the lights. He entered a passage where the underbrush thinned, the trees lengthened, and their trunks fattened. He walked over level ground, with views of the stars in patches. This was easily the best terrain he'd encountered and must be the heart of the valley floor between the hills. Stopping, sitting cross-legged, Bo dug out his compass and penlight to orient himself north. He turned the small light on for only an instant.

A gunshot rang out of the south.

He flung himself flat to the soft ground, shoving the compass and light in his vest. Facing the direction of the report, Bo put his M-16 in prone firing position, cheek to the stock, and glared deep into the darkness, vague and long.

Two hundred yards off, six flashlights swept the ground left and right and into the trees. Bo cussed himself for not checking his surroundings before he sat and turned on his light. He'd gotten too focused on reaching Dash 2, believing the VC didn't even know to look for him.

He'd just blown that with a one-second glance at his compass.

The flashlight beams began to joggle, all turned his way. Their holders came at him.

Bo jumped to his feet. He turned north, with no choice but to take fast and incautious strides. In seconds he smacked straight into a tree, scraping his knuckles. He forged ahead, away from the lights.

Another tree stood in his way, followed by a hedge that snagged his uniform and made a ruckus when he shoved through. His blindness was worsened by constant glances backward to see how fast the VC were gaining on him.

Bo had no hiding place. He wasn't going to find one in this darkness and at this pace. He was making too much noise. What if he happened on some VC troops ahead? They'd hear him coming a long way off.

He moved thirty seconds ahead of the flashlights but that gap was closing by the step. He collided with another tree, knocking his elbow hard. He wasn't outpacing his pursuers, and he was moving too quickly, too carelessly, too concerned with what was behind him.

Bo stopped. He faced the advancing lights. Fear told him to keep moving. He needed to think his situation through.

The enemy had flashlights, he did not. They could dodge trees and bushes and hustle behind him. They knew where they were going, he didn't. Bo could keep on rushing through the jungle and night colliding with trees. With the amount of noise he was making, it wasn't going to take long until the enemy troops zeroed in on him stumbling ahead of them. Or he was going to stride right up on another patrol in the dark. One or the other was a sure thing.

Or he could make them put out those flashlights.

Bo wasn't afraid when he knelt and brought up the M-16. There was a certain gravity to this, an inevitability, the only move he could make. He'd faced death already today and earlier this week. He'd faced the possibility of his brother's, too. Facing it here wasn't the first time.

He braced one elbow on his knee, tracking the flashlights as they coursed in and out of the trees. Bo waited until the VC came within seventy yards. They couldn't know he was there in the dark, an American with an M-16 trained on them, or they wouldn't be advancing all lit up behind six flashlights.

Bo kept both eyes open down the barrel, unable to see his own gunsight. He didn't need to kill to make his point, but he had to aim close. The VC needed to hear the rounds zip past. Bo wouldn't know if he was lethal, and he couldn't care.

He fired once; his muzzle suppressor flashed the jungle bluish-white. The flashlight he'd targeted swung wildly sideways as if alarmed. Bo took quick aim at the next flashlight and squeezed the trigger. This light fell.

Two beams shifted to the ground, aimed at the downed VC. Then all went out except for one, which charged across the dark valley floor.

Bo took aim. The beam dodged in and out between trees, appearing and disappearing, closing in. Before Bo could draw a bead, the light extinguished.

He turned and began moving, needing to regain his advantage of distance. In seconds, Bo walked straight into another tree, banging his forehead. Glancing back, the oncoming light flicked on again, then off, too quick for Bo to dissuade the VC with another round.

This one was going to chase and not give up a clear shot.

Bo stopped in standing firing position. He scanned the blackness down the barrel.

The jungle was starless, the lone VC had dissolved among the trees and shapeless gloom. Bo could fire again, warn off his enemy, but he'd hit nothing and he might give himself away.

To the cautious sounds of leaves underfoot and snapping sticks, the VC kept coming. Nothing but heat loomed between them.

The sounds of the VC's approach stopped.

"Hey, Captain."

The call out of the black, in English, came from maybe thirty yards away.

"What you doing here, man?"

The voice moved soundlessly from right to left, circling. Bo followed with his M-16. He could fire a sweep across the words, then turn tail and run.

"Don't shoot nobody else, man."

The voice was high and thin, singsongy. It moved without haste. Bo kept it in front of his gun.

"You don't want to die, do you, GI Joe?"

Bo answered. "Do you?"

Another crackling step. Bo tracked it, not sure. He took three steps to his right, to change the place he was in the dark.

"No, man. I don't."

"Where'd you learn your English?"

"Movies. 'We don't need no badges.'"

Bo grunted, with his cheek against the stock.

"What else?" Bo sidestepped again.

"'There's no place like home.'"

"No, there's not."

The voice glided more to Bo's left, patient, the movements of a man who made little mark on the jungle. The VC's words sounded like a pal's.

"I got a favorite. Want to hear it?"

"Sure."

"'There are two kinds of people. Those with loaded guns and those who dig. You dig.'"

Bo kneeled. He flicked the switch near his thumb to put the M-16 on automatic.

Raising the barrel just enough, he fired a burst of ten rounds. His muzzle burned blue. In the lightning-fast flickers, he couldn't spot the VC. Crouched, Bo crept backward, gun up. He wasn't a digger yet.

The VC spoke from the place he'd been last. "Don't want no gunfight with you, man."

Bo kept retreating, hoping he'd not back into a tree.

The VC said no more. The flashlights all stayed off.

If the VC was following, he did it silently. In a minute, he let Bo know he wasn't going to trail him. He called through the dark in a voice that had faded far back.

"'Here's another fine mess you've gotten me into.'"

When Bo had walked enough, sure he was alone, he turned on the penlight and checked his compass, to keep heading north.

CHAPTER 42

Inside the tent, Minh stayed low beneath the hovering heat. Loi slept naked on the cot, always facedown. She curbed her urge to touch him, though he was lovely. She'd fed him and cleaned up after him; his clothes had dried, and she'd left them folded beside the narrow bed.

His breathing was even. Minh stretched out on the dirt floor to sleep, but she couldn't stop listening to his breaths so she sat up to watch him by candlelight.

She envisioned that this was what it would be like. Would there ever be a bed wide enough for two? Would she have her own cot, and would it be close to his or over here away from him? Feeding him, tending him, watching and wanting him, but keeping distance not to disturb him. These were the costs of belonging to Loi. Small things.

She blew out the candle to ease the stagnancy inside the tent, then went outside to sit in the open, cross-legged in front of the flap. The camp radiated with the scarlet of fires built under tarps. A hundred men walked everywhere among the trees, some with flashlights aimed downward. Another hundred milled around the fires and another hundred served them. A hundred fighters were in the hills with the artillery tonight, more fanned out through the valley floor and along the river to herd the American pilot, keeping him in the valley and under the guns. A thousand were in other camps by other fires she could not see through the jungle.

Sitting outside the tent, Minh made it plain where she belonged. Had Loi been disliked by his men, she could not do this; they might begrudge him having her. Minh had seen how the fighters admired Loi, the way he led from among them. She had no fears of their jealousy. She worried only about the revolution. They were all comrades, equals fighting to unify their land; the men might ask why Loi should have a woman, why more than they? If someone brought this up against her, Minh would have no answer. But the revolution was fought in books more than in the jungle; no one had mentioned it yet, and if she conducted herself the right way, quietly and resolutely, no one might.

They might look down on her, too. That would be a help, for them to view her as a possession, too small a thing to quibble over. Other officers, other cadres, the ones Loi would listen to, must see Loi as deserving, and Minh as a trifle. Maybe they would desire their own trifles, that would be best. The revolution would survive that.

What no one could know and Minh could not tell was that being owned was the price she paid for possessing Loi. In her short life she'd had nothing, truly nothing. In Hanoi the clothing, food, and coins were never hers. They'd been given but were never kept; everything she touched was gone so fast, as if it had never been in her hands at all. On the Road, in the war as a singer and actor, none of the words and tunes were hers, always someone else's, and they went through her like food, keeping her going but nothing else; she had no title to them, no home for them. Loi was to be hers more than she could ever belong to him because he was all she had.

She sat beside the tent with thirst and hunger of her own, ascetic and rooted. After an hour, still able to hear Loi's breathing through the canvas, she watched a little man in sandals—a rifle jingling on him—pull a cart up out of the darkness. He halted beside the tent, and the aromas of meat and greens stopped with him. From his wagon he plucked a tin meal box and put it warm in Minh's hands, then trundled on. She ate the stew with her fingers, saving none for Loi because this had not been given to him.

The hours ticked past and the camp did not quiet. Again, vehicles powered in and out hauling ammunition to the large guns on the perimeter and picking up fighters to transport them around the valley. Another battle with the Americans loomed for dawn.

Loi stirred inside the tent but only enough to creak the cot's wooden frame; he rolled over and stayed asleep. Minh remained cross-legged where she could hear him, just outside the canvas from his open, sleeping mouth. She credited herself with his long rest, he slumbered like someone cared for and safe, like she believed such sleep to be.

The camp's glow faded in the jungle beyond Loi's tent. She rose to stretch the kinks in her legs. She was bored and not a bit drowsy, despite the rhythms of Loi's breathing. She thought of Nhu and Yen, how might she say good-bye to them? How might she help them? Minh puffed at the thought that she was in a position to protect them. She would speak to Loi when the time was right, before they left the valley.

Minh wandered away from the tent, not far into the tangle of trees and bush in the last light of the camp's fires. She yearned to see stars, but the trees locked them out. Two more trucks rumbled into the camp, stopping near Loi's tent. She was not there to shoo them away. Should she be near if he awoke? What did he want and expect from her? How much of him was the young priest and how much the warrior, and how to serve both? How different were they, and if they struggled inside him, who would win? Minh considered jumping on the trucks to ride out into the valley, help the drivers hand out ammunition, perhaps sing for the gunners in the hills. That would bring credit to Loi as well as ease her boredom. Quickly she shrugged off this way of thinking. This was another, perhaps the biggest, cost of belonging: she must learn to be admired by only one, rely on and receive everything from one. That was something to get used to.

Minh pushed a little deeper into the woods, into the night where she needed her hands as much as her eyes to walk. She fended off trees and thorns before she walked into them. Men were out here moving, too, kicking through the foliage, talking and pissing, carrying supplies and food to the farthest rims of the camp. All acted oblivious, though several saw her. This was how her acceptance was to be expressed; Loi's men were going to ignore her.

The American pilot was out here somewhere, close. Loi had said he'd been chased and steered under the umbrella of his guns. What would happen if she stumbled onto him? Would the American try to kill her? Would he run, would others come to her defense, should she scream? Minh tried out scenarios in the dark as she walked, liking everything. This was far more exciting than plays.

She'd gone far enough. The ground began to disappear in shadow. A young man surprised her coming up from behind. He stopped ten strides back, a wooden crate propped on his shoulder.

"Hello," she said.

"Hello. Who are you?"

A fascinating question. The first time in her life Minh had to make choices to answer it.

"I'm with the division." She'd forgotten which division it was; she thought of it only as Loi's. It struck Minh as marvelous in that moment that Loi had those two things, a thousand men and her, and that they might somehow be comparable.

The young fighter nodded, little to say. He walked past her, bearing his box. She followed just to see where he was going out here in the woods. He led her to a round tent, a pale cone tied by strings around an artillery piece. The material seemed to be the same as the American parachute she'd coveted. Before disappearing, the boy told her to go back and be careful, there were holes dug out here as pens to keep animals in. Minh turned around; a small part of her was let down that the boy had said only this to her, alone and with the chance to try more.

She retraced her steps, returning to the red gleams of the camp. The comings and goings had ramped up while she'd been on her stroll. The two trucks had departed, replaced by four more that ambled like elephants among the trees and fires. Minh approached Loi's tent, where a light the color of rust bled through the canvas. With an ear to his breathing, she heard nothing. Minh eased back the flap. The narrow cot was empty, his clothes gone. A candle burned on the one table, where there were no papers, no note to Minh in his absence.

CHAPTER 43

Sol had done the right thing. He'd told Crown to instruct the unlucky PJ to lay low, get himself picked up, and get out of the valley. Sol hadn't meant a word of it; no man in his predicament could have. He wanted the rescuers to pay attention to him, not someone else. But it was what a pilot had to say.

After he cut off the radio in the dark, he sat sullen for a while. The notion that Seventh Air Force had extended the deadline because of the downed PJ rankled him. Crown said they were coming for him, at all costs. He could only wait to see how true that was.

A hundred yards east, the VC camp began to ring with preparations, like it had last night. Trucks and men rushed in and out, the zeep crews stacked fresh crates of ammo, and the campfires burned high, even under their tarps, to feed a regiment, as though the cooks weren't sure when they could do this next.

Sol was locked here; he couldn't move to another location a safe distance from the zeeps. Aside from being woozy with pain, sleeplessness, hunger, and dehydration, and the constant corrosion of fear, he had to stay in place because the PJ was coming. The glowing camp was the only landmark in the dark.

One black hour mounted on the last. Admiring the velvet darkness of the jungle, Sol ate the rest of his Charms candies and swallowed half the water in his last bottle. Hours ago he'd stopped sweating, a bad sign. He was near the end of his rope and wanted to resuscitate a little before the PJ came into play.

Easing his back to the soft ground, Sol lifted the radio to his ear. It was too soon for Hallmark to hail him, but he checked the guard freq anyway. The candy and water soothed his belly. His shoulder had gone numb. The camp and the teepees settled in for the long, hot wait for sunrise. The radio hissed. Sol, pressing it dearly to his head, heard nothing but a long shush. He closed his eyes to listen.

When he awoke the radio was dead.

He had no idea how long he'd been asleep, or how upset he ought to be with himself. It might have been nothing but a catnap; the jungle showed no signs of dawn. He was still hidden, only a little refreshed. No tiger was licking his face, the pig was quiet. The VC were bedded down. Last night he would have panicked awaking to a worn-out battery; he'd had the energy for it. Now Sol probed in the pockets of his vest, and without sitting up, without his eyes, changed the battery. He questioned his calm as exhaustion, but he was calm nonetheless.

Clicking the power switch, he snugged the radio again to his ear. Nothing but the sounds that had lulled him to sleep came from the speaker. He wanted to know the time but didn't want to risk the penlight to glance at his watch. One-handed, Sol pushed himself to a sitting position. He'd grown comfortable lying flat under the ferns, and that comfort he chalked up to being dog-tired and numb.

The campfires had all burned low, just simmering coals. The teepees stood barely visible. Sol clicked the radio's transmit button twice. He whispered.

"Crown. This is Dash 2."

The reply came immediately. "Copy, Dash. Where you been?"

The voice, even with the volume way down, came through with gratifying clarity. The battery was fresh and strong.

"Fell asleep. What time is it?"

"0020."

Past midnight. He'd been conked out for a few hours.

"Crown, any news on Hallmark?"

"He's still on the loose. Said he had a close call with the VC."

"Where is he?"

"Crossed the Trail two hours ago. He might be in range. He's hailed you twice."

"Copy. I'll listen out for him."

"Dash, how you hanging?"

"Ready to go home. You still coming?"

"Oh, yeah. Full bore."

"Copy. Out."

Hallmark's call made Sol cry.

He didn't answer the first hail, "Dash 2, Dash 2, Hallmark. You copy?" An unbidden tear warmed Sol's cheek, an unexpected knot welled in his throat. He thumbed away the tear, then struggled to sit up before whispering into the radio.

"Hallmark, Dash 2. Good to hear you."

"Yes, sir. You all right?"

"I could use a hand."

"On my way. Where are you, sir?"

"Where are you?"

Hallmark reported a dim visual of the VC camp. He'd walked for half an hour keeping the fading fires on his right and the hills to his left. In six hours the kid had covered the same distance that took Sol most of a day and night.

Sol needed a way for the PJ to find him. He'd not yet thought of a plan; he kicked himself again for falling asleep. He should have been alert and plotting.

The range for their survival radios was a quarter mile. The VC camp was visible, just barely at this hour. How to vector the PJ in? Were there more VC hunting parties? Were there more antiaircraft pieces hidden in the trees? More holes in the ground to pen other livestock? Sol had no idea. He imagined the PJ falling into another pit, on top of another damn pig.

The pig.

That screaming little son of a bitch.

"Hallmark."

"Dash, go."

"Hold on."

With his good hand, Sol rummaged through his vest for the box of .38 ammo.

"Hallmark."

"Go."

"Tell me if you hear a pig."

"A what?"

"A pig. You know what a pig sounds like."

"Yes, sir."

"I got a pig near me. It's in a hole. I'm going to make it squeal."

"Sir, won't the VC hear that? I mean if I can hear it, they can, too, right?"

"It's the middle of the night. They won't come out to check."

"Why not?"

"There's a tiger."

"A what?"

"Just tell me if you hear a pig. Ready?"

"Go, sir."

Sol sized up where the hole should be, ten yards away in the inky ground. He tossed the first round.

The pig didn't wake. The bullet landed in the slop.

Sol threw another, to no effect.

The ammo box held twenty-five rounds. He threw two at a time. The pig didn't stir. Was it sleeping, worn out, dead, or just hard to spook after Sol had fallen on him and a tiger had sized him up?

Sol tossed rounds until there were thirteen left in the box and six in his revolver.

"Hallmark."

"Go, Dash."

"Hold."

"I haven't heard anything."

"I said hold."

Sol rolled to his knees, his balance precarious. He knee-walked through the ferns, gritting his teeth.

Sliding inches at a time, Sol reached the edge of the pit. Again the hole expelled the stinks of pig and filth. He muttered, "Hey. Asshole."

Down in the dark, the pig grumbled, guttural, as annoyed as Sol.

Sol heaved a bullet straight down at the grunt.

The pig snorted, truculent and refusing to panic.

Sol wasn't going to spend any more ammo on him, not unless he shot the thing. The ground around him lacked stones. He dug out the dead battery to fling that down, and missed. The beast gave him nothing more than a snort and a whiff of methane.

Sol patted his survival vest for anything of weight. He'd buried much of the contents on the run yesterday, under the dead tree; he was down to essentials, nothing he could spare.

He spoke softly. "What's it gonna take?"

The zeep tents stood implacably dark, and the camp was tucked in for the night. Sol dug out for his penlight. Leaning as far into the hole as he could reach, he cut on the beam, just for a moment, to scare the pig.

He found the creature huddled against the wall on the far side of the pit. The beast was black and meaty with a Mohawk down the middle of his head and back. Both ebony pearl eyes glistened behind his raw pink snout. The pig gazed into the light without fear or stupidity.

Behind Sol, a voice whispered, "You might want to cut that off."

CHAPTER 44

Bo didn't know what else to do. He didn't want to scare the pilot, but the guy was shining a light.

He crept closer. Dash 2 lay on his chest, reaching a small flashlight down into a big pit, looking precarious on the ledge with one arm stashed in his vest. Any VC looking this way could see him doing this, and there were hundreds of VC around.

Bo crept the last few feet, close enough to tap Dash on the shoulder. He extended the hand but withdrew it, thinking that too startling and Dash might fall in since he wasn't bracing himself. Bo whispered instead.

"You might want to cut that off."

The pilot jerked so badly he looked like he really would tumble into the hole. Bo grabbed the collar of his vest to pull him upright. As he did, he snatched the penlight from Dash to cut it off.

The pilot sucked his teeth, hurting, as Bo hauled him away from the pit. Blinded in the remnant dark from the flashlight, he kept his hand on the pilot.

"Come on, sir, let's get under cover. Show me where."

Dash answered with a croak. "Over here."

Bo expected the pilot to stand, but the man stayed on his knees to scuttle. Bo linked his fingers inside his vest and walked beside Dash 2 into a knee-high stand of ferns. Ten strides in, Dash folded onto his back. Bo sat beside him, bending low to keep the ceiling of leaves over his head.

"How the hell," Dash panted, plainly sapped by the crawl, "did you find me?"

"I can smell a pig a long ways off." Gently, Bo patted the pilot's chest. "Though it might've been you, sir."

"I fell in."

"For real?"

"It's dark."

"Is that how you got injured?"

"Left shoulder. I think it's separated."

"Okay. What's your name, sir?"

"Rall. Major Rall."

"Airman Bolick." Bo tapped the pilot's chest again. "Good to meet you, Major."

"You, too. You gonna get us out of here?"

"That's the plan."

Bo leaned over more, over his crossed legs to put his face near the pilot's. He judged the distance by the man's breathing. Bo didn't whisper but spoke softly, to be definite. "I got morphine. You want it?"

"Fucking yes."

Bo lifted the strap of his M-16 off his shoulders to lay the gun beside him. By feel, he fiddled inside his med ruck, finding first a sling, then a pocket for one of the plastic-wrapped needles and prefilled morphine syringes.

Bo unzipped Dash's mud-crusted flight suit enough to run his hand inside, to feel the left shoulder. He probed gingerly, sensing the heat and swelling of the joint. Dash's breathing snagged. Bo traced the ball of the humerus sticking up under the skin, the orb protruding below the collarbone, clearly out of the socket.

Bo whispered, keeping his tone light. "You know that pig wasn't ever going to make a sound."

"He made plenty before, believe me."

"Pigs are smart. You were just bothering him tossing stuff at him. He'll squeal if he's scared."

Bo layered an open hand across the pilot's forehead. The skin felt dry and warm. He needed to get Dash hydrated.

From his calf, Bo slid out the long knife. He found the pilot's right hand, to put the handle in it.

"Next time, show him a big old knife like this. You'll get all the pig yelling you want." Using his teeth, Bo ripped open the morphine packet. "Good news. Your shoulder's not separated. It's an anterior dislocation."

"Why is that good?"

"Because I can do something about it."

"I assume that's the bad news."

"Yes, sir. When I tell you to, put that blade between your teeth. Bite down hard. You do everything you can to keep quiet. You understand?"

"You done this before?"

"On a dummy."

Bo rolled up Dash's left sleeve, uncapped the needle, and stuck the morphine into the muscle of his forearm. He tossed the kit away under the ferns, then sat with the pilot's arm cradled in his lap. Dash lay motionless. Bo rested his hand again on the pilot's forehead, not to feel for anything medical, just for the attachment, the beginning of the rescue.

"Where you from, Airman?" From the sound of Dash's voice, the man's eyes had closed.

"Kansas."

"You move through the jungle pretty well. How'd you figure that from Kansas?"

"My brother and I used to play in the corn."

"Younger brother?"

"No, sir. Older."

That might still be true. It might not.

Bo lifted his head above the ferns, checking the surroundings. The night was quiet, black as coal.

"What's this about a tiger?"

Dash breathed deeply through his nose, settling into the morphine. "Scared the shit out of me. And the pig."

"I reckon."

Dash chuckled, almost forgetting to whisper. "He's gone."

The pilot's left arm weighed not much. Bo patted it once in his lap, like something newborn. With his head still above the ferns, the heat made the back of his neck prickle. It used to be this hot inside the crops in August, this quiet, too. Bo never held his brother like this, who never needed to be held. The fact that his brother was lost made it easier to put him into others like Dash, to hold him now.

"How you hanging, Major?"

"Getting there. You got water?"

"Yes, sir. In a bit. When you can sit up."

Bo waited for the morphine to spread. Dash had been in this injured state for almost twenty-four hours. The tendons holding his shoulder in place were pretty well stretched; his pain was significant and obvious.

After five silent minutes, Bo slid his hand back inside the pilot's flight suit, to test the joint. When he pushed gently on the ball of the humerus, Dash went rigid. The pilot clenched his teeth and sucked air.

Bo dug back into his med ruck. He leaned his face close again. "Major."

"Yeah."

"Did that hurt as bad?"

"Take the knife from me before you do that again."

"Roger. I'm going to give you another ten mil of morphine."

"Okay."

"You got too much pain. But just so's you know, it's going to knock you out."

Dash rattled his head against the soft ground. "Then don't."

"It'll be okay."

"If the VC come back, I can't be unconscious. No."

"Sir."

"I can handle this. Go ahead."

"No, sir, you can't. Besides. I don't think the VC are looking for us tonight."

"What are you talking about?"

Slowly, to be sure Dash comprehended, Bo described his encounter with the Viet Cong hunting party a quarter mile from the camp. How the English speaker asked what Bo was doing there. How he let Bo go, so long as he went north.

"Sir, I believe they've known where you are the whole time."

Dash sank into the ground as this thought embedded itself. "No."

"Yes, sir. I'm sorry."

Dash swallowed hard, choking back the realization that he'd been the cheese in a North Vietnamese trap.

Quickly, quietly, Bo injected him with the second ten-mil syringe. Dash's breathing evened out. Bo lifted his head once more above the fronds to check their surroundings. The camp had vanished into the night. Nothing else presented itself, only a few warbling nightbirds and the chitter of some animal deep in the jungle.

One more time, Bo ran his hand up under the flight suit. He pushed gently on the warm, stretched skin above the humerus, then harder. The pilot seemed to wake.

"Hey."

"Major."

"Hey. I got a question."

"All right."

Dash licked his lips. When he spoke, he was mushmouthed. "Why Hallmark?"

"Sir?"

"Call sign. Hallmark."

Bo slid sideways toward Dash's head, keeping the man's bad arm in his lap. He planted his right boot in the pilot's underarm, his left heel in the crook of Dash's neck. The swelling in the busted shoulder gave some resistance as Bo rotated the joint; Dash bore this in silence. Bo leaned across the pilot's chest, feeling for the knife that Dash could not bring to his own lips. Gingerly, he worked the dull side of the blade between the pilot's teeth.

"Bite down."

Bo cupped the pilot's chin, to feel the jaw muscles clamp around the knife because he could not see them. With both hands, he gripped the pilot's left wrist.

"Hallmark." Bo extended the pilot's arm to a ten o'clock position. "When you want to send the very best."

Logy and deadened, Dash chuckled around the long knife.

Bo straightened his legs, and in that instant yanked as hard as he could.

The arm came a long way to him. He felt the humerus slide past the collarbone to click into the shoulder socket. Even shot up with morphine, Dash 2 went stiff under Bo's feet, his back arched off the ground. The growl around the blade was feral, muted by courage, and anyone who'd heard it would not guess it was human. While Dash gurgled saliva around the knife, Bo laid his arm beside him. He snatched away the knife, then clamped both hands over the pilot's mouth as if smothering him, and whispered shushes.

"It's okay, it's okay."

Dash shifted his breathing to his nostrils, moist above Bo's joined hands. When he nodded in the dirt, Bo let him loose.

"It's fine now, Major. You did it."

Before Dash drifted off on the morphine, Bo held up his head to pour most of a bottle of water into him. He let the pilot fade out. Once Dash lost consciousness, Bo slid the sling around his neck and arm.

He sat under the ferns in the abject dark. His hand on Dash's chest, Bo measured the pilot's slow breathing, naturally matching his own to it.

CHAPTER 45

Minh lay alone on the cot.

She slept in fits and starts, waking to every sound near the tent because each noise might have been his return. A cart rolled by, a voice, a rain shower; in the hours without light or Loi, she sought him by his scent on the pillow and sheet, then dozed without dreams.

When the cook fires started before dawn, she sat up. Minh put her bare feet on the warm dirt floor. The heat was embedded in everything.

She stood, already impatient with dusk. She pushed aside the flap to step into the morning. Around the sprawling camp and up on the hillsides where the big guns were, the first sparks trickled into the darkness. Though Loi wasn't beside her, he would be. The hours until that came around were going to be worrisome and hot.

Minh walked to a cook fire. She offered to help with breakfast for a squad of twenty-five fighters. The cook handed her a knife to chop vegetables for a stew, then a long wooden spoon to stir a cauldron of rice. Minh ate some rice before the troops arrived. She enjoyed the tools of the outdoor kitchen. The flames felt honest. She would do this kind of work wherever he took her. She'd say little and let it fall to others to tell him how lucky he was.

When the first fighters emerged from their tents and blanket rolls, Minh helped serve them. She dished out meatless stew with scoops of rice. She lowered her eyes while she served them, men who knew Loi better than she did.

Two women fighters in black pajamas with rifles across their backs appeared. They presented tin plates, their hands as big as the men's. Minh dished them food, they thanked her blandly. They were both gaunt and hollow-looking, older than Minh perhaps. They sauntered away together to eat, leaving her with the scoop held out offering more than they took.

She served others of the unit but kept watch on the two sitting in the firelight.

Minh dipped some stew for herself into a bowl. She went to join the women.

Approaching, she asked if she might sit. One pointed at the ground. "You're the singer."

"You've seen me?"

The woman nodded before returning to her breakfast.

Minh sat cross-legged. Pith helmets dangled from tethers down the women's backs, beside black ponytails. Around the big camp, the first trucks grumbled in and out. No daylight filtered through the branches above, but the morning had begun.

The women peered at Minh over their plates, held close to their mouths. They chewed and seemed to be waiting for Minh to speak first.

Their sandaled feet were no rougher than hers. Their pajamas were the same, black hair longer than hers. Their eyes were cold. Their gestures were compact and stony yet not manly, and somehow identical; they were two versions of the same thing. Minh wondered how she herself might change if she became a fighter.

She asked, "Do you hate me?"

Both women laughed like girls, behind their hands, prettily.

"What have you done?"

"Why should we hate you?"

Minh held out her bowl to divide the stew between their two plates. The women accepted with gray teeth. Minh said nothing more, as if she'd made a silly joke, and the two fighters, taking the offered food, ate stew they didn't want as her apology.

Minh had seen female fighters on the Road and in her audiences but had never addressed them. She wanted to ask the histories of these two with their features flickering. She asked instead their duties. What Loi had asked her.

"What will you do today?"

The women looked to each other to answer. One spit into her plate to clean it with a red bandanna while she spoke. "Hunt the American pilot."

"Will you catch him?"

"No."

The other licked a finger and used that to clean her plate. "When the planes come back, shoot at them."

Minh could describe diving from the ferry just before it blew up, or the bombed bunker that collapsed on her and Loi. The helicopter she might have shot down. Maybe she was already a fighter.

"I was told the American"—Minh raised a finger at the darkness beyond the camp—"is out there."

Both women looked to the valley floor at the foot of the hills.

"He is."

"How do you know?"

The woman who'd spit in her plate tucked it inside her tunic over her small breasts. "Another American was seen last night."

"Another one? Where?"

"A kilometer south of here."

"Where did he come from?"

"No one knows."

The other woman added, "He was headed this way."

Two American pilots were hiding in the jungle near the camp. Perhaps they had linked up. Was this the news that took Loi away in the middle of the night?

Minh asked, "Aren't we leaving the valley?"

The two women shook their heads at each other, then at Minh.

"There have been no orders for that."

No orders?

Loi had said the division would leave. There'd already been two days of squaring off against the Americans, a hundred explosions, and a million burning bullets everywhere. How much more? How terrible was today going to be? At the heart of it was Loi, driving madly from hill to hill, gun to gun, danger to danger in his white shirt.

What would make it stop? What would let Loi leave?

Leaving was their beginning. But he'd given no order for it.

Excusing herself from the women fighters, Minh returned to Loi's tent. As before, she sat outside it. His promise to take her with him had removed all other places for her but the one he might come back to.

CHAPTER 46

July 18

Sol floated between layers of exhaustion and morphine. He surfaced on one to find himself below the other. He let himself sleep.

At one point he became mindful of rain, a sprinkling on the fronds over his head. He thought to open his mouth to catch some of it; before the thought was complete he drifted away again. Another time his ears buzzed. He lay vaguely awake while his face and hands were smeared with something damp and his ears were stuffed with it. He tilted back into unconsciousness.

When Sol opened his eyes, he resolved not to close them again, and almost failed. What drew him to stay awake was a voice.

The sound was tinny, distant, and small. Was it a dream, or the buzzing again? The word *rescue* made him flutter his eyelids to stave off shutting them. Sol shifted his legs on the soft earth while his alertness dawned. He set his jaw against another electric pang from his shoulder but didn't get one. His left arm rested across his waist, bound and nestled.

"Hold on, Crown."

The whisper sounded close but was not his own. A hand pressed on Sol's chest, the dark orb of a face leaned to him.

"Morning, Major. Stay quiet."

Sol sucked a sharp breath, a sudden acceleration of awareness.

"We're good. Your arm's fine."

The kid, the PJ, what was his name? Hallmark.

"Help me up."

With trouble, Sol sat upright, staying under the ferns. When he blinked, his eyes felt crusty, his hands and neck, too. He was damp and smelled of earth. Mud. He'd been dabbed with it.

"What the hell?"

Hallmark spoke softly. "Skeeters. After the rain. They were sumbitches."

"Water."

The PJ handed over a full bottle. "I topped off mine and yours."

Sol took a few deep swallows then, one-handed, poured some to clean his face and clear his ears.

"How long was I out?"

"Three hours. Sunup's thirty minutes away. How you feeling?"

"A little groggy. Better. Thanks for letting me sleep."

"I had nothing to do with it. How's the shoulder?"

Gingerly, Sol tested the joint. His left hand worked without pain, and as long as he let the arm dangle in the sling, he felt nothing. A slight lift of the elbow reminded him of how much his shoulder could hurt.

"I'll make it."

"Roger."

Hallmark lifted his radio to continue conversing with Crown. The kid didn't ask more after Sol's condition or report to him what was going on with the rescue. This felt a little impersonal. Sol, who'd stayed asleep partly because he deserved it, thought the PJ owed him some company, at least some whispering conversation after all he'd been through. The significant differences in their ranks required a report.

Hallmark worked the radio, exchanging info with Crown, and largely ignored him. Sol couldn't make out Crown's low-volume responses and barely heard the PJ's mutters.

He poked his head above the ferns to check the VC camp. Through the jungle, the hillside and the valley floor flared with the day's first fires. No breeze blew any sound or smells from the camp his way. The early morning steamed from the downpour.

Sol finished the second half of the water, a luxurious feeling. He tossed the empty bottle between Hallmark's crossed legs. The PJ stopped murmuring into the radio. He cocked his head and extended one plaintive hand at the act, at Sol's disdain.

This was Sol's third day of being trapped on the ground in Laos, surrounded by enemies for every minute, scared, wounded, and alone for most of it. He'd stayed alive, evaded, hiding in the damned heart of a VC division. What was it Hallmark had said about the VC using Sol for a decoy? Bullshit. He'd faced tracers, guns, bombs, a tiger, a pit, and a pig, a busted shoulder, flashlights, rifles, and calls for "Captain." He'd run as far as he could and was going to run more today in a sling. He'd done his part. Why shouldn't he be demanding that others do theirs, why shouldn't he be a little selfish?

The answer came when the young PJ dug into his own pack for another bottle of water. Hallmark handed this through the ebbing dark to Sol.

CHAPTER 47

The pilot took the water bottle. He didn't open it, just set it beside him. It seemed more important that he have the bottle than to drink the water. He'd woken up testy.

Bo returned his attention to the radio and Crown.

The rescue mission was ready to shift into high gear at first light. A Nail flight would be on station early, reporting on weather. As the VC guns came out to play, the FAC would smoke them for the opening flights of fast movers. According to Crown, Seventh Air Force had re-upped the word: get the pilot and the PJ out of the valley "to-fucking-day." Today's assault on the VC guns was do or die. That translated to a lot of firepower headed to the valley: forty jets, eight Sandys, and four Jollys. The Thuds and F-4s would be carrying CBUs, cluster bombs that opened like a clamshell in midair to release six hundred tennis ball–size bombs that exploded on impact, firing shrapnel and thousands of shotgun pellets in every direction. CBUs were nasty, indiscriminate, and the best weapon to neutralize ground troops.

"Hallmark."

"Go."

"How's Dash 2? Can he move?"

In the blackness, sitting beside Bo, the pilot was little more than a cut-out shape. Bo lifted his head above the ferns. On the other side of the triple-layered canopy of trees, the sky showed the first pale hints of sunrise, though little light made it through the leaves; on the jungle floor, it remained night. A couple hundred yards off, the camp glowed, open for business. Dash 2 sat upright, quiet, one-armed, and a little unpleasant.

"He's good."

"Copy. You'll need to move away from the VC camp. Too many big guns there. Can you make it half a kilometer north? There's some high ground."

"Copy."

"Nail is inbound now."

Bo kept his head above the ferns, pivoting and scanning alongside Dash. An odd pair of structures loomed out of the dark, only thirty yards away. Bo hadn't noticed them last night. He whispered to Dash, "What are those?"

"Zeeps. They're covered with parachutes. Sleeping quarters for the crews."

As Dash said this, a yawn drifted out of the dark from the hidden guns, followed by the crackling of someone walking through the brush.

Bo muttered to Crown, "We can't move until the attack starts. Copy?"

"Copy. Understand, Hallmark, to be clear: the Jollys are going to want you somewhere else. I'll be up this channel. Good luck."

"Hallmark out."

Bo stowed the radio and lowered himself below the fronds. He lay on his left side, head propped on his arm. Dash did the same, arranging himself on his good right side. To keep their voices down, they lay close, stretched out like they were sharing a towel.

Dash said nothing. Just enough light dripped into the jungle to see the pilot's eyes reflect. He was looking at Bo, wanting or expecting something. The water bottle lay unopened between them.

Lee had needled Bo for wanting the pilots he rescued to be good men. Appreciative and brave men. The truth was that by the time a PJ got to them, the downed fliers were at the end of their ropes. They'd been shot out of the sky and were on the ground, out of their element; they were sometimes hurt, maybe dying, always afraid—no matter what they said on the radio. Bo's job was to be stronger, calmer, braver if called for. He didn't need to be the pilots' friend, only their rescuer. He didn't need to admire them, just save them. They'd be bound to each other for life anyway, buddies or not. Bo should need nothing back from them, for they might not have it to give. He would let Dash 2 stare at him in the rising light, wanting something. Dash could have it, if Bo had it to give.

He whispered, "We'll get you out of here soon, sir."

Another VC fighter left the gun tents, calling to a comrade. In the rising daylight, Bo and Dash lay low beneath the ferns, facing each other. For the first time, Dash's features began to emerge. The pilot was gray at the temples, crow's-feet beside his eyes from squinting above the clouds. Dash 2 was maybe ten years older than Bo, no rank or insignia on his flight suit. The pilot was lean and brown-eyed, haggard from his trial. Nothing about him was exceptional.

With dawn came the first high-pitched mumbles of Nail's O-2 Skymaster. The FAC flew far off but seemed to be threading through the valley, headed this way.

Dash whispered, "Sorry."

The camp began to scurry. More voices emerged from the zeeps. Bo poked his head up for a quick look; the gun crews pulled down their parachute tarps. Ten strides past the ferns lay the pit and the black pig.

"Sorry for what, sir?"

Dash didn't explain. Instead, with Nail's engines swelling in the distance, he asked, "What's that like?" With his good hand, the pilot touched the patch on Bo's sleeve, a white-winged angel enfolding a blue world. Beneath the globe ran the pararescueman's creed, That Others May Live.

It seemed out of place to start a conversation now, with Nail winging closer, the rescue mission starting. Dash wanted something before the bombs and guns cranked up. He'd been through the wringer and needed what? Assurance, inspiration, faith, some stamina? Bo hadn't been a PJ long enough to know what a frightened man's heart reached for.

He lay a hand on the pilot's good right arm and squeezed. Across that human bridge, Bo tried to express that throughout this dangerous day, to the end of the rescue, and for the rest of their lives, Dash 2 would not be alone.

The pilot nodded. Whatever Dash sought, Bo hoped he'd found it in time. The first antiaircraft guns boomed over the valley.

CHAPTER 48

The Americans came at first light, as Loi had said they would. While fighters spread out from the camp and the cooks killed their fires, Minh sat outside Loi's tent.

One plane buzzed over the valley. The engine drone was small and slow, the spotter plane, the American eyes that came before their knuckles.

In the hills east of the river, a few big guns took first crack at the spotter. They fired only potshots.

As the plane thrummed and the valley popped, morning light took hold above the treetops, then gradually beneath them. The camp scurried with comings and goings, trucks and shouts; tents emptied, men in black pajamas and regular uniforms jogged into the woods. Alone, the American plane swooped over the valley marking targets, drawing more fire. It made a pass straight over the camp, skimming the limbs and leaves. Minh raised her face to the sound as if it were sunshine or rain. After the plane was behind her and fading, the jet bombers returned to the valley.

Both women fighters ran past Minh, waving. They dodged into the woods, bounding north to hold the American pilots in place. With the full battle about to begin, Minh considered running somewhere, too. Was there some work she should find, or shelter? She felt conspicuous sitting with so much action and noise around her, the brawl growing on every side of her and in the brightening sky. What could she do, where could she add herself? She was untrained to fight, just as she was unsure to love. She couldn't sit much longer, but she would have nowhere to go if she stood. She chose for now to hold her place beside Loi's tent, for he was both duty and shelter for her.

Barrages from the larger guns began to swell with the light, shaking the valley. They erupted from both sides of the river. Loi's artillery pulsed, throwing up their curtains of steel. Over the southern part of the valley, the morning's first jet drilled through the shells to drop its bombs, battering the cannons in return. The plane strained to get away; the guns trailed, firing furiously to drag it back and kill it. Blasts from the artillery and bombs alike shimmied the canvas of Loi's tent.

The American assault focused against the hills more than the valley floor. Loi had tucked his guns at the base of tall stone faces, snugged them in the smallest openings on the slopes, and scattered them in the forest along the river bends. Over the past two days, Minh had ridden in Loi's truck to each. For the Americans to quiet them all would take an immense effort. Some of the cannons, like the pair in the trees on the outskirts of the camp, hadn't even spoken this morning.

Though the battle raged elsewhere, the whole valley clanged with each raid from the sky. Minh no longer heard the little spotter plane darting around; the bombs and hammering artillery masked it. The fight wore into its third day. It seemed out of all proportion over two American pilots.

A truck jolted into the camp, barely avoiding several tree trunks that would have wrecked it. Minh shot to her feet. The vehicle stopped shy of the tent, but she ran to it. Her dread mounted with every stride.

Holes speckled the driver's side door. The canvas over the bed had been perforated, one rear tire flapped, badly flat. Minh tore open the cab door. Her hands flew to her mouth to throttle a cry; Loi sat high behind the wheel, blood on his white shirt and hands.

Minh reached up to catch him should he fall. He fought for his balance climbing down. Blood smeared the seat as he slid off it. He wobbled in her arms. Loi tried to walk. She wouldn't allow it; his left pant leg glistened at the thigh, his left arm was scarlet to the wrist. She forced him to sit against the front tire.

The wounds of the truck told Minh what had happened. An explosion had gone off too close. Loi had driven into a storm of shrapnel.

She lifted his chin, raising his eyes to hers. "You came back to me."

Loi licked his lips. He seemed to be choosing his words, like a boy in trouble. "A bomb."

"I know." Minh unbuttoned his white shirt, with no knife to cut it off him. "I know."

She stripped him to the waist, working fast, not knowing how much blood he'd lost. Loi was disoriented, wanting to talk but scrambled; it amazed her he'd driven in this shape. She peeled down the bloody sleeve last; Minh chewed her lower lip as she revealed the gash in his biceps, a lipless dribbling mouth. Loi slumped bare-chested while Minh ripped his shirt into strips. She narrowed her thoughts only to rending the cloth, closing herself to the stink of blood, his pale, cool skin, and the battle raging closer.

She tightened one strip around the laceration in his arm. Minh wadded another length of cloth; breathing as hard in revulsion as Loi did in his pain, she stuffed it into the pinched, weeping hole in his thigh; her finger scraped the metal shard still inside. Loi winced and shook his head against the hot truck tire but made no suffering sound. Minh bound his leg, pulling hard to stop the bleeding; this was all she knew to do, what she'd seen done on the Road after the bombs. Tear the clothes off the injured, pack their wounds, and wrap them tight. Wait for help or keep walking.

Kneeling, Minh clenched her own bloody hands between her knees so Loi would not see them shaking. "I'm going to get help."

Loi reached his good arm for her as she stood. Minh kneeled again, to be close when he spoke.

"Someone to fix the tire."

She covered his hand on her arm. "You're not serious."

Loi bared his teeth with the effort of squeezing. "Go on."

Minh backed away to behold him. Her bandages were good, no blood seeped through yet. Loi held her gaze to say he was not dying and that she should turn and run.

The camp was mostly vacant. Minh sprinted between tents and banked fires, privy pits and wooden lean-tos. She passed many cooks and peasants from Tchepone who made the daily deliveries of foodstuffs to the camp. She dashed under the tall trees, not once under open sky. She didn't know if the camp had a hospital or where it might be, so she ran to the one place she knew other than Loi's tent, where she'd been two nights before, the headquarters bunker.

The tunnel entrance was cut into a dirt mound, capped with logs. Arriving, Minh bent at the waist not to enter the tunnel but to catch her breath.

"Loi," she shouted before she could breathe evenly. "Loi! He's hurt. Someone help."

At the mouth of the opening, Minh sank to her knees and called again. She should rush inside, insist on attention from the officers. Though she was a beggar and a singer to everyone in the camp but Loi, he was their cadre. She could go in his name, demand in his name. In the valley's distance, but not so far as before, another jet dueled with his guns.

Before Minh could cry out one more time or take a step, the tunnel answered.

"Coming."

A stout and gray man emerged, the regimental cadre who'd forgiven Loi's failing by claiming some blame and credit for shooting down American planes. He rushed up quickly, Minh didn't have time to rise. With a strong hand he scooped her to her feet.

"Where is he, girl?"

"Are you a doctor?"

"Never mind what I am. Is that his blood on your hands?"

"Yes."

"Go."

He pushed her away from him, to get her moving. Minh took off through the camp, not so quickly as she'd come because the man running with her was older and heavyset. Like a juggernaut, he jogged at a steady pace, with a hard face.

They surged through the camp, drawing attention from the cooks and peasants. She said to the cadre hurrying beside her, "Loi wants his truck fixed. A flat tire."

The political officer pointed at a half-dozen men. With only his gesture, the men fell in behind him. He called over his broad shoulder, "Good!" and ran on beside Minh.

It took three minutes to return to Loi. He slouched alone against the truck. The cadre slowed, out of breath, and dropped beside Loi. Minh stayed back with the six men who'd followed, all of them gasping.

Loi lifted his good hand to the cadre in greeting, a brave gesture. "Bao. I'm all right."

The old man pushed Loi's arm down, taking command. "We'll see."

He checked Minh's makeshift bandages. The bleeding stained them, but neither was soaked; the bleeding had slowed. Bao gave Minh an approving nod.

"Is that his tent?"

"Yes."

"Is there a sheet on his cot?"

The question asked if Minh had slept on that sheet.

She nodded.

"Get it."

When Minh had stripped the cot and returned, old Bao had lain Loi on his back. He'd removed the bandage around the thigh wound to inspect it, probing with his own fingers, which had gone scarlet.

Minh laid the sheet beside him.

"As it turns out, I was a doctor. So we're all lucky today. He'll be fine. Some stitches. I need to pull that shard out of his leg. You did well."

Bao rose to stand back, kindly giving Minh a moment with Loi while he busied himself with orders to the six cooks. He told them to find a jack and a spare tire.

The blood on Minh's hands had not dried, nor had the blood on Loi's. When they touched, their hands were tacky.

"He says you'll be fine."

"Thank you."

"Your mother will have to make you another shirt."

"She already has. I lost four in Khe Sanh."

In the wordless moments between them, the guns of the valley called out. Another jet shrieked down, more bombs blew, and the catastrophe of the morning bellowed its loudest.

"Loi. Listen to me. There's been enough. Catch them."

"No."

"Then let them go."

Minh spoke of the pilots, but she meant herself and Loi. Let us go.

He clasped her hand tighter. The blood between them cinched their palms.

"No."

Minh whirled on Bao to ask for his intervention. He didn't wait for the question to answer her.

"He's not going to die from stitches."

The old cadre stepped up to replace Minh. She didn't give ground, and the old cadre bumped her.

"I need to take him now."

"Stop him."

"I don't think that's possible." With none of his sternness, Bao patted her arm.

He eased Minh aside to spread the sheet on the ground. Bao and the cooks lifted Loi onto the white linen. The cadre and three men hoisted the corners of the sheet to carry Loi away. The other three remained behind, scratching their bearded chins, mumbling to one another for a way to fix the flat.

Loi and his bearers disappeared into the camp among the trees and tents.

Minh faded away from the truck and the muttering cooks, toward the deeper jungle. The female fighters were out there. The American pilots were there, too, fooled into believing they were hunted. Above the trees, where the daylight glinted and the battle waged, the spotter plane flew Minh's way.

CHAPTER 49

Sol whispered to Nail 44 the same thing he'd told the seven other FACs he'd worked with over the past three days. "Negative on the smoke. Too many unfriendlies close by."

The O-2's dual props hummed closer over the valley. Without a visual through the forest canopy, Sol had no chance to hack Nail when he flew past. The PJ sat with his head just above the ferns, keeping watch on the jungle while Sol handled the radio.

"I got a lot of bombs to drop up here, Dash. I need a tally on your exact location. If no go on the smoke, give me an option."

"What's your altitude?"

"Three thousand."

"Drop to fifteen hundred. Direction find on my count."

"Copy. What's the bad news with that?"

"You're going to draw fire from a pair of ZPUs seventy yards northeast of my location. When they open up, you mark them. Bring in the fast movers. Once the gunners are busy, Hallmark and I will make our move. Over."

Sol sat up. The sling snugged his arm to his side, the move was pain-free. In the clearing, the zeeps had been quiet all morning; none of the jets or Sandys had challenged them. As Nail's engines headed their way, the crews scurried around their guns, sensing their turn had come.

"Dash, ready for your count."

Sol whispered, "One, two, three, four." He counted up to ten, then down to trigger Nail's directional finder. He stopped when the FAC's hum disappeared under the opening blasts from the twin ZPUs. With the zeeps baying, Sol raised the volume and pressed the radio to his ear.

". . . getting hosed. Nail, do you copy?"

No more came from the small speaker. The voice hadn't been Nail 44's but probably his wingmate, the high bird. Nail 44 didn't answer, and he didn't hail Sol.

The ZPUs' eight barrels sawed hard, firing and recoiling; each gun spit silver tracers and gray threads of steel. Above the trees the O-2's engines howled; Nail stayed in the fight for long minutes until his engine noise faded under the pounding guns. Sol didn't hear him again until the zeeps quit firing. When they did, Nail sounded far away.

Sol lay back under the ferns; Hallmark kept watching, as if stunned. Sol didn't hail Nail 44. No sense listening to another pilot explain that the area was too hot.

"Crown, this is Dash 2. Copy?"

"Go, Dash."

"What happened?"

"Nail 44 got a chunk of his tailpiece shot off. He had to RTB."

Sol had pushed the FAC into taking on the zeeps. It was a relief that he'd gotten away. But Seventh Air Force had given the rescuers to the end of the day. That day was half over.

"Nail 69 is high bird. He's escorting 44 out of the valley. He'll turn around and be inbound in a few mikes. Can you stay secure?"

"Roger, Crown. But we're ready to go home."

"Understood, Dash. Out."

Hallmark whispered. "Now what, sir?"

"Another FAC's on his way. We wait."

"Not sure we can do that."

"We got no choice."

"No, sir. I mean, take a look."

Carefully, Sol came upright in the ferns.

Out of the south, ten VC in coolie hats wended through the trees; across their shoulders stretched wooden yokes from which hung buckets. They were hauling water from the river to the camp. At most, they were five minutes away.

From the opposite direction, a pack of twenty fighters picked their way through the forest. In the hush after the zeeps had fended off Nail 44, a single rifle popped.

"What's the plan, sir?"

Sol patted the M-16 across Hallmark's chest. "You got a full magazine in that?"

"I do."

With his one good hand, Sol pulled the .38 from its shoulder holster. "If it comes to it, we run at the waterboys. Shoot our way through if we have to." Even to himself, he sounded cowboyish. *Shoot our way through,* what a phrase.

"That's south, sir. Crown wants us to head north."

"Crown's not down here."

"Okay, the waterboys. How's the arm?"

"It'll do."

"Good."

"Listen to me. If I can't keep up, you go on."

Hallmark scowled. His head, like Sol's, seemed to sit on a green platter of fronds. "Would you do that, sir? Run off if I couldn't keep up?"

Sol shook his head at the mystery of his courage, wishing to be surer of it. "I hope I would not."

"So that's settled."

Nail 69 wasn't going to show in time. The bucket bearers had advanced inside two hundred yards from where Sol and Hallmark hid, the VC hunters, three hundred.

Sol tested his shoulder. He could go.

CHAPTER 50

A truck arrived carrying wounded and stacked corpses, then another.

The battle over the valley was plainly furious. It rattled in the sky. Minh saw it in the bloody truck beds where the injured and the dead rode together into camp. She sat by Loi's tent watching the cost grow, a toll that had included Loi.

The three cooks found a spare tire, a jack, and wrenches, and set about fixing his flat. Minh rose to walk somewhere else. She would argue with Loi if she saw him climb back into his truck.

On the outskirts of the camp, a pair of cannons stood in a clearing with a view of the sky. Neither gun had fired all day. Now their crews scrambled to get ready. Minh stopped at the edge of the trees where she could watch the sky with them.

When the American spotter plane entered their range a kilometer away, the gunners opened up. Even with her hands over her ears, the twin weapons made an awful racket. All eight barrels shot so fast the air above them warped from the heat. The spotter plane ducked and twisted, dodging their bright spans of fire. Brass casings ejected from the cannons to mound and sizzle in the small clearing. The gunners whirled handwheels to swing their guns up or down, left or right, while loaders readied the next crate of ammunition. Both crews, ten sweating men, toiled and fired at a remarkable rate.

The American plane fought hard to circle the clearing, dancing away from flashing tracers, retreating then surging forward, probing to find the way in. The gunners guessed where the pilot might turn next and barely missed many times. Coming out of an upside-down spiral, the plane turned wrong, into a glowing torrent waiting for it. The plane dipped, cat-quick, but its tail got nipped and a piece spun into the air.

It dove straight at the jungle. Both gun crews cheered, thinking they'd shot it down. At the last instant, the spotter plane leveled off below the tips of some trees, hiding inside the canopy, taking an incredible risk to get away. The guns stopped firing with no target; Minh pulled down her hands. The spotter plane popped into view only after it was out of reach.

The eight barrels crackled as they cooled. With the confrontation won, the ten gunners looked at her. Minh held her ground to let them look.

One of the gunners called for Minh to sing. With no planes in the air, he walked away from his cannon to invite her again. Two of his shirtless crew came with him, also asking.

They knew her. Everyone knew her.

CHAPTER 51

Bo drew in his legs, able to jump quicker off his knees than from his rump. Dash gathered himself awkwardly. Bo worried the pilot was shaking the ferns too much.

The water carriers closed in from the south, inside a couple hundred yards, just two minutes away. Out of the north, the armed group of searchers advanced more slowly. They combed the brush and shot their rifles up into the trees.

Dash pressed the radio flat against his temple to listen wordlessly. He told Bo nothing of what he heard, if he heard anything.

Immediately after the zeeps chased off Nail, after the echoes died, the valley fell into an eerie quiet. Last night, in the dark hours Bo had been by himself, the stillness and silence of the jungle felt protective. Now he had the pilot beside him, ten artillery gunners nearby, a camp for hundreds in sight, ten water bearers, and two dozen VC zeroing in on him, and the only noises were random rifle shots and Dash's quick breathing. Bo didn't like it; this quiet resembled the plains, that electric hush before a tornado.

He tapped on his M-16 to burn off his nerves. Dash swiveled his head between the two groups, the waterboys and the hunters, measuring the distances. Dash was a major, Bo an airman. Bo was a PJ, trained to operate and fight on the ground, Dash was a jet jockey with a bad wing. Bo had a rifle, grenades, a pistol, two good arms, and hadn't been on the run for three days. He wasn't sure how well Dash was going to handle command under the pressures walking their way.

Dash waited long enough with the radio. He pressed transmit and whispered, "Crown, Dash 2. We got a situation on the ground. I need close air support. And I need it now."

The pilot's jaw muscles worked before whispering again.

"That's not going to be soon enough."

Dash listened more, then lowered the radio, something fatalistic in how he tucked it into his vest. He picked his revolver off the ground.

He breathed, "Okay."

The pilot cocked his head to tune his ears to the valley for the same emptiness scaring Bo. No one in the sky was rushing to their rescue.

"If we get separated, lay low. We'll find each other."

"Copy, sir."

Dash coiled beside Bo, hefting the pistol one-handed; the sling put his balance off-kilter. About to go into combat, this pilot wasn't the man Bo wanted next to him. He wanted his brother. Or Lee, who was mean about death.

The water bearers and the hunters advanced, both within a hundred yards. The odds of the two groups passing by without someone tripping over Bo and Dash were slim. Bo tried to focus on a strategy, on what to do, but his head filled with a train of questions. Was Dash going to give the signal to run or shoot? What if Bo disagreed? What if Dash moved too soon or waited too long? What if Dash couldn't keep up, like he said? What if Dash got hit and fell? What if Bo could still get away, would he stay back with Dash and get himself captured or killed? What was his duty, his oath, if his sacrifice was pointless?

Next to him, Dash appeared cool and ready, the way pilots always seemed to be. He'd taken control of the radio communications, and that was fine. He'd been on the ground for three days, he knew what he was doing. Crebbs never sounded ruffled, not even at the stick of a dying Jolly. Bo exhaled, and with that long breath, let his questions go. He'd stay with Dash, his rescue, and see what came of it.

The waterboys trundled through the trees; the VC hunters called ahead in their slow march: "Captain. Captain, where are you?"

Dash dropped his head below the greenery. "Get down."

Bo was slow to do this. It might be better to keep an eye on the VC approaching from both directions, to gauge when and if the moment came to rise up firing and hightail it. Bo was girding himself for the fight and the run, while Dash chose more of what he'd been doing for the past three days, hiding.

Bo took one last look at his enemies left and right. He figured the next time he saw them, they'd be trying to kill him.

As Bo lowered his face through the ferns, a voice fluttered and lilted among the trees, like butterflies. A woman's voice, singing. Bo eased his eyes above the fronds.

The ten waterboys stopped. All turned their long yokes and full buckets to the song, coming from the clearing where the zeeps stood guard over the camp. The VC hunters stopped in their tracks, too, and put their backs to Bo. Dash stayed below the ferns, but Bo couldn't lower his head, not yet. He risked being seen, but nobody was looking his way. One by one, the gun crewmen, bare-chested in the sun, drifted from their posts to follow the song into the forest shade.

The singer floated around bushes, swung an arm around tree trunks, weaving her way closer to the water carriers and the hunters, trailed by the gunners.

She could sing. Her voice was strong and foreign, but to the VC she was compelling. She gave her song interpretive movements as she walked, waving her hands like banners, stepping high, turning little pirouettes. Bo dared to lift his head higher to see her better. The girl was maybe his own age, insofar as he could guess about a Vietnamese. She was small like the men, in black pajamas like them. Dark eyes and black hair highlighted skin paler than theirs, a thin frame, but not so hardened as the gunners' and searchers'. The waterboys were older men. All set down their yokes to join the gunners and searchers. When they met around the singer, the waterboys offered their buckets and ladles. The girl sang as the forty men drank. They held out hands to greet each other, and nodded to the girl to say thank-you. She was the first thing Bo had found beautiful in Vietnam or Laos.

Beside Bo, Dash's head popped up. He whispered, "What the hell?"

Bo let the scene explain itself.

"Sir, I think this might be our shot. You up for moving?"

Dash shook his head, no.

What? This was their chance to sneak away, this sudden and unexpected distraction, the water buckets and the singing gal, backs turned. The girl was sent from somewhere, and Bo and Dash ought to take advantage of this break. They needed to go, right now. Stay low and creep away, run if they had to. But they might not get another opportunity this good.

Dash raised the radio to his lips. Bo could no longer see the girl inside the circle of black pajamas. Another song began, slower and sad-sounding.

CHAPTER 52

Sol clicked the transmit button twice to announce himself. He whispered, "Crown, Crown, this is Dash 2. Copy?"

"Copy, Dash 2. Read you Lima Charlie. Where are you?"

"Same place, haven't moved. Seventy yards west from a pair of ZPUs. One hundred yards northwest of a VC camp."

"Copy. Nail 69 is inbound. When he's on scene, can you smoke your position?"

Sol pulled his thumb off the talk button to let his frustration ebb again with this inquiry.

"Negative."

"Copy. What's your status?"

"I want you to relay something to Nail."

"Go ahead."

"Tell him to climb right now, before he gets anywhere near me. Ten thousand feet. Make no noise on his approach through the valley."

"He'll need a visual to locate those guns, Dash. Can't find them if they're not firing."

"Negative. Tell Nail that when he gets close, I want him to dive, steep, and hail me. I'll give him a count. I'll guide him right down on the zeeps."

"What's up, Dash?"

"There's a chance he can mark the guns without getting fired on. I have a visual on the crews. They are not at their stations. Repeat, the guns are not manned right now. If Nail comes in high, they won't hear him. Over."

"Copy, Dash. Will relay."

"Tell him to get here fast."

"Should be inside five."

"Copy."

"Stand by, Dash."

Sol lowered the radio to check his watch. 1310 hours. White rods of sunlight penetrated the triple canopy. A river of heat flowed through the green jungle; even with Hallmark's water in him, Sol hadn't started to sweat again. Some young VC woman had walked out of nowhere to sing and dance like a wood elf; forty hunters, water bearers, and gunners milled around her. Everything felt a bit dreamy.

Hallmark was right. If they snuck away right now, they might make it. All eyes were on the girl.

The PJ nudged him and murmured, "Major, what are we doing?"

"We're going to stay a little longer."

"Sir, we need to go. While we can."

"Not until the attack starts."

Hallmark gazed at the earth, at his own knees, to avoid whispering what he was about to with eye contact. "Sir, due respect. Maybe you're not thinking clear."

Again, Hallmark could be right. Still: "Beg pardon, Airman?"

Hallmark looked up. He was in the same noose as Sol. Fair enough. "My opinion, sir. We can go."

Sol wanted some water from one of those buckets. He wanted to sleep a full night in a safe bed and stretch out his left arm. He wanted to write his dad. The kid wasn't wrong. They could go, right now.

But the VC had trapped him and used him to kill good pilots.

"One of three things is going to happen here. We're going to get out alive. We're going to get killed or captured. Or Seventh Air Force is going to blow us up. But I'm not leaving until those two guns are out of commission. I'm not listening to any more crashes. Fuckers want to use me for bait? Let's see how that works out for them. You make up your own mind, Airman, I'm okay with that. But I stay. Understood?"

Hallmark looked young when he put his tongue between his teeth to nod in Sol's face. "Roger, sir."

The PJ came down off the perch of his knees, his hands eased on his rifle. He seemed to hear something he liked from Sol, something that surprised him. Sol wanted to pat Hallmark on the shoulder, but he had only one hand to do it and that hand held the radio.

Among the trees fifty yards away, the girl stopped singing. The searchers and gunners dropped ladles into the buckets. Nail was still three minutes out.

"Oh, Lord," Hallmark muttered, "I hope she knows another song."

CHAPTER 53

The two women fighters were the first to see and hear Minh. They turned her way, leading their squad of twenty guns. The water bearers came to her, too, gliding through the trees, their wooden yokes like wings. They set down their buckets in the shade on the edge of the clearing and offered ladles to the hunters and gun crews so they could drink. As she sang, Minh watched the two women fighters. They were treated without distinction by the men, not eyed or spoken to with any trace of contrast. Minh remained unsure if this ungendered sameness was for her.

When she finished her second song, the artillery gunners applauded. Minh was identified with them, she'd been watching them fight. The water bearers clapped very lightly, perhaps with arms too tired. The hunters stayed quiet, as was their skill.

Minh tried to peer past the ring around her, to catch a glimpse of two American pilots escaping into the woods. This was the place where Loi had goaded them through the valley, outside the camp, under his guns. As long as the Americans remained here, Loi would climb back into his truck.

The water carriers made ready to continue to the camp, bending for their yokes. The hunters and gunners dipped for their last sips, then dropped the ladles into the buckets. Minh raised her hands to show the forty men she was ready to sing more for them, but all looked ready to return to their tasks.

As the gathering began to shuffle, the two women fighters strode into the center of the breaking ring. Each bowed her head to Minh. Together, without words, they laid their rifles aside. In curiosity, the men stopped leaving, and the circle firmed again. Minh backed away to stand in the ranks and watch with the rest, but with one eye on the jungle.

Together, the two women lifted their pith helmets off their backs. They kneeled side-by-side with the helmets held by the brims like scoops. In high chiming tones, they sang "The Rice Drum Song":

> *My love he's got a little drum,*
> *Oh how he plays his love-a-drum drum.*
> *Love-a-drum drum,*
> *Love-a-drum drum.*
> *Come and see the boys and girls.*
> *They cross the stream*
> *To find their dream.*
> *Drum-a-drum drum,*
> *drum-a-drum drum,*
> *drum-a-drum drum.*

As they sang of their love and his beating drum, the women performed a traditional dance, of maidens in a village rice paddy. Some fighters knew the tune and sang along, while others swayed their hands to the cadence, dancing with the women in small ways.

Minh covered her mouth, laughing into her fingers. She wished she could go with the women when their dance was over, walk the valley as far as they walked, and talk with them the rest of the day. She would return to Loi clearer-headed. These two women warriors danced and sang. Who could understand her better than them?

Three of the bare-chested gunners on the rim of the circle backed away, without disturbing the dance. They drifted across the clearing toward their two artillery pieces. In the daylight, gazing into the sky, they pointed, shouting.

"Plane!"

The women stopped their performance, the ring of men disappeared. The water bearers scrambled for their yokes, then flew toward the camp, sloshing on their way. The hunters hurried to the clearing with the rest of the gunners.

The two women were the last to go. In tandem, they touched Minh's arms, as if the dance continued and this was part of it. What were they saying? Come with us? Stay here? They left in matching strides, hustling with their rifles for the clearing.

Minh turned to the jungle to see if she might now catch the Americans sprinting away through the trees. Nothing moved in the green shadows, nothing disturbed the sparkles of sun on the leaves.

She called into the jungle.

"Đi Đi."

Go away.

Behind her, the gunners shouted orders back and forth while the hunters spread across the clearing, aiming into the sky. Minh lost sight of the two women.

In the camp, Loi's truck was gone.

Minh had come to the place where she had no power except to beg. Without pride and with her heart, she called out again. *Go away.*

In the clearing, the hunters' twenty rifles opened up, *dit dit dat*, cracking apart the valley's short-lived quiet. Above the trees, too high for Minh to see, another spotter plane swooped down on them.

Minh stood rooted in place, needing the Americans to run away. Before she could shout again or pick a direction to run herself, a streak of flame and a brilliant flash struck the clearing. On instinct, she expected a great explosion and concussion; her knees bent on their own. She collapsed backward, sitting up. Instead of a blast and a fireball, a plume of silver sparks blew into the air, a million flaming dots that arched and spread, then drooped like a white, burning palm tree.

The tiny fires crackled and doused, leaving a dense white cloud that obscured the clearing. The two artillery guns did not shoot, and the rifles stopped. Through the smoke, no one could see the spotter plane power away. They could only hear it.

CHAPTER 54

The clearing vanished inside Nail's white phosphorous smoke. No one there could see Bo and Dash if they took off now. Only the girl might catch them running.

She seemed adrift without people around her, standing in a blowing haze, in a jungle, in a war.

Only seconds after Nail's willy pete rocket hit, a jet engine rumbled high above, louder until it was matched and muted by the thumping roars of the two zeeps opening up. Eight barrels fired into the white mist, swiping furiously and blindly at the rumble of the diving jet.

Dash paid no attention to Bo or the girl. He kept the radio pressed to his head, whispering to Nail. He displayed no intent to move.

The girl stood with her back to Bo, too close to the guns, inside the blast zone. Bo tensed, thinking he could reach her in time. Didn't he owe her that? She'd saved him from the hunters and the water carriers, though she couldn't know it.

It was a crazy idea, a denial of the battle and a risk of the rescue. She was his enemy and that had meaning. Dash, reading him, pushed his sling against Bo's ribs, shaking his head, no.

The two zeeps shut down. In the valley and facing hills, the many other big guns took their shots while the jet bottomed out.

Suddenly, the gunners and hunters in the clearing sprinted out of the last coils of smoke. They ran toward Bo and Dash. The pilot reared his head above the ferns, radio glued to his lips but whispering nothing while the bombs whooshed in.

All the VC dove to the ground, disappearing into a trench that Bo hadn't known was dug there. That was their tactic; work the zeeps to the very last moment, until the bombs were on their way down, then bolt for cover. They were protected from everything but a direct hit.

Not the girl.

She stepped both ways, stumped, not knowing where to run, into the forest or toward the trench that she, too, seemed surprised at.

Bo braced for the blasts, sorry he'd not saved her, not sure he could have. Dash ducked.

Out of the trench, a VC fighter, thin and nimble with a black ponytail bouncing on his back, sprinted for the singer. She seemed to awake and ran to him. Together, they leaped into the trench the instant the whistling stopped.

CHAPTER 55

The F-4 pickled both its five-hundred pounders wide right, not by much, thirty yards. The two zeeps were left undamaged and a crater fumed in the clearing. Sol whispered to Nail a bomb damage assessment of zero. The FAC copied and cursed in reply.

While Sol worked the radio, all the VC gunners and hunters clambered out of the trench. They raced back to their zeeps and the open sky, even before the last bits of earth and grass filtered down on them. In seconds, they were firing thousands of rounds and white tracers at the F-4 showing its belly while it strained to climb.

Nail 69 told Sol he would pass the BDA on to the F-4's wingmate, lined up next.

"Negative, Nail. Hold Fox 4."

"Go, Dash. What do you need?"

Under the booming of the zeeps and the laboring jet, Sol described to Nail the VC tactic he'd just witnessed, how with bombs on the way down they bailed on their guns to duck into the trench. If Nail kept calling down conventional ordnance, it was going to take a direct hit on both artillery pieces to wreck them. With so much antiaircraft in the valley and the facing hills, the bombers were releasing their loads above five thousand feet, a safer distance but with decreased accuracy.

"I want CBUs." Cluster bombs.

"Dash, you're pretty close to those zeeps."

"We'll be here all day waiting for somebody to put a big one down their throats. Let's take out the gunners."

"Your call, Dash."

Sol described the location of the trench: twenty yards west of the zeeps, just inside the treeline, closer to where he hid in the ferns with Hallmark.

Nail copied. He said that Sol had balls. Sol answered that what he had was a deadline and no choice. "Pick someone good, Nail."

"Copy. Stand by."

The last of the white phosphorus smoke drifted away from the clearing. That didn't matter. The stacked-up bombers had their marker, the crater from the Mk-82s. And the zeeps were marking themselves, firing hot at the climbing F-4.

Sol monitored the FAC's chatter with Viper, Vixen, Bolo, Catnip, Lobo, and Dixie flights, all Thuds, Fox 4s, and Navy A-7 Corsairs. Nail asked who had CBUs and who had experience with them, warning the bombers that Dash and Hallmark were on the rim of the blast range.

Next to Sol, the PJ kept his opinion to himself.

Two more heads appeared above the VC's trench, the singer girl and the ponytailed fighter who'd saved her. Both climbed out of the ground. Under the clangs and crackles from the clearing, they seemed to have a heated exchange. The fighter broke it off, then jogged away to the fight.

The singer walked deeper under the trees, toward the pig pit. The closer she came, the more her features were defined in the broken jungle light, a girl darkened by the war, made lean by it. Sol put down the radio to pull his .38 from its holster. He lowered his chin beneath the ferns, keeping the girl in view. The PJ didn't raise his rifle.

She stopped on the other side of the pit, just twenty yards away. Behind her, not just in the clearing but in the hills, the valley's artillery hammered at the sky. That meant the next jet was on its way down. He'd have to release the CBUs at a low altitude, under a thousand feet, to keep the bomblets grouped. The girl motioned into the jungle and the deeper shadows, a broad wave to be seen from a distance.

She shouted, *"Dee dee."* The meaning was plain. *Go.*

Hallmark whispered, "She yelled that before."

The PJ shifted as if about to spring. Sol set down the pistol to put a hand on the boy.

"Stay put."

"Sir, she's not trying to catch us. She's trying to save us."

That might have been so. Or one more VC trick, like the calls for Captain.

"Sir, she's unarmed."

Sol didn't need to explain himself. Dead Sandy 3 and Sandy 5 didn't either. For three days on the run, Sol had experienced things he would never forget. Ever. This girl, armed or not, was on the wrong side of that.

Had she really been trying to save them? Was Hallmark right? Why would the girl do that?

She was likely dead if she stayed where she was or jumped into the trench with the others. Sol, with everything else, was going to remember it for the rest of his life, and question it.

He pulled his hand off the PJ.

CHAPTER 56

The men in the trench with her bounded out and raced to the clearing before the American jet could escape. One of the women fighters jumped up, too. The other, Minh held back.

"I want to thank you. For coming to get me."

The crags in the woman's face deepened, her gray teeth showed. "Are you trying to get yourself killed? Why are you out here?"

Minh touched the fighter's hands. "Can I stay with you? For a little while?"

"Let me go."

The woman climbed out of the trench. Minh scrambled after her.

"I only want to talk."

The fighter closed the gap between them, almost pouncing. "You want to talk?"

"Yes."

"What can you talk to me about?" She looked Minh up and down. Her eyes held dismissal like a man's and the spite of a woman's. Minh tried to speak; the fighter cut her off. "What can you talk to me about?"

The woman pointed toward the jungle. "Who were you telling to go away? The Americans?"

"Yes."

"Why?"

"Because when they're gone, this stops. I've seen the bodies coming into the camp. For what? To shoot down another plane? Hasn't there been enough?"

"You can say when there's been enough? You?" The fighter tapped her own breast. "You think I'll agree because I'm a woman?"

The fighter backed away, pointing at Minh.

"You don't know me." The woman swept an arm across the jungle, the war. "You don't know anything about this. Go find a bunker. Stay in it." She raised her rifle to show both the gun and her big hands, before running for the clearing.

In the clearing, the artillery and hunters fired without cease, a locomotive of noise; cannons boomed in the hills to shake all the leaves. Another plunging American jet screeched down. Minh stepped deeper into the woods where the American pilots must be. The immensity of the jungle and the battle in the valley said she was small; the woman fighter had said she was foolish. That woman would die in the war, would die as she was. Minh could do nothing about it except try to stop it from being today.

Minh stopped at the rim of the pig pit. The black pig below looked up, clever enough to see she posed it no threat.

Again, Minh shouted into the woods.

"Đi Đi."

She could barely hear herself. The war rang louder than her voice.

On the far side of the pig pit, in the center of a jade swath of ferns, two heads popped up. One disappeared quickly back into the leaves. The other rose far enough, kneeling in the ferns, to reveal his chest and arms. She caught her breath at the first American she'd ever seen. A rifle hung around his neck, but his hands were not on it. He was young like her, flush and well-fed, what an American ought to look like.

He pointed to the sky, then waved her away as she had done to him. He called some warning, but she heard only the guns and the jet.

Minh mirrored his gestures, to make him run while no one was looking but her. Why were they still here? Go. They needed to go. They were the cause of the fight. They had trapped her in this valley.

She waved harder, almost arguing with him. The American quit his own motions, to stand to his full height, hidden by the leaves only from the waist down. He showed himself to her in some sort of offering, asking for what, trust? The American pressed his hands together, joined under his face. He yelled, this time loud enough for Minh to hear.

"Đi Đi!"

In the clearing, all the guns quit.

With his last gesture, the American jabbed his arm at the camp. He lowered himself into the ferns, leaving his head up just enough to watch her.

CHAPTER 57

The thousand little bombs spread into a circular pattern, like blackbirds over a field. The girl had already run out of the blast range while the gun crews and hunters raced for their trench.

Dash dug his chest into the soft earth. Bo wanted to burrow down, too, but he couldn't look away from the clearing and the zeeps. What if some panicked VC overran the trench to bolt through the jungle, what if he came too close? Bo kept watch, ready to shoot anyone who might stumble over him.

Each bomblet erupted into its own small fireball, a string of detonations. Shrapnel and pellets ripped leaves apart and felled the runners in repeating, battering, deafening bursts. Half the VC made the trench in time, diving in at the last second.

Blue orbs the size of tennis balls rained on the clearing; the zeeps vanished inside the flashing blasts. Hundreds of bombs broke through the canopy, bursting when they hit the ground. Many others landed and bounced, steaming and vying to open, waiting.

A dozen bomblets followed the VC into the trench.

The dirt walls blinkered the punch of the explosions, making them narrow and high, orange sleeves of fire with bits of men in them.

A tap on Bo's arm made him jump; he'd not wanted to see this horror. The pilot had shifted to his knees, ready to run. There wasn't time to tell Dash what he'd just witnessed, to purge it immediately. Dash rose to his feet and glared down, wondering why Bo wasn't standing, too.

Bo got up. In the clearing, the last bomblets rocked the guns; a smoking few VC struggled out of the ditch. The barrage had lasted seconds, but Bo shivered as if from a daylong fever.

Dash took two steps to lead the way out of the ferns, then froze in his tracks.

One bomblet, rolling fast and fuming, either a dud or alive, had jumped the trench to bowl toward them. The ball came close, ten yards. If it went off, they stood inside its killing range.

Bo lunged at the pilot to knock him over. Dash had the same thought and spun on Bo to bring him down. They collided, cracking heads. Bo, smaller but a better tackler, drove through and landed on top. Dash grunted from the fall.

The bomblet blew, muted. Bo seized up like he'd done on the penetrator, waiting for a bullet. Under him, the pilot went rigid in his own astonishment.

When the blast cleared, Bo rolled off the pilot to a chilling scream. He scanned Dash for injuries.

Again, the pilot had the same instinct. In his sling, Dash struggled upright to check on Bo. "You okay?" the pilot asked through the wail. Bo nodded, their faces close together.

Haze from the detonation swirled over the pig pit. Bo and Dash together paused in amazement at their luck. Both muttered, "Holy shit."

Bo helped Dash to his feet.

The pilot stepped out of the ferns. He drew his revolver to fire once down into the hole, silencing it, then jogged north into the jungle. Bo followed without another look at the ruins of the clearing or the many bodies moving and still.

CHAPTER 58

Sol called a halt after a hundred-yard sprint. He ducked under a thick blooming bush. Hallmark slid in beside him. Instantly, the PJ trained his rifle on guard for pursuers.

Sol's shoulder ached from the jostling. He stopped to gather himself. And he wanted more bombs.

He whispered into the radio, "Nail 69, this is Dash 2. Copy?"

"Lima Charlie, Dash. What's your status?"

"On the move north. Headed for the high ground."

"Copy. How'd the CBUs do?"

"One hundred percent BDA. The zeeps are down."

"Excellent. You got a plan?"

"Roger. How far is the high ground?"

"Half a klick, north from the clearing."

The faint thrum of Nail's engines came from the west, along the valley ridge. The FAC was skimming the hills, staying out of the valley floor for now. Ten thousand feet over his head, his jet firepower circled and waited.

"Nail, here's what we're going to do."

"Go."

"Hallmark and I need to move fast. You're going to clear a path in front of us. I want Mark 82s in a line between us and the high ground."

Hallmark's head swiveled to Sol. "What?"

Sol had no spare hand to wave the PJ off; he released the transmit button to say "Shut up."

The growl of Nail's engines increased noticeably. The FAC was winging closer, already sizing up the job.

"Copy, Dash. How do you want it to go down?"

"Smoke the hilltop where you want me and Hallmark to get picked up. Vector your payloads on a salient fifty yards to the east of the line between the clearing and the high ground. I want the jungle hammered, Nail. Plow everything up. I want every fucking VC head in front of us in a hole. Copy?"

"Fucking copy, man."

"How long do you need to set it up?"

"Give me five."

"Make it happen. Out." Sol set the radio on the ground, freeing his good hand to hold up the index finger to Hallmark. "Before you say anything, listen to me. And put your eyes back on your weapon."

"Roger."

Sol whispered to the side of the PJ's head, "If that was a trap back there, then we're out of it. They might want to keep us in it. Or they're sick of us by now. Either way, we're not going to stroll out of here, you and me. They're coming after us, you know it. We're going to have to run for it."

"Through bombs?"

"Beside them. Hopefully."

"You got a lot of faith, Major."

Sol pinched the cloth of the PJ's uniform. It wasn't so weighty as armor but was still a protection, a symbol of duties owed to and from them. "Isn't that the point of putting this on?"

Hallmark nodded over the breech of his rifle. "I reckon."

CHAPTER 59

A truck surged into camp, then past it into the jungle. Minh ran after it, believing Loi had not seen her.

The vehicle powered through the foliage, knocking aside bushes and saplings. When it encountered a barricade of trees the grille couldn't squeeze through, it stopped. Wearing a black pajama tunic, Loi climbed down into the wild undergrowth. He reached up to the cab for a long stick. Using it as a staff, he pushed his way toward the clearing.

Running, Minh batted at branches; her calls to Loi didn't slow him. He forged ahead with a limp, left leg bandaged. Another white wrap circled his left arm.

When Minh caught up, she looked for some way to touch him, but Loi drove the stick into the ground and slogged on behind it.

He asked, "Are you all right?"

"Yes."

He asked nothing more; pain put his focus on moving. The twin artillery pieces stood a hundred meters ahead through trees and snagging thickets; Loi had missed the path trying to ram his way to them in the truck. He hobbled on, wordless through the woods. She didn't feel ignored by his silence; it was her place to hurry along beside him, seeking to prop him up. Minh was his, and that made him hers.

Above the canopy, the spotter plane seemed to be returning. If it flew elsewhere, she would know the American pilots were gone.

Loi didn't falter with his stick but drove toward his guns. The smoke was gone from the clearing, and the sun had returned. Both cannons looked scarred and chipped but able to fire if they had men around them on the black-tipped grass. The trees nearby were scorched and skinned.

Loi burst out of the bushes near the trench. Behind him, Minh shook off the last branches. One of the woman fighters was the first to look up.

At her knees lay the other woman, cut apart. One of the little bombs must have landed on top of her in the trench. She'd been struck neck to foot. Only her head was not a mash of ruby and bone; her face had been left intact, a macabre and cruel result.

The dirt walls of the ditch were blackened and gouged. More bodies lay on the bottom, gunners and hunters alike, rifles still strung around some opened chests. Another dozen wounded were being tended to by the ten left unscathed.

Loi stood over the scene in a terrible silence. The wounded and the whole riveted their attention on their cadre for help or orders, how to avenge this. Loi stamped his staff once.

The female fighter stood. She confronted Loi with eyes rimmed wet, close enough for Minh to smell the explosion on her. "Did your woman tell you what she did?"

"No."

"She let the Americans escape. Ask her."

"You tell me."

Loi didn't command this of Minh first but insisted the woman fighter make the accusation.

"I saw her do it. She told me she did it."

Loi's fingers lifted and fell around the staff, the only outward sign of his reaction.

"How?"

"She sang. She had us all gather around." The woman bit her lip and jerked a breath. Her gaze tumbled to her gutted friend. When her eyes rose, they landed like fists on Minh. "She let the pilots get away."

"Why?"

Again, Loi addressed the woman. Because the fighter would not say the true answer, Minh spoke for herself.

"I saved you."

She searched his face for anything but found it empty, as scoured as the clearing. Loi's promise was broken; he was gone without her.

He asked Minh, "Did they leave?"

The American spotter plane circled to the north.

"I think so."

Loi leaned the wooden staff at the woman. He did look like a priest. "You. Take everyone who can run. Chase the pilots down." Loi listened to the drone of the American spotter plane. "They went north."

"When we catch them?"

"Kill them."

The fighter lost no time, not over her dead friend or with Minh. She would mourn with her rifle, her bloody hands.

She rounded up those still mobile, pulling them away from bandaging and soothing the wounded. The woman fighter lifted weapons off the dead for the two gunners who had no guns of their own. Without looking back, the ten unhurt Viet Cong hurried into the jungle.

Loi and Minh were left alone with the wounded and the dead. He bent to one corpse with a jagged stump where a foot ought to be. From the man's belt, Loi tugged a pistol.

Minh could run. But where, to what?

He faced her. "You disobeyed me."

"Like the gunner in the hills?"

"Yes."

"Is that all I am to you?"

"No. But you don't know what you just did."

"You would have died in that truck. In the hills. What I did was save you."

"I did not come to war to be saved."

"I love you."

"Or loved." He limped toward her, raising the unblinking pistol. "You wanted an end, Minh. Here it is."

Should she kneel? Plead? She couldn't stop her knees from shaking. She could only stop them from bending. "I didn't know what else to do."

"What makes you think I do?"

She hadn't considered this. Loi might be lost, like her. Was that why he clung so hard to the rules? To God? For a time, to her?

Loi fired.

The air ripped open beside her head, then slammed shut as the bullet zipped into the jungle.

Loi almost tripped, unbalanced by the shot. One tear glimmered down his cheek.

He fired again. The bullet banged over her head into the trees.

Minh's bladder opened, warm as her own tears down her leg.

Loi lowered the barrel over her chest and thighs. He fired at her feet. Minh jumped, she couldn't help it. The round drilled into the soft earth. In the echo, she backpedaled. This seemed what Loi wanted; he motioned the gun at her for more steps away.

"Leave the valley."

Not alone. Not the way she had come. "I want to go with you."

As if struck, Loi leaned more on the staff. He considered the pistol, lifting it partway. "Go back to Hanoi."

"I can't. Please."

"If I ever see you again. If I hear about you in the south, anywhere. I'll have you killed. You understand?"

Who could understand this? They loved each other. What was stronger than that, what could overcome that? "Loi." His name was all she could utter. Saying anything else would make her a beggar again.

Minh did not take another step backward. Loi centered the gun on her chest. There was her answer. The war that could not fit in their two hearts fit in his hand.

"Go now."

The gun barrel didn't waver, and Loi was done crying.

CHAPTER 60

Dash tucked away the radio, with no more to say into it.

Bo came out of his crouch under the bush. "Good luck, Major."

"You, too." The pilot got on one knee. "Now."

Bo yanked the ring pull on his flare to ignite the day end. He tossed the canister ahead into the forest just as the carrot-colored smoke gushed out. Quickly the mist swirled into a bright column that reared through the branches and dense leaves, riding up into the afternoon sun.

This marked their position in the jungle for the two dozen orbiting planes, and for every VC inside a square mile.

Immediately, a Skyraider's roar leaped into the valley. The A-1 zoomed down from the hills, throttle to the stops, headed their way at treetop level. Sandy had been lurking over the ridges. When he saw the signal that the twin zeeps were out of commission, he darted in.

On every wooded side of Bo and Dash, small-arms fire crackled. At least a hundred Viet Cong were scattered in the nearby woods. Sandy took them on, strafing the emerald forest ahead of Bo and Dash, thrashing it with thousands of 20mm rounds to clear the way for their run.

Dash held out his good hand to keep Bo in place while the A-1 stitched the tangled ground beyond the orange smoke flare, speed and steel in his passing. Once Sandy pulled out of his run and banked away to clear the area, a jet bomber's plunging whine ignited the valley's artillery.

Dash tapped a fingertip on Bo's leg. "Get ready."

Bo cringed at the shrill, lethal whistle coming his way. No man wanted to be where he could hear the fall of bombs. The big guns boomed in the hills. In the surrounding jungle, the small-arms fire stopped, like Dash said it would.

Dash jumped up.

"Go."

Bo took off in the lead. He bolted into the orange cloud, an oily smoke, and held his breath until he came out the other side. He clutched the compass. Dash had made it clear; it would be a deadly mistake to veer off their straight-line sprint to the high ground.

Bo tore into the jungle, using his rifle to block and bash his way through the undergrowth. He almost slipped on the damp jungle floor cornering around trees. Bombs railed to his right, a screaming jet labored to climb, and every instinct told him to get down, bury his nose in the loam. Behind him, Dash shouted, "Run, run, run," either to himself or Bo.

The first explosion was a lightning strike. Fifty meters through the bush, a gout of white light burst into a blazing red. The blast knocked Bo off-balance, making him catch himself against a tree trunk; his ears felt cuffed and his face stung, singed by the heat flash. A hair-raising concussion splintered trees, spraying Bo with leaves and whirligigs of wood. Lopped branches, some on fire, sailed past. Bo ran wrapping his head, trying to protect his skin and eardrums as the second bomb exploded. Another blazing burst split the woods to his right, flinging it in flaming pieces as he surged through the shock wave.

Bo sprinted without looking back at Dash, unable to detect the pilot through the eruptions. He kept to his feet, but if he'd been alone he might have crumpled, so terrifying was the run. Another A-1 charged in low to demolish the jungle in his path. Another jet streaked down. Bo dreaded and marveled at the ordnance being laid down to protect him and Dash, the rattle of Sandy's guns, followed by more five-hundred-pound bombs whistling down to his right.

One after another, four more explosions tore up the woods, more flames in the center of thunderous blasts that nearly knocked Bo over. With every detonation, a storm of wild slivers slashed through the brush; some nicked Bo's cheek, others his ear and neck, the rest bounced off his arms trying to fend them off. Palm trees tipped and crashed with great commotion.

Without breaking stride, Bo checked the compass. He veered ten degrees left; he'd gotten too close to the target line.

Behind him on the valley floor and in the hills to the west, the antiaircraft guns intensified their fire, trying to bring down the two jets clawing for altitude. Everywhere, small-arms fire popped. The VC were out of their trenches now and back in the fight.

Bo ran in the traces of Sandy's guns, over busted stalks and denuded trees, under strips and dots of light where the A-1's cannons had punched through the canopy. The forest grew sparser; not far ahead, the sun dappled on the tips of tall grasses.

At the edge of the clearing, Bo quit running. He glanced back for Dash. The pilot wasn't there. Bo knelt to stay under cover before entering the field. Dash surprised him by rushing up. The pilot grimaced from the sling and his shoulder that must have been zinging him. The right side of his face was cut up and glowed pink from the bombs.

Dash folded to his knees. Bo met him with a water bottle out. Dash was sweating again, a good sign. Catching their breath was difficult for both of them in the sopping afternoon heat.

Dash panted. "Not dead yet."

Bo unbuckled his helmet to pour some water over his own head. Dash waggled fingers for Bo to dump the rest over him.

Looking down his M-16, Bo scanned their surroundings. The valley had gone quiet, marred only by Nail prowling the ridges. Beyond the treeline, the clearing was five hundred yards wide, all open, sunny ground and eight-foot-high grasses that would make it hard to be spotted, or to spot any enemies inside it.

Across the meadow, the ground rose to a hill. A single spindly tree stood at the crest in the last wisps of smoke from Nail's willy pete rocket.

"What's the plan, Major?"

They'd been lucky to make it this far, running alongside bombs, and the trickles of blood on both their flushed faces showed the truth of that.

The pilot tugged the radio from his vest. He whispered, "Nail, this is Dash 2. Copy?"

The pilot held the radio too close for Bo to hear Nail's answer. Dash did most of the talking.

"I have a visual of the high ground, half a klick north of our position. There's open ground in front of us. Before we move, I want you over our heads. You spot for us, we go. Copy?"

Dash waited, Bo with him, until the pilot said, "Dash 2 out."

The steady hum of Nail's engines turned in their direction. In the clearing, the grass was green and above their heads. The pilot drew his pistol. Bo edged in front.

"I'll go first, sir. We walk in there, no running. Too easy to get separated. Stay on my six. Okay?"

Dash didn't look confident with the pistol. His inexperience on the ground showed, and he had only one good hand to control the gun. In grasses like these, like in a cornfield, a fellow could get claustrophobic, jumpy.

"Sir, maybe put that away. If we bump into something, I got it. If we need you to take that out, you'll know it."

"What are you saying, Airman?"

"I'm saying, sir, that this is what I'm trained for."

Nail emerged from the trees at two thousand feet. The FAC banked into a spiral over the clearing.

Dash stowed his pistol. He patted Bo's arm. "I need that hand for the radio anyway."

"Absolutely, sir. Ready?"

"On you, Hallmark."

Nail drew no fire from the field or the surrounding jungle.

Bo stepped from under the trees to the wall of grass. Nail orbited low enough for Bo to see him salute.

CHAPTER 61

For the first time in three days, Sol walked under an open sky. The sun seared the top of his bare head and heated the moribund air inside the grass. Around his feet, insects cricked, alarmed at the intrusion. The ground felt solid and baked. Sol was glad to be done with damp and shadow.

Hallmark was right; running through these stalks would've been a mistake. If he let the PJ get more than a few yards away from him, Sol would lose him entirely and be left aimless in the field. Visibility was down to the PJ's back and the cloudless opal sky. He and Hallmark left a trail of crushed grass.

Over their heads, Nail flew a tight circle. If VC were in the grass or moving near the hill, the FAC would spot them; the trade-off was that enemy troops in the area could also see the O-2 orbiting and figure the escaping Americans were under him. The transit through this field was going to take two minutes. Nail had a pair of Jollys inbound.

Sol stayed on the PJ's tail, almost striding on the kid's heels. He held the radio to his ear in case of an alert from Nail. The PJ pushed his rifle sideways in front of him, plowing through the grass.

Nail checked in to say they'd covered a third of the distance, on a beeline straight for the one-tree hill. Hallmark, who did not check his compass or take his hands off his weapon, had an uncanny knack for these high weeds, some Kansas skill. Sol spoke in a full voice, the first time in three days he'd done that, too.

"You're doing a good job."

Before Hallmark could answer, a sound like ripping fabric tore through the grass. A rifle barked from the treeline. Another bullet zipped past, wavering the stalks. Another rifle popped.

The radio erupted in his ear. "VC in the grass! Dash 2, VC in the grass! Coming out of the trees! They're following your trail. I count eight, ten! Copy!"

The clatter of Nail's engine hiked up a notch, as frantic as his voice. Blind in the elephant grass with Hallmark, Sol's gut leaped into his chest as he transmitted, "Copy."

The PJ swung behind Sol, weapon leveled. The kid slapped the compass into Sol's left hand, the one in the sling.

"Head north, Major. Run."

"What? What are you—"

"Go, sir. I'm good."

Another bullet clipped the grasses. The world spun the way it had when Sol's jet got hit—he had to find order with all the gauges going crazy and his plane dying around him. Just as suddenly, just as completely, everything in this field went wrong.

Hallmark grabbed Sol by the vest, to shake and wake him. "Sir, we're dead if we don't split up. You gotta go."

Sol glanced at the compass in his palm, not to show him the way to run but as the thing Hallmark had handed him, his life.

The O-2 zoomed lower. Sweat dripped into Sol's eyes. "Nail said there's ten of them. They were behind us in the trees."

"Okay. Go that way, Major. I'll see you on the hilltop."

Sol took off running through the whipping grasses, in the direction the PJ pushed him.

CHAPTER 62

There was no manual for this. Bo couldn't be sure of any of his decisions. He knew for certain only two things. The VC had more guns than he did. And he knew how to play hide-and-seek in a cornfield.

He split off the path of broken stalks he and Dash made. The VC were going to follow that. Moving toward the sun, Bo high-stepped to keep from knocking down the grasses, reducing his footprints through them. He juked left and right as he moved, baffling his trail, leaving little behind him to track.

Nail continued to circle over the field, but Bo couldn't deal with the radio right now, couldn't pull his attention off the battleground or his hands off the M-16. His vision was limited to three strides in every direction except up; Nail circled five hundred feet over his head, making it hard for Bo to hear the sporadic gunshots and the bullets looking for him.

Should he run for the high ground? Then what? What if the VC raced for the hill, too? Could he defend it against ten rifles waiting for the Jolly to arrive, just him and one-armed Dash with his pistol? Probably not. That would be a hill they'd both die on.

Dash had one chance for rescue: Bo had to keep the VC bottled up in the grass. It helped him wrestle down his fear to know he had only that choice. Once the Jolly was on scene, Bo could focus on getting himself out of here.

First, he had to let the VC know he was in the field with them. Not just hiding, but seeking.

He spoke to himself to hear his own resolve.

"Okay."

He'd skulked far enough west. Walking backward, crouched low, Bo fired four rounds into the stalks, spreading them wide to cover the range of the field behind him. Immediately, he bolted away from his firing position, east for twenty yards, then slid and rolled to his belly. He fired three more times, aiming across the paths of the other bullets to make the VC wonder how many Americans they were following.

AK-47s answered. Shots whizzed through the blades, a swarm of waist-high rounds that scissored the stalks where Bo had just run. He flattened to the soil while the bullets scythed the field. All the firing came from the direction of the trees. The troops were advancing in a skirmish line abreast—it made sense; anything else and they risked shooting each other in the elephant grass.

All at once, the shooting quit. Someone had issued an order. The VC were within earshot of each other's voices, bunched. They didn't like being in this field either.

Nail orbited in a tight bank. Bo wasn't in contact with the FAC pilot; why was he still up there? Dash 2 should be close to the hill by now. The Jollys couldn't be far away. What was Nail doing over Bo's head?

Another volley of automatic fire erupted from the field. Again Bo hunkered into the dirt. None of the stalks shuddered, and the zing of bullets was missing in the grasses.

They were shooting up, out of the field.

Nail surged past, even lower than before. He was drawing fire. The gutty FAC was doing the same thing for Bo that Bo was doing for Dash. Buying time. Keeping the VC off him.

Bo had gone less than halfway through the field. He couldn't make a run for it yet, not until he heard the rescue Jolly inbound. Rushing for the hill too soon would bring the VC behind him. Once the chopper arrived and Dash was onboard, Bo could hightail it through the grass. He had no other plan, and he wasn't too thrilled with that one.

Until then, he had to engage the VC.

What were they expecting him to do? Lie in ambush, dodge, run away?

Bo lifted his boots high as he stepped, doing all he could to kick over no stalks, leave no trace. He put the afternoon sun off his right shoulder and walked toward the enemy.

He angled his torso sideways to wedge through the grasses. He didn't focus on the stalks at eye level but watched their tufted tops, the places where the tremble of a passing man would most easily be seen.

Bo fired once from the hip, straight ahead to tell the VC he was still in there with them and to go slow. He sideslipped to get away from the spot of the report, then continued to steal forward.

Nail buzzed past at two hundred feet, his lowest altitude yet. Again he drew fire, making himself a decoy. The stalks were so high and the fighters so short, they got off only quick shots as the O-2 streaked past.

Ahead of Bo, the tips of the grasses shook, green filaments flipping into the air as Nail made the VC swing their rifles, gunning for him. Bo fired a burst into the stalks.

The VC guns quit shooting into the air. A confused pall hung over the stalks, motionless moments where Bo knew he'd hit someone. He spun and, as fast as he could, raced through the grass.

He ran a serpentine route, bashing down the stalks, losing the sun, getting away. Bo skidded onto his chest as bullets rippled the grass behind him. He rolled onto his backside, jutting the M-16 between his spread knees, aiming down his path of broken stems. No one followed. The AK-47s blasted away, stabbing the field for him. Bo panted so hard his ribs rattled the grass beside him.

The VC were pissed off or frightened; either way a lot of rounds drilled through the field. Bo slammed a fresh twenty-round magazine into his rifle. He didn't return fire; his own reports would have been lost in the din of so many AK-47s. He couldn't crawl off, either. That would shimmy too many stalks and give him away. He could only lie on his butt, M-16 pointed into the weeds, grit his teeth, ready to kill, and bear the bullets boring through the field around him.

Again, the guns quit firing all at once; the VC were near enough for Bo to hear the shouted order, a high and commanding voice, a woman's.

He lay inert, too close to his enemies to make the slightest movement. The VCs' sandals smacked the soles of their feet, stems waggled just yards from where Bo's trigger finger tightened. This close he could fire, take out a few more.

But then what? Run? Probably die on the spot. He couldn't risk that, not until he heard the Jollys incoming. If he was going to lay it all down, Dash was going to get away safe. That much, and only that, Bo promised himself.

The sounds of the VC sneaking through the grass passed him. Bo eased to his feet, standing on the stems he'd crumpled. The tracks of bullets showed on the stalks, a hundred green scratches.

In a group, the VC had caught up with Bo, hadn't seen him, and walked past him. The swish of the grass was the only sound they made, no verbal commands, no clatter of weapons. Bo moved in their wake, treading just as carefully in the broken lane of their steps. The VC walked on, staying silent and huddled.

They were headed north, straight for the hill.

They'd spotted Dash's trail.

Nail powered in low again, daring the VC to shoot at him. This time they refused to take the bait. They must have figured the American in the field with them was dead, gone, or too afraid to take them on.

Bo crept behind them, sliding forward through the stalks. He tingled, alert that any moment he might push through the grass and see a black pajama shadow looking back at him. Nail soared over the northern rim of the field, above the high ground. He was marking the pickup zone for the steady eggbeater thrum that finally droned over the field, a Jolly sweeping down from the valley's western ridge to retrieve Dash.

Through the wall of grass, the woman fighter's voice issued another terse order. Rifles jostled. The stalks rustled louder and sandals flapped. The VC broke into a flat-out run across the field. They'd heard the chopper, too.

Bo had to stop them, slow them, or Dash was dead.

He could fire through the grass from behind, but the odds of hitting anyone were slim. He could radio Nail, call the Jolly. Warn them. That would take time he didn't have.

Bo took off behind the running VC, not sure what he was going to do when he caught them. He slung his rifle across his back to pump both arms for speed.

He was bigger, stronger, and faster than the Vietnamese, gaining on them in their sandals, lugging Kalashnikovs. Bo had maybe fifteen seconds until the field ended and the VC hit the base of the hill. He bolted over the bent green swaths of the VCs' wake; he caught glimpses of loose dark clothes and the backs of little men, black hair, brown necks, all sprinting to beat the chopper to the high ground. A hundred yards ahead on top of the hill, a spindly tree presided over the field. No sign of Dash. The Jolly grew louder, closing the distance, *bop bop bop.* Nail zoomed low across the knoll with nothing more he could do for Bo, fixed instead on the pilot's rescue.

Bo could pull up, sling the M-16 into his hands and shoot at the VC, turn them around, buy a piece of a minute, maybe die for it. That still wouldn't work; he'd have to get all of them to protect Dash, and he stood no chance of that. Running flat out, he had to get in front of them. Beat them to that tree. With the few seconds he'd gain defending the hill, the Jolly and its guns might arrive.

Bo plucked from his survival vest two grenades. Using his teeth, he pulled both pins. He ran for all he was worth, more than his own life, through the blades that smacked his face and nipped his lips, running until the black pajamas were just ten yards in front of him.

Without slowing, Bo underhand tossed one live grenade; it vaulted over the heads of the VC. He heaved the second grenade farther, then leaped with arms out into the grass.

The grenades blew one after the other. Even before he stopped skidding, Bo slapped the ground and jumped to his feet, on the move. He slung his weapon off his back to charge into the rising smoke and falling green confetti. Entering the haze, he blasted the M-16 to kill or wound or confound, anything to keep the Viet Cong on the ground and let him race past. He shot from the waist, not slowing enough to center targets, then fired over his shoulder behind him. When his ammo ran out, not breaking stride, Bo flung the rifle again over his shoulder to free his hands and fly as fast as he could to the hill.

Eighty yards away, the rescue chopper settled into its hover, broadside to the field. The rotor wash shook the last leaves off the scraggly tree. A flight engineer stood in the Jolly's door lowering the penetrator. Bo sped over the last stretch of grassland; the ground began to slope to the hilltop.

He had no idea if the VC were still chasing him or how many. From his vest, he tugged his last flare. Bo pulled the day ring and tossed the canister behind him.

He barreled up the steepening ground, drawing on the last of his stamina; his lungs burned in the afternoon heat. The grass thinned to rocky soil and scrub brush. Bo shortened his strides and gasped for breath. Sweat poured into his eyes, an empty rifle bounced on his back. He broke out of the last tall stalks.

On top of the hill beside the tree, Dash 2 left the ground, riding the penetrator up to the Jolly. He clung to the collar around him with his one good arm. Bo slowed to a jog, gassed. He was no longer in the cover of the field but laboring up the incline in plain view. With the flare billowing orange smoke behind him, Bo dodged right, then left, into a bullet.

The round caught him in the center of his left hamstring. The hit brought him down hard, like a tackler behind his knee. Instant pain outweighed him, rammed him facedown into the pebbly ground. Bo had to pry himself up to roll over, forced his eyes open. Adrenaline and fright squeezed him, made him rigid and alone in his hurt. The pain was immense, far bigger than his leg, bigger than him. He clung fast to his senses; all of them threatened to be torn from his grasp and leave him blacked out. In what felt like a muddy motion, Bo raised his head to survey the situation. He could drag himself to his feet, he'd played football hurt lots of times and knew how to do it. But he could only hobble up the hill, make himself a bigger target. Bo expected to see the little VC fighters run out of the grass, firing their AKs to finish him, but the long slope stayed vacant, only bushes and rocks and Bo on it. Below, the high grass wavered from the chopper's downdraft, with no black pajamas visible.

Another bullet zinged at him, puffing in the dirt where it struck. The VC were staying inside the stalks, shooting at him from cover. Bo lay flat on his back, plastered to the hillside, wincing into the hot blue sky. He could do nothing but bleed and seethe while waiting for the next, or last, bullet from the field. He tipped his head back to catch an upside-down look at Dash 2 being pulled inside the Jolly. Another bullet pinged off a rock. Bo's grief at dying eased. His promise and his oath were kept. His parents could honor that.

Something flashy rolled past him, then another glint. Bo muscled himself up to his elbows.

The grasses trembled from the downblasts of the hovering chopper. But something else bent the stalks and chewed at them. With the bullet in his leg twisting like a spear, Bo struggled to sit up. He pivoted against the pain, taking it head on, to look behind him.

The Jolly had rotated its backside to face the field. On the lowered cargo door an airman knelt behind the spinning six barrels of a mini-gun, lambasting the field and showering the hill with spent casings. The chopper floated down the slope, tracing the incline in reverse, fifteen feet off the ground. The minigun blazed back and forth, mowing the field. Bullets streamed over Bo's head with the anger of a kicked hive.

Deftly, the Jolly spun sideways to the field so the port minigun could take over laying waste to the grass. The same airman stood at the grips, firing with enthusiasm. Even with so much firepower shredding the stalks, another bullet struck the dirt inches from Bo's heel. He lay back to make himself smaller, feeling hectic and faint.

The Jolly's sky blue belly slid directly above him. Bo knew and loved this view, the one from the penetrator that told him he was doing his job. Dust stung his cheeks. He lay an arm across his face and shut his eyes. He wasn't in the air but wounded on the ground. The intolerable wind whipped his uniform and dried all his sweat. Bo didn't know if he was still being shot at.

He wasn't dead but he was lifted. He stood, though he could not. Bo opened his eyes to see who was yanking him around by the vest. A shout cut through the gale of propellers and bullets.

"Come on, Kansas. Time to go."

CHAPTER 63

The last VC fighter wasn't easy to spot in the field. Small in black clothes, he rose out of the stubs of grass scorched by Hallmark's grenades. In a blink, he stumbled into the stalks, looking hurt but moving.

The Jolly's gunner hadn't seen him. Sol pointed, but the airman wore a helmet and goggles, was plugged into the chopper's intercom, and both hands gripped the smoking minigun. He was done shooting at the meadow; he'd already shot it up plenty. No bodies showed from his bullets. The VC troops attacking the hill had stayed in the weeds, and if they got killed, they did it out of sight. The gunner nodded to Sol in the way that said, "Go sit down."

Sol didn't sit, too nervous. He shuttled between the portals of the shuddering, hovering chopper. The flight engineer reeled in the penetrator; Hallmark and the PJ ascended the final few feet. The ugly tree on the hill reached to the Jolly, shaking a bare branch like a scolding finger.

Sol mumbled to no one, "Let's go, let's go." All the backs of the Jolly's crew were turned away from him—the FE and gunner, both pilots in the cockpit, even the PJ and Hallmark dangling outside the door. Everyone attended to the last of the rescue, and this kept Sol's own from being completed.

He shouted and had only one arm to wave when the VC stood up in the grass at the rim of the rocky slope. The Jolly's gunner saw him and swung the minigun around to shoot, but too late; the VC, the unkillable dark ghost with a ponytail down his back, peppered the chopper. A stretch of holes opened in the fuselage beside the starboard door.

The gunner yelled into the intercom. Before the flight engineer could finish hauling Hallmark and the PJ through the door, the Jolly spun on its axis and throttled up. The steel floor tilted sharply; Sol had to brace himself to keep from spilling over, making his bad shoulder spike. With one good arm, he could do nothing to help the FE manage the penetrator inside. As the chopper fled, the minigun reached for the VC on the side of the hill; the fighter's Kalashnikov stayed at his shoulder, the gun's bore sparking until he was out of sight.

The chopper climbed fast, making for the ridge. Sol slid down against a wall while Hallmark and the PJ were tugged inside. Another chopper, the high bird, flew alongside in formation. Two A-1 escorts zoomed in left and right. A gauzy strip of mist trailed the Jolly, obscuring the disappearing Lao valley.

Sol sat by himself near the cargo door. The FE, the gunner, and the PJ ministered to Hallmark. The kid had taken a bullet on the hill; Sol had seen him go down. He wanted to slide up there, check on him, thank the kid, thank everyone. Hallmark lay flat on his back getting his leg bandaged; the men kneeled around him. This was Hallmark's world, these were his brothers. Sol climbed to his feet, wanting some water and something to eat. The wind tunneling through the chopper's open bay did little to lower the temperature; the heat was as awful up here as it was in the jungle. Everyone had it tough. Sol made up his mind finally to become a Nail pilot, to join the force that rescued others from Vietnam. He'd had enough of jets and the lonely curve of the earth.

Sol watched the valley that had failed to kill him roll away. Something was off about the stripe of haze, the contrail behind the Jolly. He eased out onto the ramp, careful with only one hand to hang on.

The cloud wasn't mist or engine exhaust. It was streaming from the Jolly's undercarriage.

Sol made his way forward. Hallmark had been shifted onto a stretcher. The kid was pale but awake and smiling when Sol grabbed his hand.

The flight engineer, the gunner, the PJ, all got off their knees. They patted Sol on the back, avoiding his bad shoulder. He wasn't one of them but their goal, the downed pilot they'd taken back from the jungle and the enemy. Tomorrow there'd be another. Sol didn't mind. He was glad for the kid and envied him the company of these men.

Sol shouted to the flight engineer, tapping his own ear. "Intercom."

The FE lifted a pair of headphones off a hook, plugged them into an outlet, and handed them over. Sol pressed the push-to-talk. "Jolly pilot, this is Major Rall."

The sizzling response took a moment. "I know who you are, Major."

"You do?"

"Yes, sir. I damn well volunteered as soon as I heard who it was."

Sol backstepped to the center of the airframe. From the cockpit's left seat, in an Army flier's helmet and behind black spectacles, the sergeant Sol had ejected from the mess hall grinned back at him.

"Can I get you anything, Major? You comfy?"

Sol wanted to laugh, something he felt he'd forgotten how to do. This was like hazing.

"Tell me about the fuel leak."

The sergeant pivoted back to his controls. "That last bastard put a few holes in the main tank. We're dropping forty pounds a minute."

Ten gallons. The chopper was losing fuel faster than it was burning it.

"It sounds like we're not going to make it back."

"Got a tanker inbound. No problem, Major. We'll be on the tit the whole way." The sergeant glanced back at Sol one more time, pleased with his pun.

Sol accepted a bottle of water from the flight engineer, then returned to the cargo gate to sit. He left the operation of the Jolly to the crew, and left Hallmark to them as well. The kid was feeling better; he managed to sit upright to talk with the PJ who'd gone down the penetrator to get him. The two spoke seriously, exchanging something intimate. Sol knew little about Hallmark, despite their perils together. He'd like to fix that, but once the chopper landed at Nakhon Phanom Air base, they'd go their separate ways. Sol's home field was Takhli. He'd have to catch a ride there. Maybe Daniels or Beach or Friedman would come get him.

The crew grew antsy about the fuel leak. The cloud behind the chopper flowed thick and gray. All the crew kept watch for the tanker. Sol stayed off the intercom, but the Army pilot must have been preparing them for bailing out if the C-130 didn't show soon. The men brought out their emergency chutes. The FE dropped one near Sol. Minutes later when the tanker appeared out of the south and caught up with them, the crew cheered, even the pilots up front, which told Sol what a close call this had been. The Army sergeant plugged his refueling probe into the tanker's drogue on the first stab; the crew settled down. Hallmark laid back on his stretcher. The PJ, who'd not left the kid's side since plucking him off the hill, came to stand over Sol. He handed down a silver flask. Sol took a good sip of whiskey while the PJ considered him, perhaps through a lens of things Hallmark had said about how Sol had handled himself on the ground. The PJ, older than Hallmark and with a boxer's nose, took the flask back with pursed lips and a thin smile. Sol was worthy of being rescued, certainly, but was he worth the kid taking a bullet?

At the C-130's speed, the Thai border was a half hour away. The rescue mission wasn't over until the low bird touched down. Until then, they were flying at ten thousand feet over Laos, bleeding out and sucking in fuel, followed by another chopper and two Sandys.

Sol didn't leave his seat near the cargo ramp. The chopper with all its doors open was too breezy and noisy for conversation; this was a place for taciturn men who did more than they said. In the flowing heat he watched the mountains and jungle spool far beneath the chopper, late on a sweltering and crystalline afternoon. Again, Sol considered going to speak with Hallmark; he didn't want to seem an ingrate. But what could he say, or shout? Thank you? The young PJ knew Sol owed him his life. Sol was going to be one of many before the kid was through with Vietnam. Maybe that was what he ought to go say.

Behind the Jolly, the two A-1s peeled off together. The high bird banked away, too, departing with them. Sol got to his feet just as the Jolly shuddered. The C-130 reeled in the long hose of its refueling drogue, then banked away to accompany the Sandys and the high bird.

The pilot had detached from the tanker. The Jolly flew alone, unescorted and leaking fuel. The Thai border was still fifty miles away and the contrail of fuel hadn't slowed. The Jolly began to shed altitude, an emergency descent.

Sol hurried forward past the flight engineer shrugging on his parachute. The PJ was helping Hallmark into his. The FE shouted for Sol to go back to the rear and get into his chute.

Sol shoved into the cockpit. The bank of gauges spun with the chopper's quick descent, the pilot worked the radio.

Sol shouted, "What's happening?"

The copilot whirled on him, aghast that Sol was there. He thumbed Sol back to the bay, hollering. The Army pilot kept his focus on the stick and his throttle, flying through eight thousand feet.

Sol held his ground and gripped the cockpit doorframe for balance. He shouted again at the copilot.

The man yelled, "We got incoming MiGs! Now go back, Major!"

Sol hurried out of the cockpit into the bay. The crew was finished buckling themselves and Hallmark into chutes. The PJ stuffed extra ammo magazines into his vest; Hallmark reloaded his M-16. Sol grabbed the headphones again and jumped on the intercom.

"Sergeant, this is Major Rall."

"Not now, Major."

"What's this about MiGs?"

"Major."

The chopper buffeted badly on the way down. With only one arm to catch himself, Sol sat beside Hallmark near the port door. Hallmark said something to him, but Sol didn't hear it under the earphones. It was probably concern, because that's who the kid was. Up in the cockpit, the sergeant turned the stick over to the copilot, then came back on the intercom.

"All right, Major."

"What's the situation?"

"Red Crown reported two MiGs scrambled out of Hanoi. They've been monitoring our chatter, they know we're sucking fuel. They'll be in range in three minutes. I sent everybody else out of the way. We're heading for the deck. Go put your chute on because I have no fucking idea if we'll make it. That's it."

Sol pushed to his feet, using Hallmark's shoulder. He rapped the kid on the back, in case he never got to say more. Sol unhooked from the intercom and rushed to the cockpit.

Standing behind the Army sergeant and his copilot, Sol held out the microphone plug. He backhanded the copilot in the arm for his attention.

Both men turned on him, angrily.

"Plug me in. Plug me in now." Sol shook the plug as the altimeters displayed the chopper's dive through seven thousand feet.

The Army sergeant snatched the cord from Sol's hand. He yanked out the copilot's headphone jack to ram Sol's plug into its place. The copilot returned to managing the controls, plainly disgusted and scared.

The intercom sputtered. "What, Major?"

"Broadcast me on UHF."

"I got MiGs on me, man."

The fuel gauge read a quarter full, plenty to reach the Thai border, but not with a plume of fuel flowing from the Jolly's punctured gut. They had two minutes before the North Vietnamese jets showed up. Sol had beaten Seventh Air Force's deadline to wind up on a rescue chopper that had two minutes to find a spot to land or bail out over the Lao jungle. Two minutes, if they had that much flight time left.

"Do it, Sergeant. I can't explain."

The Army pilot shook his helmeted head; behind his black glasses he glared with the same look as before, the one in the mess hall that said *You don't know what the hell you're doing.*

The sergeant reached across the console to the copilot's radio frequency dial. He gave Sol the okay sign.

Sol thumbed the push-to-talk. In his calmest pilot tone, he transmitted.

"Red Crown, Red Crown, this is Dash 2. I'm a flight of two F-105s. We are tracking a pair of MiGs on radar towards westbound Jolly. We have a full load of Sidewinder missiles and are making a run on them. Firing afterburners to intercept."

The trick, the real prank that Daniels could pull off because he was crazy, was to get the MiGs to buy it.

The Army pilot, quick on the uptake, switched his own radio to UHF.

"Dash 2, this is Jolly 8. I have a tally on you. Looking sweet. Good hunting."

Red Crown, the Navy ship monitoring from the Tonkin Gulf, stayed off the air, trying to figure why it had no blips for a flight of two F-105s in the area, or they knew it was a ruse.

Sol pushed his luck. "Red Crown, Dash 2. Preparing to engage two MiGs."

Sol balled his fist in the sling while his other hand manned the transmit button. The chopper fell through a layer of mist at six thousand feet. Sol peered behind him into the Jolly's bay. The flight engineer, the PJ, Hallmark, all watched intently.

"Dash 2, Red Crown."

"Go, Red Crown."

"MiGs are breaking off. Repeat, MiGs breaking off and headed back to Hanoi."

The chopper pilot punched the air. The copilot, left out of the conversation, opened his hands for someone to fill him in. Sol transmitted.

"Copy, Red Crown. Dash flight RTB."

"Dash 2, state your exact location."

Quickly, the sergeant yanked Sol's cord out of the console. He motioned the copilot to plug back in, then eased the stick to level the Jolly off at five thousand feet. The Army sergeant wasted no time contacting the C-130 tanker to hurry back.

Before leaving the cockpit, Sol took a handshake from the pilot. There was little time for congratulations, the chopper remained in danger of running dry. In the windy bay, Sol shouted to the crewmen and Hallmark what had happened. They were happy with Sol but more so with each other. Sol returned to the cargo ramp to put on the emergency parachute. Two minutes later, the men turned exultant when the big tanker roared in front of them, and the Army pilot, again on his first try, stuck the trailing drogue.

Sol sat alone. Though they were still over Laos, he felt safe in the Jolly. He looked back out the open ramp and was comfortable, not wanting to think about anything ahead. The dead were going to stay that way, and the rest would heal. His past three days were over. The next year in Vietnam was not.

CHAPTER 64

Nakhon Phanom Royal Thai Air Force Base
Nakhon Phanom, Thailand

Two fire trucks and three ambulances awaited the Jolly. Bo thought they were there for him and Dash, but the flight engineer reminded them they were setting down in a pool of their own leaking fuel. The instant the chopper's wheels touched the tarmac, the FE and Lee handed down Bo's stretcher to a pair of medics who jostled him away fast. Bo had some morphine in him and the bullet pain wasn't too bad. Another medic led Dash away to his own ambulance. The fire trucks began to hose down the gas as the Jolly's blades slowed.

Lee didn't let Bo's ambulance take off but told the driver to give him a minute. He ran to speak with Dash and the Jolly's crew, then jumped in the rear of Bo's ambulance with a slap on the vehicle's metal side.

The medic inspected Lee's bandage around Bo's wounded thigh. He left it alone, judging the bleeding under control. Lee molded a hand on Bo's shoulder. In the chopper on the way out of Laos, Lee had told him in his croaky cigarette voice that all Bo had done in the past twenty-four hours—forgetting to take off his gunner's belt before bailing out, remaining on the ground to find a pilot next to a VC camp, running through bombs, running after the VC in the grass field—all that was stupid, brave, and a hell of a thing. Bo thanked Lee for coming down the penetrator to fetch him under fire. After that exchange, there was no need between the two to cover the territory again. The hand resting on Bo's shoulder said only that Lee had gotten both ambulance drivers to agree to go to the Officers Club first.

"Let's see if we can do it this time without getting in a scrap."

"He's only got one arm."

"I wasn't thinking about him."

Maybe it was the morphine, but Bo took a few tries to form the word. "Me?"

"You got rescued, Kansas."

"I got a bullet in my leg."

"I know. It's gonna hurt."

The medic patted Bo's other shoulder for the sympathy he wasn't getting from Lee, and to assure him that it wouldn't matter if his bullet came out in surgery an hour from now or in two hours after a drink.

When the ambulance stopped, Lee hopped out into the slanting sun. He didn't reach for the stretcher handles but extended an arm for Bo to walk with him into the Officers Club. This made sense; no one was going to tip a stretcher over the bar.

Bo hobbled out of the ambulance on Lee's strong arm. The pavement held on to its heat just like the jungle, without the shade, without the quiet. Carrying the round in his leg into the O Club felt like a fuck-you to the VC who'd shot him.

Dash's ambulance pulled up; in the daylight without everything else going on, Bo realized how filthy and drawn the pilot was. He'd need some hospital time, too. A jeep delivered the Jolly's Army pilot, copilot, and flight engineer. Together, they entered the club. Both ambulance drivers took off, shouting they'd be back.

Dash led the way into the air-conditioned bar. At round tables without linens, fifteen Air Force officers sat behind sunglasses, cigarettes, sandwiches, and beers. Every crew-cut head looked around; a bedraggled pilot in a sling and a limping PJ meant free drinks. On the cheap paneled walls of the O Club hung all the colorful crests and mottoes of the bomber and fighter groups and air-rescue services based at NKP, each squadron's emblem painted on a plywood shield. Behind the bar, the three-foot-high stuffed Jolly Green Giant wore his leafy toga and held the rescue-count chalkboard, reading 146.

From a dirty pocket, Dash produced a fold of cash. He smacked it on the lacquered wood surface, telling the little Thai bartender that every man in the bar could drink until the money was gone. Lee leaned Bo against the bar. He put his own wad of cash on top of the pilot's, announcing that everyone in the Officers Club could have a few rounds on him, too.

Lee was the most experienced at the ritual. He'd been on a few of the rescues enumerated on the stuffed green giant's chalkboard, so he orchestrated the series of events. First, the Jolly's crew gathered around Dash and Bo to drink the first round, all brown-liquor shots set up by the Thai bartender.

Dash proposed the first toast, to Sandy 3 and Sandy 5, who gave their lives for him to stand there and drink to them. Every man in the club hoisted his shot and downed it in one swallow to make the drink harsh and manly, in memoriam to the two fliers who died that way.

Bo, the youngest in the bar, on one leg fresh after being shot by the enemy, sent his drink down like the others. A few of the freeloading pilots gave him quiet appreciations, like "Way to go, PJ," and pats on the back. Lee took the shot glass from Bo to turn it upside on the bar. "Morphine and booze," he said. "One and done."

The Army pilot described Dash throwing him out of the USO show. Dash downed another shot and, one-handed, began to unzip his flight suit, shouting that the pilot could see all the boobs he wanted. Lee turned Dash's glass upside down, too, citing dehydration and general principles.

The fifteen pilots in the club came around the bar to collect their drinks and hear the stories of Dash's tiger and pig, Bo's gunner's belt, crossing the Ho Chi Minh Trail, and the bullet in his leg right now. One of the gathered pilots raised his beer bottle to the Jolly's two pilots, the flight engineer, Lee, and Bo. He claimed that he was number 99 on the chalkboard and was proud to raise his glass to the courageous bastards of the rescue forces.

Lee muttered to Bo, "How you feel? Holding up?"

Bo was a little drowsy. "I don't feel nothing."

"Good. Be right back."

Lee left Bo leaning one-legged against the bar. He clapped once. "Major."

Dash put down his water glass.

The Army pilot, copilot, and FE divvied up appendages. Lee stayed on Dash's bad shoulder. The Thai bartender cleared glasses out of the way. Dash looked unsure. The four hoisted him just enough to clear the bar top, then heaved Dash onto his good, right side. He landed with an *oof* behind the counter on a rubber mat, but got back to his feet well, brandishing his sling. The crowd whooped while Dash erased the stuffed giant's chalkboard and scrawled *147*.

Lee turned on Bo. "Not the toughest thing you've done today. Come on."

The crewmen were careful to toss Bo low, the way they'd done Dash, to land on his good side. He caught himself with his hands, but the landing cost him a wicked stab in his thigh. The pain didn't peak too sharply because of the depressants in his blood. Bo got a raucous cheer from all, even the little barkeep, when he wobbled to his feet and scribbled *148*. Lee came behind the bar to help him limp out.

Lee's money was finished. The bespectacled Army sergeant dug into his own pocket. He tossed a wad of bills on the bar to buy another round for everyone. While the Thai bartender poured, the two ambulance drivers peeked inside the O Club. Lee waved them to stay by the door.

The Army sergeant stepped into the center of the gathered men. He raised his shot glass to tell one more story. This one-armed major, after surviving three days on the ground in Indian country, saved all their lives in a wounded chopper with two MiGs bearing down on them.

"That was some fast thinking. Hooah, sir."

The pilot, copilot, FE, and Lee all hopped up on the bar to sit in a line. Lee snagged the back of Bo's collar to drag him up, too. Bo bit back a squeal but jumped on his one leg to sit beside Lee. Together, all the gathered fliers and rescuers raised their glasses to Dash. Bo had nothing in his hand, so saluted. Lee said that wouldn't do and ordered him a full shot glass.

"Fuck it. Go to sleep."

Bo and all of them drank to the beaming pilot Dash 2. One by one with his good hand, Dash pushed the chopper crewmen backward over the bar. They rolled and landed in a laughing heap.

Bo was last. Dash pressed his palm over Bo's heart. He paused just a bit, just enough to make it permanent, then pushed Bo over.

CHAPTER 65

July 20
Trường Sơn Road
North of Binh Tram 17
Laos

Beyond Tchepone, no one walked north.

Behind her, the war sucked on the Road like a ten-thousand-mile straw, drawing everything to it, trucks on worn springs, bicycles on rag-wrapped wheels, men and women on strong legs. No one returned to Hanoi for medical care, no one visited families, the dead were not taken home. Every bit of flesh and metal in their millions that went to the war stayed there.

Each step Minh took away from the South branded her. The elderly dipped coolie hats over their eyes to hide from her. Young women lowered their gazes to their own trudging feet. Young men wondered at her shame and muttered things. Truck and ox drivers did not give way. Livestock bleated as if she were hurting them.

Night fell. Minh walked alone without sleep or company. She moved against a current of vehicles with their headlamps hooded. Packs of burdened bicycles made her step to the shoulder to wait as they floated past, bathed in yellow lantern lights.

It might have been midnight when the Americans destroyed the valley. A drumroll of rumbles began, thirty kilometers behind her. Each boom was no different from thunder, except there were a thousand of them. The jungle canopy hid the bursts and flashes that would have shown they were not lightning.

The bombardment lasted only a minute, and when it was done, Minh was breathless. Who had escaped and who was dead? The woman fighter, the old cadre Bao? The gunner crews, cooks, the water bearers? Did Loi lead the division out of the valley? Or did he stay to fight even the final bombers?

Minh couldn't know. Loi's life was undetermined, but his love was not. He did not want her. She walked north away from him, not pondering Loi's survival, because the room he took in her heart did not depend on it.

Loi would die in the war. He knew it. That was why he took her into his tent. What power did he have over her now? None that she did not carry with her. If Minh dropped it here, it would lie in the Road.

At daybreak Minh walked into the rising jungle heat. She asked a passing shepherd for water and was given it, but not conversation.

Midmorning, she stopped in the middle of the Road. She faced north into the flow of soldiers and black-clad farmers, carts, and goats. Minh had walked fifteen hours away from the whisk of Loi's bullets.

People and bicycles slipped past, the stink of animals drifted around her. No one brushed her aside and, once she was still, no one judged her standing there.

She spread her arms wide, to show they were empty. Minh sang a patriotic song because this was the Road.

People slowed to listen to her voice that had been in the war. A few walkers and bicycles halted at first, then many, until she attracted a crowd.

Under the arching jungle canopy, she sang, mindless of the traffic backing up. A girl with steel bars on her back lay a biscuit at Minh's feet. A young soldier tossed a bloom he'd plucked from the woods over the crowd's heads to her. An officer, an upright man, shouldered through to ask Minh to move to the side, but please to continue.

She did as he asked. The Road resumed and the officer, after listening some, touched his forehead in salute and walked away south.

Minh sang into the hot afternoon until her voice tired. Passersby, old and young, gave her ample food and water. An old village woman stopped to talk. Minh asked for none of it.

In memoriam
Sandy Bolick

HISTORICAL NOTES

Chapter 1

On January 2, 1968, weeks before the start of the Tet Offensive, the first team of the first squad of the first platoon of Lima Company, 26th Marine Regiment, was in a forward listening post on the western edge of their regiment's position at Khe Sanh. Late at night, the four Marines in the listening post detected movement in the jungle. After a call for identification was answered with a burst of gunfire, the four Marines returned "a terrific volume of automatic-weapons fire." At dawn, twenty meters from the Marines' forward position, four pajama-clad North Vietnamese officers and one tall Chinese official were discovered in the jungle, riddled with bullets. All their map cases had been opened and emptied.

The song lyrics in this chapter are the actual lyrics to the North Vietnamese patriotic song "Fly to the South."

Chapter 2

In 1968, a USO show at Phan Rang air base was interrupted when an Air Force officer removed an Army dust-off (medical evac) pilot from the event for "whipping down the panties" of a Filipina dancer. The pilot returned ten minutes later with two Army colonels in a jeep towing a 155mm howitzer. The colonels demanded the sergeant be returned to his seat. Pandemonium broke out among the soldiers and airmen attending the show, with half clamoring for the colonels to shoot the cannon, the rest rushing for the doors or ducking under tables. Order was restored when the apologetic Air Force officer restored the Army pilot to his seat.

Chapter 3

In 1968, a C-130 cargo plane over Laos took a 37mm round in its starboard engine, setting it ablaze. Immediately upon seeing the fire, the loadmaster bailed out. When the loadmaster did not answer intercom hails from the cockpit, the navigator went back to the cargo bay to find him. Seeing the flaming engine, the navigator, too, jumped out. Next, the copilot left the cockpit to go looking for the rest of the crew. He tripped coming down the stairs and knocked himself out cold. When the copilot awoke, unsure how long he'd been unconscious, he jumped out of the injured bird. Finally, the pilot, discovering he'd been left alone in his dying plane, bailed out.

After being shot down over North Vietnam, an Air Force pilot evaded capture in the jungle to await the USAF rescue force. Enemy troops walked within yards of his hiding spot. Panicked, the pilot leaped up, .38 pistol in hand, and began to run and fire into the air, "not in any particular direction or toward any destination. He didn't aim the pistol at anyone or anything. He just ran and shot his gun." Later, the pilot claimed to have "just felt better running and shooting." Several enemy soldiers also began to dash about. The pilot described the scene as Keystone Cops.

Chapter 4

The North Vietnamese Army operated FEGs, front-entertainment groups, made up of men and women who performed for the troops moving along the Trường Sơn Road (known by American troops as the Ho Chi Minh Trail). Each FEG had responsibility for a hundred-kilometer stretch of the Road, spanning several binh tram rest stations.

Chapter 5

The ruse of drawing out MiGs by false radio chatter was used by Air Force Major Robert Lodge, flying an

F-4D with the 555th "Triple Nickel" Tactical Fighter Squadron. He first attempted it while escorting an AC-130 Spectre gunship. Over the UHF channel, Lodge rebuked his wingman, Lieutenant Martin Cavato, for going bingo on fuel, suspecting that the NVA Air Force was monitoring their radio chatter. Lodge was correct; a pair of MiGs launched from Hanoi to attack the abandoned C-130. When Lodge's and Cavato's Phantom jets wheeled around to confront them, the enemy MiGs turned away.

Chapters 5–11

In May 1968, U.S. Navy A7A pilot Commander Kenny Wayne Fields was shot down over Laos during his first combat bombing mission. A forward air controller had spotted a ferry and an underwater bridge crossing the Xe Banghiang River in a valley west of Tchepone; the Nail pilot called in Fields and his wingmate Iceman, USN Lieutenant Fred Lentz, to attack these two targets.

Fields described his incredible adventures in the Lao jungle evading enemy troops in his superb book, *The Rescue of Streetcar 304*.

Chapters 19–21

During the first hour of the attempt to rescue Fields, an A-1, flown by USAF Major Bill Palank as Sandy 5, took enemy rounds to his engine and left wing. He was forced to return to NKP in Thailand, where his engine seized the instant he set down.

A second A-1 pilot, Major Ed Leonard, flying as Sandy 7 on his 257th combat mission, defied the order at dusk to RTB. Leonard informed Fields on the ground that he thought he could still pull the rescue off in the fading light. In his attempt to locate Fields, Major Leonard was shot down. He served five years as a POW.

Chapter 23

After Fields had evaded capture during the first day and was on the run at night, he was asked by Crown how many campfires he could see. Fields answered, "Hundreds." Seventh Air Force quickly surmised that Fields had been shot down by a North Vietnamese division that had fought for six months at Khe Sanh, then slipped away into Laos to refit. The U.S. military had lost track of them, and determined that Fields was hiding in the middle of what Seventh Air Force called "the Lost Division."

Seventh Air Force sent down word that the rescue force had twenty-four hours to get Fields out of the jungle before an Arc Light (B-52) mission carpet bombed the entire valley. The deadline was extended twice, as the effort to rescue Kenny Fields grew in immensity and proved increasingly costly and difficult.

Chapter 26

On the move during his first night in the jungle, Fields happened upon two ZPU antiaircraft guns on the outskirts of a large enemy camp. Both weapons were masked beneath teepees made from downed pilots' parachutes. Moving slowly, picking his steps through the dark, Fields almost tumbled into a pit dug to pen a pig.

Chapter 32

On the second day of the rescue mission, USAF Major Mel Bunn, flying as Sandy 5, was shot down in his A-1 Skyraider. Bunn ejected; his chute became entangled in the tall jungle canopy. He dangled under his chute for half an hour until a Jolly rescue chopper arrived. The rotor wash from the big helicopter caused Bunn's chute to slip off the branch, and Bunn—reaching for the penetrator with one hand, holding a pistol in the other—fell fifty feet to the ground. He lay unconscious for minutes until he revived. Bunn was able to climb aboard the penetrator and was rescued.

Chapter 36

On November 5, 1965, Sandy 12 took fire over North Vietnam during the rescue search for an F-105 pilot. During the mission, CH-3 chopper Jolly 85 came under intense ground fire. Oil and fuel streamed into the cabin as one engine caught fire. At four thousand feet, Jolly 85's pilot ordered his crew to bail out. The flight engineer, Staff Sergeant Berkley Naugle, exited through the crew door, expecting to parachute to the ground. Instead, Naugle found himself still attached by his fifteen-foot gunner's belt harness to the out-of-control Jolly. The abandoned and careening chopper towed Naugle several miles through the air until he was able to release the buckle at his waist and engage his parachute. The event, while terrifying for Naugle, was also fortunate, because Jolly 85's death throes had carried him far from where his three fellow crewmen landed. After a pitched battle between NVA troops and several rescue A-1s, Naugle was rescued, while the rest of the Jolly's crew were captured and spent seven years as POWs.

Chapter 40

On his second night on the run, Kenny Fields had close encounters with both a leopard and a tiger.

Chapters 57 and 58

After observing the enemy's tactic of diving into trenches after each diving jet had released its payload, Fields called down cluster bombs (CBUs) close to his position. The thousands of bomblets were the best way to knock out the enemy troops manning the many antiaircraft guns in the valley and hills.

Chapter 60

While running among the explosions, Fields was wounded by a detonating CBU.

Chapter 63

In June of 1972, USAF Captain Lynn Aikman's F-4 was jumped by a MiG. Aikman was shot down over North Vietnam. Inside the hour, Jolly 73, flown by

USAF Major Leo Thacker out of Nakhon Phanom air base, arrived on the scene to rescue the badly wounded pilot Aikman. Sergeant Chuck McGrath, a PJ on the low bird, had won the coin flip to be PJ 1. As McGrath rode the penetrator down into the jungle, the hovering Jolly came under severe ground fire, damaging the hoist. Jolly 73's flight engineer was forced to sever the penetrator cable, leaving McGrath on the ground with the pilot. Jolly 73 also took a hit in its main fuel tank, causing a leak.

Aikman and McGrath were rescued by the high bird Jolly 57, flown by USAF Captain Dale Stovall. Returning to Nakhon Phanom, Jolly 73, losing fuel in a dramatic white contrail, plugged into an HC-130 tanker for the flight home.

Out on the Gulf of Tonkin, the radar operators on that day's Red Crown, the USS *Sterrett*, reported the launch of a MiG 19 out of Hanoi. The Russian-made enemy jet streaked west at 400 mph toward Thacker's stricken Jolly 73, Stovall's Jolly 53, and the cumbersome HC-130 tanker. Both choppers disconnected from the tanker, knowing that if they did not, they would be sitting ducks for the incoming MiG.

Ten minutes away, flying his F-4 Phantom, in line awaiting refueling near the Thai border, USAF Captain Steve Ritchie heard the MiG warning from Red Crown. Ritchie would soon become America's leading ace fighter pilot in Vietnam with five confirmed MiG kills. On this day, he borrowed a trick from his former Triple Nickel squadron mate Bob Lodge. Despite the fact that his F-4, even on afterburner, could not possibly beat the MiG to the slower Jollys and tanker, Ritchie radioed

Red Crown that he was only one minute out, had the MiG on radar, and was preparing to intercept.

The MiG flew within five miles of the fleeing tanker before it fell for Ritchie's bluff. Red Crown announced the enemy jet had broken off and returned north.

Chapter 64

The tradition of tossing rescued fliers over the Officers Club bar existed at Nakhon Phanom air base. Once behind the bar, the saved flier erased the number on a chalkboard held by a stuffed Jolly Green Giant, then recorded the number of his own rescue.

Chapter 65

After Fields was rescued, a search was conducted the next day by a Nail and two Sandys of the five-square-mile area around the enemy camp where Fields and Ed Leonard (Sandy 7) had been within a mile of each other. Finding no trace of the Sandy pilot (who'd been taken prisoner by then), an immense B-52 carpet bombing obliterated the Xe Banghiang River valley and any enemy troops still there.

Note: The 325th NVA Division was engaged in later battles of the Vietnam War, including the 1975 Spring Offensive in the Hue-Da Nang Campaign.

ACKNOWLEDGMENTS

No novel of this scope can be written or published without an immense amount of research. No writer can do that work effectively alone.

Neither Brady Rall nor I had ever ridden motorcycles. This surprised me about Brady, my former Virginia Commonwealth University honors student, because he is a very cool young man. I am neither young nor cool. The two of us took our motorcycle training on Saturday and Sunday, got our driver's licenses with the *M* for *motorcycle* issued on Monday, then rode out of Saigon with nine million bedlamites on a Thursday in June of 2015. This was our first time out of a parking lot, nor had we ever shifted past third gear. Brady rode with me fourteen hundred miles north to Ho Chi Minh City, one of the most arduous and dangerous endeavors of my life. He never wavered or disappointed me as a friend and protector, especially after I laid down my bike outside Hue, unleashing a storm cloud of bruising and swelling from my right hip to the ankle. Thank you, Brady. You are my first choice the next time I do something this ill-advised.

My dear friend and colleague, and also very cool fellow (meaning he grew up riding motorcycles), Dr. Tim Hulsey accompanied me from Ho Chi Minh City back south to Saigon, another fourteen hundred miles, this time through the mountains. Tim is wise, funny, daring, and a lover of ideas and experiences. The same way I felt about Brady, I can't imagine how I could have pressed on through that experience without Tim's counsel and humor.

Army Major Rachel Landsee is my ally, first editor, and key adviser. Her reading of *The Low Bird* manuscript and her advice throughout the book and beyond into life have been, and I hope will remain, irreplaceable. She has opened her family to me, bringing her husband, Adam, and children Tess and Hugo into my world; when I'm in their company, I feel like I've climbed a great height and can see faraway things.

USAF Lieutenant Colonel John McElroy and Captain Chris Baker are warriors I admire and friends I love. They have my back on all my PJ books; it means a great deal to know I can go to them to be told how to write my novels, and afterward I receive all the credit for their ideas. Be safe, boys.

My dearest friends Lindy Bumgarner and Captain Mike Beach never let me forget that I have a place in their hearts.

Agent Luke Janklow and his assistant Claire Dippel allow me the luxury of writing without worry over the difficulties and vicissitudes of the publishing business. Thomas & Mercer editor Gracie Doyle, erstwhile editor Alan Turkus, and freelance editor David Downing have all been key and enthusiastic boosts to the book. They deserve credit as well as thanks.

The VCU Honors College lets me teach there. You'd have to actually do this to know how sharp those young minds can keep you. Go, Rams. This, from a William & Mary guy, is something.

Dick Robertson and Nathaniel Shaw keep me dreaming of very big stages. Thanks, gentlemen.

Finally, I want to thank the Virginia military veterans and the service family members of the Mighty Pen Project, who honor me by being my students, plus the Podium Foundation and James River Writers. These three organizations make me as proud as any page I put my name on.

DLR
Richmond, Virginia

ABOUT THE AUTHOR

New York Times bestselling author David L. Robbins has published thirteen action-packed novels, including *War of the Rats, Broken Jewel, The Betrayal Game, The Assassins Gallery,* and *Scorched Earth.* His latest literary efforts explore the adventures and extraordinary talents of the U.S. military's most elite Special Forces group, the U.S. Air Force's pararescuemen, known as the PJs, serving under the motto That Others May Live. An award-winning essayist and screenwriter, Robbins founded the James River Writers, an organization dedicated to supporting professional and aspiring writers. He also cofounded the Podium Foundation, which encourages artistic expression in Richmond's public schools. Lately his charitable energies have gone into creating the Mighty Pen Project, a writing program for Virginia's military veterans. Robbins is an avid sailor on the Chesapeake Bay and extends his creative scope beyond fiction as an accomplished guitarist. He currently teaches advanced creative writing at Virginia Commonwealth University Honors College. Robbins lives in his hometown of Richmond, Virginia.